CLIVE CUSSLER

THE
CORSICAN
SHADOW

BY DIRK CUSSLER

G. P. PUTNAM'S SONS
New York

PUTNAM
— EST. 1838 —

G. P. PUTNAM'S SONS
Publishers Since 1838
An imprint of Penguin Random House LLC
penguinrandomhouse.com

The Library of Congress has catalogued the G. P. Putnam's Sons hardcover edition as follows:

Names: Cussler, Dirk, author.
Title: The Corsican shadow / by Dirk Cussler.
Other titles: Title appears on item as: Clive Cussler the Corsican shadow
Description: New York: G. P. Putnam's Sons, 2023. |
Identifiers: LCCN 2023036252 (print) | LCCN 2023036253 (ebook) |
ISBN 9780593544174 (hardcover) | ISBN 9780593544181 (ebook)
Subjects: LCGFT: Action and adventure fiction. | Thrillers (Fiction) | Novels.
Classification: LCC PS3603.U8428 C87 2023 (print) |
LCC PS3603.U8428 (ebook) | DDC 813/.6—dc23/eng/20230822
LC record available at https://lccn.loc.gov/2023036252
LC ebook record available at https://lccn.loc.gov/2023036253

First G. P. Putnam's Sons hardcover edition / November 2023
First G. P. Putnam's Sons trade paperback edition / August 2024
G. P. Putnam's Sons trade paperback edition ISBN: 9780593544204

Printed in the United States of America
1st Printing

For Lauren and Bryce
Mes belles princesses de joie

CAST OF CHARACTERS

1940

Marcel Demille Chief Curator of the Musée de l'Armée in Paris

André Carron Assistant to Demille at the Musée de l'Armée in Paris

Eduard Martin Vice President of the Antwerp Diamond Bank

Georges Lamotte Banker with the Antwerp Diamond Bank

François Mailleux President of the Antwerp Diamond Bank

Paul Rapine Undersecretary in the French consulate to Bermuda

NATIONAL UNDERWATER AND MARINE AGENCY (NUMA) TEAM

Dirk Pitt Director of NUMA

Al Giordino NUMA Director of Underwater Technology

Rudi Gunn NUMA Deputy Director

Summer Pitt NUMA Special Projects Director and daughter of Dirk Pitt

Dirk Pitt, Jr. NUMA Special Projects Director and son of Dirk Pitt

Hiram Yaeger NUMA Director of Information Technology

Harvey Boswick Captain of the NUMA research ship *Pelican*

Ben Houston Captain of the NUMA research ship *Nordic Star*

Keith Lowden Captain of the NUMA research ship *Havana*

Meisa Noriku Marine Archaeologist on the NUMA research ship *Havana*

LAVERA EXPLORATION COMPANY

Yves Villard CEO and owner of Lavera Exploration

Henri Nassar Ex-commando and head of security

Hosni Samad Ex-commando and Nassar's second in command

Tomas Helmsman aboard the cruise ship *Hydros*

FRANCE

Brigitte Favreau Oceanographic researcher at the Le Havre Marine Institute

Raoul Vogel Le Havre journalist and informant

Pierre Roy Seine River vendor aboard his boat *La Rose*

Charles Lufbery Captain in the French National Police

Jules LeBoeuf French underboss in the Corsican mafia

Maurice Hauser Jeweler in Le Havre

Allain Broussard Brewer of calvados and nephew of Eduard Martin

Jacques Lurel Harbormaster of Le Havre

Monsieur Dumont Director of Les Invalides complex in Paris

UNITED STATES

Claude Bouchet Contract industrial spy

St. Julien Perlmutter Nautical historian and longtime friend of Pitt

Eric Watson Security technician for New York–New Jersey Port Authority

Dario Cruz U.S. Army captain at West Point

Steven Schauer Civil engineer for the Rondout Bypass

Murphy West Point cadet

Blake West Point cadet

OTHERS

Ahmad Hamid Egyptian wheat farmer in the Sinai

Dan Durkot Section chief for U.S. consulate in Bermuda

Waynne James Commander of the Coast Guard cutter *Venturous*

Doris Director of the Caribbean Children's Rescue in Martinique

VESSELS

Avignon Ferry sunk in the English Channel in 1940

Jupiter Aged cargo ship attacked at Le Havre in 1940

Pelican NUMA survey vessel operating near Le Havre

Cornwall Sunken Channel ferry containing diamond cases

La Rose Seine riverboat owned by Pierre Roy

Nordic Star NUMA research vessel operating in the Irish Sea

Mary Spring Cabin cruiser sunk in the Irish Sea

Chamonix Black cable-laying ship owned by Lavera Exploration

Cardiff Merchant ship sunk by collision in the Irish Sea

LÉ *Samuel Beckett* Irish Naval Service patrol ship

Mont Blanc Oil tanker owned by Lavera Exploration

Shearwater High-speed Channel ferry at Isle of Wight

Hydros Former Greek islands cruise ship

Venturous U.S. Coast Guard cutter

Moselle Survey vessel owned by Lavera Exploration

Surcouf French submarine launched in 1929

Naugatuck Towboat in Long Island Sound

Thompson Lykes American freighter that may have collided with the *Surcouf*

Havana NUMA research ship in the Caribbean Sea

Sokan French Martinique customs patrol boat

PROLOGUE

Attack on Le Havre

Marcel Demille rubbed his tired eyes for the hundredth time. Fatigue draped over him like a heavy cloak as his hands resumed their grip on the thick steering wheel. The moonless black night didn't help his weariness, leading his eyes to transfix on the weak yellow beam of the truck's headlights. He felt like he was driving through an endless amber tunnel.

Since early afternoon, Demille had driven the Renault cargo truck toward the port city of Le Havre. He had expected to reach the city hours ago, not anticipating the human tide of refugees in his path. They had clogged the road for most of the journey, men, women, and children. All poor, tired souls, many from Holland and Belgium, fleeing the German blitzkrieg. Well after midnight, the road had finally cleared, as the newly homeless took to the adjacent farm fields for a few hours of sleep. At last, Demille found some speed and the miles soon began to pass.

He downshifted as the truck lugged while cresting a small hill, the physical movement of changing gears helping him stay awake. Demille turned to the passenger beside him . . . and from the corner of the windshield, a blur of color caught his eye.

It was a baby carriage rolling across the roadway, its green, ruffled top caught in the truck's headlights.

Reaction overtook thought as Demille stomped on the heavy truck's brakes, rising off the seat to force his full weight onto the pedal. The younger man half dozing beside him, a cap low over his eyes, flew forward against the dashboard. He jerked awake, suppressing the impact with an outstretched arm as an over-and-under shotgun slipped from his knees onto the floorboard.

The Renault ACG truck shuddered across the damp asphalt as its wheels locked. Demille had a sudden fear their crated cargo in back might smash through the cabin and crush them. But the truck had not been traveling fast enough to shift the load, and the big vehicle skidded to a stop intact. Just a few centimeters from the front bumper, the baby carriage rolled to its own lazy halt.

A wide-eyed young mother in a dust-covered dress ran up and grasped its handle, staring up at the headlights. Demille slumped against the steering wheel, waiting for the pounding in his chest to subside. The woman merely checked the baby in the carriage, then proceeded to the side of the road as if nothing had happened. She pushed the stroller down the hill as two small boys trailed behind her, dragging heavy suitcases through the dirt.

"My God," André Carron said from the passenger seat. "They could have all been killed." He regained his seat and placed the shotgun back on his lap.

Demille wiped his palms across his pant legs and put the truck back into gear. "It is not their fault," he said, easing onto the accelerator. "Everyone's world has been turned upside down these past few days. No one is thinking straight."

The rapid success of the German offensive had caught everyone off guard. Although France had declared war on Germany months ago, after the Nazi invasion of Poland, there had been few actual skirmishes between the two countries.

Confidence had been high that France was safe behind the Army's Maginot Line and its fortifications that stretched across the border with Germany. The large French Army had quickly been mobilized and positioned along the border, ready to repulse any German advance. As months had slipped by, people began calling the apparent stalemate the Phony War and a wary sense of normalcy returned to everyday life.

In Paris, Demille had resumed his daily duties at the Musée de l'Armée, where he worked as the chief curator. The museum's most valuable artifacts had already been crated and shipped to the South of France for safekeeping, much as the Louvre had done. Too old for the Army, Demille remained in Paris and kept the museum running, aided by André Carron.

Like most Parisians, Demille thought the Allies would repel any German offensive. The government, the newspapers, and the man on the cobblestone street were all certain. Time was on the side of France.

All that changed on May 9, when the Germans burst across the borders of Holland, Belgium, and Luxembourg. The French Army marched into Belgium to blunt the assault, leaving the rugged Ardennes Forest on their right flank sparsely defended. Days later, a surprise assault through the forest by three Panzer tank corps struck like a knife to the heart. Within two weeks, the French and Allied forces found themselves bottled up in Belgium, thoroughly routed. The road to Paris was left entirely undefended.

As the City of Light approached its darkest hour, its citizens fled. A mass of humanity sought safety in the South of France. With the train system overwhelmed, evacuees clogged the roads from the city, the wealthy in their motorcars, the less affluent in horse-drawn carts. Those less fortunate dragged their belongings behind them. The Parisians joined throngs of Dutch and Belgian civilians who'd already spent days on the road, fleeing the invasion. It was called *L'exode*, and would include more than six million French civilians.

Demille had considered boarding up the museum and joining the exodus. Then a letter had arrived, hand-delivered by a young Army officer in a crisp blue tunic. Demille had to read the short missive twice, rubbing his finger over the signature of General Maxime Weygand, France's military commander in chief.

The task seemed impossible, yet here he was just hours later, driving the back roads of Normandy in the middle of the night, feeling as if he carried on his shoulders the weight of the country.

With the approach of dawn, Demille quickened his pace, pushing the truck at top speed through the sleepy farmlands. Soon afterward, he reached the village of Quillebeuf-sur-Seine, where he woke the local ferry pilot, asleep in the cabin of his vessel, and paid for transit across the placid river.

The port city of Le Havre appeared in the distance a short time later, a plume of dark smoke rising from its center. Demille drove nearly to the city center before turning toward the harbor. The normally bustling commercial center looked like a ghost town. Demille guided the truck west, making his way to the waterfront.

Le Havre's port facilities sprawled over several man-made basins, and Demille had to stop for directions to locate the one in the center of the complex, named Vauban.

Carron looked over the expansive facilities as they drew near and shook his head. "Where are the ships?"

"All of the people we saw on the road from Paris," Demille said. "They have already evacuated. The ships, too."

Carron sat upright in his seat, at full attention for the first time since they had left the French capital. "What are we looking for?"

"A Channel ferry called the *Avignon*."

Sirens sounded nearby, and the black smoke they'd seen earlier now drifted over them from the shifting winds. The day before, German bombers had struck several oil storage tanks north of the port, and they continued to burn.

Demille found the quay alongside Vauban Basin and pulled to a stop between two empty berths. The dock was strewn with a jumble of pallets, crates, and travel trunks. Farther down the quay, a handful of small fishing boats were tied to the dock, near bundles of nets and stacks of lobster traps. A stale amalgam of salt water, diesel fuel, and rotting fish filled the air. Absent, however, were any large ships.

But that hadn't deterred the mass of waiting refugees. Families, businessmen, and displaced foreigners alike were camped on the wharf, many still asleep under blanket tents, while others brewed coffee on small fires. Some young boys with dirty, sullen faces stared at Demille with idle curiosity.

An uneasy feeling of defeat struck the museum curator as he stopped the truck and climbed out.

"Stay and watch the truck," he called out to Carron, who had also exited the vehicle and was striding about, stretching his legs.

Demille stepped to the edge of the quay, which was restricted by a tall wire fence. He followed the fence to a ramp that passed a small wooden structure. A large red sign on the roof proclaimed *Capitainerie*. Demille knocked on the door and stepped inside.

An overweight man in a dirty striped shirt and suspenders was just entering the office from a rear kitchenette, a demitasse of coffee wedged in his thick fingers.

"Good day," Demille said. "I am looking for the steamship *Avignon*. I was told it would be departing this dock later today."

The port master parked his large frame behind a messy desk, then took a sip of his coffee. "You and a hundred other people," he said, waving a hand toward the quay. He then looked Demille up and down, his lips drooping into a frown. Dressed in freshly polished shoes, a tailored suit, white shirt, and polka-dot necktie, the visitor was clearly a Parisian. The harbormaster gave Demille a smirk. "The *Avignon* will not be departing Le Havre today, or any other day."

"What are you saying?"

"She was sunk in the Channel following an attack by German aircraft yesterday afternoon."

Demille felt his legs wobble, and he collapsed into a worn chair
opposite the man. "I . . . I have an important cargo that was to be
shipped to Britain on the *Avignon*." He felt in his breast pocket for
the letter from General Weygand, but declined to share it.

The harbormaster gave him a look of indifference. "Every shipowner with an ounce of brain matter evacuated in the last few days.
Even the Navy ships have left. The *Avignon* had a good ferry business
going, being pretty much the last regular vessel in play." He took another sip of his coffee. "They charged triple the normal fares to England and got it. But I guess they paid the price."

"There are no other options?"

The fat man picked up a clipboard and held it close to his face.
"There is a tramp steamer due in this morning with a load of Bra-
zilian rubber. The *Jupiter*. She'll be your best chance . . . If she shows
up. Berth two." He pointed out the front window.

Demille nodded and rose to his feet. "I will wait. Thank you."

At the truck, Carron sat on the running board, smoking a cigarette. "Find our ship?"

Demille shook his head. "It was sunk yesterday."

"We can keep driving. Cherbourg . . . Or maybe Brest?"

"There's another ship due in today, the *Jupiter*. We'll wait for her."

Less than an hour later, a large cargo ship crept into the basin and
tied up at berth two. Built in 1926, the *Jupiter*'s best years were long
behind her. Her black hull was streaked with rust and her dirty white
topsides cried for a coat of fresh paint. Heavy black smoke curled
from an upright funnel banded in red and gold, wafting over the
dock. A tough-looking crew of Portuguese merchantmen took to the
assorted derricks that sprouted from her deck and began off-loading
a cargo of Amazon rubber.

The quay came alive with the people camped near the ship. They

rushed toward the gangway with their belongings in hope of gaining outbound passage. A burly stevedore blocked their path until the ship's executive officer arrived and attempted to impose order.

He was a young bearded man with heavy gray eyes. He shouted at the refugees in broken French.

"Back, I say. Everyone back on the dock. We are not a passenger ship, and our outbound cargo will put us full up." He raised his arms in a stopping motion. "We'll only have room for a limited number of passengers."

Cries and murmurs sprang from the crowd, but they obeyed the officer and formed an orderly line. The XO disappeared into the harbormaster's office for a few minutes, then returned with a foldout desk he set up by the gangway. One by one, he listened to the refugees' tales. Most were turned away, but a few lucky souls were allowed to board.

Demille waited patiently near the back of the line, but grew distressed when the line began dispersing. Everyone was being turned away.

"We are full and can take no more," Demille heard the officer say to a large Dutch family. He repeated the words when Demille reached his place at the front of the line.

"I have an urgent cargo from Paris," Demille said.

The officer looked the curator up and down, but shook his head. "I'm sorry."

Demille reached into his pocket for a note that was attached to the letter. "I have a travel authorization from General Weygand." He looked the man in the eye. "My cargo was to have sailed on the *Avignon* to England, but she was sunk yesterday."

"The Channel is a dangerous place now." The man took the note and studied the document. The *Jupiter* was a commercial ship, so a government travel authorization meant little. But the French government would guarantee payment. Accepting an important cargo at the

last second, in wartime conditions, would justify a hefty premium in transit fees.

"You are Marcel Demille?" he asked.

"Yes, sir."

"And how large is your cargo?"

Demille pointed to the Renault. "It nearly fills the back of that truck."

"Very well. Our holds are accounted for, but we can lash it to the deck. I'm afraid your accommodations will have to be with the ship's crew." He turned to a burly crewman near the ship's rail. "See to it that this man's cargo is taken aboard once the holds are secured."

The officer turned back to Demille. "One more thing. The *Jupiter* is not sailing to England. Our next port of call is Bermuda."

Demille looked down and nodded, then turned away. Bermuda? Was he making a mistake?

He shuffled back to the truck and waited as the *Jupiter* completed loading its holds. When the hatches were sealed, Demille was waved over and he backed the Renault to the paved edge of the dock. A derrick was swung toward the truck and a line lowered. A pair of crewmen climbed into the back of the truck and secured a rope sling around the crate.

Demille paced the concrete dock, watching as the sling was attached to a hooked cable. The derrick operator applied tension to the cable and drew the crate out of the truck. But he underestimated the weight, pulling it out too quickly. The crate's leading end tipped down and hit the concrete quay.

Demille stared in horror as the end section of the crate splintered and swung forward like a hinged gate. He yelled and waved his arms at the derrick operator, who calmly lowered the crate to the ground.

"Heavier than it looks," said one of the crewmen, who tried to peer inside. "What do you have in there? A cannon?"

Demille turned to Carron, then back at the man, staring. "The crate must be repaired at once."

The *Jupiter*'s executive officer, back aboard the ship and hearing the commotion, stepped to the bow. "Get that crate aboard," he shouted. "We must get underway."

"Your men have damaged it," Demille yelled. "It must be repaired before it is moved again."

The officer squinted at the crate, then barked at the two crewmen ashore. "You men take care of that. Quickly."

As the crewmen hustled to grab some tools, Demille snuck a peek inside. The contents were wrapped in heavy tarps, concealing any possible damage, but everything appeared intact.

Demille pushed the splintered wood against the opening as a rakish blue car sped onto the wharf and stopped beside the truck. The front license plate had red numbers on a white field, the standard in Belgium. A slight, well-dressed man climbed out of the coupe and gazed at the *Jupiter* and the surrounding waterfront.

"Is that the *Avignon*?" He stepped closer as he pointed at the tramp steamer.

"No, it is a vessel called *Jupiter*. The *Avignon* was sunk by the Germans yesterday."

The two crewmen reappeared with some short planks and a toolbox and set about hammering up the crate.

"Do you know its destination?" the man asked Demille.

"Bermuda. But I don't believe they are accepting any more passengers."

The man glanced at the ship. "Bermuda will do." He faced Demille and Carron. "Are you both boarding the ship?"

"I am," Demille said, "but André here is not."

The Belgian approached the younger man. "I have a nephew near Rouen. Could you arrange to have my car transported to him?" He pulled out a business card and a Belgian thousand-franc note.

"Yes, of course." Carron eyed the banknote. "I can drive it there myself."

The man wrote a name and address on the back of the card and passed it with the money to Carron. The young Parisian eyed both sides of the card as he pocketed the money.

"Yes, Monsieur . . . Martin," Carron said, reading the name printed on the front.

Martin handed him the keys to the car. "Please show the vehicle due care. I had it custom ordered."

Martin stepped to the car and retrieved two hard-sided cases from the backseat, along with a small overnight bag. As he closed the door, a siren sounded, followed a few seconds later by the thump of a distant explosion. All eyes turned to where a plume of black smoke arose from a far section of the port.

Demille spotted two dark objects in the sky, growing larger. Seconds later, they materialized into a pair of bent-wing Junkers Ju 87s, which roared overhead. Demille nervously eyed the black-and-white crosses on their wings. One of the planes still carried a bomb on its undercarriage.

The German dive-bombers, known as *Sturzkampfflugzeugs*, or Stukas, flew to the end of the commercial dock, then separated. The one carrying the bomb turned in a graceful arc, seeking higher altitude. The second plane made a more abrupt turn, maintaining its low altitude as it banked over the harbor, then aligned perfectly with the *Jupiter*.

"Cast off!" the ship's exec yelled. "All crew aboard. Prepare to get underway." As he rushed for the bridge, he paused by the derrick operator. "Get that crate aboard now and secure the crane."

As the derrick operator began taking up the line's slack, the two crewmen dropped their tools and sprinted toward the gangway. They didn't run far before diving behind some rusty bollards. Machine-gun fire rattled from overhead as the Stuka approached. The dock,

the deck of the ship, and then the wharf exploded with shrapnel as the twin 7.92-millimeter MG17 guns opened fire. The bullets walked a seam of destruction across the wharf before the plane pulled up and continued toward the city skyline.

As the plane roared by, Carron and Demille dropped to the ground and rolled under the back of their truck. Screams erupted from the refugees fleeing the attack or caught in the melee. The Stuka vanished over the hill, and for a moment there was peace. Then chaos erupted.

Shouts rang across the *Jupiter*'s deck as crewmen tried to release the mooring lines. In front of the two men, the crate slid across the tarmac as the derrick operator took up the lift cable again. Demille jumped up to close the gap . . . but hesitated when he heard a moan to his side.

The man named Martin lay on the ground near his car, breathing heavily. Demille rushed over to offer aid, but there was no hope. Martin's white shirt was stained red, his suit coat peppered with holes. Demille slipped an elbow under the man's neck and raised his head.

Martin's eyes were glassy, but they focused on Demille with a momentary fierceness. "My bags . . . They must leave the country." He turned and coughed away a spittle of blood. "Take them with you. Please. My bank will come for them later."

Demille gazed at the stricken man, his own heart pounding. "Yes," he said.

Martin gave a faint smile, then the life ebbed from his body.

"Marcel!" Carron shouted. "You must get aboard the ship."

Demille gently lowered Martin's head to the ground, then picked up the two heavy cases. He turned to see his crate dragging across the dock before being lifted into the air. The two crewmen assigned to help were already back on the ship and pulling in its gangway.

"Grab that hammer," he shouted to Carron, motioning toward the tools on the dock. Demille rushed to the moving crate and forced Martin's two cases inside.

Carron joined him with the hammer and a handful of nails. "I will secure it. You get aboard."

Demille patted his assistant on the shoulder. "Be well, my friend."

The *Jupiter* was beginning to pull away by the time Demille sprinted onto the berthing dock. He glanced to his left as the big crate rose off the quay and dangled in the air, swinging wildly. The damaged end appeared mended, Carron having pounded in several nails on the fly.

Demille sprinted to the edge of the dock and leaped across several feet of open water. He fell hard against the side rail, knocking the wind from his lungs. He nearly slid off and into the harbor, but a crewman grabbed him by the collar and hoisted him onto the deck.

"Cutting it close, mate," the seaman said.

Demille pulled himself to his feet and nodded thanks. His eyes were already on the suspended crate. Its gyrations slowed enough for the derrick operator to drop it onto the bow deck, just ahead of the forward hold. He held his breath, but the crate held with no further damage as the line above it fell slack. On the dock, Carron waved farewell, and the curator returned the gesture.

But his sense of relief ended when a mechanical wailing sounded from high above. The second Stuka had circled overhead, climbing in altitude to fifteen thousand feet. Its pilot then rolled the plane into a vertical dive, its nose aimed at the *Jupiter*. As the dive-bomber accelerated, a pair of small sirens on the undercarriage, called Jericho trumpets, released a shrieking wail that rose in volume and pitch as the aircraft plummeted.

Black smoke belched from the *Jupiter*'s funnel as the captain desperately backed the ship from the dock. Through the smoke wafting overhead, Demille watched as the warplane descended toward them. When a bomb sprang free from the Stuka's undercarriage and the plane begin to pull up, Demille dropped to the deck and rolled against the crate.

The bomb seemed to hang in the air as the *Jupiter*'s propeller dug fiercely into the harbor's water under full throttle, gradually tugging the old ship away. By the barest of margins, it escaped a direct hit.

The bomb struck the water just a dozen feet from the *Jupiter*'s vertical bow and detonated with a thunderous roar. The ship shuddered as a fountain of water sprayed Demille and his crate, but the Jupiter remained intact. The old steamer turned and reversed engines, making its way across the basin and toward open sea. The Stuka, absent more bombs and low on fuel, gave up the attack and flew east toward a captured airfield in Flanders.

The *Jupiter*'s executive officer appeared on deck and rushed to help Demille to his feet.

"Are you all right, sir?"

"Yes," Demille replied, patting down his clothes. "I wasn't expecting the war to come to us this morning."

"It has arrived for all of us, I'm afraid." The officer pointed at the large water-soaked crate. "A close call for your shipment. May I ask what you have in there that is so critical to take from France?"

Demille took a second to glance at the coastline of his beloved country receding behind them. He then turned to the officer with a forlorn gaze.

"This," he said, rubbing the side of the crate with reverence, "is nothing less than the soul of France."

PART I

Drive into the Seine

1

PALMACHIM, ISRAEL
February 15, 2025

A bright half-moon cast silver rivulets across the Mediterranean Sea, illuminating two dark objects gliding to shore. Black inflatable boats, each holding six commandos, motored through the light surf under near-silent electric power. As the fiberglass hulls scraped the sandy bottom, the men leaped out and dragged the boats ashore, concealing them in a tide-cut gully.

Each man peeled off a loose black jumpsuit, revealing a uniform of desert camo beneath. They pulled on sand-colored balaclavas, over which they tied green headbands marked with Arabic script and the logo of an armed man holding a flag and the Qur'an. It was the emblem of the militant wing of the Palestinian Hamas organization known as the al-Qassam Brigade.

The two teams assembled before their leader, a thick, commanding man with dark brooding eyes. Henri Nassar raised a hand as he faced the men.

"We will meet back here in ninety minutes," he said in a low voice, "and not a second longer. You know what to do. Move out." Lebanese by birth, Nassar had been raised on the brutish streets of Marseille. His youth was filled with a litany of assaults and petty crimes

until he was fingered in a local gang killing. The charges were dropped when he agreed to join the French Army. It gave him a sense of discipline that complemented his tough street smarts. He soon found himself an airborne soldier in the Foreign Legion and discovered he had a natural talent as a warrior.

Assignments in Afghanistan, Chad, and Mali molded his skills and made him an attractive candidate as a private mercenary. After several years in Africa fighting on both sides of the law, he found an even more lucrative position in corporate security. He occasionally rued the job's boredom, but his employer operated on the dark side, allowing him back in the field, where his heart beat fastest.

As the first commando team moved out to the south, Nassar led the second team inland, following a narrow drainage basin ankle-deep with water. They followed the cut for half a mile, then climbed its low bank and emerged on a rolling terrain of scrub brush and dust. A paved road crossed their path, angling north to an immense industrial compound illuminated by rows of lights on tall poles. The Sorek Desalination Plant was one of the largest reverse-osmosis facilities in the world. Drawing in seawater from the Mediterranean, the plant produced 165 million gallons of fresh water a day, more than twenty percent of Israel's municipal drinking water. The fenced and guarded compound stretched for one-third of a mile, containing dozens of open treatment basins and several huge buildings housing thousands of semipermeable membrane units that filtered the seawater under high pressure.

Nassar led the team along the side of the road, moving well past the main entrance, then crossed the asphalt and circled around the back side of the complex. The commandos moved quickly down the length of a high chain-link fence until Nassar stopped opposite a large metal building. At his signal, two men ignited heavy smoke canisters and tossed them over the fence. As a thick white cloud filled

the air, a third man attacked the fence with wire cutters, carving a large hole.

The commandos scurried into the complex, sprinting through the smoke to the edge of the building. Motion detectors on the fence failed to detect them through the smoke, so their presence would be discovered only by chance monitoring of surrounding video feeds by the guards at the front entrance.

The team moved to the end of the building, then separated into two groups. Three men moved south, toward a natural gas–fired power plant that provided electricity to the facility. Nassar and two others followed close behind, then peeled off to a metal-sided building with several large white pipes protruding from one side.

It was the main pumping station, the heart of the whole operation. Inside, thirteen massive pump units sucked in water from the sea and directed it under high pressure through various filtration stages and the reverse-osmosis system.

Nassar entered through a side door, hesitating at the scene within. The high-ceiling area contained a maze of pipes running in all directions, interconnected to a row of large pumps on the main floor. It was hot and noisy, as the electric pumps were in full operation.

Nassar scanned the three-story interior. Two men in yellow hard hats stood nearby, monitoring a control panel. A third man, high overhead on a catwalk, walked slowly while consulting a clipboard. Nassar raised his rifle at the man overhead, while his fellow commandos approached the control panel. Gunfire erupted as each let loose with their AK-47s, cutting down the three technicians. As their gunfire ceased, the clipboard fell from above and clanked onto the floor beside Nassar, followed by steady droplets of blood. He sidestepped the splatter and approached the console, confirming all pumps were running, while his two comrades went to work. They jumped into the recessed bed that held the red pumps, opened their

backpacks, and retrieved small bundles of Formex P1 plastic explosive, one for each pump.

The charges were affixed with a small timer and detonator that required only a simple activation. The two moved from pump to pump, slapping the sticky charges to the base of each machine and activating their timers. They had crossed half the bay, when a distant alarm sounded.

Nassar moved to the door and waited, his gun ready, while the last charges were placed. When the other two men joined him, he burst out the door onto the tarmac. A small security truck with a flashing orange light on the roof was just skirting the building. The driver hit the brakes at the sight of Nassar. The truck's passenger jumped out, brandishing an Uzi, followed a few seconds later by the driver. The first man stepped away from the truck, yelling at Nassar in Hebrew.

Nassar responded with twin salvos, cutting down both men with deadly accuracy. He stepped close to the fallen security men as the two other commandos rushed to his side. The passenger lay dead near the truck's grille, but the driver still lived. Slumped against the front fender, he held his stomach with a bloodstained hand. One of the commandos raised his gun to finish the job, but Nassar waved him off. He wanted the security man to remain alive as a witness.

Nassar stepped to the front of the truck and raised his weapon toward the sky.

"*Allahu Akbar*," he shouted, then nodded at his comrades, who repeated the cry. Nassar squeezed a burst of fire from his gun for effect. Then the three men turned and took off at a run toward the back fence.

Sirens were now sounding all over the facility and multiple security vehicles could be seen prowling the far end of the compound. Gunshots rang out as they reached the hole in the fence and crawled through. The three men took a defensive position and waited.

Within minutes, they heard the footfalls of the other three com-

mandos. A security truck rounded the building to their right, catching the fleeing commandos in its headlights.

Nassar and his men opened fire, spraying the truck's cab. The windshield cracked with a half dozen spiderwebs, and the driver slumped forward. The truck veered and smashed into the building without slowing. The second commando team reached the fence opening and dashed through. Nassar led the combined teams in a measured run along the plant's perimeter, crossing the road and returning to the drainage ditch. Nassar had prepared the team with strenuous training runs, so each man held his own and the group moved as a single dark shadow.

At the beach, they rendezvoused with the second six-man team, which had arrived minutes earlier. Both teams slipped back into their black jumpsuits to resume their escape.

"Report," Nassar inquired of the other team's leader, a tall wiry-haired man named Hosni Samad.

"No resistance encountered until we were on our way out. All our charges were planted and activated."

Sirens sounded along the coastline as security forces and emergency responders converged on the desalination plant. Nassar led the commandos in hauling their rubber boats into the surf, and the stealth killers departed the Israeli shoreline as quietly as they had arrived.

A coastal oil tanker, its lights blacked out, waited for them five miles offshore. Once the commandos were aboard, the two inflatables were sunk, along with their Russian-made weapons and desert combat fatigues. If the ship were boarded and inspected, Nassar made sure there was no evidence linking them to the attack.

The commando leader made his way to the high stern bridge, where a leather-faced man at the ship's wheel turned to him. "The boss is waiting to hear," he said in a guttural voice. "Were you successful?"

Nassar eyed a wall-mounted chronograph, then picked up a pair

of binoculars. He casually stepped to the bridge wing and surveyed the largely dark coast. Soon a symphony of explosions erupted in the distance. While the fireballs appeared small on the horizon, a thundering echo still played out to their position at sea.

Nassar savored the sight for a moment, then put down the binoculars and turned with a smug grin to the ship's captain. "I think you have your answer."

2

THE ENGLISH CHANNEL
April 2025

The Normandy coastline appeared like a ribbon of caramel taffy stretched across the southern horizon. A light haze hung in the air, resisting a steady onshore breeze that gave the waters of the Channel a slight chop. The conditions were enticing enough to encourage a legion of weekend sailors to take to the waves. Billowing white sails dotted the sea as dozens of boats chased the wind. A concentration of smaller craft, their bows all perfectly aligned parallel to the coast, were engaged in a competitive sailing regatta.

Approaching from the north, a turquoise-colored survey vessel motored toward the regatta like a whale hunting down a school of mackerel. It moved at a restrained pace with a towed cable trailing off the stern into the ruffled water behind. The ship had a stout trimaran hull, allowing it to cut through the waves with a steady grace. On its modern bridge, a tall, lean man with dark hair raised a pair of binoculars and surveyed the boat traffic a mile ahead.

"They're moving off to the west as a group," Dirk Pitt said. "Hold to the survey line. If there are no laggards, I think they'll be clear of our path."

Harvey Boswick, the balding captain of the research ship *Pelican*, gave a concurring nod. "I think you're right," he said in a throaty baritone. "But if we run over a Hobie Cat, I'll be asking you to pay the damages."

Pitt laughed. As the Director of the National Underwater and Marine Agency, he was responsible for a great many assets beyond the NUMA ship *Pelican*. The federal agency commanded an entire fleet of oceanographic research ships, submersibles, and autonomous vehicles that probed the depths of the seas, tracking everything from typhoon formations to walrus migrations.

An expert diver as well as a pilot, Pitt refused to be constrained by his managerial duties at NUMA's headquarters in Washington, D.C. He was never far from the water, taking the time to personally manage field projects throughout the year. He insisted on remaining close to the action and to his devoted team of agency geologists, oceanographers, and marine biologists.

"Just keep a tight hand on the wheel," he said to Boswick. "I'll trust that you won't pick up a new hood ornament."

"Is there trouble ahead?" called a French-accented female voice.

Pitt stepped to the rear of the bridge and poked his head into a cramped room plastered with video monitors. A petite woman with straight black hair sat in front of a split-screen monitor eyeing a live video feed. Half the screen showed a deck winch and a tow cable that stretched taut through an overhead gantry at the stern, trailing into the water. The other half showed a gold-tinted sonar image of the seafloor. She glanced from the monitor to Pitt with an expectant look in her wide hazel eyes.

"There's some small-boat traffic ahead of us," Pitt said.

Brigitte Favreau crinkled her nose. The Frenchwoman was a young research scientist on loan from the Le Havre Marine Institute, a local nongovernmental organization dedicated to marine science and education. "Shall we retrieve the sonar fish?"

In her lap she held a remote power control to the winch, which she used to position a towed sonar array above the seabed.

"I don't think that will be necessary, although we might have to break off our survey line." Pitt motioned toward a wall monitor that displayed the ship's path along a baseline grid.

"If it's just some rag-baggers, give them a solid blast from the air horn and hold your course," Al Giordino said from the opposite side of the room. A bulldog of a man who managed NUMA's underwater technology division, Giordino turned from a separate display of the sonar feed and gave Pitt a devious smile.

"Good idea," Pitt said. "In fact, I'll have the captain increase speed."

Brigitte turned pale, causing both men to laugh.

"As a guest in French territorial waters," Pitt said, "it probably wouldn't be in our best interest to flatten some local sailors out enjoying a nice spring day."

Relief showed on Brigitte's face. "It would indeed be an unpleasant way to end our joint project."

NUMA's presence in France was a result of a reciprocal agreement with the French government. The French deepwater oceanographic fleet had assisted NUMA six months earlier in a project mapping underwater volcanoes in the South Atlantic. NUMA had in turn agreed to help survey a portion of the Normandy coastline for World War II wrecks, in a project administered by the Le Havre Marine Institute. Pitt had actually worked on a similar survey off the Omaha and Utah Beach landing sites some years earlier and was excited to search for more war vessels.

The newly targeted survey area was well east of the D-Day landing sites, but local lore had suggested a number of undocumented wrecks might be found in the area. Brigitte had assisted in developing the search parameters, focusing on an area that had no previous survey data. While the weather had cooperated and the survey

equipment performed flawlessly, the team was disappointed to have discovered only a single shipwreck, a small fishing boat that sank in the 1950s. So far, the theory of heavy World War II losses in the area had proven incorrect.

As the *Pelican* steamed closer to shore, the sailboats gradually made their way out of the NUMA ship's path. All except one, a red-hulled sailing dinghy manned by a pair of teenage boys, who struggled to capture the breeze.

Captain Boswick kept a sharp eye on the small boat as it finally tipped its bow to the east and caught a full gust of the onshore breeze. The captain exhaled when it cleared their trajectory and moved toward the other sailboats. But it traveled only a short distance before it cut a sharp turn into the wind, the boy at the tiller having lost his grip when jostled by a wave.

The boat froze for a moment as its sail went slack, then the current pushed its nose to the west. In a heartbeat, its sail filled again, pushing the dinghy in the opposite direction. The boat shot ahead, accelerating toward the bow of the NUMA ship.

Pitt and Boswick both spotted the reversal.

"Sonar up," Pitt yelled as Boswick flung the wheel hard over and cut power.

"I've got something," Giordino shouted while eyeing the sonar readout.

Across from him, Brigitte fumbled with the winch controls. She punched one of the power buttons, but instead of activating the take-up reel, she sent more cable spooling off the back end. Combined with the ship's slowing, the action sent the sonar towfish dropping toward the seafloor.

Giordino watched as the form of a wreck began to appear on the monitor. The image suddenly distorted. A second later, the screen turned black. He looked at Brigitte. "Did we lose the fish?"

Brigitte's heart pounded as she realized her error. She reversed the

winch control and stared at the stern's view camera feed as the cable was wound in. Seeing a yellow cable marker near the end of it, she slowed the pace, then watched in horror as a frayed and empty cable sprang from the water.

Giordino saw by her face that the sonar fish had indeed been lost on the wreck and he immediately marked their position.

Forward on the bridge, Boswick was still trying to dodge the erratic sailboat. One of the teens finally regained the tiller and turned away as the *Pelican* veered right and drifted to a halt. The boys gave a friendly wave at the NUMA ship as they finally turned on track and gave chase to the other boats.

"Picked up a few gray hairs there." Boswick rubbed a hand across the top of his smooth head. "And I don't have all that many left."

"We were due for some excitement," Pitt said. Once the little sailboat was safely in the distance, Boswick picked up speed and resumed a course down the survey line. Pitt stepped back to the survey bay. "How's the fish?"

From the blackened monitor, Giordino's arched brow, and Brigitte's somber stare, he surmised the answer.

Giordino shook his head. "French fried."

"I am so sorry," Brigitte said. "It was all my fault. I went the wrong way with the winch."

Pitt could see the devastated look in the young woman's pretty eyes. She was an experienced oceanographer who had a strong resume of offshore research work, but had admitted to little experience hunting shipwrecks.

"Kissed something on the bottom?" he asked.

"Yep, that's the bad news," Giordino said. "The good news is that it snagged on a wreck. With a little luck, it's where we'll find the fish."

He rewound the sonar's digital feed to show the bottom scan before the cable snapped. Just before the screen turned black, the shadow image of a submerged vessel's bow section appeared crisply.

"Do you have a fix?" Pitt asked.

"I can get us pretty close. Water's about eighty feet deep, so it's diveable."

"I'll have Harvey bring us around and we can take a look."

Brigitte was still ghostly pale from her mistake. The lost sonar fish was an extremely expensive piece of electronic equipment. The Institute didn't have deep pockets. Reimbursing NUMA for the cost of the unit would hit the organization hard, and possibly cost Brigitte her job. Pitt saw her concern and gave her a smile.

"Don't worry. Al and I may not catch much with a rod and reel, but underwater, we're dynamite with a fish that can't swim."

3

Captain Boswick guided the *Pelican* to Giordino's marked coordinates and stationed the ship over the site of the lost sonar gear.

On the stern deck, Pitt tossed a marker buoy over the side that was attached to a weighted line of rope. He joined Giordino in a nearby equipment bay, where the two men donned drysuits and scuba equipment. A NUMA crewman helped with their tanks and regulators, while Brigitte checked the surrounding seas for approaching marine traffic.

The two divers stepped to a hydraulic platform at the stern and lowered themselves to the water's edge. Pitt stepped off first, striking the chilly water and vanishing quickly beneath the surface.

The water was murky, and Pitt felt the immediate pull of a lateral current as he descended a dozen feet before making his way to the drop line. Giordino appeared beside him a few seconds later and gave him the OK sign. Both men cleared their ears and proceeded to the bottom.

The water clarity improved as they descended, but the depth filtered the light so that when they reached the seafloor, it resembled a

sandy desert at twilight. The barren, undulating surface extended to the full limit of their visibility, about thirty feet. There was nothing in view resembling a shipwreck. Giordino checked his wrist compass and pointed north, and the two men kicked their fins on the heading, gliding a few feet off the bottom.

Though the water was cold, the visibility middling, and the marine flora and fauna all but absent, Pitt felt a vitality surge through him. There was a thrill to venturing under the sea, even after countless dives. He felt serene underwater, while at the same time his senses were at their most extreme. Kicking through the murky water, his curious mind probed at the perpetual mysteries just beyond view in a realm that was foreign to most people. For Pitt, there was always a wonder to be found below the surface, even in a vast expanse of empty water.

It appeared on this dive thirty meters later when a tall dark shadow appeared to their left. The two divers altered course and approached the wreckage of a vessel grounded in the seabed.

It wasn't a large vessel, maybe forty meters long, Pitt estimated. Its decayed state indicated it had been a resident of the seabed for many decades. Though covered with silt and concretions, Pitt could tell it was a ferryboat, for the remains of two rusty sedans appeared on its single open deck.

Approaching from the vessel's stern, Pitt assumed the ferry had been en route across the Channel when it sank, its prow pointed toward England. As he drew closer, he noticed the transom and a large section of the stern were absent, having been roughly sheared away. The remains were not visible near the wreck.

As they approached the deck level, Giordino swam to the port side and Pitt to starboard, both scanning the wreck for the missing sonar fish.

Pitt took a moment to examine the two cars parked in tandem.

While both were sedans, they were too far deteriorated to identify their makes. Their bulbous external headlamps and sweeping fenders told Pitt that the cars dated to the 1930s. Looking closer, he saw a seam of bullet holes in one of the rusty fenders.

The missing stern now made sense. The ferry had come under attack in wartime and had its stern blown off by a bomb or an artillery shell.

Pitt rose above the old cars and swam forward, parallel to Giordino on the opposite side. He approached the bridge structure and rose over its roof, allowing him to look down on the forward deck. A touch of bright yellow caught his eye, and he observed the sonar fish below him, the remains of its tow cable wrapped around a corroded deck railing.

Giordino spotted the fish a second later and gave Pitt a thumbs-up signal before spiraling down to retrieve it.

Pitt dropped to the port bridge wing. Finding the side door open, he swam into the narrow compartment. He flipped on a dive light, as the bay was dark, even though the forward glass windows had long since fallen from their mounts. At the center of the bridge, the metal spokes of the ship's wheel had turned gray with corrosion. Behind it, in somewhat better condition, stood a large upright binnacle. A layer of marine growth covered the face of the compass inside, but the interior brass was surprisingly unmarred. Its presence told Pitt that the wreck had remained undiscovered by local divers, who would have quickly absconded with the artifact.

The deck of the bridge contained scattered debris, coated in a dark layer of sediment. Pitt wondered if the bones of the bridge crew lay hidden in the muck, but he had no interest in finding out. He turned his light overhead, noticing a chronometer still mounted above the forward windows, where his exhaust bubbles were now congregating. The hands on the timepiece were fixed at 10:40, marking the

moment of death for the ship. He eased around and crossed the bridge space. As he made his way to exit the starboard wing, his light crossed two rectangular shapes by the rear bulkhead.

He hovered over the items, brushing his hand above them to swirl away a layer of built-up silt. When the brown cloud dissipated, Pitt saw two metal valises standing side by side. He gripped the handle of the nearest one and gently pulled, expecting the piece to disintegrate in his hand. But the entire case lifted easily from the sediment. He stowed his light and retrieved the second valise, then made his way out the wing door with both cases. He kicked up to the roof of the bridge and met Giordino ascending from the deck with the sonar fish cradled in both arms. Giordino gazed at Pitt, who looked like an underwater tourist toting a suitcase in each hand, and shook his head. Together, they made their way across the length of the ferry and over the truncated stern, retracing their original path.

They swam awkwardly with their added cargoes. Battling the current, they might easily have failed to find their drop line. But both had made thousands of dives, and they intuitively compensated for the unseen current. They spotted their thin polypropylene drop line and swam to its weighted base. Giordino gathered up some slack in the line and looped a makeshift harness around the sonar fish. He left a length of line free and passed it to Pitt, who tied on the two cases. They checked their dive computers and began a slow ascent, taking a short decompression stop before surfacing next to the dive platform.

"Find some Louis Vuitton luggage for the taking?" Giordino asked as they climbed onto the stern deck and stripped off their dive gear.

"Something more industrial," Pitt said. "Made of metal, I think. Maybe they hold something that will help us identify the wreck."

"It would be nice to know who ate our sonar fish." Giordino stepped over to the side rail and yanked up the shot line. Pitt joined him to help hoist aboard the sonar, followed by the two cases.

Brigitte rushed over with a relieved look and studied the damaged sonar fish.

"You found it," she said. "*Merci*."

Pitt picked up a frayed piece of cable that drooped from the fish like a limp tail. "Outside of the snapped cable, it looks like she survived intact."

"Thank heavens," Brigitte said. "Replacing that would have cost me a year's salary."

"With a little cable surgery," Giordino said, "we'll put her back good as new."

Captain Boswick joined them on deck. "Commands for the helm?"

Pitt glanced at the low sun peeking from a wall of gray clouds. "Not much else we can do out here today. Let's head back to port and regroup."

"Tell me about the wreck," Brigitte said. "Was it old?"

"Looked to be a Channel ferry that was sunk during the war," Pitt said. "On her stern deck were a couple of cars that dated from the 1930s."

"I'll check our archives and see if I can make an identification. My initial search didn't show a ferry among the area's known wrecks."

"I don't think she's been visited until now." Pitt motioned toward the twin cases.

"These," she asked, "are from the wreck as well?"

"I found them on the bridge. Shall we see if there is anything inside?"

Pitt grabbed one case and Brigitte the other, and they stepped into a small bay off the stern that was configured as a marine lab. They soaked the cases in a freshwater tank, then used nylon-bristled brushes to carefully scrub off the exterior concretion. The cases proved to be made of aluminum, which accounted for their state of preservation. While the aluminum skin cleaned up well, they were

not ready to be opened. Each was secured by a thick padlock that required a brass key to unfasten.

"Must be something of value, with these heavy locks." Brigitte grabbed one of the padlocks and gave it a tug. "I remember my grandmother had an old steamer trunk with one of these locks. It was hard to open, even with the key."

"I suggest we take a similarly old-fashioned approach to opening it." Pitt held up a hacksaw he'd retrieved from a tool cabinet.

He applied the nubby teeth to the shank, easily cutting through a layer of rust. The inner core was still solid, and it took several minutes to sever. When it broke free, Pitt twisted open the lock, removed it, and pushed the case toward Brigitte. "How about you do the honors?"

She placed her small hands on the case and unhooked its tarnished brass latch. The lid pulled open easily, hinting that its seams had not held back the sea. That was proven by the soggy mass inside.

"It looks," she said, "to be some paperwork that has turned to mush."

Pitt gazed at the contents, a soggy brown and amber mass of cellulose that had once been an assortment of documents. It reminded Pitt of a pot of oatmeal.

"Perhaps the other case fared better." He approached the second case with the hacksaw. Its lock parted after a similar effort, and he again allowed Brigitte to open the lid.

"This one feels lighter," she said, turning the latch toward her and springing it open.

This time, she felt resistance all around. She rapped the seam of the case with her palm, then slowly pried the lid upright.

The interior was perfectly dry. It was packed with dozens of small manila envelopes placed in orderly rows. Brigitte pulled out one, finding it relatively heavy and filled with multiple small objects. She studied the sealed flap, which had a handwritten note glued over the seam.

"'Monsieur Hoffmann, 23 Rue Montagne, Antwerp,'" she read aloud. She shook the envelope, listening to the objects at the bottom rattle against the paper.

"No harm in taking a look." Pitt found a pair of scissors and snipped off a corner of the envelope as Brigitte held it out. She tipped up the bottom and watched as a dozen pea-sized rocks tumbled onto the table. They were roughly cube shaped and slightly opaque.

Pitt glanced at the soggy mass in the first case and stuck his hand into the muck. He felt along the bottom, then pulled out a closed fist. He extended his hand to Brigitte, turning and opening his palm over hers. She caught a half dozen of the same small stones. She held one up to the light, noticing it was dense and faintly translucent.

"Antwerp," Brigitte repeated. "You don't suppose . . ."

"I'm no gemologist," Pitt said, "but I think it's quite possible you may be holding a fistful of uncut diamonds."

4

A pair of seagulls wheeled overhead as the *Pelican* nosed into the narrow harbor at Saint-Valery-en-Caux just before sunset. The quaint coastal town midway between Dieppe and Le Havre was once a popular fishing port, but decades of overfishing in the English Channel had decimated the industry. The port's lone marina was now populated with sailboats and power cruisers.

As the NUMA ship reached its berth, a long-haired young man in a tweed blazer appeared on the dock, a notepad under his arm. He caught the attention of Captain Boswick, who invited him aboard and escorted him to the ship's marine lab. Pitt and Brigitte were busy photographing the underwater find, while Giordino stood nearby dissecting the sonar fish.

Boswick poked his head in the door. "There's a fellow here who says he's a reporter for the Le Havre newspaper. He'd like to do a story on your diamond wreck."

Pitt gave Brigitte a questioning look. "News certainly travels fast here."

Brigitte gave a guilty look. She had made several calls to the

Marine Institute in hope of identifying the shipwreck. She was ultimately successful, as a historian had tentatively identified the vessel as the *Cornwall*, a Channel ferry that had operated between Le Havre and Portsmouth.

"I may have mentioned the diamonds in one of my calls."

Pitt waved in the reporter, who approached with an inquisitive look. He introduced himself in rapid French, which Brigitte translated for Pitt and Giordino.

"His name is Raoul Vogel, a feature writer with the *Le Havre Presse*." She turned and spoke to him briefly.

"His cousin is a colleague of mine at the Institute. I spoke to her earlier about the wreck. Raoul happened to call her just after our conversation. He apologizes for the intrusion and asks if he could conduct an interview for the paper."

"Does he speak English?" Pitt asked.

The man shook his head. "Very poor," he said, drawing out the vowels. "*Je suis désolé.*"

"Why don't you handle it?" Pitt said to Brigitte. "It's only appropriate, as you put us on the wreck," he added with a wry smile.

"Yes, I guess it was my doing. I'll show him around the ship first." She escorted the reporter out of the bay and walked him around the vessel, the two of them conversing as they went. They returned to the lab fifteen minutes later. "Raoul asked to see the stones and take a picture," she said.

Vogel approached the open cases on the table. He eyed the loose stones and the rows of sealed packets in the dry case.

"*Je peux?*" he asked, flipping his fingers across the envelopes. He pulled out a packet from the back of the case and tested its weight. As he did so, a folded letter came with it and dropped to the table.

Brigitte scooped it up.

"Guess we missed that," Pitt said. "What does it say?"

"I believe it's written in Dutch," she said, holding it up. "I'm afraid I can't read anything other than the letterhead. The stationery comes from the Antwerp Diamond Bank."

"A diamond bank?" Giordino said. "Maybe you guys did strike it rich." He stepped over and eyed the document. "I can scan it and obtain a translation."

"And identify the diamonds' rightful owner," Pitt said. "Easy come, easy go."

The reporter snapped some quick photos of the cases and stones with his cell phone, then took a single posed shot of Brigitte, Pitt, and Giordino by their find. In the same morose manner in which he had arrived, he said his thanks and departed the ship.

Pitt glanced at his watch. "Too late to call the Antwerp Diamond Bank tonight, but perhaps we can ring them in the morning."

"Yes," Brigitte said, "if they are still in business."

"Now that everyone knows about our horde of diamonds," Giordino said, "perhaps we should stash them somewhere safe."

"The bridge is secure," Pitt said. "There's always someone there on watch."

They closed and secured the cases and moved them to a cabinet on the bridge, under the watchful eye of Captain Boswick. Once showered and dressed, they strolled to dinner at a quiet café near the marina. Pitt celebrated their discovery by ordering a bottle of Burgundy from Maison Joseph Drouhin, which Giordino supplemented with a local French beer.

"Will the sonar fish live to swim another day?" Brigitte asked.

"Without a doubt," Giordino said. "I should be able to finish rewiring it tomorrow, if you want to continue the survey. It might be nice to take a full pass over the *Cornwall* . . . But at a higher depth."

"I am sorry, again, for the damage."

"At least it happened at the end of the project," Pitt said.

"The fact is," Brigitte said, "we have covered more territory than

originally planned over the past three weeks. It is supposed to be windy with rough seas tomorrow, so I think we can conclude the project now on a high note."

"I would still call our Franco-American underwater venture a success," Pitt said. He poured the wine and raised his glass.

Their dinners arrived promptly after a shared appetizer of local oysters. Pitt and Brigitte sampled sea bream fillets with fennel, while Giordino attacked a plate of wild boar terrine.

"I'll certainly miss the food here," he said between bites. "Can you cook like this?" he asked Brigitte.

She shook her head and laughed. "I'm afraid I'm a microwave chef at best. My mother tried to teach me, but I was a tomboy growing up and just wanted to be like my father."

"What was his occupation?" Pitt asked.

"He was a Navy diver. Taught me to dive when I was twelve years old. He loved the sea and exploring underwater. He was always bringing home nautical artifacts he acquired in his travels. Ship's wheels, brass running lights, things like that. My mother hated the stuff, but I loved it."

Pitt could tell by the sudden mist in Brigitte's eyes that her father was no longer living.

"Thankfully, I didn't inherit his hoarding tendencies," she continued, "but I shared his love of the sea. So I studied oceanography and history at university, and am now happy at my work with the Institute. Although, after this project, I am now hungry to discover a meaningful shipwreck."

"You're not the first to be seduced by the sea," Giordino said, eyeing Pitt with a grin.

"What's next for the two of you?" Brigitte asked as she dug into a serving of Normandy apple pie for dessert.

"Another day or two here to break down the equipment," Pitt said. "Al's off to the Mediterranean to test a new submersible, while

I'm due back in Washington next week for a conference. I'm trying to convince my wife to fly over before then for a short vacation in Paris."

"I should hope she does not require a great deal of convincing."

"Not at all. She loves France. But work always seems to interfere with life. What is next for you?"

"Back to the Institute in Le Havre for a few days to write up our survey results, then on to an environmental impact study nearby for a proposed pipeline. Not as much fun as searching for shipwrecks. I suspect it will be a few weeks before I can assemble a dive team to fully investigate the *Cornwall*."

"Some photos of the ferry and the cars aboard it would make for a nice exhibit," Pitt said.

"Along with a sample of the diamonds." She smiled. "Especially if they are valuable."

"I sent some photos to a geologist at NUMA headquarters," Giordino said. "She should be able to tell us if they're worth anything."

Brigitte gave the men an earnest look. "I am sorry how things turned out, between the damage and the lack of shipwrecks." She knew that Pitt and Giordino were highly accomplished men and experts in their field. She had hoped for more compelling results with their assistance.

The two looked at each other and shrugged. "There's no accounting for what's in the sea," Pitt said. "As for the damage, it is just a few wires and some sheathing. Less than Al spends in a week on cigars."

They finished their meal and walked across a now quiet marina to the *Pelican*. They climbed onto the bridge, where the captain sat in a corner reading a book. "Weather forecast looks iffy tomorrow, if you had designs on a final survey run."

"I think we're going to call it good," Pitt said. "You can start thinking about your next project, Harvey."

The captain perked up. "It's the Mediterranean for me and the *Pelican*. Sunny days ahead."

Brigitte stepped toward the sonar bay. "I think I'll back up some files before turning in."

They bid one another good night, and Pitt and Giordino retired to their cabins one level below. Pitt cycled through his email and composed a note to his wife, Loren, in Washington before drifting off to sleep.

He'd been asleep for just a short time, when he was awakened by a commotion overhead. He dressed and was exiting his cabin when he heard yelling, followed by two gunshots.

Pitt sprinted up an interior companionway that fed into the sonar shack. The room was empty and the door to the bridge closed. He tried to push it open, but something on the other side was blocking it. He shoved the door open a crack and saw Brigitte's body wedged against the door.

She stirred as he called her name and she rolled to the side, allowing him entry.

"Are you hurt?" He dropped to one knee beside her.

She sat upright and rubbed her head. "The diamonds. Someone stole them." She pointed across the bridge to the wooden cabinet. Its lid was open and the two cases gone.

But Pitt's eyes lingered only a second. For nearby, Harvey Boswick, the *Pelican*'s captain, lay face down in a pool of blood.

Giordino burst onto the bridge from a wing door and took in the scene. He rushed to check on Boswick, while Pitt helped Brigitte to her feet.

"I'm okay." She held on to Pitt for balance. "A masked man came in and asked for the diamonds. There was a struggle with the captain. I tried to help him, but took a blow to the head." She looked toward Boswick with shock in her eyes. "Did he shoot the captain?"

Giordino checked for a pulse, then looked at Pitt and shook his head. Out the windshield, they saw a car's headlights flick on in the parking lot as an engine started.

"Can you call the police?" Pitt asked Brigitte.

"Yes, but please don't go. He has a gun."

She might as well have spoken to the wind, for Pitt was already out the door.

5

Pitt thundered across the gangway and turned down the dock. Giordino followed a few paces behind, having paused to pluck a set of keys from a bulkhead hook before exiting the bridge.

The parking lot was a hundred yards away, and both men hurtled across the dock like sprinters. The waterfront was deserted at the late hour, the departing car's engine the only sound echoing off the stone buildings surrounding the harbor.

As Pitt reached the quayside lot, the car sped out the opposite side and disappeared down a narrow side street. The distance was too great for Pitt to identify the driver, but as the vehicle passed under a streetlamp, he saw it was a blue four-door sedan.

He leaned against a dock rail to catch his breath as Giordino rushed up to him. "See which way they went?"

Pitt nodded.

Giordino held up the keys for Pitt to take. "Let's get them."

They hurried to the Citroën Berlingo panel van they had rented to transport their equipment and hopped inside. Common on the narrow streets of Europe, the small van was no larger than the fleeing sedan. Pitt floored the vehicle out of the parking lot. The van lurched forward, although its small diesel engine was unable to smoke the tires.

He turned onto the street and sped down it for several blocks, leaving the confines of the village. There was no sign of the blue sedan. They drove for several minutes and approached a large roundabout bisected by a larger east-west thoroughfare. A handful of lights showed vehicles traveling in either direction.

"Got a guess?" Giordino asked.

Pitt glanced down the assorted roads and eyed the taillights of a distant vehicle heading west.

"That one seems to be moving fast." He motioned toward the car's fading lights.

He carved through the roundabout, exiting onto the two-lane road running west. He kept a heavy foot on the accelerator as the small van rumbled across the Normandy countryside. It took a few minutes, but Pitt gradually closed the gap. He drew close enough to confirm it was the blue sedan, then dropped back and followed at a leisurely distance.

"Did you happen to bring your cell phone?" Pitt asked.

Giordino shook his head. "Left it on my nightstand. Next to my wallet, cigars, and French-English dictionary."

"Same here. I guess there will be no calling the gendarmes. And a nightcap on the way home is now out of the question."

"Did you get a look at the guy?"

"No," Pitt said. "But if I had to guess . . ."

"The reporter."

"He didn't strike me as the journalistic type."

"He claimed no English, either," Giordino said, "which the younger generation here all seem to know."

The glow of city lights off the overhead clouds beckoned ahead of them. Hedges and farm fields gradually gave way to houses, shops, and office buildings as they entered the port city of Le Havre. The blue sedan headed toward the city center, then turned down a cross street that led to the commercial shipping docks.

Pitt slowed the van as he followed the turn, holding back as far as he could while maintaining sight of the car.

The sedan drove past a large shipping wharf, busy even at that late hour with container ships transferring their cargo via huge cranes. It followed the road through an older section of the waterfront dotted with dark, run-down warehouses. The car pulled to a stop in front of a fire-damaged brick building, which looked to have been abandoned for decades. Despite its appearance, two modern utility trucks were backed against a pair of drop-down doors at its side.

Pitt stopped a half block away and pulled into an adjacent lot. He killed the headlights and parked behind a large trash bin. He and Giordino watched as a man dressed in black exited the sedan. He took the two stolen cases from the backseat and entered the building through the front door.

"He's got long hair," Giordino said. "Has to be that reporter, Vogel."

"Let's see what he's up to."

They crept to the side of the building. The high windows were dark, but somewhere inside a portable generator buzzed. They approached the heavy wooden front door and Pitt tried the handle. It turned freely. He twisted it slowly and eased the door open a crack. The foyer was too dark to see any details, but a faint light shone down a side corridor, while a small bluish glow appeared nearby.

Pitt pushed the door open and stepped in, Giordino on his heels. They took just a single step across the foyer, when a powerful light flicked on. The bright glow revealed the reporter against the far wall, grasping a powerful lantern with the two cases at his feet. He turned the light toward Pitt's and Giordino's faces, blinding them under its beam.

Pitt turned from the light, detecting a second man standing in the shadows of the foyer. Tall and bearded, he wore desert fatigues and brandished an AK-47, which he leveled directly at Pitt's chest.

6

"*Entrez-vous, messieurs,*" the gunman said in a deep voice while raising the weapon against his shoulder. Behind him, a monitor glowed blue with a video feed of the building's exterior.

"Pardon me," Giordino said, bullying past Pitt. "I think we took a wrong turn. We were looking for the fish market."

"Shut up," Vogel said in clear English. He reached under his coat and produced a pistol of his own. "Hold them here," he said to the man with the rifle. Vogel turned and stepped down the illuminated corridor, which was littered with empty bottles and debris. He passed a small room with a pair of portable generators, which sprouted extension cords like arms on an octopus. The lines ran across the floor and throughout the building, powering temporary lighting and the video security system in front.

He followed one of the lines into an open warehouse bay. A loading dock dominated one side, its twin raised doors revealing the two trucks parked against the ramp. One truck was filled with small wooden crates, the other showing a rack of automatic weapons.

In the center of the bay, a stack of empty pallets served as a makeshift table. Five men stood around it, studying a map under a utility

lamp. Henri Nassar was lecturing the others, but fell silent when Vogel entered and placed the two cases on the pallets.

Nassar glared at the intruder. "What are you doing here?"

"I was told I could find you here tonight."

"We are in pre-ops and about to depart. You are risking the mission and should not have come here."

"I have recovered the two cases. They contain uncut diamonds."

He opened the dry case and removed one of the envelopes. Tearing off one end, he dumped its contents onto the map. The men stared at the chunky little stones.

"All right, that's well enough," Nassar said. "But I don't have time for this now. Take them with you, and I will let you know where to meet tomorrow."

Vogel scooped up the stones and returned them to the case. He closed the lid and took a step from the table. He hesitated a moment and stared down at the floor.

"There is one problem," he said quietly.

"Yes?" Nassar said.

"Two men from the NUMA vessel followed me here. Amel is holding them up front."

Nassar's eyes turned to fire. "How could you let this happen?"

Vogel kicked at the ground. "The ship's captain was killed, and I escaped. I didn't realize anyone was tailing me."

"You killed the ship's captain and came directly here?" Nassar barely contained the anger in his voice. "There is much at stake, and you have jeopardized the security of the operation." The two men stared at each other.

"I am sorry." Vogel wilted under the man's gaze.

Nassar held his stare. "One mistake is damaging. Two is unacceptable."

In a smooth, unhurried move, he pulled a silenced Glock pistol from a side holster and fired three shots into the man's chest. Vogel

raised an arm in protest, his eyes splayed in momentary disbelief. He exhaled a burbled gasp and collapsed to the ground.

Nassar holstered his gun and looked at the men standing silent around the table. "Let that be a lesson. Our operations cannot be compromised under any circumstances." He nodded at one of the commandos.

"Have Amel bring the intruders in here."

A minute later, Pitt and Giordino were marched into the bay. Pitt looked at the men around the table. They were all dressed in desert fatigues with Arabic names stitched on their breasts. The men had hardened faces and were physically fit, cut of a different cloth than Vogel. Most wore buzz cuts and carried themselves with a calm yet confident manner.

Pitt had been around enough special forces soldiers to recognize the men were no ragtag group of terrorists, but a well-trained commando squad. And their leader, Nassar, was the coolest of the bunch.

Pitt looked past the two aluminum cases on the table to the dead reporter lying in a pool of blood. Whatever he and Giordino had stepped into appeared far beyond a simple diamond heist.

Nassar looked over the two Americans, noting they both had dark hair.

"What are you doing here?" he asked.

Pitt motioned toward Vogel. "He killed a friend of mine."

"Well then, it would seem justice has been served." Nassar turned to his second-in-command, Hosni Samad. "Do we have any more fatigues?"

Samad nodded. "There are several extra in the arms truck."

"Get two their size."

The gunman named Amel swung his weapon from Pitt to Giordino. "Are we not going to dispose of them here?"

"No," Nassar said, offering a thin smile. "I think we've just recruited a pair of suicide bombers."

7

Nudged at gunpoint, Pitt and Giordino donned the desert camouflage fatigues. Thoughts of resisting were deterred by the sight of Vogel. The dead journalist lying nearby left no question about the commandos' willingness to kill. As he struggled into a jacket sized too narrow for his broad shoulders, Giordino glanced at the Arabic name on the pocket. "I think Hakim forgot to eat his Wheaties," he muttered to Pitt.

"Shut up and turn around." Amel shoved both men against the wall with his rifle. A second gunman approached and bound their hands tightly behind their backs with a thin coil of hemp.

They were marched into the back of the truck loaded with crates and seated on a side bench. Their bound hands were then secured to a stanchion behind them.

They watched as the commando team efficiently secured the warehouse, loading the generators, cables, and lights, as well as the diamond cases, into the other truck. The last item retrieved was Vogel's body, which was dragged into Pitt and Giordino's truck and left at their feet.

"Beware of journalists bearing gifts?" Giordino asked.

"I suspect they didn't like the timing of his arrival," Pitt said. "Or ours."

"Some testy customers, if even a case of diamonds doesn't make them happy."

Pitt eyed the stack of crates that filled the enclosed truck bed. Two of the boxes were marked with French wording, followed by a pair of red flames, indicating a fire hazard. Pitt studied the label, noting the term *Formex P1* stamped on one side.

His attention was diverted when one of the gunmen climbed into the back of the truck with a pair of black balaclavas. He pulled one over Pitt's head, then Giordino's, but twisted them around so the eye and nose slits were on the backs of their heads.

The truck started a moment later and Pitt could hear a few other men join them on the bench, speaking French in low tones. The back door was slammed shut, and the truck pulled forward. As it began rumbling down the road, Giordino spoke quietly.

"Nice that they wanted to keep our heads warm, but mine smells like a dead buffalo."

"I must have the dirty socks flavor," Pitt murmered.

"Any luck with the translation?"

Pitt thought long and hard. He was jarred from his seat when the truck struck a pothole, and the memory came to him.

He leaned toward Giordino and whispered. "Let's hope our associates don't light up any cigars. If memory serves, Formex P1 is a French plastic high explosive, comparable to C4."

The two trucks worked their way out of Le Havre and headed south on the E5, mixing with sparse traffic at the early hour. The rear of the truck was noisy and uncomfortable, made worse for Pitt and Giordino by the knit head coverings. The truck gained speed, and the increased road and engine noise allowed Pitt and Giordino to converse without being overheard.

"How did an eighty-year-old box of rocks get us here?" Giordino said.

"Impeccably bad timing. How are your wrist bindings?"

"Tighter than a steel drum."

Pitt felt the wooden seat back behind them. He raised his wrists to the bottom edge and tried working the bindings against it. "Might try the seat back," he whispered, "in the event we're here for a while."

Giordino felt for the edge, then also began working his bindings against it. Seated outboard of Pitt, he caught the attention of one of the gunmen. There was no warning this time, just a rifle stock rammed into Giordino's stomach. He grunted as the air was driven from him.

"No tricks," the man yelled, then retook his seat.

"You okay?" Pitt whispered a minute later.

"Yeah. Just remind me to skip the aisle seat on the next trip."

Giordino remained still, but Pitt continued to work his bindings while blocked by his friend. He felt no progress, but it was all he could do. Bound next to a cache of explosives, he knew the coming attraction. He and Giordino would be sacrificed in a staged suicide bombing.

The truck hit another pothole, sending them bouncing in their seats. The truck eventually entered a motorway with smoother pavement and it picked up speed. Two hours later, they reached the outskirts of Paris and curled around to the southern side of the French capital. Passing near Orly Airport, they exited the highway into the suburban commune of Choisy-le-Roi.

Nassar drove the lead truck, guiding the other through a quiet residential block to a light industrial area that bordered the Seine River. He slowed while moving past a sprawling complex secured behind an iron rail fence, then turned into its narrow entrance.

A dozing guard in a small hut looked up at the appearance of the twin trucks. He scrambled to his feet and pressed a button that rolled open the entry gate. When the first truck drove through and pulled

to a stop, he stepped around its front grille. As he approached the
driver's door, the guard hesitated when he saw the driver was dressed
in fatigues and sunglasses and wore a long beard. The late-night
darkness concealed that the beard was fake.

Nassar gave the man a forced smile. "My apologies for the late
arrival, but we had mechanical problems that set us back a few hours.
A shipment of filtrate sand . . ." He motioned his thumb to the back
of the truck.

"I was not expecting any arrivals tonight," the guard said. "Do
you have a weigh bill?"

"Yes." Nassar reached beside him and picked up his silenced
Glock 19 and a clipboard. He passed the clipboard to the man, holding the pistol beneath it.

The guard reached out, frowning at a short note in Arabic script.

As the man grasped the clipboard, Nassar leveled the pistol at the
guard's heart and fired twice. He stepped on the gas, and the truck
lurched forward before the guard hit the ground, the clipboard still
clutched in his lifeless fingers.

Nassar wheeled toward the river, then turned down a road that
bisected two long single-story buildings. He drove to the end and
stopped near the corner of one of the buildings.

They had entered the grounds of the Edwin Pepin Plant in Choisy-
le-Roi, one of the largest water treatment facilities in Europe. The
plant served nearly two million residents of the Paris suburbs with
fresh drinking water. A multitude of low buildings spread across the
riverfront site housing massive tanks that separated, filtered, and
chlorinated water drawn from the Seine. As he had with the Sorek
Desalination Plant in Israel, Nassar had previously studied the layout
of the French facility and knew its greatest vulnerabilities.

He climbed out and directed the second truck, carrying Pitt and
Giordino, to park tight against a tall white building. Inside was the
pumping station for the entire complex.

Nassar returned to his truck and proceeded to a nearby building, where a handful of cars were parked out front. He drove to the side and stopped next to a side utility door. The building contained a recently upgraded system that used electrolysis to chlorinate the drinking water prior to distribution. Nassar stood guard as one of his commandos pried open the utility door with a crowbar, revealing a fuse room for the electrolytic generators.

Two other men quickly unloaded the truck's cargo: several twenty-five-kilogram fiberboard cases containing a mixture of ammonium nitrate and fuel oil. Nassar's team had stolen the industrial explosive from a Pyrenees mining company several weeks earlier. Next to it they placed several packets of the Formex P1 plastic explosives.

Nassar was taking a low-tech, high-stealth approach. Security at the facility was lax, but there would be no effort to enter any of the buildings and risk setting off an alarm to the police. The placement of the explosives and the suicide truck might not be as precise as he would have liked, but the result would still be catastrophic. The bulk of the treatment plant would be shut down for months, drying the faucets of two million Parisians.

Nassar activated a timed detonator affixed to a small amount of Formex buried at the base of the crates. He closed the utility door, returned to the truck, and retraced their route. A plant employee in a hard hat was crossing the parking lot when they drove by the front of the building, but he gave them only a passing glance. Nassar drove slowly, then turned and met up with the other truck.

In the cargo bay, Pitt and Giordino were bumped and jostled as one of the commandos dug through the stacked crates and placed a timed detonator inside a lower container. The boxes were restacked and then the two captives were freed from their seats and dragged out of the truck. Still blinded by their turned balaclavas, Pitt and Giordino were led to the front of the truck. Pitt was forced to climb into the driver's seat, while Giordino was shoved into the passenger seat and

buckled in. A roll of tape was used to bind each man's ankles together.

The commando named Samad rammed a gun into Pitt's throat to
hold him still as another loosened his wrist bindings and brought his
hands forward, retying them onto the steering wheel. Pitt was then
buckled in for added measure as Nassar's truck pulled alongside.

The commando leader stuck his head out the window, looking
wary. "What is this?"

"A more realistic suicide profile," said Samad, who stood on the
truck's running board.

Nassar gritted his teeth, then looked at his watch. "Is the detonator activated?"

"Buried deep in one of the cases, where it cannot be easily located."

"All right. Get all of the men in the back of my truck. Now."

The gunman nodded, then leaned in toward Pitt and Giordino.
"Say hello to Allah for me. You should meet him in about twenty
minutes."

The driver's door slammed shut, and Pitt heard the other truck
rumble away. He bent his head to the steering wheel, where he was
able to grasp the top of his balaclava with his fingers. He jerked his
head upright, pulled the covering from his head, and glanced at
Giordino.

"Unless you've grown accustomed to the smell of buffalo, lean
your head toward the steering wheel."

With his fastened seat belt, it was a harder stretch for Giordino,
but Pitt guided him close enough to clutch and remove his balaclava.

"Sweet mother of mercy." Giordino sucked in a deep breath of air.
"I tried not to breathe for the past two hours."

"Enjoy what you can, as evidently we only have another twenty
minutes."

Both men struggled with their bindings, but they were tightly

bound. "We're going to need a knife or a hacksaw," Giordino said. "Maybe you can drive us to an all-night hardware store."

Pitt eyed the ignition, which still held the truck's keys. "With our luck, it would be on the other side of town."

Pitt leaned forward and pressed his head against the center of the steering wheel. A deep sounding horn blared from beneath the hood, which Pitt kept activated for half a minute. The headlights of a small vehicle appeared a block or two in front of them, and Pitt sounded the horn again. But the car turned away, driving toward the front gate.

A short time later, the car reappeared, screeching around the corner with a roof-mounted light bar flashing red and blue. The security vehicle stopped well ahead of the truck, its lights illuminating the cab as a security guard jumped out. He raised a flashlight in one hand and a pistol in the other.

"Do you want to tell him this is all a big misunderstanding," Giordino said, "or shall I?"

Before Pitt could answer, the security guard fired a shot into the cab, perforating the center of the windshield. Both men tried to duck below the dashboard.

"A lucky shot into the back end," Pitt said, "and he's liable to blow us to the moon."

"About that hardware store . . ." Giordino flung his torso sideways toward the passenger door while swinging his wrists up behind him. His hands struck the dashboard, and he groped along its surface until feeling the dangling keys. He slipped the ignition key between two fingers and twisted his wrists. The diesel motor turned over twice, then caught, burbling to a low idle.

Pitt twisted his body in the other direction to bring up his right elbow. The truck had an automatic transmission with a column shift. When the motor caught, Pitt lowered his forearm onto the shift lever, pushing it in and down. The selector dropped past neutral and drive into third gear, but that was close enough. Pitt moved his bound feet

to the accelerator and mashed it down. The truck lurched forward. He twisted the wheel to bypass the security car and ducked.

The guard fired two more shots into the windshield, then retreated behind the car door as the truck approached. The truck rumbled past on the opposite side, clipping the security vehicle's side-view mirror. Pitt accelerated past the long row of buildings on either side of the road, clueless as to where they were heading. A short distance ahead, the lane ended at a crossroad. A brick building stood unyielding on the far side.

Pitt swung to the left and slowed the truck as they approached.

Giordino glanced at the speedometer. "Can you make the turn?"

"One way to find out."

Pitt let off the brake and swung the wheel to his right. With his hands tied to the rim, he could muster only a half turn of the wheel. The truck veered to the right, turning onto the cross lane, and almost immediately drifted off its left shoulder. It bounded onto a strip of landscape grass and skimmed by the brick building as Pitt twisted himself like a contortionist to turn the truck. He kept the wheel turned until the truck crossed a gravel lot and bounced onto the paved entry road.

"Exit looks to be ahead." Giordino continued to struggle with his bindings. He scanned the truck's interior for something resembling a sharp edge, but none was to be found.

In the distance, the two-tone wail of a French police siren grew louder. The paved lane led past a small guard hut and an open gate. Beyond it was another crossroad—an even narrower turn than he had just navigated. A row of thick poplars lined the far side.

"They're not making this easy." Pitt realized there was no way he could make the sharp right turn with a direct approach. He yanked the wheel to the left, lurching the truck off the pavement as he aimed it at the back of the guardhouse.

He looked to Giordino. "Any luck with your bindings?"

"None."

Pitt glanced at the dashboard. Between the instrument cluster and a wide glove box in front of Giordino was a radio and a small hinged door.

"Al, there's an ashtray next to the radio."

Pitt's eyes were back on the guardhouse as he carved a subtle arc around the back of it, then turned the wheel right, aiming for the narrow gate. Approaching from an angle, he had a better chance of completing the turn—if he could clear the gate.

Giordino held his breath as Pitt drove toward the gatepost, then swerved right at the last second. As the truck bounded from gravel to paved road, it rocked to the side, grazing the post with a metallic shriek.

Pitt turned the wheel as far as he could muster. The front fender grazed the bark off a poplar tree, then the truck broke clear, rolling freely down the narrow lane.

"It's all in the wrist." Pitt gave a half grin.

"Your high school geometry teacher would be proud," Giordino said. "As would A. J. Foyt."

"I don't think we'll be able to explain all this to the French police in twenty minutes or less," Pitt said, "so let's find a safe place to ditch this thing quickly, then find a way out."

Giordino was working on part two of the solution, bending to his side and probing the dashboard. He found the radio, then the compartment to its side. He pulled it open as Pitt acted as his eyes.

"Pay dirt," Pitt said. "In the lower right corner, if you can reach it."

Giordino groped until he touched a small round knob that he pressed in with a click.

It was a cigarette lighter, an amenity lost to most modern vehicles, but still in place on the older French truck. As they waited for the element to heat up and pop out, Pitt drove steadily down the lane. To his chagrin, the road led into a quiet residential neighborhood with

narrow streets running off either side. Streets too narrow to navigate with his bound hands.

Outside, the blare of the police siren grew louder. "Maybe," Giordino said, "they want to give us a ticket for driving at night without our headlights turned on."

The road ahead split at a Y-shaped junction, and Pitt opted for the left. As he made the turn, a police van turned onto the same road several blocks ahead. Pitt immediately pulled to the side of the road and stopped, using both of his bound feet to press the brake. He turned the wheel into the curb to hold their position, then let off the brake and ducked. Giordino held his low position on the passenger side.

The truck's headlights had not been turned on and they went unnoticed pulling to the curb. The police vehicle raced by with its lights flashing, screeching onto the grounds of the water treatment plant behind them a minute later.

"Got it," Giordino said. He snatched the lighter between his fingers as it popped from the heating element. He tried to turn the tiny red burner against his own ropes, but couldn't reach the bindings. After several attempts, he raised his arms behind him. "I'm going to have to try to burn yours first."

It took a painful contortion, but Giordino finally raised the lighter to the steering wheel and Pitt's hands. The device had lost most of its heat by the time Giordino got close, but it didn't matter. He was suddenly thrown into his seat back when Pitt stomped on the accelerator.

"What gives?" Giordino said.

"Over there." Pitt tilted his head toward the driver's-side window.

Giordino looked past Pitt to a residential side street perpendicular to their position. Halfway down the street, a man was crossing the yard of a darkened house. He stopped mid-step and pointed toward Pitt and Giordino, calling toward an idling vehicle waiting at the curb.

It was the commando truck driven by Nassar.

8

Nassar had driven a few blocks from the water treatment plant and turned down the tree-lined street. He stopped in front of a brownstone duplex he had scouted earlier. The building was gutted on the inside as it underwent a complete renovation. A pallet of bricks and a pile of old lumber sat on the lawn, while a commercial trash container occupied the front walkway.

After parking in front of the worksite, Nassar and his team stripped off their desert fatigues and false beards and stuffed them into a worn canvas duffel. In the back of the truck, one of his men began gathering their weapons to conceal them in a compartment beneath the rear bench.

Hearing the approaching siren, the men waited in the truck until the police car passed. Samad then ran across the lawn and buried the duffel bag at the bottom of a trash bin. As he stepped back to the vehicle, he saw Pitt and Giordino in the other truck at the end of the street. Nassar cursed in disbelief when he gazed into his side mirror. "Bring one of the rifles up to the cab," he yelled. Nassar quickly drove the truck onto the lawn and made a three-point turn. As he began

pulling forward, Samad caught an AK-47 tossed from the back and scrambled into the cab.

———————

Pitt was already on the move, racing ahead several blocks to a broad intersection. He was relieved to find a wide four-lane road with a dividing median. Residential apartments lined either side, and all he could see were tall buildings in both directions.

Pitt could only guess they were somewhere in Paris, but had no idea where they should go to safely ditch the truck. The lights appeared marginally brighter to the left, so he turned right, hoping to drive away from the city center.

The dual lanes gave him plenty of room to complete the turn under acceleration. He'd entered onto the Avenue de la République, a long thoroughfare that ran near the left bank of the Seine, changing names a half dozen times along the way. All Pitt knew was that it was a wide, empty boulevard that allowed him to pick up speed.

"The road's a straight shot for a spell," Pitt said to Giordino, "if you want to try burning me again."

Giordino maneuvered the lighter into its socket and pressed down. His face was mashed against the side window as he waited for the element to heat, and he glanced into the side-view mirror.

"Looks like our buddies may want to have a word with you about your driving."

Pitt looked in his side mirror as the other truck swung onto the avenue a few blocks behind, its headlights swaying across the lanes. He felt the minutes ticking down and pushed harder on the accelerator, searching for an empty field or a vacant park. But the buildings seemed to grow larger and more concentrated.

Only a few sporadic vehicles shared the roadway at the late hour, allowing Pitt to speed freely and ignore traffic lights. A glance in the mirror told him the pursuing truck was doing the same. Unburdened

by its cargo of explosives, Nassar's vehicle slowly gained on Pitt's truck.

Speeding north, Pitt was late to interpret a road sign for an intersecting freeway, and he missed an on-ramp that would have led him quickly away from the city.

As it was, the boulevard led perfectly straight for a two-mile stretch, allowing Giordino another go with the cigarette lighter. He held the heating element close to Pitt's right hand, scorching through most of the rope before the lighter grew cold. Pitt yanked on the binding until it broke free from his wrist.

"Thanks. And no charred flesh to boot," Pitt said. "Let me return the favor."

He reached for the lighter just as the truck struck a dip in the road. Both men bounced from their seats, and Giordino lost his grip on the device. It dropped to the floor and rolled beneath the seat.

"This just isn't my day." Giordino wedged his feet under the seat to try to kick it out.

Pitt groped the floor with his free hand, but came up empty. He abandoned the search when gunshots erupted behind them.

Nassar had closed to within a dozen yards. Pitt looked to see the commando Samad leaning out the truck's passenger window with an AK-47, its muzzle flashing with fire.

———

"Aim low, just at the tires," Nassar ordered, knowing they would be engulfed should the explosives detonate. He hoped to stop the truck, kill the two Americans, then make good their escape.

Samad kept his aim low, skittering shots off the pavement. As the fleeing truck's cargo bay extended well past the rear axle, the tires proved a difficult target.

Passing a traffic signal, Nassar regretted having discarded their disguises, knowing they would encounter surveillance cameras as

they approached the center of Paris. He yanked a ball cap low over his brow and pulled up his jacket collar, cautioning Samad to do the same.

Ahead of them, Pitt fought to gain separation, knowing the danger of a stray bullet. He held the accelerator to the floor as the big truck swayed down the boulevard.

Giordino shook his head at the gunfire. "Are they dying to stop us?"

Pitt could only smile at his friend's morbid question. He took a glance at his watch. They had less than five minutes until the explosives were due to detonate.

The boulevard shrunk from four lanes to two, and multistory shops and residences crowded the street as they entered the 13th arrondissement. Pitt had to swerve around a stopped news truck delivering the morning paper, briefly cutting onto the sidewalk to maintain momentum. A metallic screech sounded a few seconds later as Nassar followed suit, scraping the side of the news vehicle.

As he drove, Pitt tried to untie the binding on his left hand, hesitating when the road angled into a large, round plaza. They had reached the Place d'Italie, a major city intersection that fed into no less than eight roads splaying from its center like spokes from a hub.

"We don't seem to be evading civilization," Giordino said.

Pitt gritted his teeth. Contrary to his intent, they had driven deeper into the heart of Paris. The tall buildings that crowded the narrow streets, combined with a gloomy night mist, obscured any landmarks or sense of direction. As the time ticked away, Pitt could only try another direction and hope for the best.

He motored onto the large roundabout, dodging some smaller cars as he sped through the light traffic.

Nassar's truck followed a short distance behind. Samad fired a shot that missed to the side, then the gunman fell back into the cab as the vehicle turned.

Both trucks sped past a police car parked in front of a late-night café. The officers were inside, but heard the last gunshot. As the two vehicles roared by, they raced to their car and powered up their flashing lights and siren.

Pitt was halfway around the circle by the time the police car left the curb. He randomly chose one of the feeder roads and turned onto a dimly lit street that angled to the northwest.

Nassar followed close behind, his vehicle having gained ground through the roundabout.

"Get them now," he yelled to Samad as he eyed the police car in his side mirror. Nassar had closed in on Pitt's rear bumper and swung into the oncoming lane to pull alongside the truck. But Pitt had noticed his move and deftly drifted to the center, blocking Nassar's approach.

They parried back and forth for several blocks, Pitt wheeling from one street to another, trying to gain separation, while the police car trailed far behind. Samad continued to fire single shots, until finally hitting the mark when Pitt rounded a corner.

Pitt heard the boom of a rear tire bursting, then felt the tug of the steering wheel.

"Party's about over." He kept his foot on the accelerator, knowing their speed run would be finished once the steel wheel spat out the damaged tire. He held to the center of the road and continued to block the pursuing truck.

"Looks like a large park coming up," Giordino said, "on both sides of the road."

Pitt glanced a block ahead to see the congested buildings part. A pool of darkness encompassed the road, affirming Giordino's verdict. "Let's find a parking spot and ditch this bomb box."

He had been struggling to untie his left wrist and finally loosened the binding as they approached a parklike space with open lawns. Pitt shook away the rope as a group of pedestrians strolled along a

sidewalk on the left, and he idly wondered why they would be out so late at a park.

To his right, a pair of wide gravel walkways extended into the darkness. They both appeared empty. He knew their time was short, maybe a minute or two at most. It seemed their last and only option.

With both hands free, Pitt cranked the steering wheel hard over, forcing the truck up the curb and onto the first walkway. The gravel path ran straight and true across a neatly manicured, grassy plaza. Dust flew from the truck as it raced ahead, despite its thumping rear tire.

"*Sacrebleu,*" Giordino blurted as they sped forward.

A glimmering wall of lights rose high in the sky directly ahead of them, tracing the outline of a towering metal structure.

Pitt looked from the massive construct to Giordino in disbelief. They had somehow managed to drive the explosives-laden truck to the base of the Eiffel Tower.

9

Nassar slowed his truck near the curb, eyeing the police car behind him as he ordered Samad back into the cab with his rifle. While distant sirens could be heard converging from all points of the city, no other vehicles had yet appeared on the scene. The pursuing policemen had a choice: stop and arrest the occupants of the truck slowing in front of them or pursue the madman barreling toward the Eiffel Tower.

Predictably, the police car hopped the curb and followed the trail of Pitt's truck.

Nassar accelerated past the open space on the Avenue Joseph Bouvard, then turned south, fleeing in the opposite direction. "Call for a pickup," he ordered Samad. "We'll have to ditch the truck."

Back on the Champ de Mars, the public ribbon of green that spread from the foot of the Eiffel Tower, Pitt kept his foot on the gas. Despite the late hour, scores of tourists, lovers, and souvenir hawkers strolled about in the shadow of the thousand-foot-tall icon. Built in 1889, Gustave Eiffel's tower attracted tourists around the clock as the most-visited monument in the world.

Pitt turned on the headlights and mashed the horn, warning the

people ahead on the gravel path. The siren and flashing lights from the pursuing police car further incited people to flee the oncoming vehicles.

Having visited Paris before, Pitt now recognized the area around him. He also knew that in the short time remaining, there was no getting away from the innocent crowds in the surrounding park and streets.

"Might be getting time," Giordino said, "to find a parking space."

Pitt's mind raced for a solution. There was, in fact, only one safe place to take the truck before it detonated, but getting there would risk all. In his mind, there was now no choice.

He resisted the urge to check his watch, knowing the results wouldn't matter. They just needed another minute . . . or two. The truck rumbled ahead, its flattened rear tire somehow holding intact.

Pitt steered toward the center of the tower, skirting a small pond and continuing forward. The giant iron structure loomed overhead, its top beacon illuminating the grounds in a faint glow. As he drew closer, he could see the central area beneath the tower's support legs was fenced off, just beyond a small frontage lane.

He stood on the brake and swung right onto the lane, willing the truck through the turn as it scraped the fence near one of the tower's massive support legs. At the end of the fence, a pathway through the landscaped grounds led to the north of the tower. Pitt turned hard left onto it.

A young man wearing glow-in-the-dark bangles jumped out of the way as the truck knocked over his card table filled with plastic souvenir towers. He saved his curses for the police car that followed a few seconds later, after it took a wider turn and crushed most of his inventory.

As the truck screeched past the tower leg, Pitt held his breath with the mental image of the whole structure collapsing under the force of the detonating explosives. He followed the semicircular path to the

opposite side of the tower, finally approaching the main cross street just beyond the monument. It was Quai Jacques Chirac, a main artery that ran along the left bank of the Seine.

Pitt reached the end of the walkway and drove the truck onto the road. The ornate Pont d'Iéna bridge beckoned in front of him, arching across the Seine. It was illuminated by the flashing lights from a pair of police vehicles speeding across from the far side.

Fearing an impromptu blockade, Pitt swung the truck right onto the quai, just missing a teen in dark clothes, who whizzed past on a scooter.

"I think we're about out of options," Giordino said.

"We just need another minute." Pitt scoured the road ahead. Soon he saw what he was looking for: a small cross lane that descended down a slope toward the riverbank. Pitt swung the wheel left, whipping across the quai in front of an oncoming bus. Behind him, the pursuing police car had to brake hard and wait for the bus to pass.

Pitt steered down the narrow passage, thankful to have put some distance between the truck and the Eiffel Tower. As he reached the bottom of the ramp, the rear tire finally shredded away, dropping the steel wheel onto the pavement. Sparks accompanied shrieking metal as the truck motored ahead.

"Hope you're not planning on giving our cargo a light," Giordino said.

Pitt shook his head. "I'll have it out shortly."

The roadway led down to a riverfront quay, where several tour boats were docked for the night. Pitt held the wheel straight for the river and kept the accelerator floored, squeezing as much speed as possible from the disabled truck.

Giordino realized Pitt's intent and he braced his feet against the floorboard.

As the truck roared across the quay, Pitt aimed for a gap between two of the docked boats. Despite the lost tire, the truck had gained

speed down the ramp. The front tires bounced over a thin retaining lip at the dock's edge, then nose-dived over the side and into the Seine.

Pitt and Giordino were thrown forward against their seat belts as the truck's nose smacked the water. The cab sunk beneath the surface quickly, drawn down by the weight of the engine. The rear of the truck angled out of the water in momentary suspension, then it, too, was swallowed by the river.

The trailing police car screeched to a halt on the dock, and the two officers leaped out, guns drawn. They reached the edge of the dock just in time to see the truck vanish into the dark water. They stared dumbfounded, then looked at each other. One was about to speak, when the quay rumbled beneath their feet. A second later, the river exploded in front of them. A fountain of water shot high into the air, deluging the tour boats and riverbank. The officers were thrown back against their car from the concussion as debris rained around them. A section of the truck's tailgate descended from the heavens, landing squarely on the roof of the police vehicle.

The echo from the explosion receded, and in a few moments, it was as if it had never occurred. The truck, its occupants, and the remnants of its lethal cargo were lost to the dark and silent river that continued to flow, as it had for thousands of years, majestically toward the sea.

10

The explosion rocked Pierre Roy from his bunk. He slipped on a worn bathrobe and padded from his cabin to the main deck of *La Rose*. The slender riverboat, built in the 1940s and painted black with touches of gold trim, was docked on the bank of the Seine a few hundred meters downriver from the Eiffel Tower. Nearly as antiquated himself, Roy used the boat for his livelihood, ferrying bundles of newspapers and boxes of fresh flowers each morning to street vendors who worked along the riverbank. He gazed upriver and saw no sign of an explosion, but the nearby bridges and riversides were aglow with red, blue, and orange emergency lights. Sirens wailed from a hundred points across the city. Roy watched the scene for a few moments, then let out a deep yawn. The trouble, whatever it was, appeared distant.

As he turned back toward his cabin, something in the river caught his eye. Stray branches were common in the Seine, but the riverman's eyes saw something different. He squinted under the glow of a deck light and saw . . . two figures bobbing in the water. They were being carried by the current as they struggled to make their way toward Roy's boat. He hurried to the side of the pilothouse, plucked a boat

hook from the bulkhead, and rushed to the bow as the two men approached. There he could see a lean man struggling to grip a shorter man, helping him stay afloat. Both were pale from the icy water.

Pitt looked up as Roy extended him the boat hook. He reached up and grasped the pole with his free hand. The water's momentum carried him and Giordino to the side of the boat as Roy desperately hung on.

"*Bonsoir*," Pitt gasped, juggling Giordino with one arm while clasping the rod with the other. "Mind if we come aboard?"

"*Oui*," Roy said. "To the stern."

He walked the boat hook alongside the hull to the stern, where the two men found respite from the current. Under a dangling sternpost lamp, Roy saw Giordino's arms were limp at his sides and his hands behind him.

When Pitt let go of the hook to clutch the transom, Roy tossed the tool aside and reached for Giordino's lapel. Aided by a push from Pitt, he pulled Giordino over the low railing, and both men fell prone onto the deck. Pitt pulled himself aboard a second later.

"*Mon Dieu*. You are bound hand and foot," Roy said to Giordino. "And you as well." He eyed the tape around Pitt's ankles. "How did you both survive the river?"

Pitt shrugged, too exhausted to explain. Their escape had been oddly unhurried once the truck plunged into the river. Pitt had time to unfasten their seat belts as the cab filled with water. When the truck struck bottom, he took a last breath and forced open the passenger door. Linking arms with Giordino in the dark, silty water, he slid them out of the vehicle and pushed for the surface. With bound feet, both men had to kick like dolphins to ascend.

Highly experienced divers, Pitt and Giordino were accustomed to all kinds of water conditions. Where others might have panicked, they brushed off the shock of the cold water and the power of the current in a simple quest for survival. When they broke the surface,

Pitt had to strain to keep both their heads above water, paddling with one arm while clutching Giordino with the other. He let the Seine's current, still raging from the springtime runoff, carry them downstream before the truck's contents detonated. Roy's boat appeared through the darkness ahead and Pitt towed his bound partner toward its berth along the right bank.

Giordino sat upright and responded to Roy's question. "We're both naturally buoyant, I guess. By any chance do you have a knife aboard?"

Roy hurried to the pilothouse and returned a minute later with a steak knife and a bottle of cognac. He cut away Giordino's hand ties, then gave him the knife to slice the tape from his ankles.

"*Merci*, my friend," Giordino said through chattering teeth as he cut the tape. He handed the knife to Pitt, then rose to his feet and accepted a drink from Roy. As Pitt stood and joined them, a bright spotlight blazed across the water from the far bank. The beam swept over the stern of the riverboat, then locked onto the three figures. Shouting voices echoed over the water, then a pair of police vehicles roared up to the revetment above the boat.

Roy looked on in shock as a SWAT team raced down to the boat with weapons drawn. Pitt took a quick drink of the cognac, then raised his arms alongside his host.

"I'm sorry, *mon ami*," he said to the Frenchman, noticing for the first time that Roy was wearing a robe and pajamas. "Sometimes, it just doesn't pay to get out of bed."

11

The heavy metal door creaked open, its hinges having last seen lubrication in the prior century. Two armed policemen stood at the threshold and motioned for Pitt to exit his holding cell. He rose from the cot and shuffled toward the door, wearing faded gray pants and a matching shirt provided by the detention center. Both his wrists and ankles were now secured by chained handcuffs, slowing his pace.

The officers escorted him down a drab cement-block corridor to a small conference room, where they removed his cuffs. Giordino sat at the table, dressed in a bright green shirt and slacks and similarly free of restraints. The French had abolished prisoner uniforms in the 1980s, opting to provide detainees with street clothes. The policemen remained at the door as Pitt entered the room.

Giordino admired Pitt's gray ensemble. "You look like a starved elephant."

"And you a lost frog." Pitt took a seat across from him.

"You might want to refrain from calling anyone that around here." Giordino spoke under his breath as a well-dressed man entered

the room and took a seat at the head of the table. He had a thin build, with cropped black hair and dark eyes that seemed touched with melancholy. He sat patiently in an uncomfortable silence as he considered the two Americans.

Captain Charles Lufbery had seen it all in his twenty-five years in the National Police. From a beat cop corralling drunks to a counterterrorism officer helping secure Paris, he had sat across the interrogation table from a wide assortment of criminal elements. This was perhaps the first time he had been surprised by the detainees facing him.

Pitt and Giordino had already been subjected to lengthy, separate interrogations by a tag team of police investigators. Their explanation of events matched known facts, and no one could deny that the duo had nearly died driving the truck into the Seine River the night before. It was now late the next morning, and neither man would have had a minute's sleep. Yet they didn't show it.

They were both rugged men, one short and powerful, the other tall and lean. Lufbery expected a look of fatigue, fear, or defiance on their faces. Instead, he saw only a calm indifference, infused with an unnerving sense of amusement. Even before the facts had confirmed it, Lufbery knew these men were no criminals.

A coffeepot sat near his elbow and he poured three cups. He introduced himself as he slid two of the cups across the table.

"No croissants?" Giordino asked with genuine disappointment.

"We can make a stop at the canteen on your way out, if you like." Lufbery spoke in a deliberate manner, his English nearly perfect.

"So we won't be charged," Pitt asked, "for swimming in the Seine after dark?"

"Not in this instance." Lufbery offered a thin smile. "The U.S. embassy has vouched for your character, in the manner of a rather thick dossier of your accomplishments. The authorities in Saint-Valery-en-Caux have also affirmed your account of the events aboard

your vessel last night. It would seem that France owes you a debt of gratitude."

"I'd settle for my clothes back." Giordino flexed his right arm, causing his bicep to pop the seam on the tight-fitting green shirt.

"We can arrange some additional wardrobe options. I would in the meantime like to offer my apologies for the death of your ship's captain."

"His murderer was in the back of the truck that blew up," Pitt said. "An alleged reporter named Vogel. He'd been killed earlier in Le Havre."

"You were a witness?"

"No, but we heard the gunshots and saw his body a short time later."

"Killed by the same characters that drove the other truck," Giordino said. "Any luck in apprehending them?"

Lufbery's eyes turned cold as he stared at the tabletop. "The vehicle was found afire behind an empty warehouse. I'm afraid we have few identifying clues, beyond your descriptions of those involved. But we are examining all data related to known extremists in the region."

"What exactly was their target?" Pitt asked.

"The water treatment plant at Choisy-le-Roi. It supplies much of the fresh water to the city. The facility was struck by a large explosion about the time you drove into the river. Thankfully, there are no reported casualties, but considerable damage was inflicted on the control operations. Much of south Paris may be without water for a short time."

"Seems an unusual target for a terrorist attack," Pitt said. "No visual displays of violence or indiscriminate killing. Any idea who these people are?"

Lufbery paused to sip his coffee. "A local newspaper received a call from an unknown Islamic group calling themselves the New

CLIVE CUSSLER THE CORSICAN SHADOW   77

Caliphate, who claimed responsibility. The call was made before the explosions, so there is some credibility. I'm afraid we have made no individual identification, but we are pursuing multiple avenues of inquiry."

"I don't believe they are Muslim extremists," Pitt said.

Lufbery squinted at him.

"Why do you say that?"

Pitt described their appearance and military bearing. "They were professionally trained and highly confident. I could be wrong, but the operation didn't seem the workings of an ideological attack."

"An interesting hypothesis," Lufbery said.

"That reporter, Vogel, didn't appear too radicalized, and he was obviously associated with them," Giordino added.

"Raoul Vogel is not his real name. It appears he used an alias to obtain press credentials, as there is no record of him outside a few articles he wrote for a Le Havre newspaper. We suspect he was using his guise as a reporter to acquire inside information to support local robberies and criminal acts. Unfortunately, I have no information on his true identity."

"A positive ID on the body is hopeless now," Giordino said. "Whatever was left of him after that blast must be halfway to the English Channel."

"True, but Le Havre is not that large a city. I am confident the local authorities will determine who he was. The recovery of your diamonds, however, may be a different story."

"They weren't ours to begin with," Pitt said. "I rather wish we'd never found them." He looked at the officer. "I think we've told you all we know."

"Your cooperation is appreciated. But I must ask one favor. I would like to see the warehouse where you were abducted."

"Certainly," Pitt said. "We could actually use a lift in that direction."

Lufbery escorted the men to the building's cafeteria for a quick breakfast, then requisitioned a car and driver and proceeded to Le Havre. Pitt's description of the building and its location were phoned to the municipal police, and several investigators were on-site when Lufbery pulled up two hours later.

Pitt and Giordino accompanied the police through the building, which had been scrubbed of any evidence. Only the dead reporter's bloodstains on the floor confirmed their account. Lufbery spoke to the lead officer as other police searched for any remaining evidence.

"The building appears clean, but it will be swept for prints," he said to Pitt and Giordino. "It's owned by a fish-processing company but has stood vacant for several years. That suggests a local knowledge and presence."

"Perhaps another connection with our reporter friend," Giordino said.

Lufbery nodded.

"Our captain was murdered as a result of their operation," Pitt said. "I'd like them all to meet justice."

"We'll pursue them to the end." Lufbery handed Pitt his business card and then shook hands with the two men.

Pitt and Giordino retrieved their rental van and drove back to Saint-Valery-en-Caux. The exhaustion of their ordeal along with a sleepless night hit them as they reached the dock.

Brigitte and the boat's crew greeted them with a warm return, but were shocked to hear of the night's events. Brigitte turned pale at the news of the reporter's death.

"All of this killing over some diamonds," she said. "It is a miracle you both survived."

"It's a bigger miracle that the Eiffel Tower is still standing." Giordino gave Pitt a sideways look. "But I did get a nice tour of Paris out of the deal."

Pitt motioned for Brigitte and the *Pelican*'s executive officer to

meet him on the bridge when the rest of the crew returned to their duties. "I didn't want to bring it up in front of the crew," Pitt said, "but what of Captain Boswick?"

"The police questioned everybody," the XO said, the shock of the incident still etched in his face, "and an ambulance took the captain away."

"He was taken to the morgue in Le Havre and will be transferred to a local mortuary after an autopsy," Brigitte said. "I told the police that the captain's body will need to be transported to the U.S. for burial, and they've agreed to help with the arrangements."

"Nice of you to think of that," Pitt said. "Boswick was a good man." Recalling the scuffle on the bridge, he eyed Brigitte for injuries. Her hair was disheveled and her eyes bloodshot. Pitt could also tell she'd had no sleep. "You sure you weren't hurt in the attack?"

Brigitte shook her head. "No, I just took a blow to the head." She rubbed the top of her scalp. "I think I was more shocked than anything."

Her eyes drifted to where Boswick had fallen after being shot. Unlike at the Le Havre warehouse, the bloodstains had been scrubbed away after the police had left.

"I think we all need a chance to rest and recoup," Pitt said.

"Yes," she said. "I would be grateful for some sleep." Brigitte moved to exit the bridge, but hesitated when Giordino entered with a bemused look, carrying a sheet of paper.

"Sorry to intrude on the slumber party," he said. "But I just received some ironic news."

"What's that?" Brigitte asked.

Giordino arched a thick brow. "It seems the so-called diamonds we recovered are virtually worthless."

12

The banker sat perfectly upright, as stiff as the hard maple chair that supported him. He looked in the general direction of the man seated across the desk, but didn't engage his face. Instead, the banker's eyes wandered from the desk lamp built from a nautical signal light, to a letter opener fashioned from a boarding pike, to the dusty model of an oil tanker on a rear bookshelf. He gazed everywhere but into the cold gray eyes of Yves Villard.

"I'm sorry, Monsieur Villard." He eyed the pike and hoped it wouldn't be thrust into him at his pending words. "The board of directors has reviewed your company's request, and I'm afraid their determination is final. No more credit can be extended, and you will be deemed in default if your existing loans cannot be made current by the end of the week."

He opened a thin binder and skimmed the first page. "The total debt balance now stands at 27.45 million euros. Absent a payment, the bank will have no choice but to place a lien on your fleet." He caught himself too late and cleared his throat. "I mean, the company vessels not under impound."

He closed the binder, gripping it tightly as he found the nerve to face his client and await the reaction.

Villard said nothing, but he didn't have to. Even sitting still, he exuded power, authority and, now, anger. This was all the more impressive considering he was approaching seventy years of age. His stout body was fit and seemed to strain at the seams of his dark wool suit. His black hair was barely tinged with gray, his tanned face nearly wrinkle free.

Only his hands showed the rough life he had endured after decades at sea, starting as an apprentice seaman while in his teens and building his company from scratch. Thick and meaty, his hands were gnarly and scarred from years of manual labor. The banker looked from Villard's hands to his eyes and found an intensity that proved the man had not yet given up living on his own terms.

"We're a seismic exploration and oil transport company," Villard said in a deep but surprisingly calm voice. "Our ships are our means of survival. You kill the ships, you kill the company."

The banker nodded. "Our management is sympathetic, but they don't see a way forward, given your situation."

"Our attorneys are working to address the matter."

"The bank's contacts believe that Interpol is unlikely to free the Marseille vessels in the foreseeable future, given the nature of the allegations."

"The accusations are localized to a few rogue employees," Villard said. "The management of the company had no involvement or knowledge of the activities." That was a lie, but the authorities had so far been unable to establish a link to the company's founder and CEO.

But it little mattered. By all appearances, it seemed that Lavera Exploration Company was about to succumb to a triple death blow. A slump in oil prices a few years earlier, from increased U.S. production and Russia bickering with OPEC, had been followed by a nosedive in demand during the pandemic. No sooner had the following recovery and Russia's invasion of Ukraine bolstered world oil prices than the bulk of the firm's fleet was impounded by Interpol in Marseille.

No less than twelve tankers, four survey vessels, and a pipe-laying ship were discovered transporting large quantities of Venezuelan cocaine and Mexican methamphetamines to Western Europe. A monthslong investigation by undercover French operatives had resulted in mass arrests and a seizure of the vessels.

Over the course of a decade, smuggling had become Lavera's most lucrative source of income. But the company's founder was more than a roughneck or drug mule. Yves Villard was a man of vision. A chance discovery on one of his seismic exploration vessels, utilizing proprietary remote sensing technology, had sent him chasing the future. His illicit drug money was not wasted on yachts or private jets, but invested for the long term in specialized vessels, expanded field surveys and, most of all, offshore leases. The leases were collected at strategic locations around the world and were the linchpin in his dream of a global monopoly. He had applied all of his drug profits and leveraged the company's assets to lay the groundwork for a future empire. But he had been caught flat-footed by the drug bust and his dreams were now unraveling before his eyes.

Villard had actually been scheming his exit from the drug trade, banking on some potential international contracts, when the seizure occurred. Now it was too late. The impounding of his ships had brought him to the brink of financial ruin, and only a small army of lawyers was keeping him out of jail.

Villard picked up the pike and tapped the blade against his open palm. "We have a number of new business ventures that are poised at a critical juncture and offer a highly lucrative revenue stream unrelated to oil." *And unrelated to drugs,* he thought.

"Yes, we have seen the projections," the banker said. "They appear speculative, and a questionable source of revenue for quite some time."

"That is not true. In fact, we have an opportunity in Israel for an immediate deal, and possibly in Egypt as well." Villard glanced from

the banker to Henri Nassar, who sat quietly at the side of the office. The ex-mercenary, wearing a conservative sport coat strained by his thick build, sat motionless for a moment. He lightly squinted at Villard, then nodded his head in exaggerated agreement.

The banker missed the exchange, but it didn't matter. He had delivered his message and now focused on his escape from the office. "While it does sound promising, I'm afraid that unless you become current on your present obligations, there is nothing more the bank can do."

He stood and tilted his head at Villard. "I wish you the best of luck, sir." He moved swiftly to the office door, letting himself out without a backward glance.

Nassar rose and closed the door, then slipped into the banker's seat.

"Pigheaded imbecile," Villard said. He stood and approached a side window while gingerly rubbing his spine. A tumble down a flight of stairs a few years earlier had left him with chronic back pain and a heavy reliance on oxycodone. He straightened himself and peered out the third-floor window toward one of Le Havre's marinas. It was full to the brink with small pleasure craft. The winds were blowing strong today, deterring all but the hardiest sailors from leaving their berths.

Villard gazed to the southwest at one of the commercial wharfs, where a large container ship was being off-loaded. His own dock lay slightly beyond, a small wharf that stood empty. He stared at the horizon, lost in thought, then shuffled back to his desk.

"We are on the cusp of triumph," he said softly. "Our future wealth could exceed that of the richest oil companies. Yet fools like him refuse to see it." He dropped heavily into the tufted leather chair. "Are we not well positioned in Israel?"

"Very much so," Nassar replied. "The Sorek Desalination Plant is critically damaged. Media reports suggest it may take upward of a

year to fully restore its capacity. As we suspected, Hamas is widely being blamed." Nassar paused to offer a self-satisfied grin. "We also have a preliminary agreement for our proposed pipeline to tap into the pumping station near Ashkelon. The politicians are clamoring for solutions, and we are the only ones poised to offer one. But our lease request is still under government review with the Energy and Water Resources Ministry."

"When do you expect approval?"

"There should be a ruling within the week."

Villard nodded. "Once we have that in hand, we can go public with our proposal. The Knesset will be falling over themselves to approve a deal, and we'll have our cash river, so to speak."

Nassar cleared his throat and gazed at the floor. "There may be some potential hurdles with the lease. As a foreign entity, we will be subject to opposition."

"Opposition that will fade with desperation. And we have two commission members in our pocket with subsidiary construction contracts." Villard tapped his fingers on the desktop. "Politicians, regulators, and government bureaucrats. They should be easier to manage than the cutthroats we've been dealing with the past few years."

"Perhaps, but they are not as reliably motivated by money."

"It is all we have left now, Henri. I'm afraid the equity shares I have given you in Lavera Exploration aren't worth a rusty chum bucket at the moment."

"The timing of it all is unfortunate. We are very close to success."

"The undercover police raid . . . it is a disaster," Villard said, his voice rising in anger.

"A costly loss, but it could have been worse," Nassar said. "At least there were no personal recriminations."

Nassar was right. Villard had avoided entanglement when his fleet manager had been killed in a gunfight during Interpol's raid. The dead man had conveniently taken the fall for Villard.

"Yes, that has been our only luck. But that business is dead now, as it should have been long ago." Villard glanced at a wall portrait of a woman seated in a spring garden. It had been twelve years since his wife had died. She had been the one virtuous thing in his life, the driving force for a life of dignity.

His decency had vanished with her death, and he'd thrown himself into a despondent chase for money and power, legally earned or not, as a salve to his emotional pain.

"It is fortunate," Nassar said, "that the exploration business has provided a path to redemption."

"Yes, but while the demand for oil will eventually evaporate, the thirst for fresh water will only grow. Still, as you've heard, we are now facing bankruptcy at the hands of the bankers. And without any cash flow, we will lose the global assets we have worked so hard to obtain."

"I can meet with that fellow privately." Nassar raised his brow with knowing menace. "Convince him to reconsider."

Villard shook his head. "It would do no good, as they would just send somebody else. We need that contract with the Israelis. That will buy us time on our debts and pave the way for a similar deal in France. From there, we can expand around the globe and build true dominance for the future."

"Any hope of recovering the Mediterranean fleet?"

"No," Villard said bitterly. "My legal efforts to halt the auction have failed. The vessels will be sold shortly, and the proceeds given to the government enforcement agencies. I lack even the funds to make a lowball bid."

"There doesn't appear to be much time to appease the bankers," Nassar said.

"If things get delayed in Israel, I may have to go see the Ox. He might consider a bridge loan, given the profits he's made off our transportation network."

Villard sat back and turned a critical gaze to Nassar. He'd hired the Lebanese man for security when he'd first ventured into the world of illicit drug trafficking. But Nassar had proven himself much more than a security guard, providing muscle to delinquent creditors or creating accidents to undermine partners or competitors. He had a knack for reading people and managing deals and was never hesitant to kill, if need be. His work had been impeccable. Until now.

"I was hoping for a seamless operation here in France, but the plant attack at Choisy-le-Roi was a fiasco," Villard said. "I want to know why. Let's start with Vogel." The old man's gray eyes turned cold as he waited for an explanation.

"Vogel appeared at our pre-mission briefing, just as we were about to depart," Nassar replied. "He was followed by two Americans, nearly blowing our cover. He claimed to have stolen a fortune in diamonds from their boat."

Nassar raised one of the aluminum cases from the floor and set it on Villard's desk. He opened the top and retrieved an envelope, showing Villard the pile of opaque stones at the bottom. "Uncut diamonds, he claimed, found by the Americans on a shipwreck."

Villard examined the stones, then closed the case. "I know an old diamond merchant. I'll have him take a look. But that still doesn't explain why you killed him."

"The compromise to the operation was unsettling. He was a punk and a drug user, too untrustworthy to the operation."

"Perhaps, but he had contacts in Le Havre that provided useful information on police and maritime activities. I didn't wish to lose those resources."

Nassar nodded, not willing to apologize.

"Given the results of your operation," Villard said, "perhaps it was not altogether a poor decision. Which brings us to the fact that these two underwater explorers took a driving tour of Paris with our explosives."

"I thought their remains would prove valuable as evidence of a suicide bombing. I still don't know how they escaped, but at least the vehicle was fully destroyed."

"The media have taken the bait that a new Islamic terrorist group, the New Caliphate, is responsible, so we appear fortunate at the moment."

"Yes, but I am worried about those two Americans. They saw little, but they are dangerous. It would be prudent to eliminate them."

Villard rubbed his chin. "Yes, but it's too high a risk at the moment. Keep an eye on them, however, and we will deal with them at the appropriate opportunity. In the meantime, I'd like you to follow up with our Irish Sea project."

"You wish to proceed?"

"You heard the banker. We have no income stream and no prospect of renewing our Mediterranean trafficking. We need contracts now. It's time to accelerate our activities on all fronts, in any manner possible. What is the status in Egypt?"

"I didn't want to draw a link to the Sorek attack, so we deferred action in the Sinai during our last voyage. However, I have an inside source at the Bahr El-Baqar facility who has been provided with the necessary materials to create an incident. He is standing by for instruction."

"Have him initiate action at once."

"I will draw up potential action plans near our sites in Greece, Italy, and India. I have also been in contact with a source in the United States, who may be onto some valuable data there. A risky locale, but a huge potential payoff."

"We have little left to risk. Regrettably, it seems there may be little demand today for what we have to sell." Villard held up the pike and eyed its razor tip. "But tomorrow, we will make it so the world is on its knees and begging."

13

EL MAREH
NORTH SINAI, EGYPT

The predawn explosion rattled the shutters on Ahmad Hamid's cinder block house. The Egyptian farmer had already risen and washed, and completed his Salat al-fajr morning Muslim prayer, when the distant boom sounded. He opened the front door and padded barefoot onto the soft dirt, his eyes scanning the horizon with a wary squint.

The landscape around him was dark, as was to be expected at the early hour. Flat farmland surrounded him, dotted by a dozen of other small farmhouses, a few showing interior lights flicking on with the first stirrings of the day. A half-moon overhead illuminated the orderly fields of wheat that surrounded each house, their protruding golden crowns wavering in a light breeze.

Hamid took a deep breath, smelling the earthy aroma of the wheat stalks and reminding himself how lucky he was. Like most of his neighbors, Hamid was a recent immigrant to the northern plains of the Sinai. He had grown up in a faraway village near Faiyum, west of the Nile River. For decades, his family's multi-generation farm had produced rich crops of corn, cotton, and wheat. But slowly and steadily, the irrigation waters from the distant Nile, fed to Hamid's

farm via a long and expansive canal system, had withered to a trickle. The family farm had to be abandoned when the fields gradually turned to dust.

It was a problem plaguing much of Egypt. A booming population, combined with a Nile River that was shrinking due to climate change and the opening of Ethiopia's Blue Nile dam, created extreme water stress for the desert nation of over 100 million people. Yet innovative solutions were creating new agricultural oases in formerly barren regions.

In the northern Sinai, cotton, barley, and wheat fields now sprouted from the desert as a result of the government's mega El-Salam irrigation project. Reclaimed runoff and capture of the Nile's last drops before entering the Mediterranean were transferred across the Sinai Desert to create new green lands.

Hamid and his neighbors were the immediate beneficiaries, struggling farmers who had been relocated from afar and given the chance to start fresh. Hamid's family's hardships would soon end, he thought, as he eyed the robust fields of his first crop planted in the Sinai. But then his eyes caught a small yellow glow on the northern horizon and his heart sank.

The flickering light told him it was a fire, no doubt associated with the earlier explosion. And the location was exactly where the Bahr El-Baqar waterworks was situated, a massive treatment and pumping facility that provided water for much of the northern Sinai. It served as nothing less than the lifeblood for the reclaimed region. He watched the distant blaze, hoping he was wrong, but a tiny voice behind him proved otherwise.

"Baba, there's no water."

Hamid turned around to see his six-year-old daughter in the doorway holding an empty teapot. He forced a smile. "We'll have tea later, Safiya."

He moved to a protruding pipe and gate valve at the edge of the

wheat field that provided irrigable water to the fields. With trembling hands, the farmer spun open the gate valve. A brief splurge of water rushed from the pipe, then quickly diminished to a slow drip. Hamid stared as the last few drops splattered on the dusty soil. He grimly closed the valve.

As the fire still burned far away, he knew it meant one thing. Disaster. The wheat crop would quickly be ruined without irrigation, along with the crops of a thousand other farmers in the region. The image of the dusty family farm left in Faiyum played on his mind as he looked across the fields of wheat. How many others would face starvation and ruin . . . or worse?

Hamid slowly staggered back to the house. His daughter still stood in the doorway, watching him with a downcast face.

"Are we going to have to move again, Baba?" she asked in her small voice.

Water in the form of tears appeared in Hamid's eyes.

14

F lemish Dutch?" Pitt asked.

"A dialect spoken in the Flanders region of northern Belgium." Giordino held up a copy of the letter found in the diamond case, which he had run through a translation app. "It's the language used in the letter."

Both men were seated on the bridge of the moored *Pelican*, while Brigitte stood near the helm with a cup of coffee in her hand.

"What does it say?"

"It's from the president of the Antwerp Diamond Bank, dated 9 May, 1940. It is addressed to two of the bank's vice presidents, one named Lamotte and the other, Martin. Here, I'll just read it."

Giordino cleared his throat. "'Gentlemen, the board of directors has approved the immediate evacuation to England of the bank's tangible holdings. Mr. Lamotte is hereby instructed to depart at once for Normandy with the bank's depository holdings of industrial diamonds. Immediate passage is to be taken on the first available England-bound vessel.

"'At the same time, Mr. Martin is instructed to depart with the gemstone repository, once final deposits have been received and

inventoried, as expected in the next forty-eight hours. Passage has been booked for Mr. Martin on the *Avignon* at Le Havre for twelfth May. Deliveries in both instances are to be made to the Bank of England in London on Threadneedle Street. Signed, François Mailleux, President, Antwerp Diamond Bank.'"

"The business card inside the case," Brigitte said. "It had the name Georges Lamotte."

"Lamotte was the banker carrying the industrial diamonds," Giordino said. "That must be what we found."

"Further confirmed," Pitt said, "by the fact the shipwreck we found was named *Cornwall*, not *Avignon*."

"Are industrial diamonds worth anything?" Brigitte was equally disappointed to learn that their discovery did not consist of uncut gemstone-quality diamonds, but the more common industrial variety often referred to as *bort*. The NUMA geologist Giordino had contacted in Washington had sent a confirming analysis based on a photographic review of some sample stones.

"They're worth a fraction of a gemstone's value," Pitt said. "We were just involved with a deep-sea diamond-mining group out of Australia. They indicated that up to eighty percent of all mined diamonds are unsuitable to be cut into gemstones. As I recall, good industrial diamonds are worth only a few dollars per carat."

"So the two cases that were stolen?" Brigitte asked.

"Worth a few thousand dollars at best."

"A paltry sum," Giordino said, "for the life of Harvey Boswick."

Pitt gave a tight-lipped nod.

"I wonder if the guy with the gemstones made it safely to England," Giordino said.

"Martin was his name. What was the ship he was to sail on?" Brigitte opened a laptop computer.

"The *Avignon*," Pitt said. "Out of Le Havre."

Brigitte accessed a ship registry website administered by the

French Archives Nationales. Her brow raised when she discovered a passage. "It says the *Avignon* was a Channel ferry and postal carrier built in 1933 and owned by a subsidiary of the Red Star Line. She could accommodate forty-two commercial passengers and operated primarily between Le Havre, Southampton, and Portsmouth."

"Did she survive the war?" Giordino asked.

"No. She was attacked and sunk by German attack planes in the Channel." She looked up from the computer with a shocked look in her eyes. "And it happened on twelfth May, 1940. The very day Monsieur Martin boarded the ship with the bank's gemstone diamonds."

15

A light mist hung over the English Channel as the *Pelican* knifed through a flat gray sea. Pitt stood on the bridge, cradling a mug of coffee and gazing at the green-frosted coastline of France a mile off the port bow. The bridge wing door stood open, allowing a cool breeze to cross the compartment, carrying the faint odor of seawater.

The environment was an elixir to Pitt. Nothing calmed his nerves, cleared his mind, or energized his soul like being on the water. Since his first tumble into the ocean on a Southern California beach as a tyke, he had been mesmerized by the sea and its underwater world.

He'd learned to scuba dive at an early age, which had fueled a passion to explore the depths. Later, as a pilot in the Air Force, he made the most of his billets in Greece, Hawaii, and Southeast Asia to explore the underwater attractions, diving with locals or exploring on his own. In the years since, as the Director of NUMA, his passion had never waned.

"For a man nearly blown apart in the Seine a day or two ago, you're looking well this morning." Brigitte entered the bridge with less vigor, her hair tousled and dark circles under her eyes.

"I credit the sea air," Pitt said. "You sleep well?"

"Yes, but I didn't expect we'd get underway so early. I heard the engines start up at five o'clock."

"I thought we'd get an early start since you were supposed to jump ship today. Al and I worked up a search grid for the *Avignon* based on your findings and some info from the NUMA database." He motioned to a workstation that displayed a digital map of the coastline east of Le Havre, overlayed with a small, shaded offshore box.

"It doesn't appear she was very far from shore when she sank."

"Less than five miles," Pitt replied. "There were eyewitness accounts from people in the village of Saint-Jouin-Bruneval, so she couldn't have been too far out."

"Then there's a good chance we can find the wreck." She gave a hopeful smile.

The change in plans to search for the *Avignon* did not come as a shock to Brigitte. In the few weeks she'd worked with Pitt and Giordino, she had seen their persistence. Even their pursuit of the journalist who stole the diamonds was no surprise. Both men carried a palpable sense of right and justice, as well as something more. A sense of innate courage, it seemed.

"The diamonds," she said. "You really want to find them?"

"I'm sure they belong to someone else," he said, "but it makes for a nice mystery to solve. Plus it gives us the chance to check Al's patchwork on the sonar fish."

They sailed toward Le Havre along the Côte d'Albâtre—the Alabaster Coast—which blunted the sea with white chalk cliffs like those of Dover. Off the small farming village of Saint-Jouin-Bruneval, the *Pelican* slowed and began its search for the shipwreck. The newly repaired multi-scan sonar unit was deployed off the stern, and the vessel began a box grid survey running four-mile-long lanes.

They searched through the morning, taking shift breaks with other technicians on the crew. At two in the afternoon, Giordino

called out from the sonar shack that a target had appeared. Pitt stepped to the sonar monitor in time to see a fuzzy, linear shape passing off the screen.

"It's about eighty meters in length," Giordino said. "Same as the *Avignon*. We'll get a better look if we circle back on our port side."

Pitt relayed the instructions to the helmsman, and a few minutes later they passed directly over the wreck. The sonar image showed a clear outline of the ship's bow and stern, but the center section was blurry, as if covered in mud.

"Looks like it could be our wreck." Pitt glanced at the surrounding seas, noting a light surface chop. A small tanker was passing to their north, while some fishermen in a small powerboat were motoring to their west. "Conditions look adequate. Let's see if Brigitte wants to join the dive."

A shot line with an attached buoy was tossed over the target, and the three divers quickly followed suit, stepping off the *Pelican*'s lowered stern platform into the brisk water. A dive flag was hoisted above the ship as it drifted safely away from the divers, holding position a hundred yards downwind. The water was clearer than on their last dive, but the current stronger. The three divers kept a hand on the drop line to stay together until they reached a sandy bottom, thirty meters deep.

Pitt saw a dark object to their left and swam in its direction. It wasn't the wreck, but a funnel dislodged from the ship. The rusted mass had myriad irregular holes and indentations, indicating violent damage before it hit bottom. Past the funnel, Pitt saw the ship itself, a mahogany-colored mass rising from the sand.

The *Avignon* had been built in 1933 of a standard British merchant ship design. Two large holds were positioned in front of a raised center bridge, followed by a third hold aft. The wreck had settled into the seabed from the scouring force of the current, its main deck rising only a dozen feet from the surrounding bottom.

As the divers approached the hull and ascended to deck level, Pitt noticed two things. The first was the ship's orientation. He checked a compass heading on his dive computer and confirmed the vessel's bow was pointed toward Le Havre.

As they kicked their fins against a head current, the second thing Pitt saw was the ship's utter destruction. The muddy sonar image they had viewed of the amidships reflected the fact it was nearly obliterated. The center of the ship, where the superstructure had once stood, now appeared as an empty crater covered with sand and concretions.

If this vessel was indeed the *Avignon*, then the story matched. This ship, Pitt saw, had likely suffered a deadly bombing at the hands of the Luftwaffe.

It also meant their diamond quest was for naught.

Giordino looked at Pitt and shook his head. If the diamonds had been stored in the bridge or an adjacent cabin, they would have been scattered in a thousand directions and now buried deep under sediment. But proving as much would take a major excavation.

Though disappointed with their find, the divers proceeded to survey the rest of the ship. They swam over thick links of anchor chain coiled near the bow, then past towering derricks that rose into the gloom like thin sentries. Pitt noticed the stern's hatch cover had been knocked ajar when the ship sank, leaving a narrow gap with the deck. He turned on a flashlight and slipped through the opening to see what cargo the ship was carrying.

The deep compartment was filled with pallets of bricks, disintegrating sacks of cement, and other building materials. Pitt moved his light across the hold, revealing a dozen or so orderly piles of the materials.

A separate object caught his eye in the corner and he went to investigate. Tied against the bulkhead by thin, rusty chains were four small engines. Pitt approached one and wiped his hand across the

top, swirling away the silt. A circular emblem on the valve cover appeared of a woman on a horse. The word *Godiva* was inscribed above and *Coventry* below it. Pitt recognized the logo from the Coventry Climax company, which had made lightweight fire pump engines. In the 1950s, similar motors were appropriated for sports car racing by the likes of Lotus and Cooper, who found monstrous success due to the engine's power-to-weight ratio.

Pitt detected another light and turned to see Brigitte poking her head into the hold and tapping her wrist. He glanced at his orange-faced Doxa dive watch to confirm their bottom time, then ascended from the hold. They met Giordino on the deck above, then made their way over the remnants of the side rail. Retracing their route past the funnel, they spotted their drop line and swam with the current to its base.

Brigitte gripped the line and led them in a measured ascent, stopping at the fifteen-foot mark for a five-minute safety stop. They inflated their buoyancy compensators and surfaced to spot the *Pelican* a short distance away. Its prop began to churn at their appearance, making a beeline for the buoy marker.

Much closer to them, the powerboat with the fishermen appeared to be drifting in their direction. Pitt noticed a muscular man on deck staring at them through binoculars while speaking to the pilothouse.

The powerboat instantly throttled up, its twin outboards whining with high revolutions. As the boat surged forward, it didn't turn away from the divers, but steered directly for them.

Giordino shouted a warning to Brigitte, who had drifted a short distance away. Pitt pulled the dump valve on his buoyancy compensator, purging the air with a rush. He plunged under the surface and angled toward Brigitte's position.

Giordino followed suit, but was fractionally closer to the charging boat, which had borne down on them in a heartbeat. Giordino had

barely gotten himself inverted, when the boat smashed into his up-raised feet and fins.

Close by, Brigitte was still struggling to purge her buoyancy compensator, while kicking forward. A hand gripped her harness from below, and she felt herself get yanked underwater as the boat roared by less than a meter away. She peered down to see Pitt pulling her to a safe depth as she finally drained the air from her vest.

He pulled her across from him and looked into her face to see that she was all right. She nodded, noting in the fraught moment that his green eyes were remarkably calm. They descended another few feet, then kicked over and met Giordino at the drop line. The boat took another pass directly overhead, then sped away as the *Pelican* approached the buoy. Pitt ascended first, making sure the surface was safe before motioning for the others to join him. They made the short swim to the NUMA ship's dive platform and were elevated to the stern deck.

"Anybody get his license plate?" Giordino said as he rubbed his bruised feet and ankles.

"Some drunken fishermen, I think," said the *Pelican*'s executive officer. "I warned them off just before you surfaced, and they complained that you were fouling their lobster traps."

"They didn't look like lobstermen," Pitt said. "Brigitte, are you okay?"

"Yes. And thank you for pulling me down. I was slow to deplete my vest."

Pitt and Giordino stepped to the rail. The powerboat was now a small white dot on the horizon, speeding toward Le Havre.

"Some associates of our friends from Paris, perhaps?" Giordino asked.

"Could be. Maybe they're unhappy that we borrowed their truck."

"I don't blame them," Giordino said. "Their insurance probably didn't cover the loss."

Brigitte joined them at the rail after toweling her hair. Her fear had turned to anger. "There seem to be a lot of dangerous fools prancing about my country."

"I'm afraid you don't have a monopoly there," Giordino said.

"If they are hunting for the diamonds, I guess they are out of luck," she said. "Unless they want to vacuum the entire wreck site."

"They'd be wasting their time," Pitt said.

Brigitte gave him a quizzical look. "Why do you say that? Do you think that was not the *Avignon*?"

"Yes, I'm quite sure that's the wreck of the *Avignon*. But I can say with some confidence," he added, "that Mr. Martin and his cache of gemstone diamonds were never aboard her."

16

QUEENS, NEW YORK

Claude Bouchet checked his appearance in the van's rearview mirror a final time. His short hair was stylishly cut and gelled, and his beard neatly trimmed. Both were colored jet-black, courtesy of a men's hair dye. It took a few years off his forty-year-old face, along with the women's concealer that hid the dark circles under his eyes and the seams around a widened prosthetic nose. Combined with a pair of colored contact lenses, it completely changed his true appearance.

Bouchet prided himself on the ability to change his looks. His attire was equally well choreographed. Threadbare blue blazer, gray polyester pants, tired oxford shirt, and a dark coffee-stained tie. It was city-cop perfect.

He popped some chewing gum into his mouth for effect, then locked the white rental van and strolled toward a twenty-story glass office building, carrying a soft leather attaché case. The building was in a large 1960s development called LeFrak City, situated in the Queens borough of New York a few miles south of LaGuardia Airport. More than a dozen brick apartment buildings towered over a recreation plaza recently renovated with a pool and several sports

fields. Bouchet smiled at some kids playing soccer and entered the drab office building adjacent to the residential area.

A taciturn security guard made him sign a visitor's log before he caught an empty elevator car and rode it to the eleventh floor. The doors opened to a corridor filled with office suites all leased by the New York City Department of Environmental Protection. Near the end of the hall, he found a wall plaque labeled Office of Water Supply Management and he entered through the door.

A plump woman with purple highlights in her gray hair looked up from her counter desk in annoyance. It was five minutes to four on a Friday and she was in the midst of painting her fingernails. She casually reinserted the brush in the bottle as she asked what he wanted.

"I'm Officer Mike Brown with the NYPD," Bouchet said with a practiced Brooklyn accent. He quickly flashed a replica police badge he'd acquired off the internet. "I have an appointment with the assistant deputy water supply commissioner."

"Sure. This way."

The woman rose fanning her wet fingernails and led him down a hallway. Bouchet was glad to see that most of the offices they passed were empty, their occupants having left early ahead of the weekend. They reached a corner office and the secretary knocked on the open door.

"An Officer Brown to see you," she announced, then slipped past Bouchet to return to her desk, still fanning her nails.

Brown entered the office to find an attractive middle-aged woman of Puerto Rican descent seated behind an executive desk. She stood as Bouchet rushed over and shook her hand.

"Thank you for seeing me," Bouchet said between chomps on his gum. "And sorry I'm late for our appointment. Big wreck on Queens Boulevard."

There was in fact no wreck on Queens Boulevard, Bouchet having intentionally arrived late in the day.

"There always is on a Friday," the woman said, motioning for him to take a seat.

"I'll try not to take up much of your time. As I said when I called, I work in the NYPD's Counterterrorism Bureau. I'm on a task force with the mayor's office, and he's asked for data on the vulnerabilities in the city's water supply system."

"We just made a presentation to the mayor's office a few weeks ago." She studied Bouchet's face a moment. "I don't recall your presence there."

Bouchet swallowed hard. "I was on a field assignment at the time."

"If you had attended the briefing, you would know that we prepare an annual report on the city's water vulnerabilities, from the collection points in upstate New York to the distribution network in the city. I believe I left a summary of our presentation at the meeting."

"Yes. But I was told of the detailed report and was asked to obtain a copy," he lied. "That's why I'm here."

Bouchet couldn't help but smile to himself. A detailed written report of New York City's water vulnerabilities. It was better than he had thought. A copy of the report would earn him a hefty bonus.

As a contract industrial spy, Bouchet had multiple clients around the world. He would usually have to spend months working undercover in a company before gleaning valuable competitive data. This job, for a French client, was funded as a short-term gig, and it looked like he would make the score in less than an hour.

The woman took a key from her desk and unlocked a file cabinet behind her. She produced a thick bound report with an emblem of the New York City Department of Environmental Protection on the cover.

"This is a classified document. I'll have to obtain permission from the department head to release a copy. I'm afraid I'll also have to confirm your position with the mayor's office."

"Certainly," Bouchet replied with a friendly nod. But inside, he

was silently cursing. The report was lying on the desk just a few feet away. The payout for it would be lucrative, but his cover was about to be blown. He should just get up and walk out the door now. He knew where the report was stored. He could break into the office over the weekend and steal it.

But something triggered inside of him. Arrogant pride. He was good at industrial espionage. He had clients paying him top dollar and he had never failed. The data he sought was right there. It was Friday and the office was empty. He would finish the job now.

As the woman picked up her desk phone and dialed a number, Bouchet calmly slipped a hand into his leather case. He suddenly let the case slip off his wrist and fall to the floor. In his hand, he held a suppressed Ruger SR22 compact pistol. He calmly raised the weapon and fired three shots into the chest of the assistant deputy water supply commissioner as she looked up in shock. One of the hollow-point bullets punctured the left ventricle of her heart with a nickel-sized hole, killing her instantly. As she slumped onto her desk, Bouchet deftly clutched the phone out of her hand and hung it on the receiver. Grabbing the report, he tucked it into his leather case and slipped out of the office.

The secretary was still working on her nails when he reached her desk.

"Quick meeting," she said.

"The commissioner was most helpful."

"Have a nice weekend."

"I shall," Bouchet replied, the first honest thing he'd said all day.

17

The café had been selected for its location in an inconspicuous village midway between Paris and Le Havre, and for its highly regarded coq au vin. Villard and Nassar arrived ten minutes ahead of their scheduled luncheon time, but the Ox was already waiting, seated at a rear table with his back to the wall.

With a flabby face and long, stringy hair, Jules LeBoeuf did in fact resemble the ox that his surname denoted. A wide frame and massive belly only added to the likeness. But the bovine term could also be applied to how he managed his illicit business affairs. He gored and trampled anyone who stood in his way.

An underboss in the Corsican mafia, LeBoeuf operated in the northern regions of France. He dabbled in the usual illicit trades: extortion, racketeering, and prostitution, with some ventures into cybertheft. But he had found the most profit in the smuggling trade, be it foreign drugs, banned hydrofluorocarbon gases, or even humans.

LeBoeuf had personally approached Lavera Exploration during the oil glut of 2016, when Villard's tanker fleet lay at anchorage, collecting dust. Transporting a single block of heroin from Karachi to Marseille had saved Villard from bankruptcy and set him down the

path of drug trafficking. A brief run of riches had followed, but now Villard again faced ruin.

Villard stepped to the back of the restaurant, skirting a trio of LeBoeuf's armed goons at a table that blocked his path. He stood for a second before the fat man in a mark of respect, then dropped into a chair opposite him.

Nassar had followed into the room a few steps behind. He gave a faint nod to the three bodyguards, then took a seat at the bar. A tall mirror behind the shelved bottles gave him a clear view of the room.

"Yves," LeBoeuf said with a snicker, "you are looking well, for a man with no money." He reached across the table with a short dinosaur arm and poured Villard a glass of white wine from a half-empty bottle.

"You arrived early." Villard eyed a half-devoured plate of mussels in front of the big man.

LeBoeuf wiped a dab of cream sauce from the corner of his mouth and belched. "I just wanted first crack at the Moules à la Normande." He pushed the half-eaten plate across the table.

Villard ignored the mussels and took a sip of wine.

"You do not appear to be in want."

LeBoeuf laughed. "When a roadblock appears, one simply takes another path. There are many merchant mariners happy to boost their profits. I'm talking with some people in Jakarta who may find gain from your loss."

"Yes, it is my loss," Villard said, his lips tightening, "although you enjoyed much of the gain."

"We all weigh our risks and rewards, do we not? But tell me, will your Mediterranean fleet be released or is it gone forever?"

Villard shook his head in a slow and painful reply.

"Very unfortunate. We had a nice conduit in the works." LeBoeuf signaled a waiter, who collected their lunch order. "And another bottle of Vouvray." LeBoeuf drained the remains of the bottle into his

glass. When a new bottle was procured and opened, LeBoeuf probed Villard with his dark eyes.

"So you are in a bind, my friend," he said softly. "How bad is it?"

Villard gave him a grim look. "With the bulk of my fleet impounded, I have no cash flow. I have been investing in a new venture, but because of the financing, that is now in jeopardy."

"Ah, yes, your water business. That was some serious bungling in Paris the other night." He turned and gazed at Nassar with an amused look.

Villard said nothing, choking down LeBoeuf's admission that he knew all about it. "I have specialized pumping stations," he said, "on order in three countries that are necessary to complete the systems. They are the key components beyond our earlier capital investments."

"I thought your projects were five or ten years in the future."

"Events have forced us to accelerate our plans."

"And to accelerate market demand?" LeBoeuf grinned, revealing teeth stained brown from methamphetamine use as a teen.

Their food arrived, sparing Villard from answering. LeBoeuf knew why he was there and kept him wriggling like a worm on a hook.

The Ox waited until their meal was finished before firing the question. "So, Yves, how much is it that you need?"

Villard didn't answer directly. It was a dangerous gambit to come to LeBoeuf for money. The terms would be ugly and the consequences for default potentially fatal. But he had no other choices.

"Before the collapse of the market and the initiation of our joint venture," Villard said, "the oil exploration business provided me a prosperous career. I didn't know at the time that the data we acquired, combined with the knowledge we have today, could create an entirely new opportunity that will make your drug-trafficking business look like peanuts.

"We've identified targets of opportunity that have the potential to

produce billions in revenue—and all of it legally. Climate change has forced an end to Big Oil, but is creating an ever greater thirst for fresh water." He hesitated, putting his hands on the table and looking Le-Boeuf in the eye.

"I need forty million euros to keep the banks happy. Our project in Israel, once it goes online, will repay that inside of a year."

"That's a sizable loan," LeBoeuf said. "I read your forecasts, and they could all be fantasy. Nevertheless, I am prepared to loan you thirty million euros, repayable in forty-five days with a fifteen percent note. Any default and you shall sign over all remaining company assets. I'll have the funds wired to you by the end of the day." He reached a chubby hand across the table, an insidious glint in his eye.

Villard reluctantly shook hands, pulling away with a smear of cream sauce from the mussels LeBoeuf had been eating.

"Thank you, Jules."

"Of course. Just don't disappoint me in forty-five days. Can you pick up lunch?" LeBoeuf hoisted himself from the table and carried a glass of wine toward the bar. He stopped, downed the contents, and set the glass on the bar near Nassar. LeBoeuf slowly waddled out of the café, his three soldiers following behind him.

Nassar approached Villard, who remained at the table, staring vacantly at the uncleared lunch dishes. "Get the car," Villard said quietly.

Nassar exited the café and walked to Villard's Mercedes a half block away. A plumber's van was parked across the street, an emblem of a pipe wrench and toilet plunger displayed like crossed swords on the side. Inside the van, a man pulled off a set of headphones and hit the stop button on a recording device. "LeBoeuf has left the building. That's all for us."

A second man powered off a video camera aimed at the restaurant. "Anything incriminating from the Ox?"

"I'm not sure. We better send a copy to Paris. Perhaps they'll be able to identify the other two men he met for lunch."

The video man looked at his watch. "Team Two is on surveillance until midnight. We're not on our next assignment until nine a.m. Let's have some lunch."

The first man nodded. "As soon as they've all left, let's try the same place. Those mussels looked *magnifique*."

18

Villard was waiting out front when Nassar pulled to the curb.

"Did he agree to the loan?" Nassar asked as he drove away.

"Yes. Thirty million. More than I anticipated. But a short window for repayment."

Nassar motored north from the village, passing lush fields of green farmland.

Villard stared out the window, his gaze returned by a small herd of Jersey cows grazing by the roadside. "When do we hear back from the Israeli authorities?"

"The Israeli cabinet is meeting later today, when the water resources minister is scheduled to pitch our proposal. We should hear something soon."

"We need quick approval and a contract," Villard said. "Time is not on our side."

"But the minister is. He will push hard for its implementation."

When they reached the outskirts of Le Havre, Villard directed Nassar to the old city center. Much of Le Havre had been bombed flat during the war, then rebuilt in a modern but drab style reminiscent of East Berlin. Nassar drove to a small area of the business district that had survived the destruction.

CLIVE CUSSLER THE CORSICAN SHADOW

Villard guided him to a large stone building on Boulevard de Strasbourg that was constructed in an art deco style. Several ground-floor shops lined the street, and Nassar parked in front of one labeled *Hauser Jewelry*. It had been Villard's favored jeweler when birthday shopping for his late wife.

The proprietor was a ninety-two-year-old man named Maurice Hauser. He resembled Albert Einstein in his later years, with a shock of wild gray hair and bright eyes that gleamed through thick spectacles.

"Mr. Villard, you've come to pick up your valuables." The old man scurried into a back room and emerged with the two diamond-filled cases recovered from the *Cornwall*. He set them on a glass counter.

"These cases survived quite well underwater all those years." The old man tapped the stouter of the two. "A pity that the cases are probably worth more to a collector than their contents."

"What are you saying?" Nassar frowned. "They are full of uncut diamonds."

"Diamonds, yes, but they are nothing more than bort."

"Bort?"

"Non-gemstone-quality diamonds or fragments," he said. "They constitute the majority of all mined raw diamonds. The contents of the two cases combined are worth around twenty-five hundred euros."

Nassar's jaw dropped. "That's all?"

"I'm afraid so. Their only value is for industrial use. But there is a fascinating story behind these particular diamonds."

Villard gave Nassar an icy glare, then nodded at the old jeweler. "Go on. What is so interesting about these worthless stones?"

"They come from the Antwerp Diamond Bank, which served the diamond merchants in the city before World War Two. When the Germans invaded Belgium on their way to France, there was much panic. I was a small boy and still recall my mother's angst at the sudden shortage of food at the grocers." A faraway glint came to his eyes, then he

rapped on the counter. "You see, my father and uncle were both diamond cutters in Antwerp. The merchants and cutters often kept much of their inventory at the bank for safekeeping. To the bank's credit, they whisked the diamonds out of the country as the invasion unfolded, in an attempt to keep them out of the hands of the Germans."

"Do you mean," Villard asked, "the more valuable gemstone diamonds?"

"Yes. But even industrial diamonds had considerable value at that time. This was well before the advent of the synthetic diamonds used for industrial applications today. They were so important to the war effort, in fact, that the British sent a commando team into Amsterdam in 1940 to retrieve a large cache of industrial diamonds from under the Germans' noses." He patted the side of the open case. "The Antwerp Bank attempted to transport these to safety, but as you found, they were lost in the English Channel."

"But you said the bank's gemstone diamonds were evacuated as well," Nassar said. "Could they have been on the same boat?"

"It doesn't appear that way." He pulled out the faded letter found in the dry case. "My Flemish is rusty, but from what I could decipher, a bank executive named Eduard Martin was to transport the gemstone-quality diamonds on a separate vessel sailing for England, the *Avignon*. I happen to know those diamonds vanished as well."

Villard wrinkled his brow. "How would you know that?"

"Because, believe it or not, some of those lost diamonds belonged to my father and uncle. I have a cousin in Brussels, a history professor at the Université Libre de Bruxelles, who compiled a detailed family history. We lost many relatives to the death camps," he said in a low voice. "I recall reading in his account how my father and uncle had received insurance payments after the war that helped them reestablish their businesses.

"I contacted my cousin, and he knew the whole story," he continued. "The Antwerp Bank's diamonds were transferred to France

by the bank's vice president, Eduard Martin, but he's thought to have been killed en route to England. The diamonds disappeared. The insurance company investigated the loss after the war, but no recovery was made and they paid out two and a half million euros in claims. My uncle grumbled that they only received half value, so the total lost diamonds were actually worth around five million euros."

"A hefty amount, even today," Villard said.

Hauser gave a warm squint. "Particularly if you consider their current value. You see, gem-quality diamonds today are worth roughly ten times their value in 1940."

"You mean they would be worth fifty million euros?" Nassar's downcast face brightened.

"I would imagine so."

"What do you think happened to the diamonds?" Villard asked.

"Most likely at the bottom of the sea, like the others." Hauser reached under the counter and retrieved a large envelope. "My cousin had a copy of the insurance company's investigation and emailed me a copy. I only skimmed it, but I read that the ship Martin was to sail on, the *Avignon*, was also sunk by the Germans."

He slid the envelope across the counter and smiled. "Since you found the unloved diamonds on a shipwreck, perhaps you can find the valuable ones, too."

Villard found no amusement and stood with his arms folded.

"Can I show you anything else while you're here?" The old man motioned toward a display case filled with diamond rings.

"No," Villard said. "Thank you for the information, Maurice. You can keep the bort and cases for your efforts." He plucked the insurance report off the counter and exited the jewelry store with Nassar in tow.

When they climbed back into the Mercedes, Villard asked, "Could the Americans be searching for the gemstones? Why were they diving again in the Channel?"

"It is possible," Nassar said, "but my men say they recovered nothing from the site and have returned to port." As he spoke, his cell phone buzzed with a text message.

While Nassar checked his phone, Villard pulled out the insurance report and glanced through it, noting that one section of evidence was an interview with Le Havre's harbormaster.

Beside him, Nassar's face turned ashen. "Sir, there is bad news from Israel. The prime minster has elected to defer all national infrastructure projects until the next fiscal year, due to budget constraints."

Villard slapped his palm on the dashboard. "What about the emergency water shortages?"

"A water treatment facility in Haifa has excess capacity and has been tapped to provide relief, while other sources are being diverted. Our agent reports our project is still viewed favorably, although there are concerns about the environmental impact." Nassar lowered his voice. "The delay will be at least six months."

Villard stared out the windshield. In his younger days, he would have exploded with rage. Age had dimmed his passion, but elevated his reasoning. Some events were simply beyond his control. But his anger still ran deep. This news meant the potential end of his business, and possibly more.

"There is some positive news," Nassar offered. "My contact in the U.S. has provided a secret report that we can use to exploit our holdings there. I've identified a potential target that could produce a truly significant outcome."

Villard's fingers trembled as he clasped the insurance report. He took a deep breath. "Our only option is to accelerate any available opportunity. Put an operational plan together for it. At once."

He tossed the report onto Nassar's lap. "And unless it can produce fast results, we'd better do one more thing. Find those gemstone diamonds."

PART II

The Shearwater Ferry

19

ST. GEORGE'S CHANNEL
THE IRISH SEA

Summer Pitt stood at the stern rail of the NUMA research ship *Nordic Star* and eyed a world of gray around her. A lumpy gray expanse of sea melded into a drizzly mist falling from thick steely clouds overhead. The monochrome environment was a Prozac-inducing moment, bleak enough to take down the sunniest Pollyanna. But not for Summer. She shook off the oppressive gloom by taking in a deep lungful of sea air and releasing it in a satisfied sigh. She was happy to be at sea doing what she loved best, even if the weather was dreadful.

An oceanographer and the daughter of Dirk Pitt, Summer had spent the past three weeks crisscrossing the Irish Sea, measuring sub-surface currents, water temperature, and acidity levels. Early evidence had suggested a potential slowdown in the currents of the Gulf Stream that were accountable to climate change. A continued slowing of the Gulf Stream portended dramatic effects for both sides of the Atlantic, including rising seas and more severe storms. The preliminary findings made Summer more depressed than the weather.

Nevertheless, she couldn't help noting that during the course of the expedition, she had glimpsed the sun only once. The rest of the

voyage had been carried out under dark, rainy skies that cast the sea in a cold, leaden hue. Having grown up with her twin brother in Hawaii, she admitted to herself that she longed for a cloudless sunny day.

Her eyes were drawn to a frothy circle of water off the stern as a small yellow submersible emerged from the depths in a welcome burst of color. The pilot guided it alongside the ship, where waiting crewmen hoisted it aboard.

When the vessel was secured to the swaying deck, the top hatch popped open and two men in blue jumpsuits climbed out. The first was a young man with shaggy hair and wide eyes who clutched a camera. He had a radiant grin as he spotted Summer and rushed over to her.

She returned the smile. "How was your first submersible dive, Diego?"

"It was awesome. I captured some great stills of a cuttlefish on the seafloor. I can't wait to post them online. Thank you for letting me take your place." He turned and raced off to a laptop computer in his cabin.

"Looks like you suitably impressed the summer intern," she said to the second man exiting the submersible, who happened to be her brother.

Dirk Pitt Jr. was tall and lean like his sister, but carried his father's dark hair and angular features. He smiled at Summer and shook his head. "I thought he was going to wet his pants on the way down when the claustrophobia kicked in, but he turned it around when we hit the bottom. Thankfully, there was some marine life about to help calm his nerves."

"I don't suppose you collected any data during your joyride."

Dirk gave his sister a hurt look. "Current, temperature, and salinity readings during descent and ascent are on the hard drive, and a water sample is on the manipulator." He pointed to a hydraulic arm on the front of the submersible. "The other data's all on board. Just

CLIVE CUSSLER THE CORSICAN SHADOW

don't lose our place on the *Ford v Ferrari* download we watched on the ascent."

Summer rolled her eyes. Her brother was serious about his work, but also had a mischievous side. "Thanks. I already know, by the way, Ford won the race at Le Mans."

"Don't tell Diego," Dirk said. "He doesn't have a clue." He looked at the scattered whitecaps on the surrounding waters. "We might want to squeeze in one more dive here before moving to the next target area."

As if on cue, the deck vibrated from the thrust of the ship's engine, and the ship keeled as it turned in a southwesterly direction.

"Apparently the captain has other designs," Summer said. A hand-held radio on her belt buzzed with static, then a voice called out. "Summer, can you and Dirk please report to the bridge."

They made their way forward across the turquoise-colored research ship. Designed for coastal research in northern latitudes, the *Nordic Star* had a reinforced hull that made her a formidable ice-breaker when the need arose. To aid in its survey work, it carried multiple ROVs and AUVs, in addition to the yellow submersible parked on the stern deck. Built to a design featuring high automation, the ship required a working crew of only ten, along with its comple-ment of research scientists.

Dirk followed Summer onto the bridge, where the ship's captain was examining a map of the Irish Sea on a flat-screen monitor. Ben Houston looked up and waved them over. The ex–merchant marine captain was a jovial, energetic man who battled a receding hairline and an extra ten pounds around his midsection.

"Sorry to pull off-site," Houston said, "but we just received a Mayday call."

"What's the nature of the emergency?" Dirk asked.

"We don't exactly know. It was a truncated message from a woman calling for help. She didn't provide a vessel name, but I

suspect a small craft. She only indicated her location was approximately eighteen miles east of Rosslare Harbour, which is on Ireland's southeast coast. She's fallen silent since." Houston motioned toward a crewman on the ship's radio who was attempting to hail the other vessel.

"Where does that put her in relation to our position?" Summer asked.

"About ten miles due north of us." Houston stabbed the monitor with his finger. "We should get close in about twenty minutes."

Summer eyed the position on the chart. It was within a restricted area marked No Fishing or Dredging.

The *Nordic Star*, pushed to its top speed of twenty-six knots, covered the distance in a shade less than Houston predicted. All eyes on the bridge scanned for signs of a distressed vessel, but the only thing afloat was a large black ship conducting underwater operations a half mile to the southwest.

Houston slowed the vessel and was marking their position, when Summer pointed off the bow. "There's something in the water. Possible debris."

The ship eased to a halt alongside three small items: a seat cushion, a yellow rain jacket, and a half-empty plastic water bottle.

"Certainly could be from a small craft," Summer said as a crewman fished out the jacket and cushion with a boat hook.

Dirk noticed the direction of the current and focused on the black ship in the distance, angled perpendicular to the *Nordic Star*. He recognized it as a pipe-laying ship by a high circular framework on its stern deck that resembled a Ferris wheel. "It looks like the current is running from the south or southwest," Dirk said. "If that debris is from a boat, then it likely went down somewhere between us and that black ship."

"Let's see what she knows." Houston eyed a nearby radarscope,

which showed the other ship's position and speed, as well as her name, *Chamonix*. He hailed the ship over the bridge radio and inquired if the Mayday call had been received or if they had seen a vessel in distress.

The reply came in a gruff, French-accented voice. "We received the call, but were unable to respond due to ongoing subsea operations. We have seen no nearby traffic. What is the name of the vessel in question?"

"I don't have that information," Houston said.

"Understood. I will post lookouts. *Chamonix* out."

"We've got the equipment to find a vessel if it sank nearby," Summer said. "Why don't we conduct an underwater search ourselves?"

Houston nodded. "I'd like to make a wider-area surface search first and advise the Coast Guard about the debris we found. Once we're satisfied there's no one still in the water, we can deploy the sonar."

The *Nordic Star* circled the area in ever-widening arcs without sighting any vessels or debris. An Irish Coast Guard helicopter appeared, performing the same task at altitude. When the search turned up empty, Houston returned to the spot where the debris was found.

Dirk and Summer lowered a towed multi-beam sonar unit off the transom, and the ship pulled forward at a steady crawl. The siblings retreated to a small operations bay near the stern deck, where they could review the sonar's readout. Less than an hour later, the shadowy image of a small boat appeared on the bottom.

"She measures about ten meters," Dirk said, gauging the size with a scale at the screen's bottom. "Would seem to resemble a standard cabin cruiser."

Summer gave a grim nod. "The boat looks intact and the image crisp, as if it hasn't been sitting there long."

"Could be. We'll need a visual to know for sure."

They relayed the wreck's position to the bridge, then retrieved the sonar fish. Dirk began prepping the submersible for another dive, while Summer climbed to the bridge.

"An Irish Naval Service cutter is due on-site shortly," the captain said. "I'll advise them we've found a potential wreck."

"We'd like to take a closer look with the submersible," she said. "Dirk is prepping it now."

Houston wasn't surprised at their initiative. He'd worked with Dirk and Summer on multiple projects and knew their dedication was no less than their father's.

"I'll park us on the marked position when you are ready to deploy."

Twenty minutes later, Summer was looking out the viewport of the two-man submersible as a wave washed away the gray sky overhead and the vessel slipped underwater.

"Depth is showing at one hundred eighty meters," Dirk noted from the pilot's seat. "Should be a quick ride to the seafloor."

Summer flicked on a bank of exterior floodlights as a dark gloom enveloped their descent. The visibility was still murky as waves of tiny suspended particles and dissolved organic matter washed past the lights like a sandstorm. The seabed appeared a short time later, a hardscrabble bottom with no marine plants and only a few scattered fish.

She poked her nose against the viewport, but saw no sign of the boat. "Current probably pushed us off during our descent. Target should be to the south."

Dirk engaged the rear thrusters. He spun the submersible to the designated heading, then propelled them forward, skimming a few feet off the bottom. A white boat soon materialized from the murk, sitting perfectly upright on the seafloor.

As Dirk had predicted, it was a small wooden cabin cruiser, long in the tooth, but looking prim and orderly. A bold name in cursive gold paint across the transom proclaimed her the *Mary Spring*.

Dirk hovered above the stern, where they could peer across the small open deck. A cooler was wedged under the gunnel on one side, while some fishing gear appeared on the opposite rail. In between, a dead man lay face down on the deck.

Summer grimaced at the sight, tightly gripping the armrest of the copilot's seat.

Dirk inched the submersible closer, but they were unable to view the man's facial features or discern obvious injuries. The victim's leg was pinned under a bench seat, holding his body in place. Around his wrist was a strap to a single-lens reflex camera that lay beside him. Summer gazed past the body to the rear of the cabin . . . and pointed to a linear seam of small indentations on the bulkhead. "Those look like bullet holes."

Dirk eased the submersible toward the boat's port side and saw more of the same damage. Not only was the cabin pockmarked with small holes, but the side of the hull was, too.

"Concentrated gunfire on the hull," Dirk said. "If that's what it was, it looks to be enough to have flooded the interior and made her sink."

He continued circling, passing around its bow and back along the starboard flank. When they approached the cabin, Summer held out a hand for Dirk to slow. He brought the submersible to a halt, then inched it close to the cabin's side window.

Inside, a dark-haired woman was sprawled on the floor. Unlike the man, she lay face up, exposing a terror-stricken face and a blood-marred blouse. She clutched a radio transmitter, its coiled cable leading to a shattered console on the helm.

Summer turned to her brother. "They look like a couple out for an afternoon cruise. Why would somebody murder them?"

"No telling. Hopefully the police can piece something together."

"Do you think the black ship had something to do with it?"

Dirk shrugged. "Hard to imagine. This looks more like a pre-

meditated hit. The boat could have been shot up earlier and drifted a while before sinking. Perhaps the woman regained consciousness briefly before they sank . . ."

"Maybe, but that radio set looks pretty demolished."

Dirk backed away from the death scene and adjusted the submersible's ballast to place it into a slow ascent. He and Summer rode in silence as the vessel climbed. When they broke the surface, they found themselves facing the *Chamonix* in the distance.

Summer stared at the large black ship and felt an unnerving sense of dread.

20

The *Nordic Star* remained near the wreck site as the Irish Naval Service patrol vessel LÉ *Samuel Beckett* approached and took a detailed radio report. Captain Houston watched as a search and rescue dive team was assembled on the stern of the cutter, preparing to recover the bodies from the sunken cabin cruiser.

Houston turned to Dirk and Summer on the bridge beside him. "There's nothing more we can add. We have one more environmental site we're scheduled to investigate before we are due to head back to Southampton. It's about an hour away."

Dirk stared across the choppy seas to the pipe-laying ship. "I'd like to know what the *Chamonix* is doing out here, working in a restricted area."

"They appear to be anchored up," Summer said. "Have they held the same position?"

Houston checked the radarscope and nodded. "Pretty sure they've stood pat since we arrived."

"I'd like to drop the sonar," Dirk said, "and take a pass by them on the way out of Dodge."

Houston shrugged. "No harm, as long as we run at a safe distance."

A few minutes later, a towfish was deployed off the stern and Dirk turned the sonar to its maximum range as they pulled past the *Chamonix*.

"Look at that." Summer motioned toward the monitor. "There's another wreck, sitting right underneath the *Chamonix*."

It appeared on the screen as a thin sliver. Dirk lowered the range setting, which enlarged the image at the far edge of the monitor. The ship lay on its side, its topside configuration hidden in the shadow of its hull.

"Looks to be about sixty meters long," Summer said. "Should we have the captain make another pass?"

Dirk recorded the wreck's position. "Not a pass, but a closer inspection."

Houston was less enthused when they presented their request. "The *Chamonix* was none too happy when we skittered past them. Radioed us to veer away on account of their underwater operations, although I didn't see any sign of activity in the water."

"You were a hundred meters off?" Summer asked.

"Still close enough to rile their feathers. But they're actually underway now." He pointed out the rear bridge window at the black ship. A churn of white water appeared off its stern as it slowly got underway. "It appears they are departing to the east. You sure you want to make another dive?"

"No harm in taking a quick look," Dirk said. "But we don't need to advertise the fact. Can you slow us down, then circle back once they're out of sight?"

Houston checked that the Coast Guard cutter was still in the area and agreed to the request. Fifty minutes later, Dirk and Summer were back in the submersible, scanning the familiar beige seabed as they skimmed above its surface, heading toward the unknown shipwreck.

The dark form of the vessel appeared out of the gloom, and Dirk guided the submersible to its elliptical shape. The facing hull

was colored a grizzly brown, thick with concretion, indicating the ship had been submerged for many decades.

Dirk steered along the lower hull, then circled around the half-buried bow. He let out a low whistle as a mangled section of the bow appeared under their lights.

"That's some ugly damage."

He positioned the submersible near the ship's side rail. A deep, rectangular gap in the hull about twenty feet from the bow extended a similar distance aft. Thick orange rivulets of rust seeped from the jagged edge like icicles on a cabin roof in winter.

"Collision damage," Summer said. "That's what sent her to the bottom."

"I bet it happened in the fog."

Aside from a rash of stormy weather and rough seas, Dirk and Summer had incurred several days in the Irish Sea filled with heavy fog. Back in the days before shipboard radar, they knew, collisions at sea had been an all-too-common occurrence.

The gash extended well below the waterline. Dirk pivoted the sub so its lights illuminated the length of the deck. The vessel was a merchant ship, with a high center bridge sandwiched between two large holds fore and aft. Ghostly derricks stood sentry alongside each hold, rust-stained cables dangling from their arms.

"The forward hold must have flooded at impact," Summer said. "I bet she went down in a hurry."

Dirk brought the submersible alongside the forward hold, which beckoned like an open garage door, its hatch having been tossed aside during the sinking. The submersible's lights exposed a half-empty compartment holding a pyramid-shaped mass covered in sediment on the lower-side bulkhead, the load having shifted.

"Dry bulk?" Summer asked.

"Could be. Anything from grain to gravel, I suppose. It doesn't appear there's been any salvage interest here." He backed the sub-

mersible away and traversed the ship's length, passing by the rusty superstructure and the stern hold. He eased past the fantail and hovered above the transom. "Can you make out a name?"

The paint had vanished long ago, but Summer eyed the faint raised metal beading of the ship's name. She tilted her head as she called out the nodules. "C-A-R . . . *Cardiff*, I think. Or something close to that."

"That gives us something to go on."

Dirk guided the submersible for another pass along the tilted deck and approached a flat slab of steel on the seabed. It was the hatch from the stern hold, lying top-down beside the ship.

Dirk hovered above it. "Note anything interesting?"

Summer studied it a moment. "It's the stern's hatch cover, but there's very little corrosion and no sediment on its exposed underside. As if it fell off recently."

"Or was just removed," Dirk said.

He raised the submersible to deck height and approached the open hold, poking its prow into the dark space. Unlike the forward hold, the rear compartment was filled with a jumbled mass of debris. Thick, rusty chains dangled from the upper bulkhead. Large pallets still clung to the vertical floor, glued in place by concretions, while others lay heaped at the lower end of the hold.

Dirk eased the submersible into the hold for a closer look. The thrusters began to kick up sediment, so he moved and hovered in small increments, approaching the main mass of debris slowly. Some of the loose pallets, free of sediment, appeared in an orderly stack in the corner.

"Looks like the *Chamonix* was doing some salvage work in here," Summer said. "Must be something of value."

"Given the pallets and chains, I'd say it was something heavy. Maybe large equipment."

Summer pointed at the debris pile. "That's all they left untouched. Can you take us in for a little closer look?"

The hold was spacious enough for the submersible to maneuver in it. But Dirk remained wary of entanglement with the hanging chains and moved cautiously toward the pile of debris. From her copilot's seat, Summer activated the submersible's manipulator, an extendable hydraulic arm mounted in front. She extended the arm to a section of broken pallet and clasped it with the manipulator's titanium claw. Even under the light touch, the decayed wood disintegrated.

Dirk smiled. "Rock-crusher grip you have there."

"There's not much integrity. Surprising any of this wood has survived."

"Probably treated with creosote. Plus, it may have been protected from the forces of water movement in here until the hatch was popped."

"Perhaps the sealed condition also minimized the presence of wood-eating microorganisms," she said. "Let's try for a thicker piece."

She grasped a heftier slab of wood at the base and nodded at her brother. He inched the submersible rearward, pulling the timber with it. A cloud of sediment filled the water as Summer cast the wood aside.

Dirk reversed course, and as the water cleared, a pair of metallic objects appeared in the debris pile. Summer cleared away some smaller sections of wood to reveal two steel drums. They lay in a horizontal position with chains wrapped around them and secured to a decaying pallet underneath.

Dirk shook his head. "Just some rusty drums, probably full of fuel oil. That wouldn't be of any interest to salvors."

"Maybe they're part of a cleanup effort. Or there was something else stored in here."

"Apparently everything of value is gone now." Dirk backed up the submersible to exit the hold.

Summer raised a hand. "Hold up. I can see a set of markings on one of the barrels."

She pointed to a spot of color beneath the chains wrapped around the nearest drum. Dirk moved in again and Summer extended the manipulator toward the loose band of chains. With practiced dexterity, she pulled them aside, revealing a speckled band of green paint that had been protected from decay.

"Oh, no," Summer exclaimed, examining the exposed section.

Overlaid on the green patch was a yellow rectangle with a black trefoil design in the middle. Although the emblem came from another age, its meaning was perfectly clear.

It was the international warning symbol for radiation.

21

The leaves of a towering sycamore rustled in the breeze as Pitt stepped under their shade to admire a tall marble monument. It was engraved *Jeremiah Winslow, 1858.*

"He was a well-known American in Le Havre's history," Brigitte said. "He came from New Bedford and established a whaling fleet here in the 1820s that grew to be the largest in France. Winslow was quite a wealthy man."

"Whaling was an extremely lucrative business in the day," Pitt said. "A successful voyage could net the crew and owners over fifty thousand dollars."

"That's a lot of blubber," Giordino said as he joined the pair.

They stood in the Sainte-Marie Cemetery a mile north of the Le Havre waterfront. Built on a gentle slope, the picturesque grounds reflected the varied history of the port city. Veterans from both world wars were buried alongside the whalers, fishermen, and merchant traders who founded the city.

But the visitors had come there to search for a specific grave. NUMA's Director of Information Technology, Hiram Yaeger, had discovered a burial record for a man named Eduard Martin in the Le

Havre cemetery. The same name as the diamond-transporting bank executive from Antwerp.

Pitt was sure of his assessment that the *Avignon* had been on approach to Le Havre when it was sunk. The orientation of the vessel combined with the British pump motors carried in the hold told him the ship was inbound, which meant Martin had not yet boarded her. He tasked Yaeger to search for records of other vessels that were outbound from Le Havre near the same date.

Yaeger had taken the extra step of running Martin's name through every French database he could access. The mystery deepened when he discovered a grave under Martin's name in one of Le Havre's cemeteries.

"The guide indicates that Martin's grave is just up the hill." Brigitte consulted a printout from the cemetery's website. Pitt and Giordino followed her as she trekked up a short rise, passing small family mausoleums and ornate individual grave markers toward an area of open manicured lawn.

The grave markers showed it was a more modern section of the cemetery, the inhabitants buried in the twentieth century. Among a row of simple headstones, Brigitte found the grave of Martin.

"'Eduard J. Martin,'" she read. "'Born sixth March, 1892, died twelfth May, 1940.'" She turned to Pitt. "The *Avignon* was recorded as sinking on May twelfth. He died the same day."

Pitt stared at the simple marker. "This must be our man, but perhaps I'm wrong about the ship. She could have turned back to Le Havre after she was attacked." He looked at the adjoining grave sites to see if there were other victims of the *Avignon* buried nearby. None showed a related date of death.

Giordino shook his head. "I don't think so. The damage on that ship gave no appearance she had time to turn around. I think she went down in a heartbeat. And you found those British pump motors in the hold. Maybe she was sunk in the early morning on approach?"

"There is much confusion in wartime," Brigitte said. "It could also be that the attack occurred the day before, but word didn't arrive in Le Havre until the twelfth and that's how it was recorded. Either way, it means that Martin could not have boarded the *Avignon* carrying the Antwerp diamonds. But he died at the same time. So where did the diamonds go?"

"Perhaps only Martin knows," Giordino said as they gazed at the grave of the Belgian banker.

Pitt pulled a folded paper from his back pocket. "Hiram identified someone he thinks may be a relative of Martin who lives in the area. No phone number or email, but an address near a town called Routot."

Brigitte pursed her lips. "I think I know where that is. On the way to Rouen, less than an hour from here."

Back at their rental car, Pitt took the wheel and drove them southeast from Le Havre, crossing the Seine and following its snakelike route toward Paris. They entered a rich agricultural region of Normandy filled with broad fields of wheat, flax, and barley.

Brigitte guided him to the rural town of Routot, then east down a narrow lane. Her cell phone's GPS led them to an old white farmhouse and barn tucked against a forest of beech and oak trees. Across from the house, several acres were filled with mature apple trees, their branches overflowing with late-spring blossoms.

Pitt parked on the gravel drive in front of the house and Brigitte knocked on the door. A fit, middle-aged woman with dark hair answered with the hesitant smile of someone expecting a solicitor.

"We're looking for Allain Broussard," Brigitte said, glancing at the note from Yaeger. "For a historical research project. Does he live here?"

"Yes. You'll find my father in the barn," she said. "The entrance is on the side. Go on in."

Brigitte thanked the woman, then proceeded to the large structure

with Pitt and Giordino. Built in the traditional French farm style, the barn was made of local limestone in a clean, rectangular shape with a high slate-tile roof. An open sliding wooden door around the corner beckoned, and the trio stepped inside, expecting to find a dirt floor and stacks of baled hay.

Instead, the interior resembled a modern fabrication lab. Bright overhead lights illumined a spotless open bay with a polished concrete floor and white walls. A large stainless steel tank sat in the middle, linked by pipes to a round copper pot. Nearby, an open vat sat wedged beneath a large press. Only the back wall showed a nod to the past, with several rows of stacked oak barrels.

An elderly man in dark overalls was pushing a tool rack across the floor and glanced in surprise at the visitors. For a man of ninety, Allain Broussard was spry and clear eyed, moving without apparent difficulties.

"*Bonjour,*" he said, a smile emerging from beneath a thick gray mustache.

Brigitte returned the greeting as she introduced herself and the others.

"Americans?" he asked Pitt in studied English.

"Yes," Pitt said. "We'd like to ask you about Eduard Martin."

Broussard searched his memory, then his face lit up like the Eiffel Tower on Bastille Day.

"Come to my office. We'll sit and talk there."

He led them to a glass-walled office at the end of the building. Slightly less modern than the work bay, it had a long bookshelf filled with textbooks and bottles, fronted by a massive oak desk. The guests took their seats in comfortable armchairs facing the desk, while their host ducked into an anteroom. Broussard returned with a bottle and four brandy glasses.

"I hope you will share a drink." He poured a healthy sample of

brown liquid into the glasses and raised his. "*À votre santé*," he said. "To your health."

A burst of tart apple inflamed Pitt's tongue, followed by an aftertaste that nearly curled his toes. He set down the glass and smiled. "That's far and away the best apple brandy I've ever tasted."

Giordino agreed. "I'd call it some serious jet fuel."

"*Merci.*" Broussard gave them a happy grin. "It's called *calvados* here in Normandy. I've been making it for more than fifty years. Much more profitable than selling apples," he said with a wink.

"So, you have asked me about Eduard Martin," he continued. "That is a name from my past that I have not heard in many years. What is your interest in my uncle?"

Pitt glanced at the others, then relayed their discovery of the industrial diamonds on the *Cornwall*. He showed Broussard a copy of the letter from the Antwerp Diamond Bank and described their fruitless dive on the *Avignon*.

"We just came from his grave in Le Havre," Pitt said, "which indicated he died the same day that the ship sank."

"He did not die on a ship," Broussard said. "My uncle was caught in a German air raid in Le Havre and killed on the docks. He was trying to leave France, perhaps on the *Avignon* or another vessel."

The old man shook his head as the memories returned. "I recall attending his funeral with my mother. It was a hasty affair, given the events of the day. The entire service lasted barely five minutes."

"Did you know your uncle well?" Brigitte asked.

"No. He lived in Antwerp, so I met him only a few times. A serious but very capable man. He was my mother's older brother, and she was very fond of him. I remember how upset she was that no other family members could attend his funeral."

"Did you know," Giordino asked, "that he was carrying a fortune in diamonds when he came to Le Havre?"

"We learned of this only after the war when the insurance people came around asking questions. They searched his car, and we heard from a friend in Le Havre that they even exhumed his grave. But I don't believe the diamonds were ever recovered."

"What do you think happened to them?" Brigitte asked.

Broussard tilted his head. "I cannot say with any authority, but I suspect they were taken to Bermuda. From there, I have no idea what became of them."

"Why Bermuda?" Pitt asked.

"The day my uncle was killed, a man arrived at our farm driving his car. His name was André Carron. André worked for a museum in Paris and was helping transport something out of the country." Broussard took a sip from his glass. "He never told what it was, but acted as if it was very important. He described how my uncle arrived at the dock with great urgency just before the German planes attacked. They were all trying to board a departing ship when the attack started. My uncle Eduard was badly injured, and in his last breath he gave André our address and asked him to bring his car here."

The tragedy of the memory lifted and Broussard's face brightened. "André stayed on the farm with us for almost two years. He was afraid to go back to Paris. My father had already been called up to the Army, and my mother was terrified to be left here alone, so he agreed to stay on as a farmhand. He was great fun. He taught me how to smoke and play cards," he said with a wink.

"Did he ever talk about the diamonds?" Brigitte asked.

"No, I don't remember anyone mentioning diamonds until the insurance men showed up years later. But my mother spoke of something after they left. When André informed her years earlier of her brother's death, he told her that Eduard had two boxes in his car that he insisted be put on the ship. They were apparently consigned with André's shipment. My mother often thought they may have contained the diamonds."

"So they were possibly sent off on another ship," Brigitte said. "Do you know which vessel?"

"I'm afraid I have no idea." Broussard poured a second round of brandy and held up his glass. "I call this Viviane's Nectar, after my late wife." He laughed. "She actually hated the stuff."

"You mentioned Bermuda," Pitt said. "Is that because this other vessel sailed there?"

"Yes, that must have been the case. You see, a coworker of André's departed with his museum shipment and ended up in Bermuda. If my mother's speculation was correct, then Eduard's cases were carried on the same ship."

"How do you know," Giordino said, "that it went to Bermuda?"

"André and his boss would correspond. I was always excited to see a postcard arrive from Bermuda, showing a sunny beach or such." He motioned toward the far end of the barn. "I took all the letters and put them in the trunk of the car after André was killed. Would you like to see them?"

When Brigitte nodded eagerly, the old man rose and strode from the office. The startled visitors rushed to keep up.

"Was André killed in the war?" she asked as Broussard led them out the barn's main door.

"Yes. The Nazis picked him up one day and shot him along with a few other men from town. My mother told me later that he was active in *La Résistance*."

He led them along the length of the barn, turned the corner, and stopped in front of a pair of wide double doors built into the end of the building. He slid them open to reveal a long, narrow tack room filled with harnesses and bridles hanging from a weathered wooden wall.

"André built this so the Germans wouldn't confiscate my uncle's car." Broussard reached beneath a horse blanket to a slim cutout in the wood. He gripped the indentation and pulled forward. The entire

back wall swung out on concealed hinges, revealing a stall-sized space occupied by an old blue car.

Pitt's jaw nearly dropped when he saw the horseshoe-shaped radiator grille on the front of the car. "It's a Bugatti."

"Well done," Broussard said. "A Type 57C from 1939. The body was built by a Swiss coachmaker by the name of Gangloff."

The two-door coupe had a long hood and streamlined fenders, giving it a more modern appearance than its age would suggest. The original blue paint was dull, and the wire wheels showed smudges of rust, but the car was otherwise immaculate.

"Very stylish," Brigitte said.

"Yes, she is quite lovely," Broussard said. "And she still runs like a top. Many times after the war my mother wanted to sell it, but I always talked her out of it. As a boy, it was the most beautiful car I had ever seen. It is still beautiful, I think, but at my age, I find it difficult to drive."

"If you want a kind home for it, you could sell it to Dirk," Giordino said. "He keeps a few old cars in his garage."

Pitt beamed at the vehicle, knowing it would be a fine addition to the collection of antique autos he kept in a hangar in Washington. "You said it is a Type 57C. So it has a supercharger?"

"Yes, it is quite fast, like all Bugattis." Broussard opened the hood, revealing a gleaming straight-eight engine with a small supercharger mounted to its flank.

Brigitte was less impressed. "And the letters?" she asked.

"Of course." Broussard stepped to the rear of the car, turned the handle, and opened the trunk. Inside was a cardboard box containing shoes, clothes, and other personal effects of Carron's. Beside it, an open shoebox held about a dozen letters and postcards.

"André had no family that I could find," Broussard said, "so I still have some of his belongings." He picked up the shoebox and plucked

out a postcard. "This was the first one he received." He passed it to Brigitte.

The card's front had a simple drawing of a palm tree. Brigitte flipped it over, seeing it was addressed to André Carron in Paris. The postmark from Bermuda was dated 15 July, 1940.

"'Dear André,'" she read, translating to English. "'After an arduous voyage, Jean d'Eppé and I have reached safety. Not in England, as intended, but Bermuda. Given the recent events, I think it is for the best. A French envoy here, Monsieur Rapine, has been most hospitable, providing me a room in his bungalow and safe accommodations for Jean. We shall remain here for the time being. I hope you had a safe journey from Le Havre and remain well in Paris. The news of the occupation is ever more distressing. Marcel.'"

Broussard thumbed through the remaining cards and letters, admiring a photo of Whale Beach on Bermuda's west shore. "The rest are in a lighter vein, although he discusses leaving Bermuda later on. My mother wrote him a note, telling of André's death, but I don't believe we ever heard back from the man."

He handed the box to Brigitte. "Go ahead and borrow them. Maybe you'll find a clue to the diamonds." He turned to Pitt. "I'll charge the battery, and you can take the Bugatti for a test-drive when you bring them back."

"You've got a deal." Pitt shook the man's hand.

"Thank you for your help," Brigitte said. "You have been very kind."

"And thanks also for the brandy," Giordino said.

Broussard smiled. "If your friend buys my car, I'll put a case of Viviane's Nectar in the trunk."

"In that case," Giordino said with a grin, "consider it sold."

22

The slim concrete building towered over the landscape of Le Havre's port facility like an NBA player at a petting zoo. At its summit, a circular glass-walled control bay overlooked the surrounding area. The interior was packed with radar, navigation, and communication systems, which allowed a skilled set of operators to monitor incoming and outgoing traffic while keeping a keen eye on approaching weather conditions.

The control tower employees weren't guiding commercial jets, but an endless stream of container ships, tankers, freighters, and cruise ships.

The *capitainerie,* or harbormaster's office, managed the arrival of more than six thousand ships a year at the sprawling facility, which encompassed the largest container port in France.

Wearing a brown Dior suit, Villard entered a drab office complex at the base of the tower with Nassar at his side. They were escorted to the private office of the habormaster, a short, slab-faced man named Jacques Lurel.

"Monsieur Villard, it is good to see you again," he said at the door. But the shiftiness in his eyes said otherwise. Lurel was well

aware of Villard's troubles with the law and was leery of his presence. He hotfooted the visitors to a secluded table in the far corner of his office.

"Jacques, I need your help with something," Villard said. "We're searching for the whereabouts of a lost cargo and would like to check your historical records."

"Everything is computerized now." Lurel pointed to a monitor on his desk. "If you have the date and transit info, I can retrieve the records on my computer."

"We are interested in outbound traffic on or around twelfth May, 1940."

Lurel leaned back in his chair. "Nineteen forty? That's quite a while ago." He thought for a moment. "We have some scattered prewar dock records in the basement that survived the bombings. I'll have someone check."

He rose and phoned his secretary with the request, then returned to the table. "It will be a few minutes. May I ask the nature of the inquiry?"

"A cargo of interest was scheduled to ship from Le Havre on a vessel named the *Avignon*, but she was recorded as sunk by the Germans while crossing the Channel." Villard set Hauser's insurance folder on the table. "Insurance records indicate the goods likely reached port on the twelfth and were awaiting transit when they vanished. It was originally believed the cargo was lost on the *Avignon*, but the insurance investigators determined the ship may have been sunk while inbound, before reaching Le Havre that day. If that is the case, it goes to reason the cargo may have been placed on another vessel."

"That would be logical. It was a perilous time for France and many were fleeing to England any way they could. It was certainly not an orderly evacuation by that point. Did the insurance company identify another vessel?"

"The investigation did not occur until after the war, when most of Le Havre was nothing but rubble. The report indicates they found no additional information."

"Some of our wartime documents were stored by individuals in their homes, only to be returned to our office years later. Perhaps that will be the case here."

Lurel poured the men coffee while they waited. "I'm sorry to hear about your troubles in the Mediterranean, Yves. Is there a resolution in sight for your fleet?"

Villard gritted his teeth. "*Les poulets* will never return my ships. I'm down to a handful of operating vessels."

"I hate to bring it up, but your storage yard on the east channel? Your lease payments are six months overdue."

An uncomfortable silence filled the room. "I will take care of it," Villard said in a strained voice.

"I noticed some activity there the other day," Lurel said. "A large delivery of pipe."

"We have a local project we hope to be initiating shortly."

Lurel's secretary entered the office carrying an oversized book. The green leather binding was battered, looking every bit the survivor of World War II. Lurel opened the cover, revealing a handwritten title page that was equally distressed.

"'Harbor Master's Logbook, Port of Le Havre, 1938 to 1940,'" Lurel read. "It appears you may be in luck."

Villard and Nassar sat forward as Lurel rifled through the pages.

"Very little commercial activity in mid-May," Lurel said. "By then the region was close to falling into the hands of the Germans. Many inbound vessels would have redirected to Cherbourg or Saint-Malo farther west."

He pressed his finger to one of the pages. "Here we are, twelfth May. There are entries for just two vessels. A British collier, noted as damaged, arrived at Bellot Basin for repairs. And a merchant vessel,

CLIVE CUSSLER THE CORSICAN SHADOW

the *Jupiter*, arrived at eleven o'clock. The log says she departed at twelve thirty."

He looked up from the page. "A note here says it departed under urgency and without picking up a harbor pilot, due to a German air attack."

Villard's tired face lit up. "Yes, that must be the one. Is there any detail about her?"

"She was Portuguese. Took aboard a shipment of tires and chemicals, along with forty-seven passengers. She departed the Quai d'Escale bound for Bermuda."

"There is still the question of the earlier ship," Villard said. "Is there reference to the *Avignon* on or about that date?"

Lurel scanned the surrounding entries. "Yes. It seems she was scheduled to arrive on the twelfth. A notation indicates that she did not appear."

"Where was she to berth?"

"In Vauban Basin. Right next to the *Jupiter*, it would seem."

Nassar smiled at the harbormaster. "May I?"

He snatched the logbook from Lurel and pulled it across the table. Gripping the pages with the May 11 and 12 entries, he carefully ripped them from the book, then folded and stuffed them in his pocket.

"Now, here," Lurel said, "those are official records!"

Nassar rose from his seat and leaned toward the smaller man, glaring eyeball-to-eyeball.

"I shall gladly return the pages when we have found what we are seeking."

The harbormaster shrank into his seat.

Villard offered a feeble thanks for the information, and the two visitors departed.

On the street below, Villard turned to his underling. "It would seem likely the diamonds were placed aboard the *Jupiter* for evacua-

tion. If the ship suffered a similar fate as the *Avignon*, then those diamonds are still out there."

"At least no one else knows they were placed on that ship." Nassar patted his pocket. "I will find out all I can about the *Jupiter*."

Villard stopped to watch a fully loaded container ship exit the harbor on its way to the English Channel. "Lurel may try to impound our pipe inventory for nonpayment of our land lease. Where is the *Chamonix*?"

"She completed the salvage project in the Irish Sea and is now at the Isle of Wight. The recovery was a success."

"Have her come to Le Havre and collect the pipe inventory before Lurel can impound it. Then move her out of port. Perhaps we'll soon be able to proceed with the Normandy pipeline operation."

"I'll notify her captain." Nassar paused. "Has there been a positive movement with the Paris officials?"

Villard gave him a hard look. "No, their water crisis has been averted . . . for the moment. We need to give them another kick. Have some of the radioactive material sent over anonymously, but not on the *Chamonix*. We can fashion another freshwater scare."

"Perhaps a spill into one of the city reservoirs?"

Villard nodded. "Yes, that might work. Put an operation together. Something you can pull off as soon as possible. But first," he said, watching the gleaming white container ship make its way toward the open sea, "find out what became of the *Jupiter*."

23

The *Nordic Star* approached the port of Southampton, England, late on a hazy morning. The NUMA research ship threaded its way through the local marine traffic to dock at a reserved berth opposite the port's bustling commercial wharves. Two large cruise ships were moored at the nearby Ocean Dock, which in the last century was known as the White Star Dock. It was from there in April 1912, the *Titanic* had departed on her ill-fated maiden voyage.

A handful of visiting scientists stood at the rail, eager to exit the *Nordic Star* and return to their academic homes with their newly acquired field research. A new cadre would be joining the NUMA ship in a few days for its next project, tracking pods of blue whales near Iceland.

Summer sat in the sonar bay, where she should have been completing their report on the Gulf Stream flows in the Irish Sea. Instead, she was engaged in some online snooping about the shipwreck they'd examined. While they had reported their findings to the Coast Guard, she was bound and determined to learn more about the wreck.

Dirk stepped in with a mug of coffee and looked over her shoulder at the screen. "The *London Times* from April 1959?"

"It contains an article about our shipwreck in the Irish Sea. The *Cardiff* sank in 1959 with all hands after striking an oil tanker. The ships apparently collided in rough seas and thick fog. The tanker limped intact to Wexford, Ireland, after a fruitless search for survivors from the *Cardiff*."

"Does it mention her cargo?"

"The newspaper says the *Cardiff* was carrying a shipment of Welsh barley."

"Maybe in her forward hold, but not in her stern."

Summer searched for data about the restricted sea zone where the wreck had been located. She found a hit in a British Admiralty report that cited the *Cardiff*'s sinking. It justified the restricted area by confirming the wreck contained hazardous materials.

An hour after tracking down related leads on other government websites, she discovered the full truth. Highly radioactive plutonium waste from Britain's nuclear weapons research program had been shipped on the *Cardiff* to be deposited at a deepwater dump site in the North Atlantic.

Dirk shook his head. "Nice that they were just planning to pitch it over the side."

"Unfortunately, it was a common occurrence in the day. More than a dozen countries used to dump radioactive waste and munitions at sea until it was outlawed in the 1980s. The Brits apparently failed to locate the ship back in 1959, or deemed it too dangerous to salvage, so they just drew a big restricted area around it and let it lie."

"Apparently the *Chamonix* didn't deem it too dangerous to salvage, if in fact that's why they were there. I wonder what their story is?"

While Summer continued to research the shipwreck, Dirk sat at another terminal and tried to chase down the *Chamonix*. "She was built in 1997 and purchased by a large engineering company for use

in Southeast Asia. It was recently sold to a French entity called Aquarius International."

Summer pushed her chair back and rubbed her eyes. "I can't find anything that suggests a license or operation has been authorized to recover any radioactive wastes from the Irish Sea."

"A bit unusual," Dirk said.

"It could be a Navy operation."

"Perhaps, but I doubt they'd be using a French vessel. It's not even a salvage ship."

"Let's assume," Summer said, "they were salvaging it illegally. Is that enough reason to kill the people on the *Mary Spring*?"

"No. But the fellow on the stern had a camera. Maybe he'd simply been taking pictures of an unusual pipe-laying ship and his act was misinterpreted."

"Or he saw something more than that. What do you think we should do?"

"I think," Dirk said, examining his computer screen, "we need to take a quick run over to the Isle of Wight."

Summer gave her brother a quizzical look. "Why's that?"

"Because according to the marine vessel automatic identification system, that's where the *Chamonix* docked six hours ago. Just down the road from us."

Summer gave an impish smile. "I'd love to see the island. I always wanted to attend the Isle of Wight music festival."

"Not until June, I'm afraid."

"Well, we do have some free time before the next project kicks off. Just promise me we won't get in any trouble."

"Trouble?" He laughed. "That's your middle name, not mine."

24

Dirk and Summer borrowed a loaner car from the port authority and drove across the complex to the main ferry terminal. They boarded a Red Funnel ferry for the twelve-mile journey from Southampton to the Isle of Wight. The two stood at the rail and watched the coastal scenery pass by as the ferry made its way into a strait called the Solent that separated the island from mainland England.

The waterway was crowded with tankers and cargo ships, as well as a few sailboats taking advantage of a sunny day. They crossed the narrow strait and approached the northern tip of Wight. Barely twenty miles across, the island was popular as a vacation spot and a haven for boaters, in addition to attracting visitors for its celebrated annual music festival.

The ferry entered the mouth of the Medina River, which divided the port city of Cowes sharply in two. Racing sailboats and power yachts were moored in the river as well as at myriad shoreline marinas. Cowes was well known for its annual sailing regatta, held since 1826, which attracted sailors and celebrities from around the world.

The eastern bank of the Medina showed the town's more industrial nature, with large warehouses and boatyards. It was here that Summer spotted the *Chamonix* berthed at a long dock beside a small coastal oil tanker.

The ferry motored past the two vessels, allowing Dirk and Summer a long look. There was considerable activity about the tanker, but the *Chamonix* looked deserted.

"I guess we didn't need a car," Dirk said as the ferry nosed ashore to a terminal on the river's east side, just a short distance away.

Summer disagreed. "I came to sightsee. A quick look at your ship, then we're off for a drive around the island."

Between the ferry terminal and the *Chamonix*, Dirk eyed a warehouse building with a huge Union Jack painted on one end and a banner advertising it as a classic boat museum. Docked at the waterfront were an assortment of antique sloops, yawls, and other racing sailboats. Once they drove off the ferry, Dirk turned and motored past the museum. A small open boatyard occupied the next waterfront lot and then they reached a high-walled compound. The *Chamonix* was moored out of view on the opposite side.

Summer pointed at a large coil of concertina wire that topped the block wall. "Not the welcoming types. I guess this is as close as we're going to get."

Dirk drove farther, turning into a narrow entrance secured by a gatehouse. He stopped at a lowered wooden barricade and was approached by a sour-faced security guard.

Dirk flashed an eager smile. "I'm here to look at a boat for sale."

"There are no boats for sale here," the man replied.

"Isn't this the East Cowes Boatyard?"

"No, this is a private facility."

"Who owns it?" Dirk asked.

The guard lowered his hand to a belt-mounted radio. "I must ask you to please turn your car around and leave."

"Well, that wasn't very informative," Summer said after Dirk duly backed away. "Let's go see the rest of the island."

Dirk drove a short way down the road, then parked on a side street. "If not the front door," he said, "then maybe we can see something from the side."

Summer shook her head at her brother's stubbornness, but followed him out of the car. They walked back to the compound, following the side wall to the waterfront. It extended several feet past the raised dock, offering no place for a foothold to see around it.

"You'll have to go for a swim," she said, "if you want to see more from here."

Dirk glanced in the other direction. "No, I think we can take a peek without getting wet."

He led her across the neighboring boatyard, where they entered a disheveled office at the front of a small warehouse. A teenage boy with crooked teeth greeted them as they stepped in.

"I'd like to inquire if you have any small boats for rent," Dirk asked.

"This is a boatyard, mate. We store and repair boats."

Summer gave him a sultry smile. "You sure there aren't any we could borrow for a short ride?"

The youth tapped his fingers on the counter. "Come to think of it, we've got a small dory out back I could rent. Twenty quid for an hour."

"We'll take it." Dirk placed a twenty-pound note on the counter.

They found the boat behind the building tied to a small floating dock. The rowboat was about fifty years old and had an inch or two of water sloshing around in its bottom.

"I think you got taken," Summer said as she climbed into the front. "We'll never make it back."

Dirk took the center bench seat and placed a pair of oars into the locks. "We don't have far to go."

The private compound was barely a hundred feet downriver. Dirk

rowed into the river's center and let the current carry them slowly toward the facility. A long warehouse stretched the length of the dock, with a wide sliding door open at the center. A cargo truck was parked near the doorway, its bed covered in a blue canopy with a white stripe.

At the dock, the *Chamonix* and the tanker were moored bow to stern, both facing the Solent with the tanker positioned in front. The pipe-laying ship still appeared deserted, while a few men were milling around the dock beside the tanker. A wisp of smoke carried across the water from its funnel, and the deep throb of its idling engine suggested the ship had either just arrived or was preparing to depart.

"I'd like to know what they did with the salvaged material." Dirk craned to see the deck of the *Chamonix* over its high freeboard.

"I may regret pointing this out, but there's a dock ladder beneath the bollard securing the ship's stern line."

Dirk squinted, then smiled. "I like the way you think."

He rowed alongside the *Chamonix*'s hull, then followed its rounded stern to the dock, keeping in the shadow of the towering ship. When the rowboat bumped against the pylons, Summer tied a painter to a rusty steel ladder that descended from the wharf. The dock itself was nearly ten feet above them, which kept their boat well concealed from the workers in the compound.

Summer stood and grabbed the ladder, then turned to Dirk. "I think I'll let you go first."

He grinned as he slid by her and scampered up the ladder. Some large crates and pieces of industrial equipment were scattered along the dock's near side. Closer to the open warehouse door, the blue truck obscured much of the view toward the tanker. Some more pallets and a small utility van were parked near its bow.

With no one in the immediate area, Dirk climbed onto the dock. Summer got up the nerve to follow him as he walked alongside the *Chamonix*, examining its equipment-filled deck.

He approached a metal gangway and zipped aboard. Feeling

conspicuous with her long, flowing red hair, Summer stayed on the dock and ducked behind a giant spool of cable.

On the ship, Dirk skirted around the massive high reel on the stern deck that was used to lower welded sections of pipe to the seafloor.

He noticed an open hatch near a deck crane facing the dock and slipped to its side. Looking inside, he found it empty. But a movement caught his eye: a crewman on the opposite side of the deck. Dirk ducked behind the hatch cover and waited as the man stepped toward the blockhouse. Once the man was out of sight, Dirk returned to the gangway and met Summer near its base.

"Find anything?" she asked.

"No. If it was aboard, then I think it has already been off-loaded. Let's see if we can get a peek inside the building."

He led Summer across the narrow dock to the warehouse wall and moved along its length. They reached the front of the blue truck and squeezed along its side to the building's open bay door. Dirk stopped and peered around the corner. A forklift was parked just inside. Nearby wooden pallets were stacked high with dry goods, while racks along the back wall held twenty-foot lengths of pipe in varying diameters.

Voices echoed from inside, but Dirk couldn't see anyone near the door. Summer tapped him on the shoulder, and he turned to see her pointing at the truck. Its back end was open, and a loading ramp was extended to the ground.

"They may have loaded it in the truck," she whispered.

She hopped onto the ramp and climbed inside, snaking past a stack of cardboard boxes. A second later, she poked her head out at Dirk. "There are two large yellow containers in the back. I'm going to take a closer look."

As she ducked back inside, a voice rang out from the warehouse. "Hey, you."

Dirk stepped away from the truck as two burly men exited the

building. They had dark features and wore military-style buzz cuts. The man who spoke carried a clipboard, while the second man pulled a pistol from a holster and leveled it at Dirk.

Dirk raised his hands and stepped forward, taking a quick glance at the back of the truck. Summer had squirmed into the back of the cargo bay, hiding herself.

"What are you doing here?" said the man with the clipboard.

"Don't shoot," Dirk said. "I'm just here to pick up some motor-cycle parts . . . A shipment of sprockets from Ducati."

The clipboard holder looked around the dock, then turned to the gunman. "Take him inside." He retrieved a handheld radio and spoke into it in French. A minute later, Hosni Samad emerged from the tanker and crossed to the warehouse. Inside, Dirk was being held against a slatted crate filled with gray boxes that were marked as industrial explosives.

The commando looked at Dirk with irritation. "How did you get in here?"

"I walked through the front gate. Can you have him put that thing away?" Dirk tilted his head toward the gunman. "And what about my parts? They should have shipped in from Genoa."

Samad pulled aside the man with the clipboard. "Is this true? Did the man wander in here?"

"No. I radioed the guard. No one has been allowed to enter from the street."

Samad gazed at the truck's open door, then glanced at his watch. "Have the containers been loaded?"

"We were just preparing to close up the back."

"Get it on its way then. It's supposed to be on the Chunnel train at two o'clock."

"What about him?" he asked, motioning toward Dirk.

"I'll take care of him. Just get the truck on the road."

"Yes, sir." The man scurried over and secured the ramp, then

closed the truck's back doors. He spoke into his radio, and two men ran up from the tanker. After a brief conversation, they climbed into the truck and started it.

From the warehouse, Dirk could only watch with dread as the truck rumbled off the dock, knowing Summer was locked inside. His attention was quickly diverted to Samad.

"Who are you, and why are you here?" the commando asked.

"I'm a courier. I was told to pick up a parts order for a motorcycle dealer in Southampton."

Samad stood close to Dirk. The American accent was a cause for suspicion. More disconcerting was the total lack of fear in the young man's eyes. The clipboard man frisked Dirk, removed his wallet, and handed his driver's license to Samad.

"American," he said.

Samad looked at the name on the license and slowly shook his head. He had read the news accounts after the thwarted attack in Paris . . . and remembered the name of the American who had driven the truck into the Seine. It was the same as the name on the license, but this was not the man he had tied up in the suicide truck.

"Hold him here." He stepped to a quiet corner of the warehouse and phoned Nassar. He returned a few minutes later with a ruthless look.

"Tie him up and put him aboard the *Mont Blanc*," he said. "We're going to take him for a swim."

25

Concealed behind the tall cable spool, Summer watched the truck roll away and counted her lucky stars. She had escaped the truck bed without being seen, seconds before the doors were closed and locked.

She'd known the truck wasn't a safe place to hide when Dirk was apprehended, as the men holding him were initially in plain sight. Summer had stayed at the back of the truck until Samad was called and everyone moved into the warehouse.

She had used the time in hiding to examine the large yellow containers at the back. They were made of a hardened polyethylene composite, shaped like a cylinder, and almost five feet tall. Running her hand across the top, she found a circular hatch and realized they were oversized storage containers for fifty-five-gallon drums.

She confirmed her suspicions when she opened a latch, revealing a rusty drum inside. It looked in the same condition as the ones they'd seen on the *Cardiff*. She quickly resealed the top, hoping there wasn't any leakage from the material inside. Under the low light, she examined the exterior of the yellow containers and found no radiation or hazard warnings.

When the voices outside diminished, she made her way to the open end of the truck and surveyed the dock. Several workers on the tanker were using a portable crane to guide pallets into a forward hold. The men with Dirk in the warehouse were no longer visible.

She slipped out of the truck and ducked beside the cab. She made it out unseen and retreated to the spool of cable. She had no sooner dropped behind it when the gunman exited the warehouse and closed the truck's doors. Two men rushed up from the tanker and climbed into the cab, and the truck drove around the warehouse and exited the compound.

Summer waited in hiding, unsure what to do. Hopefully they would just let Dirk go. But she realized that wasn't the case when he was marched out at gunpoint, his hands tied behind his back. She watched as he was led aboard the tanker and taken inside the blockhouse at the aft end of the ship.

The man with the clipboard reappeared a few minutes later and returned to the warehouse. The gunman also exited the ship, but took up a position on the tanker's gangway, watching anyone who might try to board.

They had obviously left Dirk alone, locked up somewhere in the blockhouse. Summer's heart began to pound. Wherever they were going to take him, it couldn't be good. She had to figure out how to free him, but with the guard on watch, there was no way to approach the tanker from the dock.

Fortunately, she thought, Dirk had already provided another way aboard.

26

Brigitte briefly examined the front of the postcard. It displayed a color photo of a pink-sand beach with children frolicking in the water. A label at the bottom identified it as Elbow Bathing Beach, Bermuda. She flipped it over and read the card's message written in blue ink.

> *"I feared I would experience my first hurricane, but the strong winds and heavy rains were deemed only a tropical storm by the time they struck Bermuda. The monotonous pace of the island is indeed disrupted by an occasional moment of wonder. Marcel."*

"Elbow Beach again." Giordino took the postcard from Brigitte and handed her another. "That makes nearly a dozen. Marcel could have mixed it up a bit more."

He placed the card on a scanner and made a digital copy, then replaced it in the box Allain Broussard had loaned them.

"What's the date on that one?" Pitt sat across from the pair in the *Pelican*'s sonar shack, his hands clasped behind his head.

"October twelfth, 1941. Near the end of the line." Giordino pulled out the last three postcards.

Brigitte translated the card in her hand and the next one Giordino gave her, reporting more weather and greetings from Marcel Demille.

"Here's something," she said, reading the next-to-last card. "'Seventeenth November, 1940. Apologies for my lack of correspondence. I have been fighting a stomach ailment that has made me weak. The doctor says it may be an ulcer. I met an officer from an FNFL vessel here for repairs and discussed my situation. He agreed to make inquiries about relocating Jean and me to French soil. It will most likely be in the Pacific, after a stop in Little Guinea. I am hoping for a positive reply. Marcel.'"

"Thirty postcards about the weather and finally things get interesting," Giordino said. "Guinea is in West Africa, isn't it?"

"Yes," Brigitte said. "A former French colony. But I've never heard of Little Guinea." She searched on her phone. "No such place appears in the geographic listings."

"It doesn't seem likely they'd recross the Atlantic to Africa en route to the Pacific," Pitt said. "Maybe it's the nickname of a base or facility."

"What," Giordino asked, "would be an FNFL vessel?"

"Forces Navales Françaises Libres, or Free French Naval Forces," Brigitte said. "Those vessels under the government in exile, led by Charles de Gaulle. Ultimately around fifty ships made up the Free French Navy."

"The last one." Giordino passed the final postcard to Brigitte.

She held up the same photo of Elbow Beach and laughed. "Your favorite."

"Go ahead and read it. Put me out of my misery."

"Eleventh February, 1942. A quick note to say au revoir from Bermuda. We will be departing shortly to a kindred territory. I will write again in a few weeks. Marcel."

"Apparently not," Giordino said, his hand at the back of the card box. He took a final look at the beach scene, then flipped it over to file it away. He hesitated when something caught his eye. "There's a postscript at the bottom that you missed." He handed it back to Brigitte. "Something about Mr. Martin."

"Oh, yes. 'P.S. As we have received no guidance, Jean will be carrying Monsieur Martin's luggage with him.'"

Giordino sat up. "That's some postscript. It would seem to confirm that the diamonds were in Bermuda . . . but now they're not."

She passed the card back. "The mystery deepens."

"Apparently taken from Bermuda to French soil in the Pacific," Pitt said.

"What might that have been in early 1942?" Giordino asked.

Brigitte thought a moment. "French Polynesia, most likely. Possibly New Caledonia or Vanuatu in the western Pacific."

Pitt frowned. "Unlikely they would travel to the western Pacific islands at that stage of the war."

Giordino brightened. "Tahiti it is then! When do we leave?"

Brigitte smiled and shook her head. "There are more than a hundred islands in French Polynesia. Where would you start?"

"Don't pack your flip-flops just yet," Pitt said. "It's a long way from Bermuda to Tahiti. We don't know if Demille even made it that far."

Giordino scoured the box for any stray postcards or letters. "This card is the last correspondence we have. Perhaps he never left Bermuda. Especially if he took a peek in Martin's cases while packing to leave."

Pitt glanced at his watch. "Maybe Hiram has something to add. I asked him to check the records in Bermuda while he was running down a few things for me. He's due to check in shortly."

A few minutes later, Hiram Yaeger appeared on a video screen, seated at his computer command post in Washington. A fit man with

long hair, his casual appearance in jeans and a Yardbirds T-shirt belied his brilliance at managing NUMA's vast information technology network.

"*Bonjour*." He raised his first cup of coffee for the day.

"Good morning," Pitt said, noting the time difference. "What are we missing in Washington today?"

"Let's see. The politicians are prevaricating, the media is mendacious, and the lobbyists are looting us all. Same as yesterday, and the forecast calls for more tomorrow. And you? Any more midnight tours of Paris while dressed for combat duty?"

"Al says we have to wait until Halloween before we try that again."

"I've been monitoring the news accounts and expert assessments," Yaeger said, "while Rudi has spoken with a number of intelligence officials. The French authorities seem to believe it was a homegrown attack by militant Islamic sympathizers."

"These guys weren't interested in blowing themselves up," Giordino said, "or even sticking around for the fireworks."

"The uniforms suggest a link with the Palestinian Hamas organization, rather than ISIS," Yaeger said. "There are some similarities to a recent attack at a desalination plant in Israel. No suspects yet in either case, though."

"Anything from Le Havre?" Pitt asked.

"I checked satellite images for the warehouse location where you were abducted, and it does appear a ship was berthed there a few days before your incident. It was a small oil tanker, but I haven't been able to obtain an identification or track its whereabouts."

"Thanks for checking," Pitt said.

Yaeger reached for a thick folder and cleared his throat. "As for your little treasure hunt, I'm afraid I got sidetracked by an overheated mainframe last night and conducted only a limited amount of research. I didn't find any more on Eduard Martin, beyond his affiliation with the Antwerp Diamond Bank and his burial in Le Havre."

He looked at the folder. "But Marcel Demille was a little more prominent in the data files. He was a graduate of the Sorbonne in 1922 with a degree in history. He worked for the National Archaeological Museum in Saint-Germain for several years, then became chief curator at the Army Museum in Paris, at least until 1940, when the citations in France cease because of the war."

"Any recorded appearance in Bermuda?" Giordino asked.

"I searched what I could, but many of the government archives have not been digitized and made available online. I did find a port entry record, and also a newspaper account that Demille gave a talk at the Bermuda National Library in December 1940 on behalf of the Bermuda Historical Society, where he may have been employed. But I found no official record of him leaving the country, nor a death record."

"We just found evidence," Giordino said, "that he found the beaches too crowded and may have shipped off to Tahiti."

Yaeger smiled. "I'm available for on-site data analysis."

"Let's defer any tropical travel plans for the moment," Pitt said. "Did you find anything on Demille's contact in Bermuda or his travel partner?"

"The envoy he mentioned was one Paul Rapine, an undersecretary to the French consulate in Bermuda. The consulate was shut down during the war, and Rapine appears on the Bermuda government payroll as a foreign policy advisor. He remained in Bermuda until his death in 1953. His journals and official papers are no doubt archived on the island, and would certainly be worth a look . . . on your way to Bora-Bora."

"Only if Al hijacks the plane," Pitt said. "It sounds like Rapine's records may be our best prospect for tracking down Demille's movements."

"Best I can give you at the moment," Yaeger said. "As to the other name you sent me, you indicated it was Demille's traveling companion?"

"Jean d'Eppé? Yes, he surfaced in some correspondence from Demille. He apparently traveled with Demille to Bermuda, and also departed the island with him."

"A very interesting name in French history," Yaeger said, arching his brow. "I found several people by that name in France before the war, but none showed up in Bermuda. As I mentioned, I found Marcel Demille's arrival in the Bermuda customs records. He arrived in May 1940 on a ship called the *Jupiter*. The records showed his arrival and entry, but I found no corresponding record of a Jean d'Eppé."

Brigitte pulled out the original postcard from Demille to André Carron and quickly reread it. "That's funny. He clearly states he arrived in Bermuda with d'Eppé."

"You said his name had historical significance," Pitt said. "Could it have been a nom de guerre for another passenger?"

"Quite possibly. Jean d'Eppé, or the historical Jean d'Eppé, was a famed thirteenth-century military commander under Charles I. But Max came up with an interesting coincidence." Max was the name of a holographic interface Yaeger created to communicate with his powerful computer systems by voice.

"The meaning changes if you add a diacritic mark, or accent, to the spelling of the name," Yaeger continued. "As Brigitte would know, if the acute accent, or *aigu*, is added to the first letter of his surname, you have the French word for 'sword.'" He typed *Jean d'Éppé* onto the screen for all to see.

"Jean—or John—of the sword," Pitt said.

"Exactly."

"Does that have any particular significance to us?"

"It may or may not," Yaeger said. "According to Max, Jean d'Éppé was not just a thirteenth-century French nobleman. It was also a nickname given to Napoleon Bonaparte by partisan supporters after his banishment to Elba."

"Napoleon?"

"Oh, no." Brigitte gasped. "Marcel Demille. He was the curator at the Army Museum."

"Yes," Giordino said. "But what does that have to do with Napoleon?"

"As Broussard told us, Demille and André Carron were transporting a large crate from the Army Museum," she said, "which is located at the Invalides in Paris."

"The same place where Napoleon is buried," Pitt said.

Brigitte nodded, her eyes wide in disbelief.

"So if Marcel Demille was traveling with Jean d'Éppé . . ." Giordino said.

"It could only mean one thing," Pitt concluded. "He departed the country not only with a cache of diamonds, but also with the remains of France's greatest emperor."

27

The tanker Summer sought to board was named the *Mont Blanc* for the highest peak in the Alps, the letters emblazoned across the ship's transom. Summer was less interested in the ship's name than the steel ladder welded to its stern. The metal rungs reached from the deck to the waterline, an easy access point to board the ship. But they were mounted on the starboard side of the stern, in clear view of the guard on the gangway. She'd have to stick to her makeshift plan formulated on the dock.

Summer continued to row the dory down the center of the river like a tourist. She had made a quiet escape from the dock to the leaky boat and knew it was the best way to approach the tanker unseen.

Once out of view of the guard, she turned and approached the ship. She nudged the boat along the tanker's side until even with the accommodations block, which provided cover from the gangway on the opposite side. Holding position against the hull, she grasped a makeshift grappling hook and prepared to board.

It was nothing more than a hammer she'd found atop the cable spool on the dock. It was tied to the end of the dory's thin bowline and muffled with a rag knotted around its head. Summer stood in the

boat and tossed the hammer up and over her head like a rodeo cowboy lassoing a steer.

Her throw completely missed. The tool bounced against the hull and splashed into the water.

Summer reeled it in and sat still for a moment, fearful of detection. The gentle throb of the tanker's engine covered the noise of the splash, so she tried again. Her second toss was on the mark, just clearing the top bar of the ship's railing. The hammer wasn't hooked enough to secure a footing, so Summer released more line, letting the hammer drop in a loop around the rail and back toward the boat.

She had tied the other end to an oar and raised it over her head until she could reach the descending hammer with her free hand. She then pulled on the line, yanking the oar up to the deck, where it clanged tight against the rail. Summer secured the loose line to the dory, then began shinnying up. The thin rope proved difficult to scale, so she pushed her feet against the side of the hull and walked herself up the ship's side.

It was a ten-foot climb, and Summer felt the strain in her arms. She reached for the rail and lurched herself over the side, sprawling onto the deck. She bounded to her feet and took her bearings while catching her breath. The port-side deck was thankfully deserted. Just a few feet away stood the high blockhouse and a side-entry door.

Summer moved to the door and cracked it open. Just an empty passageway. Taking a quick look around, she stepped inside and let the door close quietly behind her.

28

While held in the warehouse, Dirk couldn't refrain from worrying about his sister trapped in the truck. The prospect of the lithe redhead popping unexpectedly out the back when the truck reached its destination almost seemed humorous. But there was no humor in the armed thugs driving the truck or the possibility that she was locked up with radioactive material.

His own troubles had grown serious when Samad had ordered his hands bound behind his back and he was prodded to the tanker. As he crossed the ship's gangway, he looked toward the bow, where several men were stowing materials into a hold. A pallet dangled from a dockside crane, holding stacks of the gray boxes he'd seen in the warehouse. He also glimpsed something yellow in the hold, but couldn't make out its specifics.

Dirk was led into the blockhouse and up a companionway to a second-level deck, where cabins for the crew were fitted. His captors stopped and conferred a moment, realizing the cabins couldn't be locked from the outside. He was led to a small locker with a sliding latch door that was flung open. Inside, a broom, mop, and bucket were wedged beside a small utility sink.

"Feel free to clean up," the clipboard man said and shoved Dirk inside.

Standing six-foot, three-inches tall, Dirk banged his head on the ceiling as he crashed against the back wall. The door slammed behind him and the latch slid closed, locking him inside.

Dirk kicked over the bucket in the darkness and took a seat on it, cursing himself for dragging Summer into this. The same fate would probably await Summer somewhere across the Channel. He had to escape, if not for his own sake, then for hers. But a mop, broom, and dirty sink didn't offer much of a start.

As he thought about it, though, he decided it was better than nothing.

He stood and turned his back against the sink, feeling the bottom of the faucet. As he expected, the aged fixture had lost much of its original chrome plating, and the bottom of the spigot was coated with a rough layer of rust.

Dirk lowered his wrists and aligned the bindings against the bottom of the fixture, working them back and forth. The rusty faucet didn't cut like the edge of a Ginsu knife, but the jagged surface gradually sawed into the rope. After several minutes, one of the strands parted, and he was able to unwind the bindings.

He dropped the rope into the sink and rubbed his wrists, then pressed an ear against the door and listened for voices in the passageway. Silence. He twisted the handle and threw his shoulder hard against the door, but it didn't budge.

He took a step back and kicked with the sole of his foot, but the result was the same. The door was made of heavy maple, too thick to break, and the steel latch was securely mounted.

Dirk took a seat on the bucket and contemplated another way out. Under the faint light that spilled over the threshold, he noted the door hinges were mounted on the inside, screwed to the wood with large backing plates.

With a hammer and chisel, it would be easy to pop the bolt off the hinge. Or with a screwdriver, he could remove the backing plates. But all he had was a mop and a broom.

He picked up the mop and studied the business end. It was a classic string mop, with a few dozen cloth strands clamped between two metal tabs affixed to the handle. He realized one of the tabs might slip under the hinge's backing plate and allow him to pry it from the door.

"Clean up, indeed," he muttered as he began plucking the strands from the mop head one by one. That task completed, he slid the bare tab against the top door hinge mount and worked it under the edge. He gripped the mop handle and gave a hard pull. The mounting screws squeaked as they began to lose their grip in the door. After a few tries, the screws popped free and the backing plate fell loose. He repeated the process on the lower hinge, the mop handle splitting with his last heave.

Dirk then wedged the mop tab beneath the base of the door and yanked with the remaining piece of handle. The door notched open an inch or two on the hinged side before catching on the latch. It was enough space for Dirk to slip his fingers around the doorframe. He grabbed the edge and heaved the door back, bending the latch, while creating enough space to slip out.

He strode down the hallway and was nearly to the companionway when a cabin door in front of him opened and a towering bald man stepped out with a tray of dirty dishes. The man gazed at Dirk, his eyes enlarging at the sight of the stranger. Dirk gave him no time to react. He shoved the tray against the man's chest and followed with an overhand punch to the head.

The man was too slow to dodge the punch, but turned enough so that the blow caught him on the cheek rather than the jaw. The tray of dishes went flying, but the man stood as steady as a block of granite. Shaking off the blow, he lunged at Dirk.

Off balance from his punch, Dirk recovered enough to throw a left cross as the man barreled into him. The blow struck the man's forehead, but produced only a wince.

The bald man didn't try to hit back, but bulled into Dirk with his superior mass, driving him across the hall into the opposite bulkhead.

The air rushed from Dirk's lungs as he struck the wall. A sharp pain flared as his shoulder contacted with something at his side. Out of the corner of his eye, he saw a mounted fire extinguisher.

The bald man pinned Dirk against the wall and began pummeling his torso with body shots, stinging his ribs and stomach.

The blows kept Dirk from regaining his breath, and he began to see stars. Groping along the wall, he grabbed for the fire extinguisher, ripping it from its mount. With a single high swing, he brought the canister down onto the man's head.

A muffled clang accompanied the blow, and the jackhammer punches to Dirk's body ceased. The hefty man staggered back and collapsed to the floor.

Dirk leaned against the wall and rasped for air, each breath inciting pain from his bruised ribs. When his head cleared, he grabbed the man by his heels and dragged him back to his cabin.

The man wore a red work jacket of the type he'd seen on some of the workers on the dock. Dirk tugged it off the unconscious man and slipped it over his shirt, then donned a black ball cap sitting on the bunk. He tossed the tray, dishes, and fire extinguisher into the cabin and closed the door. Striding quickly to the end of the hall, he descended the companionway.

As he reached the lower level, he heard a click behind him. He turned as a cabin door was closing shut in the corridor. Dirk stepped to the starboard-side exit and looked outside. The gangway was a short distance away, but in the middle of it stood the gunman from the warehouse. His gun was holstered and he leaned on the rail, watching the last pallet being loaded into the forward hold.

Dirk pulled the brim of his cap low as he noticed some boxes of galley provisions stacked near the door. He picked up one of the boxes, held it high in front of his face, and stepped across the deck.

He made it two steps onto the gangway before the gunman called to him. *"Où allez-vous?"*

Dirk mumbled something in a deep voice and stepped faster. The gunman turned and faced him, blocking his path. Dirk pretended to stumble, stooping slightly. As he reached the guard, he exploded upward, driving the box into the man's torso.

The gunman teetered on his heels but managed to push the box aside. His eyes opened wide at the sight of Dirk, arms outstretched, shoving into him like a bulldozer.

The gunman had no chance. Off balance, he flipped back over the rail. He made a desperate grab for Dirk and the handrail, but missed both. His legs flew up and he plunged headfirst into the water.

A silence fell over the wharf at the sudden splash. The dockside crane halted, and the crewmen on the bow froze. Then the gunman broke the surface and began yelling and pointing at Dirk.

Workers seemed to materialize from everywhere as Dirk hustled off the gangway. He turned right and ran back toward the *Chamonix*, thinking a quick sprint to the rowboat would be his best strategy. He pounded across the wharf, reached the forward section of the pipe-laying ship, and stopped in his tracks.

Two large crewmen appeared on the ship's deck and were making their way toward the dock. But it wasn't their appearance that made Dirk stop. Peering over the edge of the dock, he realized the rowboat was gone.

He reversed course and moved toward a paved drive that curved around the far end of the warehouse to the front entrance. But the crane operator had left his machine and was running to cut him off, while several crewmen from the tanker were also scrambling to give

chase. Dirk ran toward them, then looked to his right at the open warehouse doorway.

He had one chance for escape, but it would require some luck. "Please have the keys in the ignition," he pleaded as he bolted through the warehouse door.

29

The forklift just inside the warehouse did indeed have the keys in the ignition. Dirk jumped into the operator's seat and turned the key, but the engine refused to start.

Near the back of the warehouse, clipboard man had exited a small office and was making his way across the floor. He heard the forklift's starter grind and glanced up to see Dirk behind the wheel. He charged the cab and lunged at Dirk just as the engine caught.

The man slammed into Dirk and grabbed his red jacket to pull him off. But Dirk mashed the accelerator, sending the forklift forward. The man's feet slid across the polished floor, and his grasp on the jacket turned into a hold of necessity.

Dirk had to swerve to avoid striking a pallet head-on, simultaneously jabbing his right elbow at his attacker's head. It dazed the man, but did not diminish his vise-like hold on Dirk's jacket.

Dirk zigged and zagged the forklift to dislodge the passenger, but to no effect. He had maneuvered into the warehouse interior and had to circle around several stacked crates before he could aim back toward the exit.

The man still had no footing, but he had a firm grip on Dirk with his left hand and began punching with his balled right fist. Dirk tried to ward off the blows, but took two hard punches to his already aching rib cage. He kept the accelerator down and aimed for the open doorway, skirting to one side.

The dangling man launched another strike, then glanced at the approaching daylight. Too late, he saw that Dirk meant to squeeze him against the doorway's edge. He quickly raised his legs and tried to tuck against the side of the forklift.

The doorway arrived first, clipping his waist and legs. He gasped at the impact and let go of Dirk's jacket. As the forklift broke into sunlight, his body bounced off the forklift's engine compartment and he tumbled to the ground.

Clear of the warehouse, Dirk made a sharp right onto the paved exit drive, only to face the crane operator and another crewman with a pipe wrench. He aimed the forklift directly at them, forcing them to dive out of the way. At the last second the crewman tossed his wrench. The heavy tool grazed the top of Dirk's head, leaving a thin gash, but no impairment.

Dirk sped past the tanker toward the end of the warehouse. Gunshots rang out behind him and he ducked as bullets struck the side of the forklift. A moment later, he reached the end of the warehouse and whipped around the corner, taking a last glimpse down the wharf.

At least six men were in pursuit, and an armed man was climbing into the passenger seat of a small utility van. As he left them behind, smoke began to rise from the forklift's rear engine housing and the diesel began to rattle and knock. Dirk careened around the end of the warehouse and approached the front entrance. The wooden barricade was down, and the guard was in his station house, his face pressed against the window.

The guard scrambled to the door at the sight of the oncoming

forklift, but could only watch as it plowed into the barricade. The wooden barrier exploded into fragments, a large wedge landing on the seat next to Dirk.

The small van appeared from behind the building a few seconds later, its tires screeching. The guard jumped out of the way as the van sped past, the passenger leaning out the window with a gun in his outstretched hand.

Dirk drove toward his parked rental car, but noted the van in close pursuit. With little cover on the side street, he continued toward the more congested center of East Cowes. The forklift was no match in speed, and the pursuers quickly made ground.

Dirk zipped past the boatyard, searching for an escape route as he approached the large hangar that housed the classic boat museum. Two loud pops rang out, and he ducked as the shots whizzed overhead, the gunman's aim jostled by the rough road.

As the van drew closer, Dirk made a sudden right turn into the museum's parking lot, taking advantage of the forklift's sharp turning radius. Still, the forklift tilted to one side, nearly toppling, as Dirk drove toward the waterfront.

The van's tires squealed as the vehicle followed course, but the driver was forced to brake hard and take a wider turn.

Only a few tourist cars were sprinkled through the lot. Ahead, the car park ended at a riverfront walkway. More shots sounded, and bullets struck the back of the forklift. The van had accelerated again and was just a few car lengths behind.

At the end of the lot, Dirk stood on the brakes and wheeled the forklift in a sharp U-turn, while raising the pronged lifting forks to waist height. He grabbed the wooden plank from the barricade and jammed one end onto the accelerator and the other against the seat, then jumped out the side. The forklift shot forward, straight toward the oncoming van.

The van's driver slammed on the brakes, but had no room to turn

away before colliding with the forklift. The lift prongs cut through the grille and radiator, sending up a plume of steam as both vehicles jarred to a halt. The driver and gunman, neither wearing seat belts, were thrown face-first against the dashboard. Bloodied and dazed, both men staggered from the mangled van, searching for their quarry.

Dirk was well ahead, sprinting to the museum's entrance. But he spotted a family with small children standing in the potential line of fire and he turned away from the building. He ran toward the waterfront and a large dock that housed myriad antique sailboats from the museum's collection.

While Dirk would have liked to admire the historical racing sailboats, he had his eye on another form of escape. At the end of the dock a tiny passenger ferry was showing a wisp of smoke from her exhaust, having just docked after running a handful of passengers across the river. It was a sleek vessel, with a bright red hull and white topsides. The empty pilothouse sat atop a single covered deck that seated fifty passengers. The boat's pilot, a bearded man with octagonal eyeglasses, stood beside a ticket booth as Dirk ran up.

"Is the . . . ferry . . . running today?" Dirk asked.

"The next passage will be in fifteen minutes. Fare is two pounds."

While Dirk's wallet had been taken at the warehouse, he had a few coins in his pocket. "Okay if I board now?"

"Take a seat wherever you like."

Dirk was already moving casually toward the boat, eyeing its two mooring lines. The pilot watched him for a minute, then turned his attention to two men wearing similar red jackets who ran onto the front end of the dock.

As soon as the pilot turned away, Dirk bent down and loosened the bow's mooring line, then rushed to untie the stern line. He could hear the pounding feet of the approaching gunmen as he gave the boat a hard shove and jumped aboard. He scrambled to the wheelhouse and ran his hands across the helm to the throttle control.

The drifting boat caught the attention of the pilot, who turned and yelled at Dirk. The older man started down the dock after the ferry, but was knocked down by the two men sprinting from the van.

Dirk hit the throttle and turned the wheel hard over, and the boat lurched from the dock.

The men arrived too late to jump on, but one grabbed the loose bowline sliding across the dock. He lunged for a cleat, but the line drew taut before he could secure it and he was jerked over the side. He let go of the line as he hit the water, surfacing a moment later to see the stern of the boat as it rumbled away.

Dirk glanced back to see the pilot regain his feet and storm down the dock. Dirk gave an apologetic wave, then turned and guided the boat down the river. The *Chamonix* loomed up on his right a minute later, and he brought the ferryboat close alongside it.

The pipe-laying ship was still quiet, but when he reached the oil tanker, a frenzied effort was in place to get the ship underway. Dirk smiled as he spotted the clipboard man leaning against the warehouse, clutching his side.

But as he passed by the tanker, the thrill of his escape subsided and he felt only a grave concern for Summer and her unknown fate.

30

At that particular moment, Summer was just a stone's throw away. After making her way aboard the *Mont Blanc*, she had crept into the tanker's blockhouse, checking the cabins on the first level. She found the doors unlocked and quietly went from cabin to cabin, searching for Dirk.

She had bypassed the galley and dining hall and was nearly at the end of the hall when she heard someone in the companionway. She slipped into an empty cabin as a figure in a red coat and black cap arrived at the bottom of the stairs and turned to go outside.

She waited a moment, then worked her way to the end of the hall and proceeded up the companionway to the second level. She resumed her search of the cabins, placing her ear against each door and listening before easing open the handle. Her heart pounded when she looked in the first cabin and saw an off-duty crewman sleeping in his bunk. At the next cabin, she was even more shocked to find an unconscious man on the floor amid a pile of dirty dishes and a fire extinguisher.

Summer studied his breathing to see if he was alive, when yelling erupted from the dock. A door latch clicked open down the hall, and

she hurriedly closed the cabin door and locked herself in. As she waited for the footfalls in the hallway to pass, some faint popping sounded in the distance. She hoped it wasn't gunfire.

When the passageway grew silent, she unlocked the door to leave, but noticed something in the occupant's open bureau: a pair of desert camouflage fatigues. It wasn't the color of the material that caught her eye, but an embroidered script on the breast pocket. She stepped closer and studied the garment. The script was Arabic.

A chill went up her spine. She stepped past the man on the floor, exited the cabin, and hurried down the corridor. Abandoning caution, she flung open the remaining cabin doors in search of Dirk, as she felt a growing sense of dread.

At the end of the hall, she stopped in front of a small storage locker with a damaged door. Strands of rope in the sink told her that Dirk had been there. Had he somehow escaped?

That would explain the shouting outside. And the gunshots. Dirk was already off the vessel and had no way of knowing that she was now aboard. As a deep rumble came from the bowels of the tanker and the floor began to sway, she knew one thing: she had to get herself off the ship.

Summer reached the port-side companionway, but a crewman was stomping up the steps from the first level. She returned to the corridor and ducked into the nearest cabin. She waited again, buying time by counting her breaths until she knew it was safe.

Summer tried again, returning to the stairwell and making her way down. At the main deck level, she pushed the exterior door ajar and peered outside. The view of the forward deck was a maze of pipes and valves that fed into the ship's oil storage tanks. Several crewmen lingered near the rail, chatting. One of them, she noticed, carried a holstered pistol.

More disturbing was the sight just over the rail. It was the open sea flitting by. She turned and looked aft. Not only was the dock far

from view, but the Isle of Wight was already receding in the distance. Summer looked to the rail where she had stashed the rowboat oar and spotted the remains of the bowline, its severed end flapping against the side of the ship. She would not be rowing to safety.

A strong swimmer, Summer eyed the distance to the island. If it had been August, she could probably swim for it, but the water temperature in May was only about forty-five degrees Fahrenheit. Without a wetsuit, she'd likely succumb to hypothermia before getting to shore. And that was assuming she could get over the side without being seen.

A crewman appeared near the stern, and she ducked back inside and closed the door, her heart pounding with indecision. She moved down the passageway and entered an unoccupied cabin she'd visited earlier, locking the door behind her. She took a seat on the bunk, bent over in dismay at her predicament, and ran her fingers through her hair.

Her brother's words in Southampton haunted her thoughts. "You're right this time," she muttered. "Trouble apparently *is* my middle name."

31

Dirk sped down the Medina River and entered the Solent, angling toward the English coast. The small ferry handled spryly under a light touch at the wheel. Its red and white color scheme indicated it had once belonged to the Red Funnel ferry line, the same operator he and Summer had taken to the Isle of Wight. As he passed a sleek Cossutti racing yacht tacking into the wind, Dirk noted some of the bridge markings were in Italian. His ears perked up when the bridge radio crackled with a call from the Cowes Coast Guard station to "the Red Funnel boat *Shearwater* entering the Solent."

Dirk pushed the throttle ahead. His plan was to sail to Southampton, dock the borrowed boat on the sly, and solicit police help to find the blue truck carrying Summer.

But a strange thing happened as the boat accelerated. The bow levitated out of the water and the pounding of the waves against the hull fell away. A second later, the stern rose as well, and the boat leaped forward at nearly double its speed, seeming to fly over the water.

The boat was one of a class of Red Funnel hydrofoils, originally

built for high-speed ferry service between Cowes and Southampton in the 1970s and '80s. Dirk was astounded at the sudden performance from the V12-powered craft. Absent a passenger load, it roared across the seas like a Kentucky thoroughbred at Churchill Downs. Although the Italian-built boat was over fifty years old, it had recently been refurbished by the boat museum and it ran like new.

Dirk pushed the throttle to its stops to see how fast the boat could go. It ripped over the choppy seas and raced past the sailing yacht like it was standing still. There was no speedometer, but Dirk guessed the boat was traveling close to forty knots. He aimed the bow east at a gap in the marine traffic, then stepped to a nautical chart of the English Channel on the rear bulkhead. He found his position off the Isle of Wight and dragged a finger east to Folkestone near Dover, the English terminus of the Channel Tunnel. The chart showed the distance as almost exactly one hundred miles.

Dirk returned to the helm and checked the fuel tanks. Full. His luck was holding. If only he had the time. A glance at his watch showed it was 11:45. He had just over two hours to reach the 2:00 p.m. Chunnel train and intercept the blue truck carrying Summer.

It would be close. Very close.

32

The picturesque English coastline rolled by rapidly. If he hadn't been worried about his sister, Dirk would have found pleasure in the voyage. He marveled at the hydrofoil's tireless speed and its stability in waters that were far from smooth. The boat ran even faster the farther east he traveled, due to a growing tailwind and a lighter fuel load.

Though the mechanicals had been rebuilt, the boat was still a museum piece and lacked a modern navigation system or GPS. Dirk used the chart and a compass to plot the best route to Folkestone, setting repeated course corrections to speed around the contour of the coast. He kept one eye out for marine traffic and the other on the shoreline, identifying his position by port cities and natural landmarks.

As he rounded a prominent headland called Dungeness, he spotted the famed chalky white cliffs of Dover in the distance and knew he was getting close. Ten minutes later, he approached a long concrete pier that fingered into the Channel. He curled around the end and eased off the throttle, entering the small, protected harbor at

Folkestone. The main harbor quay was empty, so Dirk ran the hydrofoil right alongside it and cut the motor.

A bearded old man with a fishing pole watched as Dirk tossed the fore and aft mooring lines ashore, then jumped off and secured the boat. No sooner had he tied off the lines than he took off running down the quay. Dirk glanced at his watch as he ran, noting he had covered the hundred miles in just over two hours. He still had time to reach the Chunnel station.

At the opposite edge of the harbor, a battered green taxi sat parked in front of a brick pub with the ubiquitous English moniker the Red Lion. As Dirk sprinted up, gasping for air, he found a frumpy man in a panama hat seated on the steps smoking a cigarette.

Dirk motioned toward the cab. "Are you the driver?"

"Aye. Are you in a hurry to get somewhere, lad?"

"I need to get to the Chunnel entrance yesterday."

"Right you go." The man snuffed out his cigarette and ambled to the car.

Dirk was already buckled into the passenger seat by the time the driver climbed in. "They charge fifty pounds for a car to make the crossing," the driver said as he pulled away from the curb. "Plus, you'll need to pay for my way back."

"I just need you to drop me where the trucks enter and board the train," Dirk said. "I'm trying to meet up with a truck from the Isle of Wight."

The cabbie nodded. "I hear the trucks go through a bloody maze to get on the train, but I'll put you as close as I can."

The entrance to the Channel Tunnel, as it was officially known, was less than three miles away, but the taxi had to loop an extra two miles to the west and enter the M20 to access the station. The taxi drove through an initial checkpoint that separated passenger cars from commercial trucks, then pulled to the side.

"The lorries are processed over there." The cabbie pointed to the other lane. "I can't get any closer without taking a ride to France."

Dirk grabbed a business card from a holder on the dash and slipped it in his pocket. "What's the fare?"

"Six-eighty."

Dirk drained his pocket of coins, which barely totaled half a pound, and held it out to the man. "I don't have time for the full story, but my wallet was lifted and this is all I have. I swear I'll mail you a twenty as soon as I can."

The cabbie had seen his share of frauds and stiffed rides, but saw the earnestness in Dirk's face. He took the coins and smiled. "Go find your truck."

"Much obliged," Dirk said as he climbed out. "How far is the train platform from here?"

"Quite a spell, maybe half a mile. Good luck."

Dirk hustled across the median to the truck lane, where a line of carriers were backed up as they were funneled into the entrance. He looked for the blue truck among the approaching vehicles, but none fit the bill. When a large moving van began pulling forward, Dirk ran to the back end and climbed onto its bumper, grasping the door handle for stability.

The truck followed a meandering asphalt path for a quarter mile, then pulled to a stop. Dirk stepped off the bumper and scanned ahead, where several long lines of vehicles stopped at a passport checkpoint. A security booth stood on the right side of each lane, processing the trucks. As he surveyed the inspection point, he caught a flash of blue.

Pulling away from another lane was a blue covered truck with a white stripe, exactly like the one on the dock. Dirk swung around to the left side of the vehicle in front of him and sprinted ahead. He cut to the far left lane and passed several waiting trucks until he reached the front vehicle stopped at the checkpoint.

Dirk positioned himself on the shoulder beside the truck's rear wheel and waited. Soon the truck pulled forward and Dirk walked beside it, matching its speed to conceal himself from the security booth. He had to run to keep pace as it accelerated, but when the truck was well past the checkpoint, he hopped a ride on its rear bumper.

He considered the relaxed security and gave thanks he hadn't tried to sneak aboard in Calais on the French side, where security was tight on account of the many migrants seeking entry into the UK. The truck traveled a short distance before the multiple lanes narrowed into one, which descended to the loading platform.

Dirk spied the blue truck as it crossed from the ramp onto an open flatbed car, then proceeded forward through a series of covered railcars. Five more trucks followed until his own was next in line. But then it was halted by an attendant directing the trucks aboard.

"Next train for you," the man told the driver. "Be about fifteen minutes."

Dirk waited until the man moved out of sight, then hopped off the truck and approached the platform. He took a step onto the flatbed car and heard an abrupt command.

"You there. Stop where you are."

The attendant glared at him from the enclosed railcar ahead. He hurried over to Dirk in broad strides. "Where do you think you're going?"

"I'm with the blue truck that was just driven aboard. I had to hop out and use the loo."

The attendant studied Dirk in his red work jacket and black ball cap. Though he sounded American, he resembled every other truck driver passing through the station.

"You quick better get on the club car, the train's about to leave. Follow me."

The man led Dirk down the platform, passing a dozen trucks

including the blue one, until they arrived at a fully enclosed passenger car. "You'll take the ride in here," he said. "Drivers aren't allowed to be in their trucks during the crossing."

Dirk thanked the man and stepped inside. The passenger car featured rows of padded seats and a small snack bar at one end. The compartment was packed with truck drivers downing coffee and sweets while waiting for the fast journey across the Channel. No sooner had Dirk stepped aboard, when the sliding doors closed behind him and the train began to move.

Dirk thought he glimpsed the truck's two drivers from Wight and he lowered his head as he made his way to the back of the car. A rear door led to the truck carriages, but was marked with a sticker proclaiming *Do not open while train is in motion* in English and French.

As Dirk reached for the door handle, a voice stopped him. "You can't go out there."

A beefy security guard in a neon-yellow vest stood by the snack bar. Dirk waited for the guard to approach him. "You can't go back to your truck until the train reaches Calais," the man said.

"I'm looking for my sister," Dirk said in a low voice. "I believe she was abducted and is being held in one of the trucks on this train. Could you help me check?"

"Have you reported her missing to the police?"

"I haven't had time. I was barely able to pursue the truck here."

"Let me call it in, then we can go have a quick look. We've got a few minutes before the train reaches the tunnel and runs to speed."

As the guard radioed his supervisor, Dirk glanced at the two truck drivers. They sat near the opposite end of the car, both staring at Dirk and the security guard with interest.

The guard led Dirk through the door a minute later and asked him to identify the truck in question. They bypassed several, squeezing past them in the narrow space to the side of the carriage.

The covered railcars were built of open steel latticework on their

sides that reminded Dirk of the bars on a playground jungle gym. The green country landscape was rushing by outside, blasting them with swirls of damp air that smelled of wet grass.

Dirk led the guard past a silver rig and trailer to the blue truck he recognized from the Isle of Wight. "This is the one."

The driver's door was unlocked, and he opened it as the security guard looked over his shoulder. The cab was empty except for some empty coffee cups and fast-food wrappers. Dirk closed the door and made his way to the rear, slapping the side of the trailer and shouting Summer's name.

The split back doors were secured by a locking pin, and Dirk was relieved to find there was no padlock on the mechanism.

"Just a quick look, lad, as we're almost to the tunnel." The guard stepped to one side. "We can request a full inspection from the French authorities in Calais."

Dirk felt the train begin a fast descent as he yanked the locking pin free and flung open the right-side door.

"Summer, are you in here?" He stepped onto the bumper and strained to see inside. He saw no movement nor detected any noise. But he recognized a new sound from outside the truck. Gunfire.

He jumped off the bumper and swung the door aside to find the security guard backed against the carriage side, clutching his stomach. A pair of dark spots appeared on his yellow vest as he gazed at Dirk with a bewildered look. He tried to speak, then took a step forward and collapsed.

Dirk caught the dead man and lowered him to the floor. He knelt beside him and glanced down the side of the truck as the two drivers approached. One of the men raised a revolver at Dirk.

He felt his ears pop as the train barreled into the Channel Tunnel with a buffeting of compressed air. An instant later, the railcar turned pitch-black . . . except for the bright yellow sparks from two muzzle flashes.

33

Dirk dropped to the floor beside the security guard as the bullets whizzed over his head. His first instinct was to search for a weapon on the security man, but as a law enforcement officer in England, the guard was unlikely to be armed. Dirk didn't have the luxury of time to be proven wrong and scrambled away from the dead man.

A large lorry was parked behind the blue truck, and Dirk rolled under its front bumper as the two men approached. It was black as night inside the railcar, with just an occasional glint of light. The tunnel was fitted with widely spaced light fixtures that flashed by as the train accelerated. The effect was like a dim strobe flashing every few seconds.

Dirk detected the legs of the gunmen as they approached the dead guard. He crawled rearward, angling toward the passenger side of the truck. He glanced back just as one of the drivers bent down and waved a cell phone light beneath the truck.

Dirk rolled out from under the lorry and began running as the light holder raised his voice. The gun barked twice, and Dirk heard the bullets strike metal beside him. Six shots, he counted to himself.

Did the man have another round left? He ducked and ran alongside the truck, then on to the next two in line. He had the sensation of running uphill, since the train was still on its descent to the bottom of the Channel. Reaching the third truck, he nearly tripped as his foot caught a front-wheel block, knocking it aside.

As a tunnel light flashed by, he noticed the truck's passenger window was rolled down. On impulse, he stepped onto the running board and slithered into the cab. An odor of dust and sweat told him it was an older vehicle, confirmed when his shoulder bumped into a manual gearshift lever. That prompted an idea.

He slid into the driver's seat, pushed the clutch pedal, and shifted into neutral. He found the emergency brake lever between the seats, held it with a firm grip, then ducked low and waited.

The man with the light appeared soon enough, checking along the railcar. Dirk waited until the phone light flashed past the truck's windshield, then he peeked over the dashboard. The man stood right in front of the truck, then bent and searched beneath. He turned and moved to the truck parked ahead, repeating the action in the opposite direction.

As he did, Dirk released the brake lever and crossed his fingers.

The truck moved ahead just a few inches, held in check by a rear wheel chock. But the train was traveling down its steepest gradient. The truck's weight and momentum overcame the rear block and its wheels rolled forward again.

With three feet between vehicles, the man had plenty of time to jump out of the way, but he never saw it coming. He stood and turned just as the rolling truck arrived from behind, catching him between the bumpers. The man's femur bones snapped on impact, and he let out a sharp wail.

Dirk set the brake as the truck bounced back, and he scrambled from the cab. A tunnel light flashed by, giving no sign of the other gunman. Dirk ran forward and squeezed between the two trucks to

the injured assailant. He moaned in pain, writhing on the floor beside his fallen phone light. Dirk picked up the light and quickly searched the man. He was unarmed.

Dirk killed the light and stood to move. As he rose, another tunnel light zipped by. In its strobe-like flash, the other driver materialized from behind the truck and lunged at him with the butt of his empty revolver.

The tunnel turned black once more, and for Dirk, the lights didn't return.

34

SEVENTH ARRONDISEMENT
PARIS, FRANCE

The gold dome of Les Invalides gleamed like firelight in the late-afternoon Parisian sun. The towering Baroque structure stood as the centerpiece of the sprawling Hôtel National des Invalides built by Louis XIV as a home for aged and disabled soldiers. While most of the complex had since been appropriated for museum displays and administrative offices, some eighty old soldiers still lived on the grounds of the fabled site.

Brigitte and Pitt climbed the steps to the main entrance, followed by Giordino toting a large aluminum case. Outside the ornate twin doors stood Captain Lufbery and a man in a brown suit, whose scowling face showed nothing but agitation. Lufbery introduced the man as Monsieur Dumont, the director of the Invalides complex.

"Thank you for closing early and allowing us in without any tourists," Pitt said. "We shouldn't take long."

"This is most unusual." Dumont shook his head. "The crypt has not been disturbed since 1861."

"As I explained to Monsieur Dumont," Lufbery said, "the mayor of Paris has expressed his gratitude for your recent heroics and

allowed this investigation to proceed privately." He neglected to reveal that he was the one who had instigated the action at the request of Pitt. "Shall we?"

Dumont unlocked the doors and led them into the grand structure. The space beneath the great dome was built in the shape of a Greek cross. Halls of marble studded with fluted columns soared to the vaulted ceiling. Pitt's eyes were drawn to the cupola and a round painting of Saint Louis entering heaven, bordered by twelve lower panels featuring the Apostles.

But the starring attraction of the structure lay below, in a sunken crypt that was excavated in the 1840s to house its honored resident. The group followed Dumont to a circular stone balustrade that overlooked the tomb of Napoleon Bonaparte.

A massive sarcophagus of red Finnish quartzite, which emulated the tombs of Rome's great emperors, sat beneath the center of the dome on a large block of granite. The thick lid was curvilinear, with raised scrolls at either end.

Giordino couldn't help thinking it looked like a giant red bathtub, but kept the thought to himself.

"Emperor Napoleon I," Dumont said haughtily, waving an arm toward the crypt.

"The Little Corporal from Corsica," Pitt replied.

The self-anointed emperor had taken the reins of France in 1799 and expanded its dominion with battlefield brilliance to rule most of Europe. Forced to abdicate after his crushing defeat at Waterloo in 1815, Napoleon had been banished to the island of Saint Helena in the South Atlantic, where he died in 1821. History turned in his favor and his body was exhumed in 1840 and brought to Paris for reburial with great fanfare.

"This way to the crypt, please." Dumont led them around the overlook to a stairwell that led to the lower level. They climbed over a low retaining wall and approached the towering sarcophagus.

Dumont turned to Pitt. "Captain Lufbery has indicated this experiment will be conducted electronically?"

"Yes, we'll examine the interior strictly by remote sensing."

Pitt motioned to Giordino, who set his case on the floor and opened the lid to reveal a ground-penetrating radar system. It consisted of a box-shaped transmitter and antenna packed beside a tablet computer.

Giordino assembled the devices, activated the battery power, and passed the tablet to Pitt. "I'll drive this time," he said with a smile, "and you navigate?"

"Sure," Pitt said, rubbing a faint cigarette lighter burn mark on his wrist with mock pain.

Pitt powered up the unit and adjusted the scale to reflect a five-meter penetration. A blank gray haze filled the screen as Giordino stepped onto the granite base and held the transmitter flat against the sarcophagus. The unit transmitted microwave radio pulses through its base, then captured the reflected radio waves, creating a layered image.

Giordino slid the unit horizontally across the side of the polished quartzite to the end of the sarcophagus, then raised the unit a few inches and returned in the opposite direction. Brigitte and the others crowded over Pitt's shoulder to view the display, which showed a thick dark line at the top of the screen and another at the two-meter mark near the bottom.

"Have you spotted his bicorne hat and riding boots yet?" Giordino asked as he worked his way up the side.

"Not yet." Pitt turned to the director. "Mr. Dumont, do you know what his coffin is made of?"

"The emperor is buried in six coffins." The Frenchman held up his hands and counted off on his fingers. "One of zinc, one of mahogany, two of lead, one of ebony, and the last of oak. One enclosed in the other, like the tombs of the Egyptian pharaohs."

"That will definitely show on the system, particularly the lead coffins," Pitt said.

But as Giordino continued to scan, nothing appeared on the screen. He ran the sensor back and forth until he extended it over his head, his reach falling short of the top. Pitt exchanged positions with him, guiding the sensor up to the lid. He stepped off the base and set the device on the floor.

"Anything?"

Giordino shook his head and showed Pitt a replay of the images. The readings were all the same: a blank void between the two sides of the sarcophagus. Brigitte and Lufbery looked on in shock, while Dumont paced behind them. "What are you saying?" the director asked.

"The sarcophagus is empty," Pitt said. "A coffin, particularly a lead one, should have appeared as a distinct object between the two sides of the sarcophagus. Their rough outlines, at a minimum, should have been visible. I'm afraid we're not seeing anything there."

"Impossible," Dumont said. "It is just impossible. Your equipment is worthless. It means nothing."

"Perhaps we can calibrate with another tomb?" Brigitte said. "Marshal Foch or Joseph Bonaparte?"

Lufbery agreed. "There is no harm in that, Monsieur Dumont. Perhaps it will prove you right."

Dumont paced some more, letting his temper cool. "Very well," he said. "This way to Joseph Bonaparte."

He led them upstairs to one of six small chapels on the main floor that surrounded Napoleon's open crypt. The Chapelle Saint-Augustin in the front corner was an open room with a raised green-marble sarcophagus in the center. Inside were the remains of Joseph Bonaparte, the emperor's eldest brother, who had served during Napoleon's reign as the king of Spain.

Pitt and Giordino activated the radar system. Giordino ran the

transmitter alongside the sarcophagus, which also required a high reach. When he completed his first pass, he turned to Pitt and knew by the look on his face that they had their proof.

Pitt turned the control screen to Dumont as the others looked on. "Again, we have the dark horizontal lines that signify either side of the sarcophagus. But as you can see here"—he pointed to a dark rectangular outline in the middle—"we have a distinct image in the middle, representing a coffin."

Dumont turned pale. "They are just lines on a screen," he said, but there was no conviction in his voice.

Lufbery approached and put his arm around the man's shoulders. "I am afraid, Monsieur Dumont, that for the sake of France, we must see for ourselves."

35

Dirk awakened to a steady vibration beneath him. It wasn't the sway of a railroad car, but the bounce of a highway vehicle. He pried open his eyes and found he was still in darkness. The whine of a diesel engine told him he was in the back of a truck.

A glint from the headlights of a following car filtered through a seam in the doors, barely illuminating the cardboard boxes stacked around him. It also revealed the dead Chunnel train security guard in the yellow vest lying a few inches away.

Dirk sat upright, and the action triggered an explosion of fireworks before his eyes. A pulse of pain erupted from the top of his skull where he'd been crowned by the handgun, and his ribs ached from his fight on the tanker. When the stars and pain subsided, he backed against a crate and rubbed his wrists on his leg.

They were bound with a heavy fabric cargo strap. He felt a smidgen of wiggle room between his wrists and decided that, with sufficient time, he might be able to work his hands free. But only after his raging headache subsided.

He felt the truck slow as it exited a highway onto a city street with

periodic traffic stops. Dirk eased to his feet and groped his way to the forward part of the truck bed, searching for signs of his sister.

He reached the twin yellow containers in back. As Summer had done, he pried open one of the lids and caught a shadowy glimpse of a rusty barrel.

As he worked the lid back on, the truck came to a sudden halt and he was thrown against the wall. A voice outside issued a command, and the truck pulled forward a short distance, then came to a full stop. When the engine shut off, Dirk made his way back to the dead security guard and resumed his position on the floor, pretending to be unconscious.

The back doors were swung open, but little ambient light entered from the nearby streetlamps. A metal ramp was pulled down and two men entered the truck with flashlights, restacking boxes to create a pathway for the yellow bins. They dragged the body of the security guard to the base of the ramp, where Henri Nassar stood waiting.

Like the others, he wore desert fatigues and a thick fake beard. "So this is the man who crushed Antoine's legs on the train?"

Nassar felt the pulse in Dirk's neck, then hauled back and gave him a stinging open-hand strike to the face.

Dirk couldn't help but open his eyes as he shook off the blow.

"I think he is awake now." Nassar leaned closer and faced Dirk. "What were you doing on the dock facility in Cowes?"

"Looking for my sister," Dirk said through gritted teeth. "What have you done with her?"

Nassar turned to the driver. "What is he talking about?"

"I don't know anything about a woman. He was at the facility and somehow followed the truck to the Channel Tunnel. We found him aboard the train trying to break inside the truck with the security guard."

Nassar glanced at the body. "Dispose of it where it won't be found."

The driver nudged Dirk. "What about this one?"

Nassar pulled a kaffiyeh headscarf from his coat pocket and tied it tightly around Dirk's neck. "Secure him to one of the barrels. We'll make him a calling card."

Four men in desert fatigues approached Nassar. "The cameras and security systems have been disabled," one said.

"Let's get moving," Nassar said, "before anyone comes to investigate."

The two yellow bins were placed on hand trucks and rolled down the sidewalk, with Dirk forced to follow with a pistol in his back.

Dirk saw they were on a quiet city side street, but he had no idea he was in Paris, let alone the 14th arrondissement. A line of low shops and buildings fronted the sidewalk, but behind them a towering earthwork rose high in the night sky.

It was the Réservoir de Montsouris, a massive water storage facility that held a fifth of the city's drinking water. Built in the 1870s, it consisted of four mammoth water storage chambers on two levels. Hundreds of stone pillars supported the interior of the tanks, making them resemble some sort of ancient temples flooded by fresh water. The entire complex was buried under a grass-covered mound that stretched the length of three football fields, which helped keep the water cool.

An ornate glass building on the west end housed the entrance, but Nassar and his men had approached the mound from the east. They broke through a streetside metal gate and moved the bins down a walkway, bypassing a secondary security gate that had also been defeated. From there, a stone stairwell ascended the thirty-foot-high mound.

Two men maneuvered each barrel up the steps, one pulling on the hand truck while the other pushed from below.

Aside from their desert fatigues, they all wore fake beards and carried AK-47s. They reached the top of the flat grass mound, which

appeared long enough for a plane to land. The group moved a short distance across the field and parked the bins beside a large circular metal plate that rose from the ground.

It was triple the size of a manhole cover and secured with fist-sized bolts. One gunman produced an oversized wrench and made quick work of the bolts, loosened on an earlier visit, then lifted off the cover with the aid of another commando.

From far below came the sound of rushing water. Nassar aimed a flashlight down the opening, which capped a maintenance access shaft. At the bottom lay one of the chambers filled with purified water—which was soon to become radioactive.

Nassar slipped off a backpack and handed it to one of the men. "Set the charges. Fifteen minutes."

The man retrieved two Plexiglas housings. Inside each was a block of plastic explosive. He inserted a digitally activated detonator cap into the soft explosive and set the timer. He then sealed the housing and placed it in one of the yellow bins. He repeated the process with the second charge, slamming the bin's lid closed when he was finished. "Both timers are running," he said.

Nassar muscled the first bin to the edge of the opening and pushed it over. It splashed into the water a few seconds later, and Nassar turned to Dirk and the man guarding him. "Tie him to the other barrel."

Dirk considered a sprint to the edge of the mound, but the guard's pistol had never left his back. He could do little but stand determined as another gunman looped a rope through a steel lifting eye on the yellow bin and tied it to his wrist bindings.

Nassar stepped close when the handiwork was complete. "Enjoy your swim," he said. "If you can hold your breath for fifteen minutes, you can witness the full show."

He raised a foot against the bin and shoved. The container of radioactive waste toppled into the opening. An instant later, Dirk was dragged with it, vanishing silently into the deep black hole.

36

D irk had little time to react. In the plummet down the shaft, he pushed himself away from the container and tried to orient his feet downward. Had he been under the bin, he would have been crushed when it hit the water. Landing on top would have been little better. But he gained separation from the bin and struck the water side by side with a blistering splash.

The entry was still painful, as he landed on his side from a twenty-foot free fall, and the shock of the cold water nearly took his breath away. But he needed to preserve every ounce of air as he was quickly pulled to the bottom. In the black pool, he had no measurement of the chamber's depth, but the pressure on his ears told him the water extended well over his head.

Finding himself on a flat stone floor, he rose to his feet and pulled the bin upright. He stretched his torso upward to test the depth, but found no air and an oppressive load holding him down. With his hands tied in front of him, he took a step back, pulling the container. The bin slid over the flat surface with little resistance, and he shuffled backward as fast as he could.

It was like backing through a tunnel blindfolded. He bumped

against a stone pillar, but felt with his back that it was a smooth support piling that offered no foothold. He continued his blind reverse shuffle, moving faster as he felt his lungs tighten. All the while, he struggled with his bindings.

The fabric ties were heavy, but he could feel the waterlogged material begin to stretch. It gave him hope he could free himself with time, but that was a luxury he lacked. As an expert diver and a strong swimmer, he knew he could hold his breath for two or three minutes. But the exertion from dragging a heavy barrel would shorten the time.

He bumped against a second pillar, then a third, bouncing off them like a steel ball in a pinball machine. His heart pounded and his head felt like it was going to burst as the oxygen in his bloodstream began to ebb.

As he brushed against yet another pillar, he slid back a few feet and struck a flat wall. He moved along its length until his shoulder grazed an angled metal bar. He traced it with the back of his arm and found it was pointed up at a forty-five-degree angle.

It was a handrail.

Dirk slid along the wall, following the rail down until his heels felt an edge and he turned a corner. He raised the back of his foot and felt it slide up and across a raised section. Steps. He quickly backed up the first step, then two more, hoisting the container after him.

His chest felt like it was ready to burst, and he purged some air from his lips to relieve the pressure. He backed up another few steps, dragging the bin after him as he felt his energy wane.

He rose another step and felt a swirling lightness about his head. Unsure if he was about to pass out, he stood upright as best he could . . . And his head broke the water's surface. He sucked in the cool, dank air, gasping until his heart stopped racing and the spots cleared from his eyes.

He pulled the bin up another step to fully clear his head from the

water and peered around. A dim light illumined the far end of the cavern, its faint glow giving the clear water a turquoise sheen. Dozens of pillars stood like a stone army, supporting the vaulted ceiling of an underground cathedral filled with water.

After a moment to regain his strength, Dirk hoisted himself and the bin up the next few steps to a dry landing at the end of the chamber. It led nowhere. He went to work on his bindings, stretching and twisting the wet fabric for several minutes until he could slip a hand free and unravel the rest. Then he remembered the explosives.

He tossed the rope aside, forced open the bin, and reached inside. His fingers curled around the Plexiglas housing and he removed the explosive device. Even under the low light, it appeared a simple device. He opened the sealed box, revealing an electric timer and a small detonator pressed into a block of plastic explosives.

Rather than risk activating the timer by trying to stop it, Dirk carefully pulled out the detonator. The digital timer was ticking down under three minutes.

He turned and tossed the detonator cap and timer as far as he could, hearing it splash somewhere in the darkness. He resealed the remaining plastic explosive and placed the housing on the landing.

He had less than three minutes to find the second drum, filled with radioactive waste, waiting to explode. He looked from the landing in the direction he had come. Had he traveled in a straight line? Which pillars had he bumped into? It was all a blur, one he didn't have time to analyze.

He climbed over the rail, dove into the water, and swam in the basic direction he'd started from. At ten yards out, he took a deep breath and kicked to the bottom.

Whatever ambient light existed on the surface promptly vanished, forcing Dirk to see with his hands. He reached the bottom three meters below and kicked along it, his arms groping ahead and to the sides.

He bounced from pillar to pillar until his breath ran out and he surfaced for air. After a few quick breaths, he returned to the bottom and resumed his blind search. The cold and fatigue began to wear on him and shortened his time underwater.

He rebounded to the surface for more air, but his thoughts were punctuated by a muffled pop and a small eruption of water off to his side. It was the detonator cap he had removed and tossed aside from the first barrel. It meant the timer in the other bin had less than a minute to go.

A brief flash of light had emanated with the explosion. It revealed a ladder embedded in the side of a pillar to Dirk's left. Ascending to the dark vaulted ceiling, the ladder marked the access shaft that he and the barrels had been dropped through.

Dirk swam toward it as fast as he could, kicked to the bottom, and made a quick circle search. His foot brushed against something, and he spun around and touched the second bin, which lay on its side. Dirk groped across the surface to find the top hatch. He pulled it open, reached in, and found the explosives box wedged against the drum.

He yanked it free, pushed off from the bottom, and clawed his way to the surface. With no time to remove the detonator, he flung the entire housing toward a dark corner of the cavern, then swam behind the nearest pillar. The box splashed as it hit the water, then a second later it erupted.

The explosion roared through the enclosed chamber like an atomic blast. Bits of stone and spray peppered the walls and water surface. The pillar in front of Dirk trembled from the shock wave. As the boom echoed off the stone walls, a high wave of water rushed back and forth like a tidal surge.

When the storm subsided, Dirk swam to the pillar with the ladder. Sirens sounded in the distance as he pulled himself from the water and slowly ascended the access shaft.

At the top of the ladder, the covering plate had been put back in place, but Nassar's men had not bolted it down. Dirk nudged his shoulder against it and pushed it ajar just enough for him to slither past. He crawled onto the grass and caught his breath, then rose to his feet as a shrill whistle sounded nearby. A powerful beam of light swept across the field, then froze on his silhouette. A rotund security guard clutching the light rushed over, yelling in French. As the man drew near, he thrust a pistol forward.

Dirk slowly raised his arms as the guard stopped a few feet away and shouted again. *"Qu'est-ce que tu fais ici?"* What are you doing here?

Dirk looked down at his sopping clothes, then shrugged. "I just came to get a drink of water."

37

While they waited for arrangements to be made to open Napoleon's tomb, Brigitte had led Pitt and Giordino to the Musée de l'Armée next door. There they toured the impressive display of military weapons used throughout French history. Afterward, they inquired at the administrative office for information about Marcel Demille. His role as museum curator before the war was confirmed, along with his disappearance in May 1940. No other information about him had survived the war.

Back under the dome, Dumont insisted that the sarcophagus opening take place quietly after dark, so the trio walked to dinner at a neighboring café. After they'd eaten, a portable crane was brought from a local construction project and wedged through a side door. A boom was extended to the center of the crypt and a cable lowered to the sarcophagus, where workers fitted a set of lifting straps around the massive lid. By the time everything had been safely arranged, it was well after ten p.m. The crane operator took up position at the controls, then sat and waited.

Dumont had not dared disturb the tomb of the great French leader

without authority from above, and soon a horde of government officials began flooding into the museum's foyer to watch the spectacle.

Brigitte, Pitt, and Giordino had to squeeze in on the main floor overlook to obtain a view. Captain Lufbery noticed them from across the room and elbowed his way beside them.

"I see the circus has come to town," Pitt said.

Lufbery nodded. "Dumont is a fool. He was afraid to investigate on his own, and now the whole city is here. He will be embarrassed now by either result."

"What is the delay?" Brigitte asked.

"He's waiting for the mayor to arrive." Lufbery rolled his eyes.

It was almost midnight when the mayor finally arrived with a small entourage, and Dumont gave the crane operator the direction to proceed. The Invalides director stood on a ladder beside the tomb, looking like a small child next to the oversized monument.

The spectators held their breath as the lift straps drew taut and the massive lid of the sarcophagus was raised. The operator held the lid up by just a few inches to stabilize it in midair, blocking the view inside. After an anxious pause, he gently pivoted the boom to one side, exposing the interior.

The great hall fell silent as Pitt and Giordino eyed each other with a nod. Then the audience let out a collective gasp.

Napoleon's tomb was empty.

The crowd began to murmur, the sound growing to a din at the shock of the empty tomb. Dumont nearly fell off his ladder before descending to the ground on wobbly legs. He was assaulted by government officials demanding answers. He had none to give and simply shook his head in defeat. At one point, he searched the crowd and meekly pointed at Pitt.

Giordino nudged his friend in the ribs. "I have the feeling you are one of the most unpopular men in Paris tonight."

"At least I'm not at the very top of the list."

As the crowd began to exit the dome, Brigitte leaned toward Pitt and Giordino. "This means Jean d'Epeé was indeed a code name for Napoleon. The diamonds must be hidden with his coffin. It is a shocking combination."

"No wonder Marcel Demille got an ulcer," Giordino said.

"Imagine the stress," Pitt said, "of babysitting the remains of an emperor and national hero."

When the dome finally emptied and Dumont was free of his last inquisitor, he had the sarcophagus lid returned to place. As he approached the group, he was sweating profusely, and his eyes bulged. "You knew this," he said to Pitt, "so you must know more. Where is he? Where is Napoleon?"

"We believe he was transported to Bermuda in 1940 by Marcel Demille, the Army Museum's director."

"I have heard old stories that they contemplated moving him at the beginning of the war to keep him out of the hands of Hitler, but never suspected it was true. Is he in Bermuda?"

Pitt shook his head. "The latest evidence we have suggests he was transported elsewhere, possibly Polynesia."

The director grabbed Pitt's sleeve. "You must help me find him. Help France find him."

"We'll try."

Dumont turned to Lufbery. "Wouldn't the government know where he was taken?"

The captain gave a grim shrug. "Perhaps. But it is a very cold case now."

His cell phone rang and he stepped aside to take the call. When he returned a short time later, his face had a deep pall.

"I have just received a call from our counterterrorism operations manager." He looked Pitt in the eye. "It seems your son has been arrested in the fourteenth arrondissement for an act of terrorism against the city of Paris."

38

Captain Lufbery escorted Pitt to a high-security holding cell at La Santé Prison in the Montparnasse district. A pair of armed guards stood aside as Lufbery opened a heavy metal door and followed Pitt inside. Dirk sat on a bunk wearing loose pants and a T-shirt, his wrists and ankles shackled.

He gave his father a wry smile as he held up his arms. "My first visit to Paris. I was hoping for éclairs and the Folies Bergère, not manacles and chains."

Pitt hugged his son. "I would have thought jet-skiing down the Seine would be more your style."

"It would have been preferable to the ride I took." Dirk rubbed the knot on the top of his head.

"Tell us what happened." Pitt pulled over a slim wooden bench and took a seat.

"I've told the authorities everything three times, but I'm not sure they believe me." Dirk proceeded to describe the discovery of the radioactive barrels in the Irish Sea and his actions from the Isle of Wight to the Montsouris Reservoir.

"It sounds like the same cast of characters that Al and I ran into."

Pitt turned to Lufbery. "Have you figured out who these people are yet?"

Lufbery gritted his teeth. "We are pursuing several leads at the moment." It was all but a declaration that they had no firm suspects.

"Have the police recovered the radioactive barrels from the reservoir?" Dirk asked.

"The last report I have is that a hazardous materials team is on-site making preparations to remove the containers."

"What do we need to do," Pitt asked Lufbery, "to get my son out of here?"

The French police captain looked at the floor. "It will take some time. I'm told the security cameras were disabled and there presently are no witnesses. Your son was the only one seen on the grounds. He will have to remain in custody until we have further information."

Dirk looked to his father with unease. "Have you heard from Summer?"

"No," Pitt said. "Where could she be?"

"She may have slipped off the truck while I was in the warehouse. The terrorists at the reservoir seemed to know nothing about her, so she must have gotten away. She left her phone and wallet in the rental car. Hopefully she found her way back to the ship in Southampton."

Pitt checked his messages, then tried calling her. When there was no answer, he phoned the *Nordic Star*'s captain, Ben Houston. He hung up a moment later with a grim look.

"The captain has been trying to reach both of you for hours. He's had no word from Summer."

"I will request immediate assistance from our UK contacts at Scotland Yard and the Home Office," Lufbery said. "We can have them search the facility on the Isle of Wight."

Dirk saw his father's face turn downcast at the news. "Go find Summer. I'll be fine here. It'll give me a chance to brush up on my language skills."

Pitt tried to smile, but his anguish was too intense to hide. He said goodbye to Dirk and left the cell with Lufbery, multiple questions burning in his head.

Who were the people that took Summer? Why had they abducted her? And where on earth was she?

39

Hiding aboard the *Mont Blanc* at sea, Summer was acting like a ghost without chains. She had locked herself in an empty cabin as the tanker departed Wight and remained secluded, strategizing an escape. But survival came first and stealth now meant everything. She kept a towel stuffed at the base of the door to conceal her cabin light and used the plumbing only when she was certain the adjoining cabins were empty. Her ears became her first line of defense, listening as the cabin doors opened and closed in the hallway around her. She catalogued the sounds, keeping a mental tab on her neighbors' schedules.

It was two thirty in the morning when she finally ventured into the corridor for the first time. The ship was silent except for the drone of its engine. Summer loosened the nearest lightbulbs in the overhead fixtures to keep the hall dim. She padded slowly down the corridor as far as the galley. The dining hall was empty, so she crept in and grabbed a bottle of water someone had left on the table. When she heard a clang of pots in the kitchen, she scurried back to her cabin.

The grumbling of her stomach eventually prompted another search for food. After an hour she tried again. This time the galley

was silent. She spotted a bowl of fruit beside a coffee urn and attacked it with vigor. Using the bottom of her shirt as a hamper, she filled it with apples and oranges. In a flash, she was back in her cabin, eating on her bunk while her mind continued to race.

What had become of Dirk? And what would the men on the ship do with her if she was discovered?

Summer didn't care to dwell on the possible consequences, so she put her mind toward rescue. A radio call for help would be the easiest solution, but any powerful radios would be located on the bridge.

No doubt some of the crew carried handheld radios. Perhaps she could subdue a crewman and take his radio? But a passing ship would have to be near, and a radio plea for help would have to be believed. It would also alert those aboard the tanker. Risky. Still, if a stray handheld radio could be found somewhere, it was worth snatching.

Better to remain patient, she told herself. Odds were that the ship would enter another port soon enough and she could jump ship without being noticed. But what if it didn't?

A toilet flushed in the cabin next door. With dawn approaching, any further explorations on the tanker would have to wait. Tomorrow night, she told herself, she would act more boldly. And search for a way to freedom.

40

Villard sat at his desk sipping his second coffee of the morning when Nassar knocked on his door at seven o'clock. The security chief entered the office without a greeting and silently took a seat across from his boss.

Villard eventually looked up from a stack of documents. The mogul's eyes were dark and sunken, and he looked to have lost weight recently. Nassar eyed an array of prescription pain bottles on the desk.

While Villard's usual intensity seemed absent, his defiance was still in place. "Report," he said.

"We met the truck from England at Montsouris Reservoir. There was a dead guard and an American in the back. They had been caught breaking into the truck on the Chunnel train. Apparently the American had earlier been detained at the dock on Wight, but escaped."

"Yes, I know. The son of the man named Pitt, who drove our explosives into the Seine." He glared at Nassar. "Go on."

"There was only one driver, as the other man had been left at a

hospital in Amiens due to injury. We entered the reservoir grounds as planned and deployed the delivered materials without incident."

"What did you do with the American?"

"He was still alive, so we tied him to one of the barrels and dropped him in the reservoir. He died in the detonation. We heard the explosion when we were leaving in the truck."

"Actually," Villard said, speaking slowly and with angst, "he survived. And prevented the release of the contaminants, if my reporting sources are accurate."

Nassar turned pale. "That can't be. There were only a few minutes, and the water was over three meters deep." His voice dropped to a whisper. "He should have drowned."

"He should have been killed on the spot before playing games. It is now a security compromise." Villard rubbed his scalp with a trembling hand. The opioids he took for his back pain made him both tired and agitated, while his financial woes tightened around his chest like a cinch on a racehorse.

"It may not be that bad," Nassar said. "The Wight facility is leased through a Panamanian shell firm, and both ships are now at sea. There will be nothing there for police investigators to find."

"But the vessels can be identified. Somebody may have tracked the *Chamonix*'s salvage work."

"Perhaps, but what can they prove? There is no longer any evidence aboard."

Villard stared into his empty coffee mug. "What about the radioactive material? Could there be residual detection?"

"The barrels were encapsulated in lead-sheathed bins. There should be no residual radioactivity."

Villard stared at Nassar with scalding eyes. "The Israelis have put us off for six months until their next budgetary cycle. Now we have frittered away our opportunity in France while risking exposure." His hand tightened into an involuntary fist. "We must abandon the

project in France for the time being. It would be best if you and your men stay out of the country."

"And proceed with the mission in America?"

"That would seem our last chance at fiscal survival. We can only hope for a rapid funding response."

"When nine million people go thirsty, there will be a quick reaction."

"Where is the *Mont Blanc* now?"

"Nearing the Azores," Nassar said, "where she is to remain moored until called upon."

"Redirect her to the United States. We will proceed as planned." He flinched and reached for one of the pill bottles.

Nassar wondered if the opioids were making Villard unstable, but it didn't matter for now. He had the shipowner's full trust and authority.

Villard sat upright in his chair and poured some pills into his palm. "On second thought, the *Mont Blanc* is now too conspicuous. The port authorities will report her presence at Wight. We should use a different vessel for moving the radioactive materials across the Atlantic."

Nassar picked up a company report from the table. "Regrettably, we have few additional vessels still at our disposal." He glanced at the document, which contained a list of the company's assets. "A seismic survey vessel in Gibraltar, a tanker in Malaysia, and the *Chamonix*." He flipped over the page. "There is another option. The Egyptian pipe-laying company you acquired owns two vessels. A freighter that's laid up in a Turkish dry dock and a small coastal cruise ship in Alexandria."

Villard arched his brow. "Cruise ships are worthless since the pandemic. A better vessel to sacrifice. Is it seaworthy?"

"She's old, but passed inspection four months ago. I can ensure she is registered to a dead-end entity before we put her to sea." He

thought a moment and smiled. "Or perhaps even link it to our friend LeBoeuf."

"Can you handle the transfer of radioactive materials at sea?"

"Under the proper conditions, yes."

"Send your team to Egypt and order the ship to sea. And reroute the *Mont Blanc*. Have them rendezvous near Bermuda, where you will join them."

"Bermuda?" Nassar asked.

"Yes. Find out what you can about the diamonds while you are there . . . Then proceed with the American operation."

He swallowed the handful of pills. As he waited for their relief, his grimace melded into a twisted smile.

41

Bleary-eyed from their late night in Paris, Pitt, Giordino, and Brigitte stopped for breakfast and coffee near Rouen before arriving at Le Havre just before noon. Pitt followed Brigitte's directions and dropped her in front of an apartment building near the city's arboretum.

"I'm not sure how soon I'll be able to see you again," she said, "as I have several pressing demands at the Institute."

"I hope it won't be long," Giordino said. "After all, we have an emperor to locate."

She turned to Pitt as she climbed out of the car. "I'm sorry about your son and daughter. If there is anything I can do to help, please let me know."

"Thanks, I shall. *Au revoir.*"

She waved goodbye, then climbed the steps to her second-floor apartment. Entering her unit, she felt something amiss. In the side bedroom, one of her suitcases lay open on the bed. She was certain she had not placed it there. Then a noise came from the kitchen.

She grabbed a heavy brass candlestick from a bookshelf and crept

down the hallway. Holding her breath, she peeked around the corner. Henri Nassar was seated at the kitchen table eating an apple.

He turned and eyed the candlestick. "Are you going to light the way for me?"

She let out a deep breath. "You would be too bullheaded to follow," she said, placing the candlestick on the table. "You know I don't like you breaking and entering."

He rose and hugged her. She returned the embrace with a passionate kiss.

"You are arriving home late this morning," he said.

"I had an engagement with Napoleon, but he decided not to show." She explained yesterday's events while brewing a pot of coffee.

He retook his seat at the table. "This friend of yours, Dirk Pitt, is certainly adept at uncovering mysteries. I hope he is less skilled at solving them."

"He has his own distractions at the moment. His son is in jail on account of a terrorist attack at the Montsouris Reservoir in Paris, and his daughter has gone missing from the Isle of Wight."

She studied his face for a reaction, but there was none. He was always a blank slate, his dark eyes devoid of emotion. She knew he acted on the wrong side of the law, but she never asked for details and he never offered any. He was wrong for her in so many ways and she well knew it. But the attraction was like a moth to a flame, and she couldn't seem to break the spell.

"So his daughter is missing," he said.

"She was tracking radioactive waste salvaged by a ship docked on the Isle of Wight." Brigitte filled a cup with coffee and passed it to him.

"Curious." His eyes flickered for just an instant before he took a sip of the coffee. "So, your NUMA friends have tracked the diamonds to Bermuda? I had just made a similar discovery, based on the harbormaster's record of vessel departures."

"A museum official named Demille accompanied Napoleon to Bermuda," Brigitte said. "We found correspondence from him while he was there. He apparently departed Bermuda in early 1942. There's reason to believe the diamond cases were secured with the emperor's coffin."

"That is unfortunate. We don't need any historical treasure hunters getting in the way of recovering the real valuables."

"There is certainly great significance to France," she said, "in recovering the remains of the emperor."

He shook his head. "A significance that will not fill my pockets. What other information does NUMA have?"

Brigitte was hurt by his tone, but didn't show it. It certainly wasn't the first time he had pressed her for useful information. They first met when he had appeared in her office at the Institute seeking offshore survey data conducted by the French government. He had beguiled and seduced her quickly, leading her to suspect he was more interested in underwater seismic studies than her personal charms. She had provided him with all the data he sought, yet he had remained in her life and the relationship had continued to flourish.

"They are interested in examining the records of a diplomat on the island who assisted the curator Demille. Paul Rapine is his name. They believe his journals may reveal where the emperor was taken."

Nassar swirled the remains of his coffee, then stood and smiled. "That is excellent information. And all the more reason why we will fly to Bermuda today."

"We? I can't. I must return to the Institute. I have reports to file and projects to organize—"

He pulled her to him and squeezed her tight. "Fifty million euros says otherwise," he whispered in her ear.

"But what about your boss?"

"If his water projects don't come to fruition soon, the mafia will be walking him like a dog."

"And the diamonds?"

Nassar chuckled. "The old goat thinks that if I find the diamonds, I will give them to him to save his company." He gave her another kiss.

Brigitte stepped back and slapped him hard.

"What was that for?" His eyes burned with anger.

"Your men almost ran me over after our dive on the *Avignon*."

"Yes," he admitted with a nod. "My fault. I wasn't clear in my instructions."

"What about the NUMA survey? Did your boss review the data I sent?"

It was the reason she had now become intertwined in Nassar's affairs. It had started innocently enough. Villard had promised a large donation to the Institute if Brigitte would steer the NUMA survey team, with their advanced subsurface technology, to a specific offshore region. It was close enough to the originally planned survey area that she felt no harm would accrue and she finessed the change through the Institute.

She made the mistake of texting Nassar about the diamonds they had found on the *Cornwall*, and the next thing she knew, Captain Boswick lay dead in front of her. She felt fear and panic at the ordeal, as well as a sense of responsibility. It all only made her more dependent on Nassar.

She was in deep now, much more than she realized. But her excitement at the dual mysteries overwhelmed her sense of guilt.

Nassar nodded. "The data confirmed what he had already planned for his pipeline. But there will be no further activity in France, at least for now. I will arrange his donation to the Institute for you as soon as I am able, but finances are tight at the moment."

"That was the deal. I only agreed to alter the survey area if the Institute received compensation."

"That's what I like about you. Always the saint."

CLIVE CUSSLER THE CORSICAN SHADOW

"I don't want to be associated with his secret activities anymore. You shouldn't, either."

He scooped her into his arms. "There is much at stake right now. But don't worry. I just have one more job to complete," he said, carrying her to the bedroom and kicking the suitcase off the bed.

42

After commandeering a pot of coffee from the *Pelican*'s galley, Pitt and Giordino sat down to the task of finding Summer. Their first update came from Captain Houston of the *Nordic Star*, who called from the Isle of Wight after filing a missing person report with the local police.

"The police said they paid a visit to the dock facility when the gunfire was heard," Houston said over a video call. "They were told Dirk shot up the facility and drove a forklift through the gate before stealing the boat museum's hydrofoil. The police acknowledged today that they've been in touch with the French authorities and are sending a detective to Paris. I think they're more interested in prosecuting Dirk than anything else."

"Do they have any reports about Summer?" Pitt asked.

"None whatsoever. I've got our consulate involved, and they've requested a warrant to search the compound, which is pending a judge's signature. But approval does not appear to be moving fast. Incidentally, we did find Dirk's rental car nearby. The police opened it up and found both their cell phones and Summer's wallet inside."

"Ben," Giordino asked, "have you learned anything about who owns the facility?"

"A local real estate company. They've leased it to a shipping company that in turn rents the storage space and dock usage on an ad hoc basis. Some outfit out of Malta has been using it for the past few months, but nobody seems to have any hard information about the company."

"Dirk said two ships were moored there. Have they been searched?"

"I'm in Cowes right now. The dock is just across the river." Houston pointed his cell phone toward the river and took a few steps closer. Across the river, a large warehouse was visible, fronted by an empty dock.

"Both ships left the dock shortly after the incident," Houston said. "The harbormaster confirmed the vessels were the *Chamonix* and the *Mont Blanc*."

"Thanks, Ben," Pitt said. "We'll try tracking them from here."

"I'll let you know as soon as I learn anything more."

As Houston vanished from the screen, Giordino tapped on a keyboard to access the AIS system. But both vessels were absent from a global map of the seas. "Went silent as soon as they left," he said.

"I'm not surprised," Pitt said. "The kids were clearly onto something. Maybe Hiram can tell us more."

They established a link with Yaeger in D.C. By the long look on his face, he was already aware of Summer's disappearance.

"How are you holding up, boss?" he asked.

"*Comme ci, comme ça*, as the locals would say," Pitt replied. "We're hunting for a pair of ships that are associated with Summer's last-known whereabouts. We have to hope she's aboard one of them."

He relayed the ships' names, and Yaeger vanished from the video screen, replaced with a view from the AIS system. Yaeger manipulated the data to find the vessels' earlier location in Cowes.

"Barking up the wrong tree," Giordino said. "Both vessels have gone silent while moving on to greener pastures."

"So we have to do things the hard way," Yaeger said. "I can start pulling satellite imagery and see if we can track their movements from up high. Most of the major ports will also have entry and departure records that are accessible," he said with a wink that signified a backdoor access. "The good news is, satellite coverage over that part of the world is strong. The bad news is that it's a high-traffic area, so a ship might get lost in the soup. Give me an hour or two, and I'll see what I can find."

"Dirk said the *Chamonix* was a large pipe-laying ship," Pitt said. "That's a type of vessel that won't vanish too easily."

"Agreed. Makes you wonder why it was being used for salvage work."

They signed off with Yaeger, and Pitt and Giordino took to their computers, using online sources and the NUMA database to glean what they could about the two ships.

The *Chamonix* had been specially ordered from a Singapore builder for pipe-laying work in Malaysia. Over the years it had passed through several hands, with its current ownership listed under a company in Beirut. The trail ended there.

The *Mont Blanc* had also been built in Asia some twenty years earlier and passed through several owners. "Guess where the current ownership is registered?" Giordino asked.

"Beirut," Pitt said.

"Yes, under the same post office box as the *Chamonix*."

Yaeger responded a short time later with similarly mixed results.

"The bad news first," he said. "There are about a hundred coastal oil tankers on the planet that match the size and appearance of the *Mont Blanc*, and it seems like half of them are plying the English Channel. I'm still pulling imagery around the Isle of Wight at the presumed time of the tanker's departure. I have about a dozen poten-

tial vessels in the region that fit the profile, but I haven't been able yet to zero in on a prospect."

"What about the *Chamonix*?" Giordino asked.

"A much easier proposition. I found her in the Channel last night. As of two hours ago, she was moored off of Antwerp."

"Commercial dock?" Pitt asked.

"No, she's in a remote waterway outside the port. Either waiting for a berth or trying to lay low. I'll email you the coordinates."

"Thanks, Hiram," Pitt said. "One more thing. See what you can find out about the ships' ownership. We traced them to Beirut, but I'd like to know who's really pulling the strings."

"Will do."

After the call ended, Giordino looked at Pitt. "Maybe we can talk to our embassy. Get the Belgian authorities to issue a search warrant like the Brits are doing."

Pitt glanced at his watch. "It's almost five. Nothing will happen before tomorrow."

Giordino saw the look in his eye and knew Pitt would not be waiting for outside help. He rose from his chair and stretched his arms. "That's fine by me. I've always had a hankering to see the diamond capital of the world by starlight."

43

The drive to Antwerp took almost four hours, even with a heavy foot on the accelerator. Pitt and Giordino traded driving to let the other catch up on lost sleep, but the effort was futile. The small flatbed truck they had borrowed at the Le Havre dock revealed its high mileage on the road. Its worn suspension transmitted every bump to the occupants, tossing them about as if they were in a blender.

Pitt was behind the wheel when they approached Antwerp just after midnight. He avoided the city proper, turning toward the sea while still a few miles west of the metropolitan area. He followed a small road past a scattering of old brick houses and open fields until they reached a small peninsula. Giordino pointed out a gravel lot beside a wide marsh, and Pitt pulled to a stop.

They had studied aerial images of the area earlier and deemed it the best place to quietly access the bayfront. Pitt backed the truck to the water's edge, killed the motor, and turned off the lights. They sat in the cab a few minutes to see if they had garnered any attention, but the night was still.

Giordino slipped on a dark bucket hat with a small lure dangling from its peak. "Ready to go fishing?"

Pitt zipped up a light jacket. "I forgot my license, so let's not get caught poaching."

They stepped to the truck's flatbed, which carried a small inflatable boat. At six feet, it was the smallest inflatable the *Pelican* carried, but still a load for the two men to carry. They slid it off the truck, dragged it to the water's edge, and climbed in.

Each grabbed an oar, and they paddled through the shallow marsh to a deepwater estuary called the Schelde. It was linked to a river of the same name that snaked through Antwerp before feeding into the North Sea.

Antwerp lay upriver, but they followed the current downstream. Pitt started the boat's thirty-five-horsepower outboard motor and propelled them toward the sea. The estuary widened as they passed the city of Terneuzen and its large port facility. The famed ghost ship the *Flying Dutchman* had originally sailed from there, but Pitt and Giordino saw no apparitions, only the city's glowing lights reflecting on the calm water.

As they passed the commercial docks filled with container ships loading and unloading cargo, Giordino assembled a pair of fishing rods and secured them to the gunnel. Past an inbound freighter, Pitt spotted a channel marker and veered out of the main waterway. A smaller passageway led around a long island shaped like a pipe wrench.

Pitt motored into the backwater channel and found it dark and empty except for a lone ship. The *Chamonix*.

The pipe-laying vessel lay moored in the middle of the waterway, its bow facing upriver. As if to keep a low profile, only a handful of its exterior lights were illuminated. But it was enough to reveal the pipe-laying reel that towered over the afterdeck, its yellow painted frame rising starkly into the night sky.

Pitt killed the motor as soon as he saw the ship, letting the tide and momentum carry them toward it. As they drifted past the hundred-meter-long vessel, they scoured the deck for watchmen. It appeared empty.

The two men quietly dug their paddles into the water and circled back to the stern. Giordino had prepared a line and grapple, but it wasn't needed. A large funnel-shaped ramp called a stinger extended from the back of the ship. It was used to guide the fitted pipes as they were lowered off the stern from the high reel. For Pitt, it doubled as a handy dock for the small inflatable.

The men rowed alongside the ramp and Giordino tied off the boat. Both men climbed to the top of the stinger and stepped onto the ship's deck.

The stern deck was dominated by the high reel tower in the center and a large crane on the port rail. A string of welded pipe was positioned near the top of the reel, where it appeared the last job had been abruptly halted.

They moved past the structure and found a massive well deck, which stretched to the forward superstructure. Inside were high stacks of forty-foot-long steel pipe and an automated station where they were welded together end to end before being fed up to the top of the reel tower. Additional inventories of pipe lay in bundles on either side of the main deck.

Pitt and Giordino took to the port rail and moved past the recessed area to the accommodations block. They crept through a side door that led into a main corridor. As with the exterior deck, there appeared to be no one on duty. They reached a large wardroom filled with comfortable chairs and a large TV blaring the replay of a soccer match. It, too, was empty.

Farther down the corridor, Pitt and Giordino took a quick step inside the ship's galley and found they were not alone. On the far side, a small wiry man in a white apron stood wiping down the dining

tables. He stopped and looked up at the two men. Pitt acknowledged him with a nod, made a beeline to a coffee urn, and poured himself a cup.

The steward worked his way closer as Giordino joined Pitt. The man wiped off the nearest table and looked up at the two men. *"Une collation?"* he asked. A snack?

The steward appeared Filipino, and Pitt thought his French sounded coarse. "No thanks," Pitt said. "Has the woman eaten tonight?"

Pitt looked for a reaction, but the crewman gave him a confused look.

"No women allowed on ship," he said in halting English.

"Tall? With red hair?" Giordino raised a palm up high.

The steward shook his head.

Pitt thanked him for the coffee and exited the galley with Giordino.

"Seemed believable enough," Giordino said, "if not altogether in the know."

Pitt had to agree. There seemed no heightened sense of security, no indication Summer was being held captive on the ship.

As he and Giordino continued down the corridor, they approached an open door marked *Operations Center.* Pitt poked his head around the corner and found it empty. He and Giordino stepped inside and closed the door behind them.

The bay was set up like a war room, with a projection screen and a large grease board at the front and an executive table in the middle. The room appeared tidy, as if no projects were in the works. Pitt examined a bookcase with engineering manuals and thick binders dated with past pipeline projects in the Baltic and the North Sea. Some coastal charts of India and Egypt were folded and stacked on top.

Across the room, Giordino studied some maps pinned to the wall. "Dirk, take a look at these." He pointed to three coastal marine

charts in one corner. Each showed angular red lines drawn from off-shore positions to the adjacent shoreline.

"Palmachim, off Israel. Mastic Beach, off Long Island. And Veulettes-sur-Mer, off Normandy," Pitt said, reading the land points on each chart. "Looks like some pipeline projects, or proposed projects." Pinned beneath each chart was a packet of environmental studies and approval certificates.

"Guess this one got deferred." Giordino pointed to a note stuck on the Israel chart with a pending date crossed out.

Pitt nodded, but his focus was on the Normandy chart. "This looks very close to the area we just surveyed."

"I'm pretty sure our search grid actually encompassed the area of that red line."

"Odd coincidence." Pitt pulled out his phone and had begun snapping pictures of the charts when the door opened and a man in work coveralls stepped in.

"*Qu'est-ce que tu fais ici?*" he blurted. What are you doing here?

"*Où est la fille?*" Pitt said.

"*Quelle fille?*" His eyes caught Pitt holding his phone up to the chart. He turned and sprinted out the door while reaching for a handheld radio at his hip. Pitt tucked his phone away.

"Perhaps we've worn out our welcome," Giordino said.

"I agree. It doesn't appear that Summer has been here. We may as well exit stage left."

They made it into the hallway, when the ship's public address system blared at high volume. "*Sécurité, envahisseurs. Sécurité, envahisseurs.*"

The two picked up their pace, running to the end of the corridor and exiting onto the starboard deck. The empty ship suddenly came alive around them. Doors clanged open, footfalls pounded the companionways, and shouts erupted throughout the superstructure. Pitt and Giordino didn't hesitate, rushing to the rail and moving aft. They

proceeded unseen past the well deck and were approaching the reel tower when a roving spotlight from the bridge caught them in its beam. Automatic gunfire opened up behind them a second later, chewing into the deck and equipment around them.

Both men dove to the deck and rolled to the side rail as a second burst sounded ahead of them. Pitt looked aft to see a gunman near the transom blocking their way with a raised assault rifle.

The security forces had materialized out of nowhere . . . and Pitt and Giordino were caught in the cross fire.

44

Tucked under the shadow of the starboard rail, Giordino grimaced as a burst from the stern shooter whistled over his head. "I guess the meter maid dislikes the way you parked," he muttered.

"And to think we forgot to get our ticket validated," Pitt replied.

Behind them, two gunmen had emerged from the base of the accommodations block. They were far enough away that their firing accuracy in the dark would be suspect. The aft gunman was the greater immediate threat. Pitt turned in his direction and saw the man was fumbling to change magazines.

"Hold here," he said to Giordino. "I'll see if I can distract our friend in back so you can get to the boat. I'll meet you off the port side if things get rocky."

Pitt rolled across to the edge of the recessed deck and dropped inside. It was eight feet down to a bundle of steel pipes, and Pitt silently cursed when he landed awkwardly and fell to his knees. But he had made the jump without being seen.

He crawled down the pipe stack and entered a catwalk that

crossed to the port side. He moved as quickly as he could while tread-
ing lightly on the latticed walkway, which echoed with each step. He
reached the opposite side, found a mounted ladder, and scurried up
it to the main deck.

The aft gunman still held his position at the center of the stern
deck, guarding the inflatable, while his companions on the other end
of the ship swept forward, closing in on Giordino's position.

Pitt looked up and formulated two plans of attack. He began by
crawling aft across the deck to a small control hut at the base of the
reel tower. He reached it undetected and crouched in front of its instrument panel to decipher the controls. He pressed a power button
and somewhere belowdecks a diesel generator sputtered to life, providing juice to the hydraulic reel. Pitt then engaged the primary
control lever, pushing it from the stop position to forward.

Overhead, the big yellow reel slowly began to rotate. The mechanism was designed to retrieve a continuous string of welded pipe
from the deck well. The pipe would be pulled up in a high arc to the
top of the spool, then lowered off the stern in an S-shaped configuration to the seabed. Deploying the pipe this way reduced the strain on
the welds and maintained the pipeline's integrity as it was lowered to
the bottom.

The only problem was that the automated operation for welding
new sections of pipe was not activated. Only a four-piece section of
pipeline was drawn up the reel. Without a counterbalancing anchor,
the section teetered at the top of the reel . . . Then momentum and the
turning wheel sent the long piece falling forward.

The pipe came crashing down the back side, plunging onto the
stern ramp, inches from where the gunman stood.

The startled gunman jumped to the side at the last second, just
clearing the pipe's initial impact. But the pipe bounced, and the gunman was caught in its rebound, knocking him to the ground. His

weapon went flying, but it didn't matter. A section of the pipe rolled across him, crushing his legs. He cried out in agony as the pipe string tumbled on, bounding down the stinger and splashing into the water.

Pitt and Giordino took off running at the same instant. Giordino used the disturbance to sprint down the rail and cut across the stern. He ran past the prone man and hopped onto the metal ramp. Sliding to its base, he jumped into the inflatable and started the motor. As he shoved off, he took a quick look for Pitt. Not spotting him on the ship, he gunned the throttle and sped downriver.

While Giordino ran aft, Pitt had moved forward, hightailing it to the large crane on the port rail. He jumped into its cab and searched the controls, but found it a more complex layout than the pipe reel. It took him a moment to find the key-activated power switch. As he twisted the key, the windshield in front of him exploded.

The two gunmen pursuing Giordino on the starboard rail had seen him climb into the cab. Pitt ducked as the shattered glass peppered his face and arms.

As he lay in the seat, he heard the engine beneath the cab start. Staying low, he reached to the controls and swung the overhead boom inboard over the deck well. As more bullets ripped into the cab, he found a toggle for the take-up spool and released a twenty-foot length of loose cable from the end of the boom.

He swung the boom in an arc past the starboard rail toward the stern, releasing a bit more cable until its hook end dangled at waist height. He brought the boom to a halt, then accelerated it in the opposite direction.

He peeked over the console as the boom swung forward, the trailing cable twitching like a cat's tail. He released a touch more and the heavy wire struck the starboard deck and skidded across it like a cracking bullwhip. The two gunmen darted out of the way from the slithering cable that could easily cut them in two.

Pitt retracted the boom and made for a second strike. But as it

moved back, the cable grew taut and the boom buckled. The extra slack had caused the cable to drop into the deck well, and the hook had latched on to something.

Pitt reversed the boom and tried raising the cable. The crane shuddered, then the take-up spool churned, pulling up a pallet of pipe from the hold.

The pallet swung wildly as Pitt raised it fast and turned the boom toward the starboard rail. This time, the gunmen were caught in the middle of the deck with nowhere to run. Pitt released the pallet, and the heavy mass crashed to the deck. The pipes broke free and rolled in all directions. A scream filled the air as one of the gunmen vanished under the assault.

Pitt didn't wait for the bounding pipes to settle. He heard an approaching outboard motor and knew Giordino had circled back for him. He jumped out of the cab and ran to the side rail. A new gunman appeared across the well deck and let out a long burst of fire. The deck sparked at his feet as Pitt climbed the rail. He took a quick step and dived over the side as a seam of bullets chased him across the rail.

Pitt caught a quick glimpse of Giordino's approach just before he struck the water. He kicked deep, then turned away from the ship and swam with all his might, staying submerged as long as he could.

Giordino had seen him jump and raced toward his anticipated point of emergence. Pitt broke the surface a few yards away and Giordino steered the inflatable alongside him. More shouts could be heard from the *Chamonix*, but no more gunfire rang out, as the crew contended with the injuries and damage to the ship.

Pitt bellied into the craft, and Giordino got back on the throttle, heading into the darkness. He drove at full speed until they were around the tip of the island, well out of sight of the ship. He continued upstream, hugging the bank until they neared their launch point.

"I bet," Giordino said, "you were a mean kid with an Erector Set when you were little."

Pitt forced a weak grin. "I always made a mess of things."

They continued in silence. Reaching the marsh, they paddled ashore and muscled the inflatable back onto the flatbed. Pitt was wet, cold, and bloodied, but Giordino could see the focused look in his eyes. He didn't have to guess where Pitt's thoughts were as they climbed into the truck and made their way back to Le Havre.

They could only be with Summer.

45

By her second night at sea, Summer had grown bolder. Food was still her first priority and she didn't have to go far to get it, as the ship's galley was just down the corridor. But as a gathering place for off-duty crewmen and the commandos she had seen aboard, it was seldom empty. Listening from her cabin and taking quick peeks down the hall, she discovered it became deserted between 3:00 and 4:30 a.m.

She struck quickly. Raiding with a trash bag, she scooped up fruit, cookies, and croissants the chef had left out for snacks. In less than two minutes, she was back in her cabin with a private stash.

She quickly adjusted to a new routine. Afraid to leave her cabin in daylight, she revised her sleep habits and became a nighthawk. The next night she was more assertive. Finding the kitchen empty, she raided the refrigerator for leftover chicken cordon bleu and dessert crepes. Devouring it back in her cabin, Summer found the French chef's cooking far superior to most commercial shipboard fare.

Fortified after her first real meal aboard, she decided to pursue her next mission: anonymity.

Still in the dead of night, Summer ventured out of the accommo-

dations block under a dark, moonless sky. She scanned the deck to ensure it was empty, then moved around the superstructure. Along the starboard bulkhead, she found several exterior storage compartments and poked through them one by one, searching for a change of attire. In a small paint locker she found a drip-spattered ball cap, which she dusted off and placed on her head, tucking her long curls inside it.

Moving aft, she approached a watertight door marked *Engine Room*. She turned the dogleg handle, nudged the door open a crack, and looked inside. A rush of warm air blasted her, accompanied by the deep rumble of the ship's diesel engine a few levels below. A grated steel landing inside the doorway led to the main engine access stairwell.

She found pay dirt on the landing. A high shelf contained hard hats, safety glasses, and ear protection devices for the engineers, while several workman's coveralls hung on hooks just below. But first she'd have to reach them.

Summer opened the door wider and spied an engineer at a panel on the deck below. She waited until he moved out of sight, then she sprang onto the landing. She selected a coverall that looked like it would fit and grabbed some safety glasses for good measure. She rushed back to the exterior deck and slipped into the garment.

Emboldened by her disguise, she returned to the paint locker and rummaged through its contents. She found a small tin of white paint, then located a brush and a can key, which she slipped into her pocket.

Summer exited the locker and looked up. The *Mont Blanc*'s bridge sat high atop the superstructure above her, offering a commanding view of the pipe-riddled forward deck.

It was too risky to make her mark forward, Summer thought, so she stepped to the rear of the structure. On the tanker's narrow afterdeck, she found a pair of large winches dominating the available space. A dozen thick mooring bitts, used to secure the ship at dock,

peppered the deck along the stern rail. To Summer, they appeared in the dark like oversized black mushrooms, but were exactly what she was looking for.

She considered the layout, then stepped to the center rail and faced forward. She opened the paint can, dipped in the brush, and painted an O on the top of the nearest bitt. She moved to the starboard rail and painted an M and an A on the two end bollards. Backtracking to the port-side bitts, she dabbled an N on one and a U on the other.

She then stepped to the winches, which stood a foot taller than her. She stood on her toes, reached up, and painted a large S on the top housing of each.

Summer hoped it was innocuous enough that a passing crewman would give it little thought. At the same time, if her brother or anyone else was looking for her, it might just provide a signal.

She briefly scanned the horizon, but the only lights came from the stars. Where was the tanker positioned and where was it headed? She shook off the questions and returned to the paint locker, where she stowed the paint and brush.

As she closed the locker door, she heard a question in French.

She held her breath as she slowly turned. A dark figure stood on the forward deck a few yards away. The red glow of a cigarette in his fingers revealed the outline of a rifle over his shoulder.

Summer's heart was pounding. She nodded at the figure and uttered the deepest "*Oui*" she could muster. Without waiting for a reply, she turned aft and casually walked away. She entered the superstructure through a side door. When it clicked behind her, she sprinted down the corridor and scurried into her cabin. As her heart raced, she listened with the lights off and the door locked.

No alarm was raised, and after a prolonged wait, Summer realized her disguise had worked. As she took off the coveralls and crawled onto her bunk, she felt a growing confidence. Somehow soon, she would find a way off the ship.

46

An unseasonal tropical storm was dousing Bermuda when Brigitte and Nassar landed at the British territory's international airport. Their rental car's wipers flipped at high speed as Nassar drove off the airport grounds. It took him extra focus to drive on the left side of the road through a raging thunderstorm, but they didn't have far to go. The journey to the capital city of Hamilton on the island's south side was less than ten miles.

"Richmond House should be ahead on the right," Brigitte said a short time later as she tracked their route on her phone.

Nassar scored a parking spot on the busy street and they rushed through the rain into a nearby office building. They took an elevator to the fifth floor, where they found the compact offices of the French consulate.

"My name is Mansard," Nassar said to the receptionist. "I had phoned about obtaining some historical information."

The receptionist checked her calendar, then placed a call. A young man, who appeared as if he had just graduated college, bounded into the foyer in an ill-fitting suit and introduced himself as the deputy

consul general. His eyes lingered on Brigitte a bit too long for Nassar's liking.

"You received my request for help?" the commando asked gruffly.

"Yes. You inquired about Monsieur Rapine. I was able to certify that he was indeed an envoy to Bermuda prior to World War Two. Unfortunately, the consulate has no logbooks or personal records of Monsieur Rapine during his time here."

"None at all?" Brigitte asked.

The young man shook his head. "There were no diplomatic relations between Bermuda and the Vichy government during the war, so the consulate was disbanded. As a result, we have very few wartime records. I did make a few calls and found that the Bermuda National Library may have some relevant data. They are located on Queen Street. I'm sorry we couldn't be of more help."

The rain was still falling when Brigitte and Nassar returned to their rental car, and she wiped some drops from her face. "I hope you didn't drag us here for nothing."

"The only clues we had led here. We will find something."

They drove across the east side of Hamilton to Queen Street, where they found the library in an attractive nineteenth-century building that had once been the residence of Bermuda's first postmaster. Inside they found a small but modern library. Brigitte led them into a side room marked *Bermuda Historical and Cultural Studies*. A mature, well-dressed woman at the counter greeted them with a toothy smile.

"Jean-Claude at the French consulate phoned about your inquiry," she said. "I was able to retrieve a number of records."

She guided them to a table with a small assortment of books and folders.

"We have a fair number of records associated with the French consulate before World War Two, and Paul Rapine in particular," she said. "He was a resident of Bermuda until his death in 1964. In

addition to his diplomatic role, he owned an import business and ran a well-known bookstore for many years. Jean-Claude mentioned you were conducting genealogy research on him?"

"Yes," Nassar said. "We're working on a family history. We found he's related to Napoleon."

The librarian gave no reaction to the emperor's name. The two scanned the materials while the librarian stepped away to reshelve a cartload of books. The archives primarily contained letters from Rapine to the Bermuda government dealing with trade issues and docking rights for French vessels, both before and after the war. But there were few wartime documents, beyond a copy of Rapine's letter of resignation to the Vichy government.

Not until Brigitte was sifting through some estate records did she come across two thin volumes.

"They are his personal diaries," she whispered triumphantly to Nassar. "One dated 1935 to 1948, the other 1949 to 1960."

He slid his chair alongside hers as she opened the first book. The passages were brief, most related to the profitability of his various businesses, with many days left blank. She skimmed the notations until reaching May 1940. "Here, on the twenty-fifth," she said, "he mentions meeting Demille and helping arrange the storage of his cargo at a waterfront warehouse."

"It doesn't sound as if he knew what Demille was transporting," Nassar said.

"He makes no other mention of it in the following days, but describes his growing friendship with Demille as a fellow patriot and countryman."

They found little of interest for several months. Skimming ahead, she stopped at an entry dated 7 February, 1942.

"The pride of the French fleet arrived today for fuel and repairs. Marcel and I dined with her captain, a pleasant man

*named Blaison. Regrettably, the news of the war is not
good."*

A few entries later, Brigitte elbowed Nassar. "Listen to this:

*'Twelfth February. A sad farewell to my good friend Marcel,
who sails with his cargo on his clandestine mission. It was a
stirring departure at dawn on our navy's great underwater
cruiser, for the glory of France.'*

Brigitte reread the last entry aloud and shook her head. "It
can't be."

Nassar gave her a perplexed look.

"The Navy's great underwater cruiser," she said. "It can only be
one vessel."

"So what does it mean?"

Brigitte looked around the room, then leaned close to him and
whispered. "It means Napoleon's tomb and the diamonds were never
recovered. They were lost at the bottom of the sea in 1942 and remain
there to this day."

47

Summer could sense dawn approaching. The air felt static, the waves seemed flatter, and time seemed to slow. There seemed a faint cosmic calmness before the birth of a new day.

Maybe it was just her heightened senses while on deck under the night sky, soaking up the salt air and temporary freedom from confinement in her cabin. Ever alert for a wandering crewman or probing eyes from the bridge, she moved with constant stealth. But she felt alive on her predawn excursions about the ship's exterior, finding more satisfaction than her daily raid on the galley.

She stayed mostly on the afterdeck, where the massive winches and bollards offered quick cover from a passing crewman. It also gave her a clear view over the rail of the vast black ocean behind her, which always seemed free of passing ships or land. She wanted to escape, but in the dark ocean there was nowhere to go. First and foremost, however, she needed a means of escape. But how?

As she turned from the rail to sneak back to her cabin, the answer suddenly appeared. Summer could kick herself. Why hadn't she recognized it earlier? Maybe the crisp air had enlivened her senses enough to fully absorb her surroundings. Or maybe it was the bright

stars that had caused her to look up for a change. It was then that she had noticed the oblong, pumpkin-orange mass overhead.

It was the *Mont Blanc*'s emergency free-fall lifeboat, mounted on a high roller frame above the stern. The boat had provisions, a motor, and a lot more agility than the tanker.

She surveyed the boat and ramp from below, then climbed a stairwell to an access platform, where the lifeboat was mounted at a sharp angle to the sea. She spent nearly thirty minutes examining its release locks and mechanisms, even climbing inside to familiarize herself with the controls.

The tanker had an additional tender mounted high near the bridge on traditional davits, so she would have to pick her escape wisely. A nearby landmass or a close-passing vessel would do. But scanning the horizon at the first rays of dawn, she saw no evidence of either, just a flat, empty sea.

She crept back to her cabin knowing she now had the means to freedom. As she lay in her bunk eating a pilfered banana, she made a vow.

Tonight, one way or the other, she would make her escape.

48

I think we've got a hit."

The image of Hiram Yaeger's tired face vanished from the *Pelican*'s video screen and was replaced by a fuzzy photo of a black ship at sea. Pitt and Giordino leaned forward to examine the image. They were groggy after their late-night visit to Antwerp, but sleep hadn't been a priority. They weren't surprised when a similarly sleep-deprived Yaeger contacted them at three in the morning, D.C. time.

"The photo is a bit indecipherable," Pitt said.

"Sorry, I've got a better one that's computer enhanced."

The image was replaced by a much clearer satellite shot of the vessel, a long white wake rippling behind it.

"I'm ninety percent certain this is the *Mont Blanc*," Yaeger said.

"Still sailing without AIS?" Giordino asked.

"Correct. I found her through sat images alone, tracing a rough breadcrumb trail back to the Isle of Wight. She's in the middle of the North Atlantic right now, heading southwest."

Yaeger used his computer skills to magnify the image.

"Looks to be riding high in the water," Pitt said. "Her tanks must be empty."

Giordino leaned closer to the screen. "Does she have a forward hold? Dirk thinks they may have loaded the radioactive barrels into a compartment near the bow."

Yaeger zoomed in on the bow, revealing the outline of a flush hold ahead of the ship's maze of deck pipes and valves. "Looks to be a small one there, as described."

He panned across the rest of the ship, then zoomed out to the photo's original proportion.

Pitt stopped him. "Hiram, close in again on the stern, would you?"

Yaeger enlarged the ship's stern in slow increments.

"See something?" Giordino asked.

"The stern bollards," Pitt said. "Some sort of lettering on them."

As the image crystallized, Giordino read out the letters on the scattered bollards. "*N . . . U . . . O . . . M . . . A.*"

"Wait," Pitt said. "Look at the winches."

Giordino spotted the large *S*'s painted on the winches and incorporated them into the full message. "It's 'SOS NUMA,'" he said excitedly. "Summer must be aboard."

Pitt sat upright and grinned, unable to hide his relief. His daughter might still be in danger, but she was alive. "Where's the nearest landfall?"

Yaeger plotted the ship's position on a map of the North Atlantic and displayed it on the screen.

"She's about midway between the Azores and Newfoundland, six or seven hundred miles from each." Yaeger added the *Mont Blanc*'s position from an earlier satellite photo. "Her current track puts her on a path toward Cuba. Possibly on her way to Venezuela for oil. But actually," he said as he enlarged the image, "if she holds to her current heading, she'll run right by Bermuda. Be there in a day or two."

"That's where we'll get her." Pitt looked at his watch. "I'll call Rudi later and see what we can coordinate between our Coast Guard and the Bermuda authorities."

"He's usually in early."

"Thanks, Hiram. Go home and get some sleep. We'll take it from here."

"No argument from me," he said as he signed off.

"I'll book us a flight to Bermuda pronto," Giordino said.

Pitt contemplated the now blank video screen, the gears in his mind churning. "Do me a favor. Reserve an additional flight, from D.C. to Bermuda."

"One person?"

"Yes . . . But you better book two seats."

Giordino looked at Pitt and smiled. "Are you thinking about Napoleon?"

Pitt nodded. "At the moment, it seems that all roads lead to Bermuda."

49

The gate attendant made the final boarding call for the flight from Bermuda to Ponta Delgada. In typical fashion, her words sounded like crypto-Martian through the fuzzy airport PA system.

Brigitte gathered her carry-on and turned to Nassar. "I really don't feel comfortable doing this."

"It is all arranged," he said, slipping an arm around her waist. "The seismic survey ship *Moselle* will pick you up in the Azores, and her captain will be under your direction. We were lucky that the ship was sitting in Spain without assignment."

"What about your boss? Won't he know that you've appropriated the vessel?"

"I told him we have a small 'import' opportunity from Colombia. He is so desperate for cash, he instantly approved."

"What happens when no product shows up?"

"I'll just say the deal fell through. Maybe by that time, we'll have found the diamonds," he said with a wink.

"I wish you were coming, too." Brigitte had considered washing her hands of everything and flying back to France. She didn't want to

proceed alone, and the Institute was already asking about her absence. She had already crossed several lines, and she feared the deepening involvement with Nassar. But going home would likely mean both a breakup with Nassar and abandoning the hunt for Napoleon. While she feared the fallout from a separation, she wasn't ready to give up the search for France's greatest treasure.

"Don't worry," Nassar said. "I'll meet you in Cartagena in a few days. The search will keep you busy. Perhaps you will even find it before I get there."

She forced a smile, gave him a light kiss, and boarded the plane.

He waited until she disappeared down the boarding ramp, then made a rapid exit from the airport. He took a cab across the island to Bermuda's commercial docks on the south side of Hamilton.

A bright yellow tender motored into the harbor and eased toward the dock where he waited. The pilot slowed just long enough for Nassar to climb aboard. The boat resumed speed and looped back in the direction it had come.

"Could you have brought something less conspicuous?" Nassar asked, motioning toward the brightly colored hull.

The pilot looked at him and shrugged. "It's what the ship carries."

The tender exited the harbor and motored south through a light swell. Three miles from shore, they approached a faded blue vessel holding station. It was a small passenger ship, just over two hundred feet long, that had been built in the 1970s to cruise the Greek islands.

Once an opulent vessel that catered to small groups of wealthy tourists, its outward appearance had succumbed to age and neglect. The ship had been relegated to a day cruiser out of Alexandria, but Nassar had been assured the operating components of the ship had been properly maintained.

He began to wonder as he eyed rust stains that descended off the hawseholes. The faded image of a chariot in the same rust color

melded against the dirty yellow of the ship's broad funnel. Even the ship's name, *Hydros*, was barely legible on her bow.

The pilot brought the tender alongside a dangling pair of davit lines. The boat was hoisted to the main deck, where Nassar acknowledged the armed crewmen working the davit, all experienced members of his commando team. He made his way to the bridge, where Hosni Samad greeted him with a lazy salute.

"Welcome aboard, sir."

"How is the operation of the ship?" Nassar asked.

"She is not pretty on the outside, but stout on the inside. The engines are strong, and she handles herself well at sea. The bilge is a bit leaky, but the pumps seem to be keeping up fine."

"They won't have to work much longer. Weather forecast?"

"The tropical storm has passed. It is clear ahead, with diminishing winds and slight seas. Perfect conditions for a transfer at sea. Orders for the helm?"

"Take us out of sight of land, then circle to the north of the island. We have a rendezvous to make once the sun goes down."

50

A white light twinkled against the black horizon, and Summer rubbed her eyes to make sure it was real. The tiny light was still there, just off the *Mont Blanc*'s bow.

She had been unable to keep her promise of escaping the evening before, as no vessels had appeared on her watch. After two hours of scanning an empty sea this night, Summer had started to wonder if she'd ever see land or a passing ship. But at last a light appeared, and directly ahead at that.

She remained in her hidden perch, watching to see if the other vessel would actually draw near.

Her desire to spot another ship had led her to the tanker's forecastle. She had crept forward the night before, eager to search the waters ahead of the ship. Slithering around a row of transfer pipes, she had come across the forward hold, where the dockworkers on the Isle of Wight had loaded cargo. She discovered a side access panel that led to the hold's interior. Using a small flashlight she found in the paint locker, she opened the panel and probed inside.

There were at least a dozen of the large yellow bins wedged at the bottom of the hold. Each, she knew, contained a barrel of radioactive

waste salvaged from the Irish Sea. But it was the accompanying cargo that made her stomach turn.

Packed beside the bins were several pallets of gray boxes wrapped in heavy plastic. Summer had to crawl into the uneven hold and approach one of the pallets to read its label. The wording was in a script she guessed was Hindi. But beneath a lightning bolt logo, she found a warning in English: *Danger, Emulsive Explosive.*

It was a commercial explosive, one that combined ammonium nitrate with oil. Any benign thoughts she might have had about the crew disposing of the radioactive waste in a safe manner vanished. They could only be combining the two elements to blow up the wastes somewhere, creating a colossal environmental disaster.

Summer's knees went weak as she considered her new responsibility. Not only did she have to get off the ship to save her life, but she also had to issue a warning to prevent the vessel from completing its deadly mission.

While making her way out of the hold, she had noticed a small platform situated above the neighboring pipes that was used as an observation post when the ship was loading or off-loading oil. It had an enclosed lower rail that concealed its base from the bridge and either side deck. Summer ran reconnaissance around the platform, then returned the next night and used it as a crow's nest.

She now studied the light on the horizon as it gradually grew larger. If there was no course change, the two ships would pass close by. The days of waiting fell away with a burst of adrenaline as her senses went on high alert. Summer waited until she caught a clear glimpse of the approaching vessel's green starboard navigation light. The ship was close enough for her to make her move.

She descended from her perch and started to move aft along the starboard rail, when a light snapped on ahead of her. A figure emerged from the accommodations block with a flashlight, its beam swaying across the deck in front of him.

Summer froze in her tracks, then ducked low. She hugged the inboard rail, backtracked to the bow, then scurried to the port side. Keeping her head down, she moved swiftly across the deck, prompted by the other vessel's approach.

She dropped to all fours and crab-crawled across the deck until she passed the man with the light on the opposite beam. Then she resumed her trek on foot.

Summer caught her breath when she reached the cover of the superstructure. She took a last peek at the approaching ship, now less than a half mile away, then climbed to the emergency lifeboat's access platform. Earlier she had examined the release mechanism and prepared the lifeboat for launch.

She unhooked a lash line that released a restraining plate, then unplugged a trickle charger connected to the lifeboat's onboard battery. As she pulled a thick safety pin from the main release mechanism, a shout sounded from overhead.

"Hey! Qu'est-ce que vous faites?" What are you doing?

Summer saw a man on the bridge wing, two levels higher, craning over the rail at her. She ignored him, opened the hatch, and climbed inside. The enclosed compartment looked like a passenger train car, with rows of aisle seats able to accommodate thirty crewmen.

Summer closed the hatch and climbed up a short ladder to the operator's seat situated in a small windowed cockpit that protruded from the top. The enclosed lifeboat was tilted at a sharp angle with its nose down, and Summer found it awkward to stay in the seat until she fastened a safety harness and pulled it tight.

The cockpit windows let in a small amount of light from the tanker's exterior lamps, enough to find and press the starter button. The inboard diesel engine turned over a few times, then caught and burbled at a low idle. Muffled shouts came from the bridge wing, but there was no stopping her now.

She reached for the release lever, a broomstick-like handle on the side of the seat, and pulled.

Nothing happened.

She felt along its side and discovered that, like the exterior release, it contained a safety pin. She popped it out of its hole, gripped the handle, and pulled it back again.

This time, it ratcheted back with two clicks and stopped. And again nothing happened.

"*Hors du bateau*," someone yelled. Out of the boat.

Then the rear hatch opened.

She pulled harder on the lever, but it had reached its stops. The beam of a flashlight splayed over the interior as the man from the deck poked his head in the hatch.

In a panic, she pushed the lever forward, then pulled it back again, hearing several clicks, then a loud clunk. The release had been designed to build tension before springing the holding blocks.

The lifeboat suddenly plunged forward. The crewman gasped and jumped back at the last second, and the hatch slammed shut. Then a moment of silence as the craft slid off its cradle and went airborne.

Summer's stomach rose as the boat plummeted sixty feet and nose-dived into the ocean. Her body slammed against the safety straps, then fell back into the seat as the lifeboat burst upright to the surface. She hit the throttle and the twenty-nine-horsepower Chinese engine propelled the boat forward.

She followed the tanker's wake before looking back through the small rear window. Several figures stood on the *Mont Blanc*'s stern deck as the distance grew between vessels. It wasn't the stealth exit she'd planned, but it wouldn't matter if she could make it to the approaching ship.

She eased the wheel to port and slowly turned the lifeboat to a parallel course with the tanker. She suspected the *Mont Blanc* had

stopped engines as she started to close on the ship. But no one was in pursuit. A running light showed the tanker's tender was still secure beneath the bridge wing, and she saw no attempts to deploy it.

Summer turned her sights to the approaching ship, which for some reason didn't seem to have moved much closer. She opened an overhead hatch and popped her head out to confirm a topside light on the lifeboat was illuminated, then steered for the outboard side of the vessel.

As she drew closer, she saw it was a dimly lit passenger ship, most of its cabin portholes dark. As she crossed the vessel's path, Summer turned on the helm-mounted VHF radio. "Mayday, Mayday. This is the emergency lifeboat off your bow in need of assistance."

The response was almost immediate. "Lifeboat, we see you and are preparing to stop. Head to our port flank for recovery."

Summer gave a silent fist pump and maneuvered the lifeboat ahead. The ship coasted to a stop as she drew alongside it, and she gazed up at the faded lettering on the bow. It was a name she recognized from her study of ancient history.

The Greek god of water. *Hydros*.

51

Two crewmen on deck with flashlight beacons guided Summer alongside the cruise ship. She climbed out the roof of the lifeboat and attached a pair of lowered cables to the lift mounts. The boat was hoisted up to the main deck and maneuvered inboard.

Summer waited until the boat touched down, then climbed out the rear hatch, eager to give thanks and offer a report on the *Mont Blanc*.

The words vanished from her lips when she was greeted by three armed men in dark fatigues who welcomed her with all the warmth of an Alpine glacier.

Hosni Samad stepped forward and motioned across the deck with his weapon. "This way."

Summer obeyed his order, wondering what she had stepped into. The answer became apparent when she was marched to the bridge. Out the window she saw the *Mont Blanc* approaching tight alongside the *Hydros*'s starboard bow. Two more men in fatigues were coordinating the approach on the bridge, while a casually dressed man oversaw the operation.

"This is the woman on the lifeboat," Samad reported to him. "She was alone."

Nassar glanced at Summer. "Yes, I've been advised."

She was held at the back of the bridge as the two ships inched toward each other until the *Mont Blanc*'s forward hold aligned with the cruise ship's open rear deck. The tanker had side thrusters for maneuvering in port, and a practiced hand at the helm kept the ship at an even distance from the drifting *Hydros*.

A crew on the *Mont Blanc*'s deck went to work, opening the forward hatch and transferring the pallets of explosives across the open water using a forward derrick. The pallets were followed by the one-at-a-time transfer of the yellow bins. The operation was concluded without a hitch, and the ships separated, each assuming a new heading.

Nassar turned to Samad. "Distribute the materials to their designated locations at once. I want it off the deck and out of sight as soon as possible. Then return here."

Samad nodded and scurried off the bridge.

Nassar approached Summer. "Who are you?"

While there was no threat in the tone, Summer could see the menace in the man. Summer looked at his blunt face and dark, hardened eyes and knew instantly that Nassar was a killer.

"My name," she said in a voice she couldn't keep from faltering, "is Summer Pitt."

A startled look crossed Nassar's face. It all began to make sense. He looked her up and down, noticing her borrowed engineer coveralls. "You boarded on the Isle of Wight with your brother?"

"I did," Summer said, unsure of Dirk's fate.

"And why was that?"

"We saw the radioactive waste being removed by the *Chamonix* at sea, then happened to see the vessel on Wight," she said. "We were curious as to the intent of the materials. Still are."

Nassar smiled. He had to admire her fortitude and cunning. But with all that she had seen, she was a liability. He should kill her now and pitch her body over the side. Yet if things went sideways, there

might be value in her presence as a hostage. And with her brother as a suspect in the Paris attack, family blame might accrue if her body was found after the end of this mission. There was also the fact she was highly attractive.

"You are American?" he asked.

"Yes."

"Well, then, it appears you will be returning home."

52

L.F. WADE INTERNATIONAL AIRPORT
BERMUDA

M r. Pitt?"
Pitt and Giordino stepped off the plane in Bermuda to
be greeted by a broad-shouldered man in a blue linen
blazer. Pitt identified himself and introduced Giordino.

"I'm Dan Durkot," the man said, shaking hands, "section chief
with the U.S. consulate here in Bermuda. I've been coordinating the
local response for the offshore interdiction. Let's get your bags, and
we can discuss it in the car."

The career diplomat, who hailed from Long Island, escorted them
first to the baggage claim, then to a gray sedan parked out front. As
Durkot drove, Pitt asked about the Bermuda Coast Guard's plans to
board and search the *Mont Blanc*.

"Actually, it will be handled by an American Coast Guard cutter,
the *Venturous*. Bermuda's Coast Guard only possesses a small number
of inshore boats. The U.S. has a long-standing policy of providing
blue-water search and rescue assistance to the country. Frankly, I was
a bit surprised at how quickly your NUMA Assistant Director, Rudi
Gunn, was able to have the *Venturous* pulled off-line and sent here."

Pitt smiled, knowing it was likely Vice President James Sandecker,

a past director of NUMA and confidant of Pitt and Gunn, who had pulled the strings.

"Since the interdiction may occur in Bermuda waters," Durkot said, "we have asked for local support. The Bermuda Police Service has assigned several officers to help with the search, along with a trained police dog."

Giordino spoke up from the backseat. "Do you have a current fix on the *Mont Blanc*?"

"We've been tracking them by flyover. The last report was that they were about twenty miles northeast of St. George's Island, so we're hoping to move quickly."

Durkot drove past downtown Hamilton, following the fishhook shape of Bermuda's lower landmass to the very western tip. He parked near King's Wharf, where visiting cruise ships normally docked, and led Pitt and Giordino to the waterfront. It wasn't a massive cruise ship waiting for them, but the gleaming white Coast Guard cutter the *Venturous*.

They were welcomed aboard by the ship's captain, a spritely sandy-haired woman named Waynne James. The Coast Guard commander guided them to the bridge, where she gave her crew the order to cast off.

"I'm told your daughter is being held against her will," James said while eyeing the ship's movement. "I can understand the urgency."

"Much appreciated," Pitt said. "Will there be any trouble catching the *Mont Blanc*?"

"Absolutely none. She's a tanker, so she's not going to outrun anybody. And she's actually headed our direction." James led the men to a monitor that showed a map of Bermuda interspersed with colored squares and triangles in the coastal waters. She pointed to a green triangle northeast of the island. "That's the *Mont Blanc*. A Coast Guard helicopter confirmed her position less than an hour ago. We'll be on her in short order."

Pitt stayed on the bridge as the cutter cleared the bay and proceeded up Bermuda's west coast. The ship rounded the island's northern tip twenty minutes later and set an intercept for the tanker.

The *Mont Blanc* soon appeared on the horizon, a light wisp of smoke trailing from her funnel. When the *Venturous* had closed within a mile, James took to the radio and requested the tanker heave to for boarding and inspection.

After a short pause, the ship responded. "Affirmative. We are reducing speed for boarding."

"What if he'd said no?" Pitt asked.

James pointed to a 25-millimeter Bushmaster autocannon on the cutter's forward deck and gave an assured grin. "A shot across the bow still works wonders at sea."

The cutter drew alongside the *Mont Blanc* as the tanker drifted to a halt. James turned to Pitt and Giordino. "I think there may be a pair of open seats on the boarding craft."

"Thank you, Commander, we'll take them."

The two men moved to the aft deck, where a boarding party was assembling beside a launch. A four-man armed Coast Guard team was joined by three Bermuda police officers. One gripped the leash on a German shepherd that barked once at the two men. They all climbed into the launch, which was lowered and released into a jittery sea.

Pitt felt a knot in his stomach thinking of his daughter as they motored alongside the tanker. An accommodations ladder had been lowered, and Pitt and Giordino followed the law enforcement officials onto the ship.

A bearded man in a ragged T-shirt identified himself as the executive officer and welcomed them aboard with mock civility.

The Coast Guard lieutenant in charge of the boarding requested that all crew members aside from the bridge staff be assembled on

deck. The tanker's crew was an international mix of men, but Pitt noticed a hardness about them beyond the norm.

A guardsman was assigned to watch the crew, while the boarding team began their inspection. Giordino followed two guardsmen aft, while Pitt followed the Bermuda team with the search dog, which had been trained to sniff out humans, dead or alive.

The shepherd showed its abilities when they entered the blockhouse and it began barking in front of the third cabin they approached.

The door was opened to reveal a groggy crewman in his bunk who had been startled awake by the barking dog. They continued their search cabin by cabin until they worked their way to the bridge, where the Coast Guard lieutenant stood checking the ship's registry and manifest.

"Anything amiss?" Pitt asked.

The lieutenant shook his head. "Everything appears in order. On their way to Venezuela to pick up a shipment of crude oil. What about the police dog?"

"Nothing yet."

"We'll check every square inch. If she's here, we'll find her."

Ninety minutes later, they had covered the entire ship without result. Pitt followed the dog through the galley, the engine room, the forward hold, and even into the bilge. He met Giordino wiping his hands on a rag after exiting one of the massive cargo tanks.

"Nothing doing in the storage tanks," he said.

After searching from stem to stern, the well-trained team came up empty. As they began to reassemble on deck, Pitt made a last walk around the stern.

He eyed the stanchions with the painted lettering that spelled out the rescue message. The white paint looked to have been applied recently. Pitt knew his daughter had been there, but now feared the worst.

He gazed over the rail at the deep blue ocean. Lost in the memory of Summer, he stared at a squall building in the distance. When the Coast Guard lieutenant called to reboard the launch, he turned toward the superstructure, but stopped in his tracks.

It was then he noticed the deployment rack over his head was missing its emergency lifeboat.

53

São Miguel rose like a shimmering emerald from a sapphire sea. The largest of the Azores islands, its volcanic mountains covered in bright layers of greenery, scratched the cloudless sky. Brigitte eyed the verdant landscape as her plane touched down at the João Paulo II Airport, wishing she was arriving as a tourist able to explore the island for fun. Instead, she felt nothing but stress at the position she found herself in.

Time was short, as there was a boat and crew heading to meet her, with a long sea voyage awaiting. She took a cab directly to the commercial docks just off the historic downtown of Ponta Delgada. The designated wharf was empty, so she lugged her suitcase across the street to a small café, where she took a seat outside and ordered an espresso.

She checked her phone and was relieved to find an email from her historian friend at the Institute. Several historical accounts of the research target were attached to the email, along with a graduate thesis about the vessel's demise.

Brigitte pored over the documents, gaining confidence in the project. The loss of the French naval vessel was still a mystery, but at least

she had a place to start searching. She finished her espresso and gazed out at the harbor.

The Ponta Delgada port had been created by an artificial breakwater nearly a mile long with a working pier built on its interior side. Cruise ships and commercial vessels used the pier for loading and unloading, while two large marinas held pleasure boats near the protected shoreline. It was one of the more orderly ports Brigitte had ever seen.

Her focus turned to a red survey ship entering the harbor, which she recognized from an image shared by Nassar. It was the *Moselle*. Brigitte gathered her things and tracked the vessel to a fuel dock. As she walked across the wharf, she noted the vessel was well kept and carried a small submersible on the aft deck.

She reached the gangway, but stopped when a shirtless crewman with a scar on his jaw appeared on the stern and glared at her. He pointed a gnarled finger at a companionway that led to the bridge.

She nodded, then hesitantly boarded the ship. On the bridge, she found the captain, a thickly bearded man with glassy black eyes, who regarded her with obvious disdain. "You're Favreau?"

"Yes. We are to undertake an underwater search."

"The boss told me. In the Caribbean."

"That's right," Brigitte said. "I'll have a location and search grid put together shortly."

"You do that. We'll be underway within the hour." He turned his back on her, focusing his attention at a yellow fuel line stretched across the forward deck.

"Can you have someone show me to my cabin?"

"Rafael," he shouted without turning around.

The shirtless man with the scar appeared and escorted her to a small cabin beneath the bridge. She closed the door, turned the lock, then wedged a chair beneath the handle.

So these were the type of people Henri worked with. And perhaps the type of man he truly was. Her stomach churned as she tried to turn her focus to the end goal. She took a few deep breaths, retrieved her laptop, and proceeded to lay out a grid to find the vessel that had vanished while carrying the remains of Napoleon.

54

P itt was on a satellite call to NUMA headquarters by the time the
Coast Guard cutter returned to Bermuda's South Channel and
approached the dock at King's Wharf. The *Mont Blanc*'s missing lifeboat had gnawed at his thoughts for good reason. Yaeger was
able to confirm that the emergency boat had been visible on the oil
tanker in earlier satellite photos.

"Did the crew have an explanation?" Rudi Gunn asked. Pitt's
Deputy Administrator at NUMA had followed events closely and
joined on the call with Yaeger.

"The captain claimed they lost it in a recent storm. There was a
recent blow around Bermuda, but it would have had minimal impact
in their location."

"Those emergency lifeboats are equipped with radios," Gunn
noted.

"If Summer was aboard," Pitt said, "she may have been afraid to
make a call with the *Mont Blanc* nearby. Commander James has
called in an aerial search and rescue, but resources are limited in these
parts."

"I'll reach out to the Navy," Gunn said. "We can get a P-3 recon-naissance craft to fly the area if the Coast Guard has not already ar-ranged it."

"What about the radioactive wastes?" Yaeger asked.

"No sign of them. And the ship was searched from top to bottom."

"It's possible I pegged the wrong ship," Yaeger said.

"No," Pitt said. "The markings on the stern had to come from Summer. She was there."

"Maybe there was a quick port call made that we missed," Yaeger said. "I'll pull the satellite photos and take another look." Nobody wanted to admit the worst-case scenario regarding Summer.

"She might already have been picked up by another vessel," Gunn offered. "I'll issue a notice with the relevant port authorities."

It was all they could do for the moment, Pitt knew. As he hung up the call, he was approached by Giordino. "I just got a message that St. Julien would like to meet us for dinner if we are able."

Pitt nodded. "Not much more we can do at the moment. I wish I had an appetite."

"Perlmutter, I think it's safe to say, will have you covered on that front."

When St. Julien Perlmutter had suggested they meet for dinner at the Waterlot Inn, Pitt correctly surmised it was one of the best restaur-ants in Bermuda. Housed in an antique cottage overlooking the water, the main dining room was spiced with nautical paintings and overstuffed Queen Anne chairs that exuded classical elegance.

Pitt and Giordino were escorted to a corner table, where a Kodiak bear of a man was seated devouring a tray full of oysters.

"Gentlemen, good to see you," he said. "Hope you don't mind that I sampled the appetizers while waiting. I worked up a hunger at the library today."

Pitt laughed to himself. Perlmutter was a first-class epicurean, and it wouldn't have been surprising if he'd already sampled everything on the menu.

"As long as you haven't drained the bar, we're good," Giordino said. He and Pitt took their seats and ordered drinks.

"How was your flight from Washington?" Pitt asked.

"Just splendid. Kind of you to spring for two seats, but I did upgrade to first class." Perlmutter's massive frame was well north of three hundred pounds and tested the legs of every chair he sat in.

"I'm disappointed not to find Summer with you," he added in a serious tone.

"She wasn't on the tanker," Pitt said. "She may have escaped in its lifeboat."

"Summer's a tough and resourceful young woman. Have no worries." Perlmutter motioned toward the menus. "What say we order, then I'll tell you what I've found about our Gallic emperor. While the steaks here are excellent, I highly recommend the jumbo scallops."

After placing their dinner order, with Perlmutter adding a bottle of claret to their request, the discussion turned to Napoleon.

"The papers for the French diplomat Paul Rapine were an excellent starting point," Perlmutter said. "The bulk of the collection is housed at the Bermuda National Library, which I visited this morning. A curious note is that the librarian indicated a French couple were in just the day before, examining the same materials. Coincidence?"

Pitt and Giordino looked at each other. "Probably not."

"At any rate, his private journal contained several references to Marcel Demille after the latter's arrival from Paris in 1940. There was mention of his imminent departure from Bermuda in February 1942, but a key page was missing from the journal. It appeared to have been ripped out."

"A national treasure is at stake," Pitt said.

"Indeed."

"So you hit a dead end?" Giordino asked.

Perlmutter took a gulp of wine, then grinned like the Cheshire cat. "My boy, I've been at this game a long time. There's more than one way to bleed the monkey. Once I had the approximate date of De-mille's departure, it was a simple matter to peruse the port and dock-age records. Fortunately, I know a historian on the island, who quickly directed me to the harbor records held at a repository on the island."

This was why Pitt had flown his old friend to Bermuda. Perlmutter was a world-renowned maritime historian, as well as a keen collector of nautical books and ephemera. His sharp mind and uncanny ability as a researcher had aided Pitt on numerous underwater projects.

"Anything from 1942?" Giordino asked.

"It being wartime and all, the local authorities kept a tight watch. The records I examined appeared quite thorough. As it was, I found an excellent accounting of the vessels that came and went in 1942."

"A list of vessels," Giordino said, "doesn't tell us which one Napo-leon hopped a ride on."

"No, it certainly does not. But in this instance, we have a notable inclusion that would appear to stand at the head of the class. You see, the majority of visiting vessels porting in Bermuda were British or American, along with some foreign tramp steamers, mostly from South America. You must remember that the Battle of the Atlantic was nearly three years on by then."

"So what sets this vessel apart?"

"Amid the myriad ships of record, there appears a lone French military craft that happened to visit Bermuda in February 1942. It was a rather astounding vessel at that, unique in all the world." Perl-mutter took a sip of his wine and wiped his mouth for dramatic effect. "It was none other than the *Surcouf*."

55

The *Surcouf*?" Pitt said. "It can't be."

"I'm afraid so." Perlmutter nodded his head, his thick jowls quivering like Jell-O.

"Wasn't she a giant French submarine?" Giordino asked.

"The largest in the world at the time," Pitt said.

"Quite right," Perlmutter said. "A three-hundred-sixty-one-foot behemoth that sported a pair of eight-inch naval guns, ten torpedo tubes, and a floatplane stowed in a watertight deck hangar."

"Sounds like the Japanese I-400 sub we found in the Pacific a few years back," Giordino said.

"Very much so, only the *Surcouf* was launched in 1929, predating the Japanese by almost fifteen years. She was quite the wonder of her day, half again as large as any other submarine ever built.

"But she had a checkered history. She barely made it to England when the Nazis invaded France in 1940, and there was a tussle with the British over the loyalty of her crew. She ultimately served convoy duty in the North Atlantic during the early stages of the war, but was often beset by mechanical problems."

"But she was here in Bermuda," Pitt said, "in February 1942?"

"Yes. She arrived on the seventh and departed on the twelfth, after undergoing minor repairs."

"The last postcard from Marcel Demille was dated the eleventh," Giordino said. "It indicated he was headed to the Pacific."

Perlmutter polished off the last of his ordered scallops and pushed away his empty dinner plate. "That would align perfectly with her final mission. She was on her way to New Caledonia via Tahiti to defend against a potential Japanese attack."

Giordino looked at Pitt with a raised brow. "We were just discussing a trip to Tahiti."

"You can forget about that," Pitt said. "The *Surcouf* never made it that far."

"You are quite right," Perlmutter said. "She was lost in the Caribbean on route to the Panama Canal. No one knows why or where she went down, and it remains one of the biggest mysteries of World War Two."

"Sunk by a U-boat?" Giordino asked.

Perlmutter shook his head. "There are no German accounts to support that. No, it is likely she suffered a nighttime collision with a freighter, although she may have ultimately been sunk in error by an A-17 attack bomber."

He leaned forward and patted Pitt's arm. "I realize finding Summer is your first priority, but I trust you will want to initiate a search for the *Surcouf* after you find her?"

Pitt gave Perlmutter a silent nod.

"Splendid. It may be a challenging hunt, but I have several research files at home that may prove helpful in determining her last location. I shall change my flight to depart tomorrow and will get cracking on it straight away."

He poured the last of the wine and raised his glass. "To the safe return of Summer . . . And a successful search at sea for the illustrious emperor."

As their plates were taken away, Giordino pulled out a Cuban Montecristo cigar he'd bought at the airport and lit it up. "Kind of ironic, ain't it?"

"How so?" Perlmutter said.

Giordino took a puff and blew a cloud of smoke toward the ceiling. "The greatest land general of the past thousand years is resting somewhere on the bottom of the sea."

56

Hiram Yaeger would never admit it, especially to his wife, but he actually loved a late-night work challenge. His department staff had gone home, the daily fires were extinguished, and it was just him and his supercomputer solving a life-or-death puzzle in the wee hours of the morning.

Like a symphony conductor directing a concert rehearsal, he manipulated the computer's electronic databases to perform myriad simultaneous tasks. One program gathered satellite images of the Atlantic around Bermuda, while another enlarged and scanned them for a small orange lifeboat. Meanwhile, he initiated searches in industry journals, port records, AIS trails, and other public records related to the *Mont Blanc* and *Chamonix* and their ownership.

Rudi Gunn stuck his head in the door at 6:00 a.m. and whistled at the computer maestro's line of empty coffee cups. "I had a suspicion you'd be at it late. I hope you're not responsible for feeding the family dog breakfast."

"Fido," Yaeger said, "can afford to lose a few pounds."

"Dirk said he'd call in a few minutes. Any luck with the lifeboat search?"

"Not yet, but I've got some additional data downloading shortly."

Gunn's face twisted with disappointment. Nobody was willing to say it, but he knew they had to consider the possibility that the lifeboat had been sunk after leaving the tanker . . . possibly with Summer in it.

"How about our two mystery ships?"

Yaeger sat upright in his chair and pulled a keyboard close. "Some interesting results in that department. If you recall, we found that both ships were purchased about six years ago and registered with a holding company in Beirut. It took some snooping through a number of shell companies, but I found the funds ultimately came from a French firm called Lavera Exploration. It's a midsize oil survey and transport company with a fleet of about twenty-five ships. Most of them were recently impounded by Interpol for abetting a drug-smuggling operation linked with the Corsican mafia."

"Who's behind the company?"

"Yves Villard is the chairman and owner. Built the company from scratch out of Le Havre. I found no record of any malfeasance up to the time of the drug bust, and he wasn't personally charged in the matter."

"Except that his remaining ships may be transporting nuclear waste."

Yaeger's computer gave a short ring, and he answered a video call from Pitt in his hotel room in Bermuda. Yaeger provided an update on the lifeboat search and the data he'd found on Villard.

"I just heard from the Coast Guard," Pitt said. "The Bermuda police took some surface samples from the *Mont Blanc*'s hold and tested them in their lab. They confirmed the presence of ammonium nitrate, a common ingredient in commercial explosives."

"Confirms what Dirk told you," Gunn said. "Not a happy combination if the tanker was carrying radioactive waste and explosives."

"They could be taking a similar approach to the Paris attacks," Pitt said, "targeting the disruption of a major water supply."

As they spoke, Yaeger expanded an AIS tracking history of the *Mont Blanc*. Since its boarding and inspection, the vessel had reappeared on the system heading for Venezuela. The previously recorded signals showed the tanker at the Isle of Wight the week before. Yaeger highlighted the historical tracking, following the ship from there to Le Havre, then tailing it down to the Mediterranean.

"When was the ship in Le Havre?" Pitt asked.

Yaeger clicked a cursor on the tracking line. "Just over a week ago."

"Not long before Al and I stumbled onto the terrorist crowd there. Show us where she was in the Med."

Yaeger enlarged the map section showing the ship's trail. The long-term tracking data showed it docked in Marseille for a week, then moving across the Mediterranean to the east. Its signal dropped near Cyprus and did not reappear until days later, entering the Atlantic at Gibraltar.

"Again, they went silent for a time," Gunn noted.

Pitt thought a moment. "Wasn't there an attack on a water facility in Israel around that time?"

"You're right," Gunn said, "a large desalination plant."

Yaeger pulled up a news account of the attack on the Sorek plant and a retaliatory rocket strike on the Gaza Strip, despite a Hamas denial. "It occurred when the *Mont Blanc* was in the region running quiet," Yaeger said.

"That's some circumstantial evidence," Gunn said. "But why pursue attacks against water facilities in Israel and France?"

"It's a good target to incite fear in the masses, if that's your thing," Yaeger said.

"True, but there must be something else in play," Pitt said. "What does the *Chamonix* tell us?"

Yaeger pulled up the AIS tracking for the *Chamonix*. Like the *Mont Blanc*, there were gaps in its satellite trail, but its record was more detailed. The history showed it was operational north of Le Havre for several weeks before its appearance in the Irish Sea.

"That area near Le Havre is right where we were surveying," Pitt said. "I recall crossing a pipeline in an uncovered trench. They must have had approval by the French authorities to work in that region."

Yaeger put the question to his computer. In short order the answer came.

"That area is part of an offshore mineral lease granted to a company called Aquarius International," Yaeger said. "Based in, you guessed it, Beirut. Same as the ships' registries. Let me see if they own any other offshore rights."

His query led to more findings. "The company has offshore lease rights in dozens of places around the world." He displayed a list on the screen. "India, Saudi Arabia, Libya, Italy, Greece, Egypt, even the U.S. off of Long Island. And look at that. Israel, too."

"It doesn't make any sense," Gunn said. "The locations all look to be inshore. Most underwater mining these days is in deep water. They'd never get environmental approval to dig up the bottom in most of those places. Same goes for oil or gas drilling."

Pitt considered the locations. "Al and I saw pipeline plans on the *Chamonix* for locations in France, Israel, and the U.S. They also had shoreline charts of Egypt and India. Maybe it's not oil or minerals they are after."

"Then what?" Giordino asked.

"Water."

Gunn scratched his head. "You mean fresh water?"

Pitt nodded. "If they're laying pipe with the *Chamonix*, it would have to be."

"From offshore?" Yaeger asked.

"Yes. Rudi, do you remember the sub-bottom survey we con-

ducted off the Aleutians a few months ago? We detected what the geologists thought was an aquifer close to the surface."

"That's right, it was a freshwater aquifer. The new survey equipment picked it up. The freshwater samples from the seepage above it were so pure, you could drink it. You think they found offshore aquifers in these locations and are trying to exploit them?"

"Their seismic survey ships might have the technology to do so," Pitt said. "Look at those lease locations. They are all places at risk of freshwater shortages in the coming years."

Yaeger pulled up a graphic from NUMA's climate modeling that showed global regions forecast to have the greatest water shortages in the next twenty years. Several red spots on the chart matched the locations of the leases.

"Israel, Libya, Saudi Arabia, India, Pakistan, even parts of Belgium and Italy . . . They're all in the crosshairs," Yaeger said.

"Undersea aquifers could be a godsend to those regions," Gunn said.

"But less so," Pitt said, "if controlled by a criminal syndicate. A tempting business that could be worth billions."

"You may be on the mark." Yaeger displayed an Israeli news article translated from Hebrew. "This is just a few days old, but indicates a contract for a freshwater pipeline and content with Aquarius International is on hold until the next fiscal year, despite current supply shortages."

"Creating their own demand," Pitt said. "I bet they're playing the same game in France."

Yaeger found similar articles in France related to an offshore water source under consideration in Normandy.

"Why resort to terrorist acts if they already have the water available to deliver?" he asked.

"The company's fleet is bottled up," Gunn said. "Maybe they're going broke and need to accelerate business."

Pitt couldn't help but think of Summer's intrusion in all this. "They seem increasingly desperate. They must have something else in the works."

"In France?" Gunn asked.

Pitt remembered the three charts he'd seen in the operations room of the *Chamonix*. Two of those locations, Israel and France, had already been attacked. Heightened security was now in effect in France, and likely Israel as well. That left just the third target, within striking range of Bermuda.

New York City.

57

Summer again found herself confined to a cabin, but absent the comfort she'd experienced on the *Mont Blanc*. The new space was tiny, just a built-in desk and a single bunk, with barely enough room to turn around. It had once served as the *Hydros*'s radio room, but had been carefully cleansed of all equipment, wiring, fixtures, and decor, save for the thin mattress on the bunk. She felt like a rat in a cage, serving solitary confinement with her only luxury being a sealed porthole.

It aided her sanity staring through the small window at the ocean by day and the stars at night. The monotony was broken by momentary bouts of terror when she was visited by her hosts at random hours. Food and a trip to the head were duly offered, and then she was sealed up once more.

She had just resumed a normal sleep pattern from her nights on the tanker and was out cold when the door banged open and the lights flipped on. Two brutish crewmen entered and pulled her to her feet. One of the men roughly pushed her toward the door while pressing a gun to her back.

Summer was guided up to the bridge, where Nassar sat at a small

chart table. The sea and sky were black outside, but she noticed a fuzzy glow of light on the forward horizon.

Nassar looked up and motioned for her to sit opposite him. He waved away the two escorts. "Coffee?" he asked, sliding a half-full mug in her direction.

She saw from a chronometer that it was two in the morning. She could use the caffeine jolt, but shook her head at the used cup.

"You are with the National Underwater and Marine Agency, correct?"

When she didn't promptly respond, he stood and opened an adjacent bridge wing door. A cool breeze blew across the compartment, causing Summer to shiver. Nassar pointed out to sea. "I can drop you over the side as easy as a falling leaf."

He said it in the calm voice of a man telling the time. But the hardened menace in his eyes told Summer it was no bluff. She shivered again, but not from the cold.

"Yes," she said. "I'm an oceanographer."

"Have you sailed out of New York before?"

"Many times. I recently worked on a beach refurbishment project in Long Island Sound."

He closed the door and retook his seat. He slid a nautical chart across the table that featured the lower Hudson River and approaches to New York City. "I have not been to your country before. Tell me about the waterways surrounding New York."

He grilled her about the marine traffic conditions and various passages around the city. When she had answered all of his questions, she asked one of her own.

"What do you intend to do with the radioactive wastes you took aboard?"

Nassar looked at her and smiled. She had no idea her brother was in a Paris jail on suspicion of terrorism. Her presence was almost too good to be true. If he could leave her remains on the ship, it would

magnify suspicion on both siblings, and Dirk would never get out of jail.

"They are simply a tool," he said, "to help create a new demand for water."

"And how are you going to do that?"

"In part," he said, "by poisoning the waters of the Hudson River for the next thousand years."

58

Villard paced the rooftop patio of his secret flat in the northern hills of Le Havre. He'd purchased it anonymously years before as a private den for romantic trysts with his numerous mistresses. The women were long gone, but the property now served as a useful hideout.

Only his private secretary knew that he was staying in seclusion here. She delivered groceries and wine every few days, leaving the supplies in a stairwell near his apartment. He spent much of his time on the rooftop, managing his remaining resources, plotting and scheming, but most of all worrying.

Villard felt like a hunted man. Much of it was borne of paranoia induced by the painkillers, but an element of it was justified. The French police had contacted his office to request an interview about two of his company's ships. They obviously had nothing or they would have barged through the door with warrants. But the fact they were sniffing around was troubling.

The failure of the Paris attacks weighed heavily on his mind. Nassar assured him security had not been compromised, but he couldn't be certain.

And what of Nassar himself? The trusted commando had not proven infallible. The situation in France was a mess, and everything in Israel remained on hold. Hopes now lay in America. But could Nassar be trusted to rectify things?

On top of that, LeBoeuf was expecting his payment soon and Villard lacked the funds to make good. He'd written a letter to the capo, sent by private courier, detailing the potential bonanzas in Israel, the United States, and planned projects elsewhere around the world. Cash flow was still a problem, so he offered up an ownership percentage in each. The silent response was not encouraging.

There was still the other chance for salvation, in the form of the Belgian diamonds. Nassar had reported finding a strong lead in the Bahamas and would be on the trail again soon. Fifty million euros would solve a lot of problems in a hurry.

Gazing at the Channel's distant gray waters, his thoughts were interrupted by the thumping of an approaching helicopter. The sound grew louder as the craft skimmed up the slopes from the waterfront. It was painted orange and white, in the colors of an air ambulance. Or was it?

Villard's heart began to pound as it tracked toward his apartment. He scrambled to hide and ducked behind a large potted plant. The thumping filled his ears as the helicopter flew overhead, continuing on its route to the Le Havre Medical Center.

Villard stayed on the ground, clutching the planter as sweat trickled down his brow. He stared at the empty sky with eyes ablaze and hands shaking. Then the anger returned.

He stood and silently cursed his foolishness, then swore at those around him. He was not ready to go down without a fight. There were still options. But they all came down to one thing:

Could Nassar be trusted?

59

Three thousand miles away, Nassar stared with frustration at the twinkling lights on Long Island. Dawn was approaching and soon the shore lights would be extinguished, along with his opportunity to sail past New York City in the dark.

Dressed in black for a night ops, he had paced the bridge like an alley cat for hours while the cruise ship drifted idly in Long Island Sound. Waiting for a suitable decoy boat to pass had strained his patience, but finally his helmsman called with a prospect.

"Vessel approaching from the east at five knots. AIS indicates she is a towboat by the name of *Naugatuck*."

Nassar eyed the vessel on the radarscope, then stepped to a computer terminal. An enlarged digital map of the area displayed tracking lines for all nearby vessels. He placed a cursor on the approaching vessel and clicked on its profile. An image of a squat red towboat appeared. Judging by its low speed, it was likely pushing a barge—exactly what he was looking for.

He grabbed binoculars, stepped onto the bridge wing, and turned toward a faint light astern. He focused on the tug's running lights,

along with a bright spotlight angled off its bow. Even from this dis-tance, he could see the shadow of a large black barge in front of the towboat.

He turned toward a crewman. "Call Samad. Tell him to bring the canister to the launch deck. We have a target."

A few minutes later, a small inflatable was lowered over the side. Nassar took to the stern while Samad climbed into the bow. He wore thick, lead-lined gloves and cradled a silver canister.

Nassar twisted the throttle and sent the inflatable scooting away from the *Hydros*. "Stay low," he said, "to avoid a radar signal."

Both men crouched in their seats as Nassar guided the boat to a point far ahead of the tug. He cut the motor after positioning them in the direct path of the barge. If they weren't detected by the tow-boat's radar, they would quickly fall under the barge's acoustic shadow. When the vessel made no deviation in course, Nassar knew they had successfully concealed themselves.

The commando leader waited until the barge bore down on them, then hit the throttle and accelerated ahead. He gradually slowed and moved to the side, allowing the black hulk to draw alongside.

On the bow seat, Samad attached a small lump of Formex P1 plastic explosive to the canister with a detonator and timer. The charge was large enough to destroy the canister and disperse its con-tents, but small enough that the blast would go undetected in the interior of the barge. He wrapped the device in black tape, then acti-vated the timer. At a break in the waves, he rose to his feet and tossed the device up and into the barge's open cargo bay.

Nassar gunned the throttle. The inflatable sped ahead of the barge, then slowed and peeled off to the side, allowing the tug and barge to pass by. The small boat returned to the *Hydros* and Nassar made his way to the bridge, checking his watch as he entered. "How far are they from the river entry?"

"Just under four miles," the helmsman said. "Another forty minutes at their current speed."

"Get us underway and take us close. I want you scraping the paint off their sides when we reach the first bridge." He glanced to the west, where the spires of New York City rose unseen in the distance. "Our newfound escort is about to lead us into the heart of the city."

60

For Eric Watson, the last hour of the graveyard shift was always the hardest. The sun had risen after a long night, and Eric's urge to go home, climb into bed, and fall asleep was at its greatest. The Port Authority security tech took a gulp of coffee from a cold mug and punched a playlist on his phone, initiating a Pink Floyd album to play softly through his earphones. It was a nightly ritual, the recording timed to end with his shift.

The Brooklyn-born technician was one of a dozen men seated among the computer monitors and wall-sized video displays in the Emergency Operations Center. They were part of the New York–New Jersey Port Authority's Incident Command Center, which monitored the safety of the city's transportation hubs and infrastructure. Housed at the Port Authority Tech Center in Jersey City, the unit's creation had been a direct result of the events of 9/11.

Watson was a bridge man, responsible for monitoring a dozen of New York City's bridges for accidents, criminal mischief, and traffic backups. A pair of computer terminals gave him video feeds from a

dozen spans, along with a data table of ever-changing background air readings.

Watson was taking a moment to update his shift log when a box on the data screen began to flash red. He shoved the logbook aside as he absorbed the alert.

"Throgs Neck," he muttered. His heart began to pound faster. There had been an alert issued last evening, and the suspected target may have come his way.

He turned to the other monitor and retrieved two video feeds from the Throgs Neck Bridge east of the city. A surface shot showed just a handful of early-morning commuters speeding across the bridge that connected the Bronx to Queens. All passenger cars, he noted, and no visible debris on the roadway.

He switched to a waterway view from beneath the bridge, the camera mounted next to an air-monitoring device. In the ruddy morning light, a large tug-driven barge passed under, its open cargo hold filled with oil drums. He zoomed in the camera lens, making out the name of the towboat as it passed, *Naugatuck*. A few seconds later, a small passenger ship entered the picture, following close beside the towboat.

Watson transferred the feeds to the large video screen at the front of the room, then barked through his headset to the operations supervisor. "Captain, we've got elevated cesium and strontium readings on the Throgs Neck. Compound levels associated with a tow barge that just passed. Towboat name is *Naugatuck*."

"Confirmed. Readings acknowledged exceeding thresholds. Stand by."

Watson waited a few moments until the police captain's voice rang in his ear. "I've called it in to maritime. Please keep a close eye on all readings. Nice work, Watson."

"Thank you, sir." The tech resumed his monitoring with a

quickened pulse and a pride-induced smile. A second later, the captain's voice blared again in his headset.

"One more thing, Watson."

"Yes, sir?"

"No more Pink Floyd while on duty, please."

61

A turquoise NUMA helicopter was fueled and waiting at the general aviation terminal when Pitt and Giordino landed at JFK Airport on an early-morning flight from Bermuda. They ditched their bags in the hangar and Pitt made a quick call to Gunn in D.C. Rudi had already notified the head of Homeland Security and a heightened security alert had been issued for all major East Coast ports and water treatment facilities.

"New York's Port Authority has expressed confidence," Gunn said, "in their ability to detect any ship approaching the city with radioactive materials aboard. They have sensors at the port's approach, and all entering ships will be scanned. They've also got some sniffer helicopters in the air covering the approach to Manhattan."

"But could an approaching ship conceal the radiation?" Pitt asked.

"They can try, but unless it's hidden in the bottom of a lead submarine, chances are good it will be discovered. The Port's detecting equipment is very sensitive."

"I'd feel better if we knew what we were looking for."

"Hiram's been working with Homeland Security to identify all inbound vessels from Northern Europe that may have had the oppor-

tunity to rendezvous with the *Mont Blanc* at sea. He thinks they have a good handle on that end. He's also been searching for vessels associated with Aquarius International and Lavera Exploration."

"We know they hit water treatment plants in France and Israel. We have to assume they have a similar objective here. Where are New York's main facilities?"

"Most of the city's water is collected in reservoirs in upstate New York and transported via three main aqueducts. The water starts out quite pure, so there are just two main facilities that treat the water along the way.

"Twenty miles north of the city is the Catskill-Delaware Water Ultraviolet Disinfection Facility," Gunn said. "It treats all of the water coming into the city, over two billion gallons a day, I'm told.

"There's another facility in the Bronx, the underground Croton Water Filtration Plant, which treats about a third of the city's water coming from the Croton Reservoir. It's located beneath the Mosholu Golf Course, so is a little more difficult to access. Homeland Security and the NYPD have posted additional security at both facilities."

"Send me their coordinates, and Al and I will take a look from the air. Any other potential targets? What about the aqueducts themselves or the reservoirs?"

"There are several holding reservoirs that could be at risk. If contaminated, those waters could be contained, so perhaps less consequential. I'll send you their coordinates. As for the aqueducts, the Delaware Aqueduct is the most critical, but like the other two waterways, it's deep underground, so it is not really accessible."

"Ask Hiram to simulate some choke points in the system and see what he comes up with," Pitt said. "We'll be in the air shortly."

Giordino had completed a preflight checklist, when Pitt approached the helicopter.

"Any reason to still go up?" Giordino asked.

"Might just be a sightseeing trip, but better to be sure."

"There are worse places to take a scenic ride."

Pitt took the controls of the Bell 505 Jet Ranger and lifted off. After clearing JFK's airspace, he flew southwest across the island-studded Jamaica Bay, rounding past Brooklyn's Brighton Beach and into lower New York Bay.

The skies were overcast, but the winds light and the visibility clear, giving them an eagle-eye view of the main shipping lanes into New York City. Flying low over the stately Verrazzano-Narrows Bridge, Pitt followed the Narrows into New York Harbor. He made a circular pass over the large container ship ports at Bayonne and Newark, then returned east to the Brooklyn port of Red Hook.

Giordino counted a dozen container ships in port or in transit on the New Jersey side of the harbor and an equal number of tankers and freighters on the New York side. "The Port Authority boys are going to be busy checking the traffic today," he said through his headset.

"Rudi claims they're equipped to handle it."

Pitt angled past the Statue of Liberty and flew north up the Hudson River proper, gliding past the towering office buildings of Lower Manhattan. The impressive city skyline would have captured most people's eye, but Pitt kept his attention on the river and the many watercraft on it: barges, ferries, small freighters, powerboats, and even a few sailboats.

They all worried him. What if the radioactive material had been transferred to a high-speed boat? Would the port sensors still react? And along with the radioactive waste, was Summer on one of those boats?

They flew past the George Washington Bridge and the upper reaches of Manhattan Island, then Pitt turned east over the Bronx. They approached the first of Gunn's coordinates, the green expanse of the Mosholu Golf Course. He hovered over a circular fenced area with several putting greens on the surface. Buried beneath was the

Croton Water Filtration Plant, carved four levels deep into the bedrock.

"Looks like tough access," Giordino said, "unless you're swinging a sand wedge."

Pitt eyed the surrounding landscape. "The Hudson is a mile or two away. They would need some additional land transportation to move the materials here."

Giordino pointed out several official vehicles ringing the area. "Security appears pretty stout."

Pitt agreed. "How far to the UV facility?"

Giordino punched the coordinates into the Bell's flight systems, and a guidance map appeared. "Just under fifteen miles."

Pitt flew north, leaving the dense borough of the Bronx to fly over Westchester County. Near the small town of Valhalla, they reached a large industrial building with a circular roof.

Giordino eyed the GPS. "That should be the ultraviolet facility."

Pitt circled above it, observing a high perimeter fence. Like the earlier plant, much of the facility was underground, where all of New York City's freshwater was subjected to an ultraviolet light treatment designed to kill microorganisms. "Looks pretty buttoned up as well."

Giordino tapped him on the arm. Pitt glanced over to see him holding up his cell phone.

"Looks like our warning did the trick," Giordino said. "Hiram just texted. The Port Authority has reported capturing a vessel on the East River containing radioactive material."

62

Pitt covered the twenty miles from Valhalla to the East River in minutes, skimming low over the Bronx as he drew near. The helicopter reached the waterway near the Whitestone Bridge, then pivoted east. Less than two miles away, another large bridge spanned the Throgs Neck Narrows, where the East River met Long Island Sound. Only, the East River wasn't really a river. It was actually a tidal estuary that carried salt water between the Sound and Upper New York Bay through a winding path that curled down the east side of Manhattan.

Pitt noted only a few small pleasure craft between the two bridges, along with a large ship moored near the northern leg of the bridge. He recognized it as the *Empire State VII*, a new training ship operated by the State University of New York's Maritime College, which occupied the adjacent shoreline.

Reaching the Sound, Pitt banked the helicopter around, tracking the river back along its westerly flow. He soon noticed flashing lights on the water beyond the Whitestone Bridge.

As he approached and flew over the bridge, Giordino pointed ahead. "Looks like someone got pulled over at Rikers Island."

The mile-long island sat dead center in the river. High walls and

fences marked the notorious New York City jail complex that occupied most of the island. But Pitt had his eyes on a barge and towboat near a prison dock on the north side, where three NYPD patrol boats swarmed around it like angry hornets.

As they passed over the vessels, Pitt and Giordino observed a large cargo of steel drums in the barge's hold.

"I wonder how many contain radioactive waste," Giordino remarked.

The captain of the tug, a bald man with tattooed arms raised over his head, stood on deck speaking to the police. At least five policemen on the patrol boats had weapons leveled at him. On the south bank of the river near LaGuardia Airport, Pitt could see a SWAT team assembling beside a hazmat response team, waiting for a prison boat to ferry them to the island.

Pitt and Giordino hovered overhead as the tugboat was searched and all three of its crewmen cuffed and taken to shore. Pitt waited for Summer to appear on deck, but no passengers appeared.

"Looks like the boys in blue have things under control," Giordino said.

"Maybe," Pitt said, "but something doesn't seem right."

"The towboat?"

Pitt nodded. "Not of the oceangoing variety. She didn't push that barge here from Bermuda."

"Might have transferred the cargo somewhere in Long Island Sound," Giordino said, "although that tug pilot didn't exactly resemble the folks we met in France."

"Ask Hiram to check all vessels that recently entered the Sound." Pitt glanced at the Bell's fuel gauge, feeling in his limbs the physical tension of flying a helicopter. "We'll go gas up at JFK."

Landing on the tarmac ten minutes later, Pitt asked the ground crew for an immediate refueling. Giordino checked in with Yaeger and hit the speaker button on his phone.

"Did you see the radioactive vessel?" Yaeger asked.

"Affirmative," Giordino said, "but we're a couple of doubting Thomases."

"You may have reason," Yaeger said. "What I've heard from the Port Authority is that the radioactive readings are widely dispersed on the barge, but not at the elevated levels first detected. I made a recent sweep of traffic and I'm seeing only a handful of large vessels entering the Sound in the past forty-eight hours. Several freighters and a car carrier were inbound for Providence and an oil tanker departed New Haven. None track to Bermuda on their AIS. The towboat and barge also originated in Providence.

"Speaking of which," Yaeger said, "I was just reviewing some satellite images to track the barge and noticed a small ship that did not appear on AIS."

"Where is she now?" Pitt asked.

"I don't know. She appeared in an image with the barge as it was entering the East River. Hold on."

The sound of Yaeger tapping a keyboard could be heard over the phone. "I ran the photo through an identity search and got a possible hit with a vessel based out of Alexandria, Egypt. The photo's coming your way now."

"That's a long way from home," Pitt said. "A freighter?"

"No," Yaeger said. "A Greek cruise ship."

63

Below the bridge of the *Hydros*, Summer stirred in her bunk. The rays of the morning sun gleaming through the bulkhead porthole cast an orange hue in the cabin. She sensed movement outside the window and leaned up, squinting toward the round glass. There was a towering concrete structure that appeared to be passing by as the ship glided forward. Summer blinked twice before recognizing it as the entrance to Yankee Stadium.

The sight made her wince. While she knew that Nassar intended to sail to New York, actually seeing the city brought home the danger. She was contemplating the meaning of their location north of Manhattan, when two commandos entered her cabin.

"Upstairs," one of them said, pointing at the ceiling.

Summer was escorted to the bridge, where Nassar stood near the helm.

"I thought you'd like to see your home." He gave a crooked smile. "It's quite an impressive city."

The ship sailed through a narrow waterway peppered with bridges and lined with industrial buildings. It was the Harlem River, she realized. Her view was disrupted when one of the commandos grabbed

her arm and jerked her to the rear of the bridge. He clasped a steel handcuff around her wrist and locked the other end to a stout brass handrail mounted to the rear bulkhead.

She watched as the ship passed under the Henry Hudson Bridge and soon entered the river of the same name. Surprisingly, the vessel turned upriver, sailing away from central Manhattan.

When the ship passed under the George Washington Bridge and the waterway traffic began to diminish, Nassar ordered an increase in speed.

The full team of commandos appeared, wearing loose coveralls over military fatigues. They moved about the ship in a flurry of activity. Automatic rifles were retrieved from a locked cabinet and extra magazines distributed. Two crewmen opened a deck hatch near the bow and removed crates of the gray-packaged explosives she had seen aboard the *Mont Blanc*. The radioactive waste, she knew, was stored somewhere at the back of the ship.

A feeling of dread came over her. She instinctively tugged at her handcuff, realizing Nassar's planned acts of destruction were about to unfold. And she would have a front row seat to it all.

64

Pitt flew the Jet Ranger west from JFK, crossing Brooklyn until reaching the tall spires of the borough's famous bridge. He backtracked up the East River from its confluence with Upper New York Bay, searching for the Greek cruise ship. He had been assured that the area around Lower Manhattan had enough radiation-detecting stations to have sniffed out the vessel if it had ventured that far south.

The lower stretches of the river were already busy with morning barge traffic as he and Giordino surveyed both shorelines. They worked their way up to Hell Gate, a small section of the waterway by Wards Island, where the East and Harlem Rivers converged. The turbulent waters at the spot had spawned shipwrecks back to the time of the first Dutch settlers. A short distance beyond, Rikers Island loomed on the horizon.

Giordino eyed the vacant waters ahead. "Our cruise ship theory may be a bum steer."

"Maybe it never left Long Island Sound."

Giordino felt his phone vibrate and retrieved a message. "Both

wrong. Hiram says the video cameras on the Throgs Neck show it passing under the bridge alongside our hot barge."

"A radiation decoy." Pitt slowed the helicopter to a hover. He eyed the dark waters of the East River beneath them, gazing down its winding path toward Manhattan. If they hadn't passed over the *Hydros* and it hadn't reversed course, there was only one other way the ship could have gone.

"Tell Hiram to check the Harlem River." He twisted the throttle on the collective and accelerated the helicopter forward.

They returned to Hell Gate and turned northwest, following the path of the Harlem River. Like the East River, the Harlem was actually a tidal strait that had been heavily rerouted by New York City engineers over the decades. The waterway that engendered Manhattan an island was crossed by no less than fourteen bridges feeding into the city from the Bronx.

Pitt proceeded up the river slowly, pausing at each bridge in search of the cruise ship.

Traffic was light on the narrow river, but the presence of a small freighter heading toward the East River told Pitt the water was more than deep enough for the Greek vessel. He followed the river for six miles until it turned sharply west over the remnants of the Harlem River Ship Canal, an expansion excavated in the 1880s to boost commercial shipping.

Yankee Stadium rose from the clustered north bank as Giordino received another text from Yaeger. "We're on the right track," he said. "There are no radiation sensors in this part of town, but a video camera on the Hudson Bridge caught them passing through about an hour ago."

Pitt juiced the throttle as the gracefully arched bridge appeared in front of them. As the helicopter passed over the structure, the mile-wide expanse of the Hudson River filled the cockpit window.

Pitt flew across the river and began to bank south, when Giordino

tapped him on the arm. "They went north," he said. "Caught on camera under the George Washington Bridge."

Pitt changed headings. He passed the GW Bridge, then flew a lazy zigzag course upriver to view both shorelines. He and Giordino observed just a single barge and a handful of pleasure craft before reaching the Tappan Zee Bridge at Tarrytown.

"We're well past the Croton plant and right off the UV facility at Valhalla," Giordino said. There was no sign of the cruise ship.

"They must be targeting one of the reservoirs."

Giordino pulled up the information Yaeger had sent earlier. "There's a large reservoir called Kensico above Valhalla, but we're already in the ballpark. The other reservoirs appear to be farther north."

"We'll keep going then."

Pitt followed the river as the urban development fell away and the lush landscape of the Hudson Valley took hold. They cautiously surveyed the waters around the Indian Point nuclear plant near Peekskill, then continued north. Nine miles on, they whizzed past the U.S. Military Academy at West Point perched on a western shoreline bluff, then flew over a large island called Constitution.

A short distance beyond, the river took a dogleg to the right. When they reached the bend, Pitt and Giordino looked ahead. Around the curve, they both saw it. A small, faded-blue cruise ship running fast upriver in the center of the Hudson.

It was the *Hydros*.

65

Pitt approached the cruise ship from high along its port flank. A diminishing wake told him the ship was beginning to slow as its bow angled toward the river's eastern bank. Pitt glanced ahead, noting a highway bridge that crossed over the Hudson less than half a mile away.

"Looks like they have designs for putting in somewhere."

"The town of Newburgh is on the left, not much on this side of the river," Giordino said, eyeing the flight system map. "Hiram's data indicates that the Delaware Aqueduct crosses under the river just north of the bridge. But it's hundreds of feet underground."

They focused on the cruise ship as they drew closer. The hull's dark blue paint was faded and chipped, while the brass rails on its main deck were dull and corroded. Even the porthole windows were frosted from years of exposure to sun and sea. But its classic all-wood design could not be faulted. From a raised prow to an open fantail stern, it carried the elegant lines of a luxury vessel.

A handful of crewmen were initially visible on deck, but they vanished as the helicopter approached. There were no passengers, either

along the deck or around a small, empty hot tub on an upper terrace. But one sight on deck stood out.

"Take a look at that lifeboat," Pitt said.

Along the ship's port deck were two white open-air lifeboats with tonneau covers over their tops. But hanging from an adjacent davit was a fully enclosed, bright orange lifeboat. It looked too large for the davit system, as it hung over the side by its lift lines rather than tucked over the deck like the others.

"Makes for a nice match," Giordino said, "for the one missing from the *Mont Blanc*."

One that Summer might have been aboard, Pitt thought. He guided the helicopter over the ship's stern, allowing him a glimpse along the starboard deck and the upper bridge.

"Look out," Giordino yelled.

Three sights caught Pitt's eye in the moments before he banked the Bell sharply left.

The first was the ship's tender, lowered just beneath the starboard deck in preparation for launching. The second was a stack of wooden crates next to the rail containing packages wrapped in gray. The third was two men crouched beside the bulkhead, each aiming an assault rifle at the chopper.

They fired just as the Bell peeled away, but they were too close to miss. One burst penetrated the helicopter's nose, shattering the avionics console between the two pilots. Another chewed up the floorboard behind them while striking the mechanicals beyond.

Pitt banked hard away from the ship. He aimed toward the western shore, then turned downriver. Beside him, Giordino furiously tried to restore life to the avionics as the consoles turned black. The acrid smell of burnt electronics filled the cabin, followed by a plume of smoke from behind the seats.

Surprisingly, the flight controls remained normal to the touch.

Then a bang erupted near the turbine. The controls began to vibrate and a whine from the rotor filled the cabin. The Jet Ranger still had lift and acceleration, but not for long. As they sped down the western bank of the Hudson, Pitt searched for a landing spot. The shoreline was blanketed with trees, so he kept over the river in case of a sudden power failure.

Constitution Island loomed ahead, and Giordino pointed out an open patch near its center. But as they flew closer, Pitt saw the clearing was a swamp pond. He clung to the western riverbank as smoke and the odor of burnt oil began to fill the cockpit. The controls in his hands turned to lead, and the turbine began to howl and grind. The entire craft began to buck from assorted failures.

Pitt spotted a small dock ahead and a bluff above it lined with buildings. But to the near side was an athletic field of open grass. As the helo shuttered, he aimed toward the clearing and yelled to Giordino.

"Brace for impact."

66

Captain Dario Cruz was marching a squad of West Point cadets to the rifle range when a sputtering sound came from over the Hudson. The Army officer looked across the athletic field and spotted the stricken turquoise helicopter. It trailed a thick plume of black smoke, with flames sprouting from the turbine housing. The thump of the rotor couldn't hide the shriek emanating from the turbine motor in its dying moments.

Cruz watched as the Bell drifted farther over the river, then banked in a sharp turn, diving directly toward the cliff face before him.

"Everybody down!" he shouted at the startled cadets. Cruz led the way in hitting the deck.

A second later, the helicopter was above them, swooping up from the river in a final power dive that gave it just enough lift to clear the bluff. The Bell skimmed a foot or two over the prone cadets, then dropped hard onto the grass a few yards away.

As the helicopter struck, the side doors sprang open, emitting a cloud of smoke, but nobody climbed out. Cruz jumped to his feet and sprinted to the chopper, expecting to help pull out the panicked or injured occupants.

As he ducked under the slowing rotor, he saw a tall man at the controls shutting down power, while a shorter man sprayed a fire extinguisher at the smoldering mechanicals. Both climbed out a few seconds later with a calm composure.

"Sorry for the haircut," Pitt said as he stepped closer. "I didn't realize anyone was in our path."

Cruz shook his head. "That was some flying. I thought you were in the river for sure. I saw a few Black Hawks get hit in Afghanistan, but never saw a recovery like that."

He noticed a seam of bullet holes across the Bell's nose and pointed at the smoking helicopter. "Did you get shot down?"

"Small arms fire," Pitt confirmed. "There's a ship upriver carrying radioactive materials. We think they're a terrorist group planning to strike at the water supply."

"There's one other thing," Giordino said to Pitt. "I couldn't tell you because our comms were out, but I saw a woman on the bridge. She had long red hair."

"Summer?"

"Can't swear to it, but I think so."

A wave of relief fell over Pitt, followed by a surge of anger. He brushed the sentiments aside to focus on a course of action and turned to Cruz. "Can you help us stop them?"

Cruz looked at the blackened NUMA lettering on the side of the helicopter, then at the two impervious pilots. He didn't know who they were, but he could tell they were not bluffing.

He nodded briskly. "Hell, yeah."

67

From her handcuffed position at the back of the bridge, Summer had caught only a glimpse of the helicopter. Still, she couldn't believe her eyes. The unique turquoise color meant it belonged to NUMA. Somebody had figured out where she was. But her joy turned to horror when Nassar's commandos opened fire on the craft.

"It is not the police," she yelled.

She strained to see the helicopter as it took fire and banked away, trailing a plume of smoke. She saw a flash of the copilot. While his face was concealed by aviator glasses, the dark curly hair looked familiar. Could it be Al Giordino?

She tried to track the Bell as it disappeared downriver, a flicker of hope in her chest. The feeling vanished when Nassar glared at her from across the bridge.

The commando leader was angry. The greatest risk to the mission had been traversing the New York City waterways, and he had accomplished that without detection. Or so he thought.

He picked up binoculars and scanned the area. There was no traffic in pursuit on the river and no threatening aircraft in the skies.

Only a fading wisp of smoke from the helicopter, which had surely crashed.

For Nassar, nothing had changed but the timetable. He had planned to moor the *Hydros* along the bank and wait for darkness before launching the strike, but there was no time for that now. The operation would commence immediately. He made a quick call to Brigitte on the ship's satellite phone, then ordered Samad to the bridge.

The adjutant apologized. "We should have splashed the chopper, but it veered away quickly. If I'd had an RPG, I would have taken it down."

"No matter now, but we will proceed at once. Set the keel and cargo charges while I see about loading the explosives." He motioned out the forward window. "The target is just beyond that bridge. I want to disembark in ten minutes."

"I'll double the time on the detonators," Samad said, then both men rushed out the wing door. Summer could see glimpses of Nassar on the deck, ordering the placement of small crates into the ship's launch.

Nassar reappeared on the bridge momentarily and ordered the helmsman to stop the ship. He reached into a cabinet and withdrew a folded flag with brass grommets.

"For *jihad*," he said sarcastically to Summer and slipped out the door. He carried the flag to the fantail and raised it on a staff angled over the transom. The breeze unfurled it, revealing a black standard with white Arabic script citing an Islamic oath called the Shahada. It was often used as a jihadist flag by the likes of ISIS and al-Qaeda. While the ship would soon be on the bottom of the river, a passing motorist would surely notice the flag after the explosives were ignited.

He returned to the bridge, where Samad waited anxiously. "Six

independent keel charges are primed, plus one in the cargo hold. The team is ready to launch the tender."

Summer followed Nassar's glance out the side window, where five commandos in tan fatigues, armed with AK-47s, stood at the rail.

"Deploy the boat," Nassar said. "Tomas and I will be there shortly."

As Samad hustled out the door, Nassar approached the helmsman. He pointed toward the Newburgh-Beacon Bridge a quarter mile away.

"Can you target one of the center bridge supports? Perhaps we can create some extra damage."

"The electronics are too old for precision, but I can aim close with the autopilot."

The helmsman waited for the ship's tender to be released, then engaged the *Hydros*'s engine. He added just enough throttle to overcome the river current at a walking pace, then set the helm on a bearing for the center bridge support.

As he did so, Nassar pulled a Glock 19 and approached the ship's radio. Using the pistol's butt, he smashed the radio unit with three quick blows, listening as the background static vanished.

He holstered the pistol, then turned and addressed Summer. "Tomas and I will be departing now. The ship is yours."

Summer swore under her breath as Nassar and the helmsman scrambled off the bridge. She could see far enough out the side window to watch the launch circle alongside to collect the two men. The boat then roared away, heading upriver and past the bridge.

Summer didn't wait for the commandos to depart before attacking the brass rail that held her captive. She tugged and twisted at the bolted end, then tried kicking it. When that failed to loosen it, she tried dropping her thigh and rear onto the railing. Repeated efforts did little more than bruise her backside. The rail felt like it was embedded in concrete.

The helm lay only a few feet away, and she tried kicking her long legs at the controls, but came up well short. She cursed aloud now, swearing at the handcuffs, the brass rail, and Nassar. While it briefly made her feel better, it didn't change the situation.

She was trapped on the bridge . . . and was going to go down with the ship.

68

Nassar gave the *Hydros* a final glimpse from the tender, then turned and faced upriver. The Newburgh-Beacon Bridge lay just ahead, and a short distance beyond, his target just off the east bank. Had he taken a second look behind, he might have noticed a powerboat in the distance, sweeping around the riverbend. It would have taken binoculars to notice several armed people clinging to the rail. Army cadets.

Captain Cruz had gulped when Pitt pointed down the bluff at a boat moored below. It was the only vessel tied up at the North Dock, which was little more than a parking lot along the Hudson. The larger South Dock was the real functioning wharf for West Point, where several official Army boats were moored. But it was nearly a mile away.

Cruz felt the urgency from Pitt and Giordino, and his own sense of action prompted consideration of the boat below. But not without pause.

"That's the commandant's personal watercraft," he said, wondering if his career would be sacrificed by borrowing it.

"I'll take the blame," Pitt said.

Before Cruz could respond, Pitt and Giordino took off at a run for the dock. Cruz reacted quickly, ordering his eight-man squad to sprint to the nearby indoor shooting range for weapons, while he followed the two NUMA men down the hill.

The moored boat was a thirty-two-foot Chris-Craft Roamer built in 1962. It was a low roofline cabin cruiser built with a steel hull. Pitt climbed aboard, briefly admiring the restored old boat with its gleaming mahogany deck and trim, and a crisp Army pennant dangling off a stern flagpole. The cruiser had a step-down cabin with galley, table, and V-berth, but its helm was on the open stern deck.

The age of the boat played into Pitt's intentions, as he assumed he could hot-wire the antique ignition switch to start the motors. He didn't have to. Two sets of keys dangled on a hook just inside the cabin door, beside a coffee mug marked with the owner's initials, CC.

As Pitt leaned in to grab the keys, he noticed a photo on the wall. It was a picture of the Academy commandant, a tall bearded man in a Hawaiian shirt, standing at the wheel of the boat with a black dachshund at his feet. He looked faintly familiar, Pitt thought, as he took the keys and inserted each into a matched pair of ignition switches. The twin Chrysler V-8 engines fired with the first twist of the keys and idled with a loping rumble.

"You couldn't find us anything from the current century?" Giordino held the boat to the dock, gripping the untied mooring lines.

"More style than we need, but it'll get us upriver in a hurry."

Pitt turned toward Cruz, who stood at the end of the dock, barking at his cadets to hurry. The five young men and three women streamed onto the dock, each holding a SIG Sauer pistol and a box of ammunition.

He herded the cadets onto the boat, where they squeezed onto the stern. A sergeant in fatigues came running up as Giordino hopped aboard with the freed mooring lines.

"Hey! You can't take that! That's the commandant's boat."

"Yeah, ain't it nice?" Giordino waved at the soldier as Pitt rammed the twin throttles forward and the old boat roared away from the dock.

Cruz turned to one of the female cadets wedged next to him. "Murphy, why did you bring pistols?"

"Rifles were locked in the armory, sir, but the pistols were out for our class. It was the most expedient act. Especially since the range officer was calling at us to halt."

"How did you get away?"

"He was at the far end of the range." She winked. "We didn't hear him."

Cruz knew there would be hell to pay for that as well. *In for a penny*, he thought. "All right," he said. "Load your weapons and stand by."

He made his way to the helm, where Pitt and Giordino stood staring ahead. Pitt guided the boat in a graceful arc to the center of the river, following its course in a gentle bend to the northeast.

"What are we up against?" Cruz asked over the roar of the engines.

"Maybe half a dozen commandos with AK-47s," Pitt said. "Expect them to be well trained."

Cruz grimaced at the challenge for his raw cadets, who had been at the service academy only a few months. "Will we try and board them on the river?"

"No." Giordino tapped the windshield while pointing ahead. "It looks like we won't have to get our feet wet."

As the Chris-Craft cleared the bend, they saw the cruise ship motoring slowly toward the bridge. And to its side, where Giordino had motioned, the ship's launch lay aground on the riverbank.

69

In a small office building near the river, Steven Schauer stood waiting for a copy machine to finish printing some engineering plans, when he heard a series of loud pops outside. It sounded like gunfire, but he dismissed the notion as he collected his copies. Then the office door crashed open and the sound of automatic-weapons fire filled the air. Screams followed.

Schauer's secretary, a stout, middle-aged woman named Martha, appeared in the copy room doorway with her mouth agape. A pair of red splotches appeared on her blouse as she took a step, then staggered toward Schauer. The civil engineer dropped his papers and grabbed her as she collapsed onto him. Catching her off balance, he fell to the floor beneath her.

More gunfire sounded nearby, then he heard heavy boots moving toward the copy room. Entangled with the woman, Schauer had no chance of escape. He felt Martha's blood dampen his shoulder as he positioned himself flat on the floor. He lay still and held his breath as the footfalls moved closer.

With his eyes screwed shut and heart pounding, he could feel the pressure on the floorboards as the gunman stepped into the room.

After the longest silence of Schauer's life, the gunman walked away and departed the office.

Schauer waited another minute, then stood on shaky legs as more gunfire erupted nearby. A side door in the copy room led to a large warehouse, and Schauer crept to the doorway. He eased the door open an inch and peered inside.

Not three feet away lay the bullet-riddled body of the warehouse foreman, a golfing buddy of Schauer's. Near the middle of the building, two men in desert fatigues stood guard with weapons drawn, while another carried in a wooden crate through an open bay door. The commando stacked the crate with several others inside a caged elevator in the center of the warehouse.

The engineer silently closed the door and retreated through the copy room, carefully stepping over the body of his secretary. In the main office he found two other dead coworkers, one slumped over his desk, the other on the floor in a pool of blood. Schauer took a deep breath and stepped to the open entry door.

He froze in the doorway at the sight of a commando guarding the parking lot to the east. Just fifty feet away, the gunman had a clear view of the office entry.

Schauer ducked back inside and considered his options. He feared drawing attention by calling 911, until he was in a less dangerous location. The office and warehouse compound had a security fence around it, and the gunman was covering the single entry road onto the grounds. But the fence didn't encompass the river side. He could escape the complex along the river, then call for help.

Schauer moved to the back wall of the office and eased open a window. He stepped on an overturned trash can for a boost, slithered through the opening, and dropped headfirst onto the ground. He crawled through some underbrush, then rose to his feet. The building gave him cover from the parking lot gunman. He ran toward the river, but had covered only a short distance when he heard approach-

ing voices. He dove into the deep grass as a pair of figures emerged from behind a tree.

Schauer raised his head and saw two more commandos, each toting a wooden crate. As they drew closer, he could hear them speaking French. Their path took them close to Schauer, but with their attention focused on the crates and the building, neither saw him.

Schauer lay still in the grass until the gunmen were well around the building's corner. He started to rise, but heard more gunfire nearby. He waited until it fell silent, then moved toward the river. He avoided the path the commandos had used and bulled through a high thicket.

He could hear the rushing waters of the Hudson as he pushed past a stand of trees, only to stop dead in his tracks. It wasn't the river that caused him to halt, but a pistol aimed at his chest.

70

"D on't move," the gunman ordered.

Schauer froze, then realized it wasn't a man aiming the pistol at him. It was a petite young woman in gym shorts and a black T-shirt with the word *Army* emblazoned in yellow.

He raised his hands and sidestepped into a small clearing by the river. Several other young, armed cadets were spread along the beach, backed by three older men. One of the terrorists lay sprawled dead next to a small boat, three neat bullet holes marking his chest.

Pitt had elected to ignore the weathered cruise ship when they drew near. He had instead aimed the Chris-Craft toward the *Hydros*'s beached tender. From a distance, they had seen several commandos come and go from the boat, but the landing had appeared empty as they approached.

That belief dissolved when a gunman sprang from behind the launch with an AK-47 and opened fire.

"Everybody down," Pitt shouted as bullets slammed into the boat.

As the cadets dove for cover, Cruz called out, "Turn to the left."

A second burst of fire plinked against the steel hull as Pitt kept his speed and turned the wheel hard over. The Army captain grabbed a

pistol from one of the cadets and rolled to the gunwale. As the boat swung left, exposing its starboard rail, Cruz rose and fired three quick shots at the gunman, then dropped back down.

He needn't have bothered ducking, as all three rounds struck the commando in the torso, laying him out.

"Nice shooting, chief," Giordino said.

"Battalion small-arms champ, three years running," Cruz said, then turned and ordered his cadets into defensive firing positions.

Pitt turned the Chris-Craft back toward shore and goosed the throttle, sending the bow onto the riverbank alongside the *Hydros*'s tender. Cruz jumped off first, fanning his cadets around on either flank.

Pitt and Giordino tied off the boat and approached the dead helmsman named Tomas who had fired on them. "Didn't we meet him in Le Havre?" Giordino asked.

"I think so." Pitt removed the commando's AK-47 and handed it to Giordino. They turned to join the others, when Murphy, the young female cadet, barked a challenge to an approaching figure.

A tall burly man emerged from the brush, his arms raised and his eyes wide.

"Who are you?" Cruz stepped closer with his weapon raised.

"My name is Steven Schauer. I'm a hydraulic engineer with the Shaft 6-B Station." He gazed at the cadets in their black Army T-shirts. "Are you with them?" He tilted his head inland.

"No," Pitt said, "we're here to stop them."

Schauer lowered his arms and sighed. "They've killed everyone. Just stormed in and shot everyone down like dogs. I was lucky to get away."

"Did you see a tall woman with them?" Pitt asked.

"No. They were all men, dressed in fatigues and carrying rifles. Like that one." He pointed toward Tomas.

"Tell us about the facility here."

"It's the Shaft 6-B Station." He saw the blank look on everyone's face. "Part of the Rondout Bypass. It's a section of the Delaware Aqueduct that carries fresh water to New York City from the Catskills. It all runs through a new billion-dollar tunnel under the Hudson River. Right here, beneath our feet."

"What is this Shaft 6-B?" Giordino asked.

"Just that, a vertical shaft. There's one here and another on the other side of the river. They were dug as end points for constructing the tunnel between them. Most of the backfill was pulled out of the other shaft, 5-B. It's a nine-hundred-foot drop on the Newburgh side and seven hundred feet to the bottom of our shaft."

"Why would some terrorists care about the shaft?" Cruz asked.

"To contaminate the water supply," Giordino said. "They have radioactive waste they must intend to dump here."

"I don't think so." Schauer shook his head. "I saw them loading small wooden crates onto the elevator. Lots of them. It looked like CL-20, some of the same stuff used by our drilling engineers during the excavation."

"CL-20?" Cruz asked.

"A high explosive that's twenty-five percent more powerful than TNT."

"What will happen," Pitt asked, "if they set it off in the shaft?"

Schauer's face went pale. "If they detonate it at the base, they have enough to set off a shock wave that will pulverize the shaft and cause it to cave in on itself. If so, there will be a massive collapse into the aqueduct, entirely damming the flow of fresh water . . . and effectively turning New York City's water supply to dust."

71

In 1842, freshwater runoff from a reservoir north of Manhattan began to trickle down a brick aqueduct into New York City. Decades of cholera, yellow fever, and unrelenting stench in the city was washed away with the arrival of reliable clean water. Over 180 years later, the New York City water supply system had grown into an engineering feat comparable to the building of the Panama Canal. Nineteen reservoirs and hundreds of miles of tunnels and aqueducts provided gravity-fed water to the city from 125 miles away. Over a billion gallons a day flowed to the city's nine million residents, carried from the pristine lakes in the upstate region.

Nassar cared little about the system's history as he stood in the Shaft 6-B warehouse. All he knew was that seven hundred feet beneath his feet flowed an enormous surge of fresh water. As he hurried his team along, he felt the rush of cool air rising from the depths of the shaft. Two of his men entered the building, each carrying crates of explosives that they stacked in a caged elevator above the shaft.

Nassar quickly tallied twelve of the crates. Each contained ten one-kilogram blocks of CL-20, enough to crumble two thousand tons of solid rock. Detonated inside the confines of the deep, vertical shaft,

the damage would be exponentially greater, creating a rockfall hundreds of feet deep.

"That's the last of it," one of the men said.

"Where is Tomas?" Nassar asked.

"Still at the landing. He wanted to conceal the tender."

As he spoke, the sound of gunfire echoed from the river. Nassar cocked an ear, then turned to Samad. The adjutant stood at a workbench across the bay unpacking a wrapped bundle from a small leather case.

"Samad," Nassar yelled. "What is your status?"

"I am just setting the detonators now."

"Make it fast," Nassar said. "It is time to finish the job."

72

The cadets moved quickly up the slope to the Shaft 6-B compound. Cruz split his forces in two to attack in a pincer movement. Outgunned and with little cover, their best tactic would be speed and surprise. Pitt, Giordino, and Schauer moved separately in a wider flank to the north, using the hydraulic engineer's knowledge of the site.

Drawing with a stick in the dirt, Schauer had sketched a map of the office and adjoining warehouse, which housed the portal to the vertical shaft. The three men were just approaching the northern entrance to the warehouse when gunfire erupted on the other side.

Cruz had sent four cadets through the office and led the remaining four toward the warehouse's east-facing open bay. As they rushed around the office building's corner, the Army captain locked eyes with the guard in the parking lot.

The commando acted first, spraying a burst from the rifle held at his waist. Cruz ignored the fire, leveled his SIG Sauer at the gunman, and dropped him with two shots to the chest. He felt a sting in his leg as he squeezed off a third shot and saw a dark spot on his thigh. His leg buckled and he dropped to the opposite knee.

"Sir," exclaimed a wide-eyed cadet named Blake, "you've been hit."

"Keep moving," Cruz ordered through gritted teeth. "Blake, lead the others into the warehouse. Shoot anything that moves."

"Yes, sir." Blake bit his lip and moved past Cruz. Scrambling through the parking lot with the other three cadets on his heels, he ran for the open bay door. A pair of muzzle flashes sparked from the dark interior, and Blake dove for the ground and rolled against a parked minivan as gunfire stitched the pavement beside him.

Blake fired two shots into the warehouse, then turned to the cadets behind him. One was sprawled behind him clutching a blood-stained shoulder, while the other two, both female, had taken cover behind a dark SUV.

"You okay?" he asked the injured cadet.

The blond-haired man grunted in the affirmative.

Blake turned to the two women. "Can you make it to that red truck?" He pointed across the lot. "Let's see if we can get them in a cross fire."

"We'll do it." The two cadets moved out, retreating across the lot, then looping around toward the truck.

Blake took a prone position by the minivan's front wheel and leveled his pistol at the open bay door, waiting for a target.

Inside the warehouse, Nassar ordered his commandos to cover the entrance.

"Who is firing at us?" Samad asked as he hunkered behind a table with a detonator in his hand.

"I don't know," Nassar said, "but they look like kids. Are you ready to set the charges?"

"One more minute."

Nassar waited anxiously by the caged elevator. The car was on a raised platform, suspended over the circular shaft by an overhead beam and cable. The crates filled with CL-20 explosives were stacked in the center.

At the far end of the warehouse, a side door eased open and Pitt, Giordino, and Schauer slipped inside. Dozens of storage crates blocked their path. They stopped in front of a low pallet and surveyed the scene.

"Those are the explosives." Schauer pointed to the distant elevator car containing a stack of small boxes. "They're preparing to blow the shaft."

Pitt studied the interior, but before he could formulate a plan, a door banged open on the far side. Two of Cruz's cadets, beefy young men who played on the Academy football team, burst through the door with pistols blazing.

They managed to take down one of the commandos by the bay door before a fury of return fire cut them down. Two more cadets had followed them to provide covering fire, but were forced to duck behind a tool bin. Outside, the other cadets opened fire, adding to the chaos.

Nassar had three commandos left, along with Samad, and they quickly counterattacked. One threw a stun grenade at the cadets outside the building, while the other two concentrated fire on the cadets by the tool bin.

"Detonators?" Nassar yelled.

Samad ran to his position with a satchel over his shoulder. "Ready to go."

"Take it to the bottom and set the charges there." Nassar hoped a stray bullet wouldn't ignite the explosives first.

Samad scrambled onto the elevator car as Nassar stepped to a raised control panel and punched the down button. The car lurched as the cable winch turned and the elevator began to descend into the shaft. Nassar bent low and sprinted toward one of his commandos crouched behind a shield of barrels.

Pitt, Giordino, and Schauer had threaded their way through the maze of crates and just reached an open view of the warehouse as the

elevator began to descend. Across the floor, the shooting had ceased, as both cadets by the tool bin had run out of ammunition.

Two of the commandos rose and began moving toward the cadets' position. One had his rifle raised for covering fire, while the other prepared to toss a grenade.

Giordino saw the cadets' predicament as Pitt rose behind him.

"Cover me if you can." Pitt sprinted across the concrete floor.

Giordino scurried after him, angling to the side so he would have a clear avenue of fire. The commandos were facing the other way and didn't detect their approach until they were near the elevator shaft. The commando with the raised rifle turned first and fired a short burst, his aim just wide.

Giordino fired back on the run as he peeled to the side and found cover behind a wheeled cart. Pitt had no such cover, but he wasn't looking for any. He launched himself at the elevator platform, diving headfirst across its surface. His speed carried him, and he slid exactly where he wanted to go.

Over the lip of the shaft and into the darkness below.

73

As Pitt disappeared into the shaft, Giordino opened fire on the two commandos pursuing the cadets. The fire selector was set on full auto, and he squeezed off a pair of extended bursts. His first salvo dropped the gunman firing at him, while the second struck the man about to hurl the grenade. The commando slumped to the ground before completing the throw, and the activated grenade rolled from his hand.

Crouched near the bay door, Nassar had raised a pistol to fire at Giordino, when the grenade detonated. The boom reverberated through the building, accompanied by a billowing cloud of smoke. Giordino used the disruption to reposition himself behind a heavy workbench that offered better cover. Closer to the explosion, Nassar coughed away a mouthful of dust, then rose to his feet in the brown gloom.

"Exfiltrate," he yelled to the gunman beside him, then moved toward the bay door. Daylight beckoned through the haze, and he sprinted out of the building with his gun pointed in front of him. A few yards outside the entrance, he broke through the dust cloud. Directly ahead, the cadet by the minivan was rubbing the smoke from his eyes, while his partner sat behind him clutching his bloodied shoulder.

Nassar fired wildly at them as he ran by, angling toward the compound's entrance. As he reached the gate, he hesitated and looked back into the warehouse.

The other commando had remained inside, intending to leave no witnesses. The gunman watched as the two cadets by the tool bin started crawling across the floor, making a bid for escape to the copy room. He would deal with them in a minute. His first priority was imposing revenge on Giordino, who had killed his comrades.

Just a few yards away, Giordino crouched behind the workbench, the AK-47 wedged against his shoulder. The dust was still settling when he found the commando in the weapon's semicircular gunsight and squeezed the trigger.

A dry click was all he heard. The commando heard the empty chamber and smiled as he located Giordino. He raised his weapon and took a step closer in order to see Giordino's face before he killed him. As he tightened his grip on the trigger, a single gunshot rang through the warehouse.

Giordino looked up at his assailant. The commando's left eye vanished in a blood-filled cavity an instant before he pancaked onto the floor.

Across by the copy room door, Captain Cruz stood leaning against the wall, his SIG Sauer at arm's length. His left pant leg was soaked red, and the loss of blood was apparent in his pale skin.

"Thanks, padre," Giordino called out. "If the Army doesn't give you a medal for that shot, then I will."

Cruz nodded. "Did we get them all?"

"Most of them." Giordino turned to the shaft portal. "You better get your kids out of here. This place could still blow."

He glanced to the elevator support and saw the lift cable still unspooling. Somewhere in the black pit below, he hoped Pitt was still alive.

74

Pitt felt like he was flying into a black hole. The light vanished as he plunged spread-eagled into the shaft. Cool air rushed against his body as he plummeted.

He had stretched for the elevator cable when he went over the side, but the reach was farther than he expected. The fingers of his right hand had just slid around the cable as gravity took hold. He found enough tension to pull his body forward and wrap both hands around it.

His palms burned as the greased cable slipped through his hands, but he was able to slow his fall. His legs dropped beneath him and he wrapped them around the cable, using his feet to slow his descent. His journey was a short one.

Within seconds, his feet collided with the block mechanism that secured the cable to the elevator's top frame. As the elevator passed a dim shaft light, he glanced below. He saw the elevator car's open roof, which allowed him to drop freely into the cage. Standing to one side was Samad, who looked up at Pitt's sudden appearance and reached for his holstered sidearm.

Pitt let go of the cable, swinging toward the commando as the elevator descended again into darkness.

His drop fell short. Pitt missed Samad, landing on the explosives stacked three feet high in the center of the cage. He used the stack as a springboard to lunge forward as Samad raised his pistol.

Pitt dove ahead with his elbows splayed. He struck the commando's forearm and knocked the muzzle aside as Samad pulled the trigger. Several shots rang out, ricocheting off the shaft's smooth stone walls.

Engaging his assailant in a clinch, Pitt dropped his left arm in a tomahawk chop, striking Samad hard on the wrist. The pistol dropped from his hand and clanged onto the floor. As they grappled, one of them accidentally kicked the weapon and it sailed over the side.

At losing the gun, Samad brought a hard counterpunch with his left fist, striking Pitt on the side of the head. The men separated and began exchanging blows. In the intermittent darkness, they punched and blocked with random effect.

Trained in kick fighting, Samad lost much of his advantage in the confined space. But his quicker reflexes delivered more accurate strikes. Pitt felt the punishment from the commando's blows, as Samad outweighed him by twenty-five pounds and was years younger.

Pitt countered by using the intermittent darkness to his advantage. He juked and slid around the cage, moving quick on his feet.

Connecting with a hard cross to the commando's cheek, Pitt took a counterpunch to his shoulder that knocked him backward. He slammed into the cage wall, and the handle to the entry door dug into his back. He reached around, turned the lever, then slid the door open as he stepped to his right.

The elevator continued to descend, reaching just past the midway point at the four-hundred-foot mark. A deep rumble echoed from below where the water rushed through the aqueduct. Pitt ducked

down as the next light approached, and grabbed a crate of explosives from the stack in front of him. When Samad's silhouette appeared, Pitt tossed the box at the commando, driving him to the left.

Samad knocked the box aside as the shaft again fell black, not realizing Pitt was already on the move. Pitt followed the cage wall to his right, then put his shoulder down and rushed toward Samad.

The commando heard Pitt's movements and pivoted to the side, but he reacted a second too late. Pitt barreled into Samad's side with the force of a charging bull. He caught the commando slightly off balance, and both men were pushed to the far side of the elevator, toward the open door.

Pitt kept driving his legs as Samad fell back against the doorframe, unable to get his feet under him. The commando took a backward step and felt only air.

Pitt thrust forward, shoving the man completely out the door. Samad grasped the doorframe with one hand and a fistful of Pitt's shirt with the other. But their combined momentum was too great.

The commando lost hold of the cage and sailed out the opening, clutching only Pitt. He felt a brief moment of weightlessness, and then the cold terror of plunging into the black void.

75

At the top of the portal, Giordino saw that the elevator cable spool was still unwinding. With an uneasy feeling, he knew the cage must be approaching the bottom. Giordino took a step toward the platform, when a deep boom erupted from far down the shaft. He froze in his tracks as the sound rattled the walls of the warehouse.

"Let's get out of here," Schauer shouted. "The building could collapse."

Giordino waited as a cloud of white smoke curled out of the opening. While the explosion was deafening, it wasn't followed by the collapse of the shaft. At least not yet.

Then Giordino noticed something odd. The cable was still spooling out, its tension indicating the weight of the cage was still attached. He rushed to the control panel, hit a red stop button, then punched a green button above it marked *Up*.

The cable reversed course, and Giordino peered over the side, straining through the smoke and darkness to spy the elevator. But he saw only the steel cable vanishing into a pool of ink.

Schauer again urged him to leave, but he remained planted,

watching the cable slowly rise. After several agonizing minutes he detected a rattling from the cage and the top of the elevator car finally came into view. Giordino looked inside and shook his head.

Seated on the crates of explosives with a bored expression, Pitt looked like a man waiting for a bus. His shirt was ripped across the chest and he was caked in a fine layer of white dust, but a faint grin crossed his lips as he spotted Giordino.

"Thanks for the lift." Pitt rose from the crates and exited the cage. "I was beginning to think it would be faster to climb up."

"We heard an explosion," Schauer said. "It wasn't the CL-20?"

"No." Pitt gave a wry smile. "It was my lift buddy. He had a satchel strapped around his neck that must have contained the detonators. I'm not sure why they were activated, but maybe the timer got triggered when I jumped into the cage . . . or he touched bottom."

"It sounded massive from up here," Schauer said. "I thought it was the main stockpile of explosives."

"Just the echo from the shaft."

"What happened to your elevator boy?" Giordino asked.

"He got careless and fell out an open door. Tried to take me with him, but I managed a hold on the doorframe." He glanced down at the shredded fabric hanging over his chest. "Looks like he owes me a new shirt."

Pitt gave a nod to Cruz, who hobbled over to join them.

"Your cadets proved themselves proud," Pitt said.

"Lost two, I'm afraid."

Pitt looked at the ground and grimaced. "I should have never asked for your help."

"You just prevented a monumental disaster. You would have had a tough time without us." Cruz turned to Giordino. "Did we get all of the terrorists?"

"All but the boss man," Giordino said. "He slipped outside after the second grenade went off."

A hail of sirens sounded, drawing closer by the second.

"I called 911," Schauer said. "Told them to send a SWAT team, ambulances, and a medevac."

"We'll need 'em," Cruz said. "A couple of the other kids got nicked pretty good."

"You might be up for the first ride," Giordino said, eyeing his bloody leg.

The Army captain shook his head. "Not today."

Pitt began moving toward the open door, then turned and called to Schauer. "Can you help with the wounded on your own?"

"Sure. What about the fugitive?"

"He shouldn't get far. But that's a job for the police. I need to get back to the river."

"Summer," Giordino said.

Pitt nodded, and the two men bolted out of the building.

76

Nassar had rushed a hundred yards down the road, when the first police car approached with its siren blaring. He ducked behind a bush until it sped by, then quickened his pace. At a residential cross street he spotted a white utility van parked at the curb. He approached the passenger door and climbed inside.

Claude Bouchet sat behind the wheel. The industrial spy's hair was dusted gray and he wore thick-framed glasses, giving him an elderly appearance. He turned and regarded Nassar with mild curiosity. "You seem to have attracted some attention," he said in French.

"Get me to the border," Nassar said, "as you've been paid to do."

"What about the others?"

Nassar glanced out the side window and shook his head. "There are no others. Now move."

Pitt and Giordino sprinted to the waterfront and cast off in the Chris-Craft. Pitt took the helm and fanned the throttles forward the instant the engines caught. The vintage V-8s snarled beneath the deck, and the graceful cruiser charged across the river.

Pitt looked upstream and found the waterway empty. Glancing astern, he spotted the Greek cruise ship to the south, bearing down on the Newburgh-Beacon Bridge at a slow speed.

Pitt spun the helm hard over. Aided by the current, the Chris-Craft accelerated downstream at more than thirty knots.

Giordino stood beside Pitt with the AK-47, reloading it with a fresh magazine taken from one of the dead commandos. "Why are they waiting down there?" he asked as he slung the weapon over his shoulder.

"Not sure," Pitt said, "but they look awfully close to kissing a bridge span."

Giordino picked up a pair of binoculars dangling from a hook and studied the vessel. "I don't see anyone on deck. It does look like she's bearing down on the center piling." He turned the glasses toward the bridge. "Limited viewing angle, but I can't make out anyone at the helm."

Pitt soon saw for himself. As their boat raced near the *Hydros*, he caught a clear glimpse of the abandoned helm. But there was someone on the back of the bridge. A tall, familiar figure waved from the rear bulkhead.

Pitt cut the throttle and wheeled the Chris-Craft along the starboard flank while Giordino covered the deck with his weapon. When no defenders appeared, Giordino passed the gun to Pitt.

"Just get her back safely," Giordino said and took the helm.

Pitt stepped to the rail as Giordino brought the cruiser alongside, tapping the cruise ship's hull. Pitt reached up and pulled himself aboard, taking a second to eye the highway bridge piling barely thirty feet off the bow. The rumble of passenger cars speeding across the motorway drowned the gurgle of the Chris-Craft's engines as Giordino pulled away.

Pitt sprinted to a forward companionway. Taking the steps two at

a time, he reached the upper landing and burst into the *Hydros*'s wheelhouse. He locked eyes on Summer with a smile, but a mix of relief and fear glimmered back at him.

"The ship is set with explosives," she said as he rushed past her to the helm.

He felt a bump through the deck as the ship nudged against the bridge piling. Pitt disengaged the autopilot, turned the wheel hard over, and increased power. A sustained screeching ensued as the hull scraped the side of the rock piling, but it was only a superficial scar.

Pitt guided the cruise ship clear of the bridge support, then aimed its bow downstream. He stepped to the rear of the bridge and gave his daughter a hug. "You're a long way from Southampton."

"I only wanted to see the Isle of Wight."

He saw by her smile that she had survived her ordeal in good order. "We really have to get off the ship now," she said.

Pitt had her slide to the center of the brass rail. He stepped to one end and raised the rifle to the bracket mounting. An earsplitting burst from the gun left a mangled hole in the bulkhead. Pitt gave the bracket a hard kick, and the rail broke from the wall. Summer was able to slide her manacled hand to the end of the rail and pull the cuff free.

Pitt stepped back to the helm and scanned the shoreline for a place to ground.

"We need to get off now," Summer reiterated. "There are explosives throughout the ship, some attached to radioactive barrels. There can't be more than a few minutes left."

"The radioactive waste is still aboard?"

"Yes. They mean to sink the ship and contaminate the river."

Pitt now understood. Nassar's plan was twofold: to block the Delaware Aqueduct of all water flowing to New York City, then permanently contaminate the Hudson River, which could serve as a

substitute water source. The city truly would be left without fresh water.

Pitt quickly eyed the riverbanks. The eastern shore was less developed and he spotted an empty marsh and inlet ahead. He turned the ship toward the spot and increased speed.

"Where are the radioactive barrels stored?" he asked.

"A cargo hold on the stern deck. They set explosives there, as well as along the keel. There's no time to find them all."

Pitt motioned for her to take the wheel. "Head for that marsh while I take a quick look. If the first charge goes up, get yourself over the side. Al is following behind."

He rushed out the side wing and scrambled down to the main deck.

As Summer watched him depart, she thought about radioing Giordino, then remembered the smashed transmitter. A glance over her shoulder told her the Chris-Craft was following close to their flank.

She glanced at a chronograph and held her breath. It had been nearly twenty minutes since Samad had set the charges. The ship could go up in flames at any second.

Pitt found the aft deck hold and pulled open the hatch cover. Inside, he saw a dozen yellow safety containers, each holding a rusty barrel of nuclear waste.

He jumped inside and made a frantic search under the low light, probing around the base of the containers. His hands found what he couldn't see: one of the wooden crates of explosives wedged at the base of a container. It was enough firepower to send the radioactive waste a hundred feet in all directions.

Pitt grabbed the case and tossed it up on deck, then scrambled out of the hold. He pushed aside the thought of the box exploding in his hands as he carried it to the port rail, opposite Giordino in the

Chris-Craft, and flung it over the side as far as he could. As the crate left his grip, he glimpsed a digital timer on the top. It read forty-five seconds. Though his heart was still pounding, he turned and sprinted back up to the bridge.

"Any idea how many scuttling charges were set?" he asked Summer.

"My French isn't reliable, but I think he said six, plus one in the cargo hold."

"No sense in us both sticking around. Get yourself over the side now." He pulled back on the throttles.

Despite his calm voice, Summer saw the intensity in her father's eyes urging her to leave. She wanted to argue and convince him they both should jump, but she knew better than to question his will. She also knew every second counted.

She squeezed her father's hand and rushed to the door. Descending to the lower deck, she climbed over the rail and jumped into the river.

Pitt watched until he saw her stroke away from the cruise ship, then he jammed the throttles forward. He looked ahead to the marsh on the eastern shoreline. It fronted a tree-covered peninsula called Dennings Point that curved into the river like a dragon's tail. Halfway down the peninsula, he spied a shallow beach oddly colored pink.

Pitt held the ship to the center of the river to gain maximum speed with the current, then made a sudden turn to port, aligning the bow perpendicular to the beach. He locked the autopilot, then exited the bridge while the ship was less than fifty yards from shore. He waved off Giordino as he climbed over the upper rail and leaped into the river, tucking his arms and legs before striking the water.

The height of the jump and the speed of the ship made it feel like he hit a brick wall. He shook off the pain, his limbs moving by instinct as he kicked hard until his head broke the surface. He had time for a single deep breath before the cruise ship erupted in front of him.

The keel charges detonated one by one, rocking the ship before it vanished beneath a cloud of smoke and debris. Pitt ducked underwater as the superstructure exploded in a fireball, sending a shower of splinters and steel in all directions. Somewhere upriver, the crate Pitt had tossed over the side joined the tumult, blasting up a geyser of green water.

Pitt remained underwater as long as he could, swimming toward the bank as the current pushed him downriver. He surfaced a few yards from shore and stroked the remaining distance until he found his footing and waded onto the beach.

The ground was pink, he saw, because it was covered with thousands of pieces of broken brick. They were the remnants from a long-abandoned factory on the peninsula that had once supplied construction bricks for the Empire State Building. Pitt made his way across the uneven surface to the smoldering remains of the *Hydros*.

The ship had plowed across the beach, its bow crunching through a heavy tree line just beyond. Flames climbed into the air from the forward deck, but to Pitt's relief, the stern cargo section remained intact, resting aground on the shallow edge of the brick beach.

Giordino ran the Chris-Craft ashore a short distance away and rushed over with Summer, carrying a fire extinguisher.

"Cutting it a little close there," Giordino said.

Pitt gave a modest grin. "I had an easy five seconds to spare."

Giordino climbed onto the *Hydros*'s deck, and at Pitt's instruction, extinguished the smoldering flames around the stern. With the fire controlled, he joined Pitt and Summer on the beach. "That would have made a real mess of the Hudson."

Sirens wafted up and down the river. A police helicopter flew low over the scene on its way to the shaft site.

Summer approached her father and accepted a soggy hug. The angst of the past days had finally surfaced in a wave of emotion, leaving her feeling completely drained. "What happens now?"

"With luck, the police will nab the commando leader," Pitt said. "He was apparently the only one to get away."

"It's a safe bet that they're through playing games with the water supply," Giordino added.

"In the meantime," Pitt said to his daughter, "you need to find some dry clothes and a new passport. I need you to get over to France as soon as you can and get your brother out of jail."

"Jail? What's Dirk doing in jail in France?"

"It's a long story."

"You won't be coming with me?"

"No." Pitt shook his head and gazed at the sweeping river with a faraway look. "Al and I are going to the Caribbean. We have a ninety-five-year-old submarine to find."

PART III

The Surcouf

77

Brigitte could not believe her luck. The fuzzy sonar image had scrolled across the tracking screen just twenty minutes before they had to pull up the survey gear and head to Cartagena. It was some kind of shipwreck . . . and a big one.

The wreck lay in deep water and the sonar had been towed close to the surface, so the image displayed was tiny. But there was no denying the distinct oblong shape. Long, smooth, and linear, with a notable hump in the middle. It could be only one thing: a submarine.

But was it the *Surcouf*? The dimensions were similar and if Brigitte looked close, she could even convince herself an aircraft hangar extended from the conning tower. She desperately wanted to drop an ROV on the site or, better yet, view it firsthand from the *Moselle*'s small submersible.

But that would have to wait. Nassar was expecting her to pick him up in Cartagena, and that was a sixteen-hour sail away. At least she could greet him with good news.

She turned from her sonar station at the rear of the ship's bridge and called to the captain. "Your men may retrieve the sonar fish now, and you can proceed to port."

The gruff captain, who seemed to haunt the bridge twenty-four hours a day, nodded and spoke into a handheld radio. He and his shipmates didn't like having a woman aboard, that was plain to see. But the brutish crew had been respectful enough to Brigitte, and to her surprise, had been ruthlessly efficient in their duties.

The underwater search could not have gone smoother. The key was where to look, and fortune had smiled upon her. Before leaving the Azores, her friend at the Le Havre Marine Institute had sent her an electronic file with a complete history of the *Surcouf* and an analysis of her sinking.

There were two theories why the *Surcouf* sank on her approach to the Panama Canal in February 1942. An American freighter, the *Thompson Lykes*, reported striking a partially submerged object off Panama on the night of February 18, which may have been the French sub. The next morning, an A-17 bomber out of Panama City reported attacking and sinking a large submarine in the Caribbean. The *Surcouf* may well have been the target of both incidents.

Brigitte pieced together the two reports and established a search area some eighty miles off the Panama coast. After just three days of surveying, and barely a fraction of the way through her planned search grid, they had picked up the target.

As the survey equipment was pulled aboard and the *Moselle* accelerated toward Colombia, Brigitte left the air-conditioned bridge and descended to the deck. She stood at the rail, the moist tropical air rushing against her skin as she looked out to sea.

A tinge of adrenaline surged through her body at the thought of the discovery. The diamonds didn't matter now. If the wreck was indeed the *Surcouf* and Napoleon was aboard, she would be the most famous woman in France.

Brigitte's excitement wore off the second she spotted Nassar standing on the dock in Cartagena. Normally buoyant and full of arrogance,

he appeared haggard and defeated. His posture was slumped, his face was drawn, and he displayed a nervousness she had never seen before.

He jumped onto the ship the second it touched the dock and ordered the captain to depart at once. Only when the ship was at sea did he pay Brigitte any heed. Nassar grabbed her hand and led her to the wardroom, where he collapsed into a corner booth.

"You look exhausted." She fixed him a coffee, then slid next to him.

He nodded with glazed eyes. "I had a difficult time leaving the U.S. They were searching all the vehicles heading into Canada, so I had to change my plans and cross the border on foot. I barely made it to Montreal in time to catch my initial flight to Havana." He neglected to mention assaulting a Canadian mailman and stealing his truck for the drive to the airport.

"Is everything okay?" she asked.

"The operation was a failure. My team is gone, and there is a high risk of exposure."

He had watched the news coverage on an airport television and had seen footage of the *Hydros* beached on the riverbank. Why it wasn't at the bottom of the Hudson, he didn't know, but the accounts mentioned the rescue of Summer. Nassar thought back to the men who had attacked from the rear of the warehouse. Could it have been the American duo from Paris?

He wrapped his fingers tight around the coffee cup. "I cannot go back to France. At least for a while. I modified the cruise ship's registry, but there's a chance someone will trace the ship back to Villard. If so, the old man is done."

That also likely meant the end of his hopes of inheriting the company or possibly arranging a buyout with LeBoeuf. Villard himself would be lucky if the authorities got to him before he defaulted with LeBoeuf. There wasn't enough left of Nassar's security team to protect the CEO, let alone his own skin, from the mafia leader.

"I'm afraid the company, and my stake in it, may be done." He gazed around the wardroom. "We're in danger here. Somebody will eventually come looking for the *Moselle*. But we have a little time. Enough to go to Caracas and dispose of it there. I have some business contacts in Venezuela who might be able to help us."

The color drained from Brigitte's face. "I don't want to hide out in South America." Then she felt a surge of anger. "You haven't even asked about the search."

Nassar gave an unenthusiastic nod. "Oh yes, our long-lost submarine. I'm afraid we won't have much time to look for it now."

"I think I found it."

Nassar sat upright. "You what?"

"We began the search using data from the Institute. I found a target just before we had to break off and come here. It looks promising."

"Show me," he said in a voice suddenly strong.

Brigitte led him to the bridge sonar station and retrieved the image of the wreck. Nassar studied it closely, comparing it to black-and-white photos of the *Surcouf* that Brigitte had printed.

He leaned over and kissed her on the cheek. "It looks very promising." With fifty million euros in diamonds, Villard and LeBoeuf would be a distant memory. "Do you have any more sonar images?"

"No, just the one."

"And the site is safe?"

"Yes. It's eighty miles from the coast of Panama. But it is deep, nearly three thousand feet. The ROV and submersible aboard the ship can handle the depth for confirmation, but salvage would be another story."

"Given what's on board," Nassar said, "that won't be difficult to arrange."

He felt like a man given parole from a life sentence in prison. He bounded over to the helm and instructed the captain to make for the wreck site at top speed.

Brigitte and Nassar were back on the bridge sixteen hours later when the survey ship approached the designated position. Brigitte was idly watching a container ship passing on its way to the canal, when she suddenly stood on her toes. "Stop the boat," she screamed.

As the captain cut power, Nassar rushed to her side. "What is it?"

She pointed out the windshield. Nassar turned and squinted out the glass. A mile beyond the passing container ship, a smaller vessel crept slowly across the horizon.

It was colored turquoise.

78

"Bombs are away," Giordino said as he entered a small operations bay on the stern of the NUMA research ship *Havana*.

"Congratulations," Pitt said from a seated console. "I think you just set a new world's record for the most fish released in the wild."

"I just hope they all remember to return to Poppa."

Giordino's fish weren't the kind with gills, but long, torpedo-shaped autonomous underwater vehicles packed with electronic sensors. They were programmed to dive deep, then skim above the seafloor, running in a defined search grid to capture the contours of the bottom.

Giordino felt like a circus ringmaster as he coordinated the launch of eight separate AUVs, then arranged their data feeds through individual frequencies and transducers. Operating the fleet of electronic fish meant they could survey nearly fifty square miles of ocean in a single day.

Giordino dropped into a console seat, grateful for the air-conditioned relief from the tropical heat outside. "It'll be another ninety minutes or so until we receive the first data relay." He config-

ured a large screen at the front of the bay with eight different sonar displays. "You think Perlmutter put us close?"

"With your arsenal," Pitt said, "I'm not sure he needs to."

For a seat-of-the-pants research project, Pitt had to marvel at what they'd accomplished. After countless interviews with federal and state law enforcement officials in New York, he and Giordino had jumped a flight to Panama City. A commuter flight then took them to the small Caribbean tourist island of San Andrés, where the *Havana* waited for them.

The NUMA vessel had just completed field trials with four new AUV prototypes, but it also carried four older models. With a software update, Giordino had devised a way to run them all concurrently. While he arranged the technical end, Pitt had conversed with Perlmutter about the *Surcouf*.

The nautical historian had also uncovered details about the submarine's potential collision with the *Thompson Lykes* and the reported bombing attack.

"The bombing location is rather vague, but the collision coordinates are quite exact," Perlmutter had said. "I might start there and work your way to the southeast, where the bomber allegedly struck."

"You think both accounts have merit?" Pitt asked.

"I do. The crew of the freighter were certain they struck a submarine, although it was the dead of night and they were running without lights. As for the bomber, the crew thought they were attacking a German U-boat. They noted it was a very large vessel. I suspect the *Surcouf* was just incredibly unlucky. The collision may have damaged her radio antenna, such that she couldn't report her condition or location. The bomber then mistakenly finished her off the next day. But it is all speculation."

"It might be much better than that. Thanks, Julien."

Pitt developed a search grid from the data, and by the time the *Havana* reached the site, the AUVs were ready to deploy. When the

first vehicle submitted its initial survey results, Giordino posted the grainy pictures on the large screen. Before long, he had eight sonar feeds scrolling by. To Pitt, it resembled a gigantic slot machine reel spinning endlessly.

Giordino adjusted the display so all of the feeds moved at the same slow speed, to allow the easy identification of a target.

"Seems like a good recipe for eyestrain," Pitt said after a few minutes.

"I've got an algorithm that will flag any potential targets so we can cycle through the data more quickly."

They took turns reviewing the sonar data, which was received in sporadic transmissions. Twenty hours later, Giordino phoned a dozing Pitt in his cabin. "We've got something."

"Be right down."

When Pitt entered the operations bay, he saw a single sonar image of a wreck enlarged on the screen. Below it, Giordino had displayed a wartime photo of the *Surcouf*.

"A match?" Pitt asked.

"The dimensions are dead-on," Giordino said. "The conning tower is a little distorted, perhaps because she's resting at an angle, but it shows a gun turret forward and an extended housing aft. By all measures, it looks like our sub."

Pitt studied the image and smiled. "It does look pretty good."

"Do you want another sonar pass?"

"No," Pitt said. "Let's go see for ourselves whether we've got an emperor's barge resting beneath our feet."

79

The *Havana*'s deepwater submersible reached the seabed an hour later. Pitt brought the vessel to a hover over the charcoal-colored seafloor that resembled the surface of the moon.

"Sonar makes her out on a heading of one hundred thirty-five degrees," Giordino said from the copilot's seat.

Pitt engaged the thrusters and propelled the sub in a southeasterly heading. If not for the submersible's exterior LED lights, the seafloor would be blacker than the inside of a coffin. Even with the lights, there was little to see. At a depth of just over three thousand feet, it was a cold and desolate landscape, contrasting with the sunbaked tropics on the surface.

As they glided above the bottom, a flat, tapered object rose slightly from the seabed. It was nearly as long as the submersible, smooth and flat . . . and clearly man-made.

"A submarine's diving plane," Pitt said.

Giordino whistled at its dimensions. "She must be a big sucker."

He saw for himself a minute later when a massive dark shadow arose from the gloom. They approached from the stern, catching

sight of the sub's twin bronze propellers rising from the sediment. Pitt ascended to its deck level and moved forward parallel to its port hull.

The submarine sat on its keel, but tilted as Giordino had predicted. But the sub was also distorted in another way.

"Looks like she was run through a meat grinder," Giordino said.

The entire surface was pockmarked with large dents, creases, and buckled steel plates, as if it had been pounded with a giant sledgehammer.

"The *Surcouf*'s maximum operating depth was only around three hundred feet," Pitt said. "She must have been crushed like a beer can from the pressure when she sank."

Any doubts about the submarine's identity were put to rest when they reached the conning tower. The *Surcouf*'s sail was built upon a long, cylindrical housing that extended fore and aft across the deck. Ahead of the conning tower, the housing morphed into a watertight turret with two dark openings, like large eyes peering toward the bow. The barrels of twin 203-millimeter naval guns protruded through the openings.

"Wicked guns for a submarine," Giordino said.

"She was originally built as a merchant raider," Pitt said, "but ultimately served on convoy duty." As they cruised around the sail, he thought of the 130 officers and sailors who had senselessly lost their lives on the vessel by accident or friendly fire.

Aft of the conning tower, the housing ended in a round steel door that swung on interior hinges. Inside, the *Surcouf* could carry a dismantled floatplane that could be reassembled and launched with a crane.

"Looks like they left the door open," Giordino said.

The round convex door was wedged open a foot or two, likely from the force of the sinking. Pitt maneuvered the submersible above the door, then slowly descended alongside the opening to shine its powerful forward lights inside.

"Perlmutter thought there were three likely places to store an over-sized coffin," Pitt said. "The fore and aft torpedo rooms and the air-craft hangar here. He believed she wasn't carrying a plane on her later voyages."

The skids of the submersible touched the deck, and the thrusters kicked up a small cloud of sediment. When the water cleared, both men leaned forward and looked into the hangar. They didn't have a complete view, but could see down most of its length to the conning tower. It was empty.

Pitt raised the submersible and continued an overhead survey. Past the sail, they crossed a long open stretch of deck until they ap-proached the bow. There they found the vessel's angled nose had been turned into a ragged mass of sheared steel. The port bow had been blown open by unknown means, whether by aerial bomb, sea pres-sure, or her own torpedoes.

Pitt glided along the exposed section, glimpsing into the interior of two of the submarine's three deck levels. He found a large gap in the exterior hull and parked the submersible nearby on the seabed.

"Time to release the hounds," Pitt said.

Giordino powered up a small ROV mounted to the submersible's frame. Using a joystick, he propelled the cabled device toward the *Surcouf.* No larger than a pizza box, the ROV was little more than a camera and lights attached to a set of thrusters.

Pitt turned on a monitor that displayed its video feed as Giordino drove the ROV into the submarine, ensuring its power cable didn't graze any jagged sections of the hull.

The ROV displayed a maze of pipes and cables along the bulkhead before it slithered into the center of the bay. From the schematics, Pitt judged it was the forward torpedo room and the video confirmed as much.

Giordino guided the ROV along the torpedo tubes, their inner hatches sealed shut. The rest of the interior was a gloomy cave with

the bulkheads, pipes, and racks of torpedoes all covered in a dark layer of silt. "Doesn't look to have been an interior explosion," he said.

"A saving grace, but the bay is empty of any large crates."

The ROV showed there was ample room in the back of the bay, but the space stood empty.

"There's still the aft torpedo room." Giordino guided the ROV back to the submersible, careful to let a take-up reel spool in its power cable. Pitt hit the thrusters and propelled them to the rear of the sub.

Because the stern was less damaged than the bow, they had to survey both sides of the hull before Giordino pointed out a buckled seam in the hull plates. "I might be able to slip in there."

Pitt hovered the submersible off the gap as Giordino sent the ROV forward, tilting it sharply to squeeze through the gap. The camera revealed a smaller version of the forward torpedo room, with similar racks of the deadly weapons. There was less covering silt, and Giordino lingered the ROV by some boots and debris in a corner that may have been human remains. Like the forward bay, there was no sign of a large crate.

"It's a big submarine," Giordino said as he maneuvered the ROV back to its cradle. "Maybe they parked him somewhere else."

"Could be." Pitt noted their battery power was waning. "Let's recharge topside, review the blueprints, and speak to Perlmutter again." He had lost none of his sense of optimism, despite their findings.

"But first," Pitt added, "how about we take back a souvenir for the people of France?" He guided the submersible away from the *Surcouf*, retracing their path to the diving plane.

"That's a hefty keepsake," Giordino said as Pitt parked the submersible next to the relic.

Giordino worked the controls of a hydraulic manipulator and grasped a hinge of the diving plane with its titanium fingers. Pitt had to completely purge the submersible's ballast tanks and apply some

ascending thrust to pull the slab from the sediment. The object finally came loose, stirring up a thick billow of silt.

As the water cleared, the submersible shuddered and wafted off the bottom. Clutching the slab like a giant pizza box, the two-man vessel began a slow and gentle rise to the surface.

80

Nassar stared at the NUMA ship through a pair of Zeiss high-power binoculars. Bright deck lights revealed a late-night flurry on the stern deck. At more than a mile away, the distance was too great to see any details, but he was sure it meant the imminent retrieval of the submersible.

"They appear to be preparing for recovery," he said.

Across the bridge of the *Moselle*, the ship's captain glanced at his watch. "The submersible has been down for several hours. It is due to surface."

The seismic survey ship had kept its distance since finding the NUMA ship near the wreck site. While Brigitte had been distraught, Nassar had viewed it as a potential blessing. The *Moselle* was ill-equipped to perform deepwater salvage, but perhaps the NUMA ship could do the heavy lifting for them. His working crew of trained commandos could take it from there.

Nassar had downloaded and studied the ship plans of the *Havana* and conducted a briefing with his assault team just in case. But his initial plan was simply to follow on the heels of the NUMA dive team and hope they exposed the tomb and diamonds for the taking.

"*Mon amour*, are you ready to make your descent?" He stepped to the chart table where Brigitte sat, and he rubbed her shoulders. Spread across the table were diagrams and photographs of the *Surcouf.*

"Have they surfaced?"

"Shortly, it would appear."

Brigitte had overcome her shock at seeing the NUMA ship and was now excited to explore the *Surcouf.* She knew she'd been the first to locate the submarine. Maybe she could still beat NUMA to the punch and claim discovery of the submarine and the tomb. All she needed was photographic evidence, hence her insistence on taking a seat in the *Moselle*'s submersible.

Nassar matched her focus as she stood and looked toward the NUMA vessel on the horizon. "Unlike our neighbors," he said, "it would be better if you deploy in the dark."

"If you're not going to take us any closer, then at least drop us up current from the site so we can drift toward it on our descent."

Nassar relayed the request to the captain, then accompanied Brigitte to the aft deck. Joined by the vessel's pilot, she climbed into a small white submersible, giving Nassar a kiss before sealing the hatch.

He watched as the submersible was hoisted over the transom and released into the sea. No sooner had the vessel vanished than Nassar received a radio call from the bridge.

"The NUMA submersible has surfaced," the captain said. "I think you'll want to take a look."

Nassar rushed to the bridge, where he found the captain peering through the binoculars.

"They've brought something up with them, but I can't make out what it is." He handed over the glasses.

Nassar took his own look. The *Moselle* was facing the NUMA ship's bow, so he couldn't see much of the stern deck, but caught a glimpse of the yellow submersible in the water with a crane dangling over it.

"Move us to the south," he said. "I can't get a clear view."

It took a few minutes for the ship to come about, but Nassar had a better perspective. The submersible was still in the water, but the crane was transporting something onto the stern deck. He glimpsed a slab-sided object as it was lowered beneath the gunwales. Was it a sarcophagus?

He refocused the glasses and looked again, but the side rails blocked his view. He watched as the submersible was brought aboard, its two occupants appearing like ants when they crawled out the hatch.

"Could you see what they retrieved?" the captain asked.

"No, but it could be what we're after. We'll have to wait for our submersible to report their findings."

A short time later, those plans went out the window. "Sir," the helmsman said, "the other vessel is on the move."

Nassar looked at the ship, then joined the captain at a radar monitor and watched the image of the *Havana* move off to the east.

"Are they repositioning over the wreck?" he asked.

"No, they are traveling away from the site." He pointed at the screen. "They're now moving off at speed."

Nassar cursed and slammed a fist onto the helm.

"They must have recovered it. Follow them at a distance and call my assault team to the wardroom. We'll have to strike them on the fly."

"What about our submersible?" the captain asked. "They've likely just reached the bottom."

Nassar's eyes were only on the fleeing NUMA ship. His gaze was steady as he shook his head.

"Leave them."

81

St. Julien Perlmutter sipped a cup of Vietnamese lotus tea and settled into an extra-wide wingback chair in his study. He set aside a thick folder on the *Surcouf* he'd assembled from his archives and began reviewing the data Pitt had sent from France, along with his own research from Bermuda. He rifled through the papers and returned again to a copy of the last two postcards from Marcel Demille.

"'We may be bound for the Pacific,'" he read aloud, "'with a stop in Little Guinea.'"

He and Pitt had performed myriad computer searches on Little Guinea, but no results had materialized. There seemed to be no known region or place by that name. Perlmutter knew the name meant something, but he couldn't put his finger on it.

He reached for a bottle of rum, a Martinique brand called Saint James, and spiked his tea with a small shot. As he took a sip, he considered the bottle, which featured a plantation house on the label. Perlmutter hoisted himself from his chair and padded to an overflowing bookshelf. He found an aged biography on Napoleon and returned to his chair.

Thirty minutes later, a broad grin spread across his face.

"I can't believe it," he said to himself. "The emperor has outfoxed us again."

———

Pitt phoned a short time later to report his discovery of the *Surcouf*. He'd barely said hello when Perlmutter blurted out, "Napoleon's not on the *Surcouf*."

Pitt described their fruitless search of the submarine anyway. "How did you know?"

"On account of Joseph-Gaspard de Tascher de La Pagerie," Perlmutter said.

"I don't follow."

"Monsieur de Tascher was a second-generation sugar plantation owner on Martinique in the eighteenth century, when the island was a French possession. La Pagerie was the name of his plantation, from an area on the island of the same name. But the plantation had a nickname," Perlmutter said. "Little Guinea. It was a reference to the African country of origin for many of the slaves who worked there. The same place name on Marcel Demille's postcard that we couldn't identify."

"Could it just be a coincidence?" Pitt asked.

"Not likely. You see, de Tascher had a daughter who was born and raised on the plantation. Her name was Marie-Josèphe-Rose de Tascher de La Pagerie."

"I don't know the name."

"History remembers her better as Joséphine Bonaparte."

"Joséphine," Pitt said. "Of course. And Martinique was still a French possession in 1942. Demille must have taken Jean d'Éppé to Little Guinea for hiding until the war was over. It all makes perfect sense if Jean d'Éppé did in fact refer to Napoleon."

Pitt was standing on the bridge of the *Havana* and retrieved a map of the Caribbean on a workstation while he spoke. He eyed the

CLIVE CUSSLER THE CORSICAN SHADOW

location of Martinique in the Lesser Antilles, the islands that form the eastern boundary of the Caribbean Sea.

"That also might explain the *Surcouf*'s sinking," Pitt said. "She may have been late in arriving at the Panama Canal because she secretly stopped in Martinique on the way. That threw off her expected arrival time and may have led to a false identification by the bomber crew."

"Precisely. Martinique was a French colony, although under Vichy control early in the war. The *Surcouf* could not, therefore, make a public arrival at the main port of Fort-de-France, but she could have surfaced across the bay at Les Trois-Îslets, very close to La Pagerie plantation."

"Where they could have off-loaded Napoleon and buried him at Joséphine's place of birth," Pitt said. "A nice romantic touch, at that."

"The logic would seem to work. I'd presume that they planted him on the estate grounds, probably in the family plot."

"The estate still exists?"

"Yes, but on a smaller scale. The remains of the estate are now a museum. I understand Joséphine is still regarded as a national treasure in Martinique, even though she is buried in France."

Pitt smiled. "Are you sure about that?"

Perlmutter laughed. "At this point, I'd be afraid to guess where any revered body is located. Sorry I created a wild-goose chase for you, but I'm delighted you found the *Surcouf*. I trust you will share your photographic records with me."

"A better-than-even trade for finding the link to Joséphine's estate." Pitt said goodbye and hung up.

Giordino approached him on the bridge. "I've got new battery packs loaded on the submersible for another dive."

"No need." Pitt relayed his conversation with Perlmutter.

"Martinique?" Giordino said. "Of course. A tropical French land, but in the Caribbean. And just when I got over my taste for snails."

He departed the bridge to secure the submersible, while Pitt gave the ship's captain, Keith Lowden, new sailing orders. As the *Havana* got underway, Pitt emailed video clips of the *Surcouf* to Perlmutter. The nautical historian had already sent Pitt additional details about Joséphine's estate, complete with photos.

After considering the information, Pitt said good night to the bridge crew and stepped onto the starboard bridge wing for some fresh air. A cool breeze blew from the sea, and Pitt stood at the rail contemplating Perlmutter's discovery. A quarter moon cast a sliver of mercury across the water. The seas ahead were black and empty, and Pitt drank in the serenity of the void. But a rustling on the adjacent companionway told him he wasn't entirely alone.

He glanced behind him as a dark shadow ascended the stairwell, cradling an assault rifle that reflected the moonlight.

82

The *Moselle* had chased the NUMA ship while Nassar assembled his assault team and prepared a rigid inflatable boat for launch. Nassar paced the bridge until his ship closed within a mile of the *Havana*. He then ordered the captain to cut power.

"Trail behind," he said. "I'll radio you once we've taken the ship."

His five-man commando team waited for him on the stern, dressed in black and armed with suppressed assault rifles. When the *Moselle* slowed, the inflatable was dropped over the side and the commandos boarded. Nassar took the tiller and ran the boat in pursuit of the *Havana*.

He motored wide, then sped ahead until parallel to the NUMA ship, where he could recon the vessel. No crew were visible on deck, which simplified his boarding plans. He could see the submersible secured on the stern deck, but there was no sign of the recovered artifact.

"The port deck is clear," one of his men confirmed. Nassar made a quick turn and ran toward the ship's port flank. Boarding a moving ship at sea was a dangerous task, but one Nassar had practiced with his men on Villard's fleet time and again. He matched speed with the

vessel and pulled alongside. A soft-tipped grapple was tossed over the ship's rail, and a member of the team quickly scaled a knotted line attached. On reaching the deck, he unfurled a stout Jacob's ladder.

Nassar led three of the commandos up the ladder, while the last man took the tiller and turned the boat away to follow at a distance. The research ship still appeared quiet, although he knew it carried a large crew. Nassar sent two of his commandos to secure the bridge, ordering them to approach from opposite sides.

With the other two men, he moved toward an open bay near the submersible. It was where the raised artifact had been stowed . . . and where he would finally put his hands on the Belgian diamonds.

83

The lone commando threaded his way to the starboard rail and began to make his way forward. At Nassar's instruction, he had coordinated with his counterpart on the port rail to enter the bridge in exactly two minutes. It gave him plenty of time to work his way to the ship's wheelhouse and prepare for the assault.

He paused when a side door opened in front of him, washing the deck in fluorescent light. A woman stepped out wearing blue coveralls and holding a camera. The commando ducked behind a capstan as the woman approached. She passed by, walking so near he could smell the lingering scent of her shampoo.

He moved forward again to a companionway that rose to the bridge. The casual voices drifting from the open bridge wing told him the team's boarding had not been detected. He glanced at his watch and saw he had just a few seconds to make his entry.

He scrambled up the stairs, eyes on the bridge door, when he sensed movement on the landing. The commando turned as a figure rose from the shadows and lunged at him with arms swinging.

Pitt struck the gunman high on the cheek, nearly sending him tumbling down the stairs.

The commando recovered and tried to pivot his rifle to fire, but Pitt pressed against him, pinning the rifle flat against his chest. Pitt used a free hand to pelt the man with a flurry of punches.

The commando released the rifle and tried to block the fusillade. But Pitt struck several stinging blows to the head, and the man felt himself waver.

He was much heavier than Pitt and used his bulk as a last measure of defense. He lowered his head and bulled into Pitt, shoving him back until Pitt's back struck the rail.

The charge threw Pitt off balance. He tried to pivot and force the gunman past him, but they were too entwined. The commando's heft forced them both to the rail, which should have halted their motion. But the commando, like Pitt, was tall, and his torso propelled their weight forward.

Both fought for balance while keeping their grip on one another, but their combined momentum had propelled them too far. Together, both men lost their footing, flipped over the rail, and vanished into the sea below.

84

The *Surcouf*'s diving plane had been too large to be muscled into the *Havana*'s main lab, so it had been positioned flat on deck just outside the bay. Crewmen had laid plastic sheets beneath it, raised at the edges to create a shallow pool so the artifact could be soaked in fresh water. Chemical baths to leach out the sea salts and electrolysis to stabilize the metal would come later at a conservation facility, but the wet bath prevented any damage in the meantime.

The woman with the camera, a marine archaeologist named Noriku, was taking photos of the metal structure when Giordino approached.

"I can't believe you pulled this up with the submersible," she said.

"It's only heavy out of the water," he said with a grin. "Looks to be in excellent condition."

"It's in great shape, except where it was sheared off." She pointed to its jagged mounting brackets.

Giordino bent to take a closer look. The pool was beginning to overflow, and he grabbed the nozzle of the hose filling it.

"Al," Noriku whispered, then clasped his arm.

Giordino looked up as an armed man in black crept along the rear bulkhead. He hadn't spotted them, as his head was turned toward the stern. That changed when he took a step closer and looked in their direction.

Giordino was already on the move. He rushed toward the gunman, raised the hose, and shot a spray of water into the man's face. The man turned away by reflex, wiping his face with one hand while raising his rifle. Giordino sprang off the deck and plowed into him chest-high, driving him hard against the bulkhead.

The air was crushed from his lungs, but he had the presence to drop a hand to his side and retrieve a holstered pistol.

Giordino struck again, driving a powerful uppercut into his midsection. The commando gasped as the pistol cleared the holster. Giordino ignored the gun and threw his weight into a hard right that crushed the gunman's jaw. The commando crumpled to the deck, and his weapons clattered beside him.

Giordino reached for the rifle and pulled the sling up and over the man's head. He heard a rustle behind him and spun as he raised the weapon, then froze.

Nassar stood nearby with a pistol pressed against Noriku's cheek and a wry smile on his face. "Drop the gun," he said, "or the woman dies."

Giordino lowered the rifle to the deck and stared at Nassar. "*Bonsoir* to you, too."

Nassar squinted in recognition, then shook off the surprise and motioned to a gunman at his side. The commando stepped over and picked up the assault rifle. As he rose, he swung the stock in an arc, striking Giordino with a vicious blow to the gut.

Giordino doubled over, but stood his ground. He said nothing, Noriku's frightened eyes deterring any further resistance.

The prone commando was helped to his feet and handed back his weapon.

As the two commandos held their guns on Giordino, Nassar lowered his pistol and approached the diving plane in the makeshift pool. "Is this from the *Surcouf*?" he asked Noriku.

She glanced at Giordino, who gave her a reassuring nod.

"Yes," she said. "We believe it is one of the bow diving planes."

He scowled. "This is what you recovered?"

A handheld radio on Nassar's hip crackled with a transmitting voice. "Commander, the bridge is secure. But Gérard is missing."

"Received," Nassar said. "On my way."

He turned to the groggy commando. "Search all of the bays here, then report to me on the bridge." He motioned for the others to move. The second commando prodded Giordino with his weapon, while Nassar jabbed his pistol in Noriku's back.

"Lead the way to the bridge," he said. "Ladies first."

85

Pitt had struck the water close alongside the moving ship. He'd felt a thump on his descent while still entangled with the commando. They both hit the water headfirst.

Pitt felt the sting of the entry and released himself from his opponent, whose grip had turned limp. In the dark water, he glimpsed the gunman's head tilted severely to one side. That had been the bump he'd felt: the commando's head striking the side of the hull as they fell, snapping his neck.

Pitt pushed the corpse aside and swam away from the ship to avoid getting drawn into its propeller. He surfaced to see the *Havana* churn past him. The vessel was traveling at better than fifteen knots, so there was no way he could catch it.

He bobbed in the frothy wake, contemplating a yell for help, when he saw two gunmen march Giordino and Noriku across the stern deck. Even if his shout was heard, no help would be tendered now.

Pitt watched helplessly as the NUMA ship sailed away, leaving him stranded in an empty ocean. The nearest land was eighty miles away, the water beneath him half a mile deep. Fortunately,

the water temperature was eighty-two degrees, deferring the risk of hypothermia . . . if he could stay afloat.

He calmly took his bearings. He wasn't far from the shipping lanes between Caracas and the Panama Canal. Could he tread water until daylight and catch the eyes of a passing ship? Possible, but it was a big ask. Just as possible was the appearance of a hungry shark.

Pitt turned west and gazed at the lights of the *Moselle* two miles distant. As the support ship for the assault team, it would track the *Havana*. Unless the NUMA ship was brought to a quick halt, he'd have the impossible task of trying to board the tailing ship on the fly.

Hope appeared dismal, but Pitt wasn't one to panic. Remaining calm would be his best course of action, he knew. Pitt wasn't a patient man by nature, but he had an innate ability to remain mentally composed.

As he contemplated his few, poor choices for survival, salvation suddenly presented itself in the buzz of an outboard motor.

86

The commando in the inflatable boat was shadowing the NUMA ship at a matching speed. To ease the ride, he had centered the boat in the flattened wake of the research ship. His eyes were glued to the *Havana*'s deck lights as he focused on maintaining a stealthy distance. The research ship began slowing dramatically, as he had expected, after receiving a radio call that the bridge had been secured. But Nassar hadn't called for his return, so he remained out of view until ordered otherwise.

He eased off the throttle, letting the rigid inflatable wallow in the slight chop. The evening was warm, the ocean calm, and no gunfire had sounded from the research ship. He let himself relax, taking in the stars that glittered through the clouds.

He was piecing together the lustrous points of Ursa Major, the Great Bear, when a hand reached up from the water and grasped the back of his fatigues. He was yanked backward by the force, his spine bouncing against the rubber hull before he toppled headfirst into the sea.

It had been a hard swim for Pitt. He had made a desperate sprint to catch the passing boat, only to watch it zip past a few yards away.

But the pilot had cut the throttle a few seconds later, giving Pitt a second chance.

His lungs felt as if they would burst as he put every ounce of energy into overtaking the slowing inflatable. He gradually gained on the craft, swimming swiftly but silently. The pilot sat on the stern bench to the left of the tiller and Pitt approached from a rear angle.

Grasping the unaware pilot, Pitt used the leverage of the tumbling man to help pull himself onto the rubberized hull and belly himself aboard. He had the throttle twisted and the inflatable racing away before the commando surfaced. Muffled by the motor, his cries went unheard by his comrades on the NUMA ship.

Pitt raced toward the turquoise vessel, but veered aside when he spotted a dark-clad gunman crossing the aft deck. As Pitt pulled out of sight, he searched the inflatable for a rifle or other weapon, but found none. The boat's emergency kit held only a stick flare, which he pocketed in case he ended up back in the water.

He swung the inflatable wide around the ship's starboard flank, then inched closer and examined the hull. There had to be a boarding device for the gunmen, and Pitt hoped it hadn't been retrieved. But he saw nothing.

He cut the throttle and let the ship pass. Its engines had grown quiet and Pitt could see the ship slowing under its waning momentum. He skirted the port flank, and there he found what he was looking for: a thick rope ladder dangling from the rail.

87

The commando Giordino had leveled earlier rushed onto the bridge with a look of trepidation. "I've searched all along the starboard deck and in the adjacent compartments. There's no sign of Gérard."

"Nothing on the radio?" Nassar asked.

"No, sir, still no response. He was expected on the coordinated strike on the bridge. He was out of sight for only two minutes. Perhaps he fell overboard."

Nassar gave a hesitant nod. "Then I hope he knows how to swim. Did you find any other artifacts?"

The commando shook his head. "We checked all the labs and bays after herding the crew into the wardroom. We found nothing other than the steel object on the stern deck."

Nassar turned and narrowed his focus. Giordino, Noriku, Captain Lowden, and the helmsman stood together under gunpoint at the front of the bridge.

He stepped close to them and addressed Giordino. "Where is Napoleon's coffin?"

Giordino shrugged. "In Grant's tomb?"

Nassar rested his palm on his holster. "Tell me what you recovered."

"The bow plane," Noriku said, stepping forward.

"And what else?"

"That was all," she said.

"You were on the submersible?"

"No, but I watched the video feed."

"Show me."

Noriku crossed the bridge to a workstation and retrieved the recorded dive video.

Nassar had her fast-forward through footage of the *Surcouf* and the recovery of the diving plane. "Where is the coffin and the diamonds?"

Noriku gave him a blank look. "What are you talking about? They found nothing like that."

Nassar paced back to the front of the bridge and turned to the captain. "Tell me why you are leaving the site."

"To take the diving plane to a conservation facility in the Virgin Islands," Giordino said.

Nassar nodded at one of the commandos, who rammed the butt of his rifle into Giordino's shoulder, knocking him to the ground.

"I asked you," Nassar said to Captain Lowden.

"It's as he says," Lowden replied. "We're headed to the Virgin Islands."

The ship was indeed on a northeast heading toward the islands. But it was only a temporary heading until the ship cleared the northern coast of Colombia and could steer east to Martinique.

"Then where is the coffin? You would not be leaving without it and the diamonds."

His question was met by silence.

Nassar waited for a reply, then whispered to one of the gunmen. The commando grabbed Noriku by the arm and dragged her to the

starboard wing door. Giordino took a step in protest, but the other gunman held him still with a jab of his rifle.

"Tell me where the diamonds are hidden," Nassar shouted, "or she will be shot and thrown over the side." He glared at Giordino. "And you, my friend, will be next."

The bridge remained silent as Nassar's anger rose. "I will ask a final time. Where are they?"

The gunman on the wing raised his rifle to Noriku's ear, waiting for approval from Nassar to pull the trigger.

"The diamonds are not on the ship," a gritty voice bellowed.

All eyes turned to the port bridge wing, where Pitt stood in the doorway. He was soaking wet and strained with exhaustion, but fire burned in his eyes.

"They're not on the submarine, either," he said. "But I know where they are."

88

Nassar eyed Pitt with a mix of anger, surprise, and revulsion. He'd thought the man had surely died in New York, but here he was. His wet clothes indicated he'd likely had a hand in Gérard's disappearance.

Nassar gave Pitt a cold glare, then motioned toward Noriku. "Tell me where, or the girl dies."

"No," Pitt said, staring him down. "You leave this ship and let my crew go, and I'll tell you exactly where it is."

"I can kill you now," Nassar said.

"In which case, you'll remain a two-bit murderer and fifty million dollars poorer."

Nassar saw in Pitt a hardened fortitude like his own. Pitt's clear green eyes showed his resourcefulness, but also his humanity. A weakness in many noble men, Nassar thought. But it was a fair enough trade. The diamonds were the only thing that mattered now, and he could take the satisfaction of killing Pitt once they were recovered.

"You have a deal," he said. "But you'll take us there in person." Nassar turned to the commando on the wing. "Release the woman.

Then secure our new friend." He pointed to Giordino. "And that one, too."

The gunman guided Noriku back to the group, then produced a pair of military-grade zip ties and secured Giordino's hands in front of him. He moved to Pitt and repeated the process as Nassar and the other commando held their weapons at the ready.

Nassar then turned to Captain Lowden. "Do not attempt to contact the authorities, or your friends will die."

He stepped to the ship's radio and fired two rounds into it. He directed one of the commandos onto the roof of the bridge, where a burst from his rifle cut down the communication and navigation antennas atop the wheelhouse.

Nassar sent the gunman belowdecks while Pitt and Giordino were separately herded to the aft deck. A burst of gunfire came from somewhere deep in the ship as they waited for the boarding team to reassemble.

Nassar saw the misgiving in Pitt's eyes. "It is not your crew," he said. "Simply slowing down the vessel."

When the gunman reappeared, the group climbed into the inflatable and left the ship. A short distance away, they heard a cry for help, and the inflatable's former pilot was spotted. The foundering man was pulled into the boat and seated next to Pitt, too exhausted to confront the man who'd nearly caused him to drown.

They reached the *Moselle* a short time later, which had been trailing two miles behind, its running lights extinguished. Pitt and Giordino were taken to the ship's galley under guard, while Nassar made his way to the bridge.

"Our submersible is asking about recovery," the captain said. "They surfaced thirty minutes ago and are not too happy to have been left alone in the sea."

"Tell them we're on our way. What's their position?"

"Eight miles due west."

They found the white submersible bobbing in an empty sea a half hour later and pulled the vessel aboard. Brigitte emerged from the hatch boiling mad.

She glared at Nassar, who stood on deck by the lift crane. "What is the meaning of abandoning us?"

"The NUMA ship moved off-site." He pointed to the research ship's lights on the horizon. "I had to ensure they hadn't removed anything of value."

He stepped close and embraced her, but she didn't return the hug.

"It was a very careless thing to do," she said.

Nassar tried to laugh it off. "So you had a brief sail in the ocean. Now tell me, what did you find?"

"It is the *Surcouf.*" Her eyes turned bright. "She is mostly intact, but heavily damaged at the bow. We peered inside where we could, but saw no sign of a large crate. The tomb may be aboard, but I have my doubts."

"That is what I hoped to hear." He took her arm and escorted her forward.

"Then where else could it be?" she asked.

"Come, the answer is waiting for us in here," he said as they reached the galley. He held the door open for Brigitte.

As she stepped into the bay, she nearly fainted at the sight of the two men seated inside.

89

Pitt and Giordino sat at a dining table in heavy wooden chairs. Their hands were still zip-tied in front of them, and their arms were bound to the chairs. They turned and looked at Brigitte with surprise.

She stared at the floor, feeling a sudden sense of shame. She followed Nassar to the table and took a seat as far from the two men as she could.

Nassar ignored the looks between them. "Your ship and crew have been released," Nassar said to Pitt. "Now tell me where Napoleon and the diamonds are located."

"Your marine archaeologist doesn't know?" Pitt nodded at Brigitte.

"She tracked them here to the *Surcouf*, as you did," Nassar said. "But you obviously believe they are elsewhere."

"Martinique," Pitt said.

"And how did they get there?"

"We believe the *Surcouf* made a stop there on the way to the Panama Canal. The side trip may have been a factor in her sinking."

"So Napoleon was buried on French soil, so to speak," Nassar said. "It would make sense. But where on Martinique?"

"Little Guinea. Or Petite Guinée, as you would say."

"The description on the postcard," Brigitte said quietly.

"And just where is this Little Guinea?" Nassar asked Pitt.

"It's the nickname of La Pagerie estate, an old sugar plantation. And the ancestral home of Joséphine Bonaparte."

"Joséphine!" Brigitte blurted. "Of course, she was from Martinique. An appropriate place to hide Napoleon until the end of the war. But why did no one know?"

"Presumably Marcel Demille sailed on with the crew of the Surcouf, intending to return to Martinique after the war," Pitt said. "Unfortunately, the submarine never made its next port of call, so the knowledge died with him."

Nassar retrieved a laptop and downloaded an image of the estate's remains, labeled La Musée de la Pagerie. He and Brigitte studied the museum's website for additional clues.

"There is the museum and several abandoned structures on the site, including a sugarcane mill," he said. "Where on the site would it be?"

Pitt shrugged as Brigitte continued to examine the site. "It indicates there is a slave cemetery on the estate near the creek," she said. "That would seem the most logical place."

"Then that is where we shall look." Nassar stood and glared down at Pitt and Giordino.

"And gentlemen," he added, "for the sake of your health, I would hope there is a slave buried there who goes by the name of Bonaparte."

90

The *Havana*'s captain tracked the dim lights of Nassar's survey vessel as it raced past them.

"They're heading northeast," Lowden said to the helmsman, who sat on the floor trying to piece together the remains of the radar antenna.

"Martinique?" the young man asked.

"Most likely," Lowden said, wondering about the fate of Pitt and Giordino.

Once the commandos had left the ship, his first task was to assess the health of the crew. Thankfully, none were injured. But an appraisal of the ship was less rosy. Along with the damage to their communication and navigation equipment, the ship's power was severely compromised.

"They shot up the main electrical switchboard," the chief engineer reported. "We can get it fixed, but it'll be twenty-four hours. Until then, we've got no propulsion and only the auxiliary generators for lights and internals."

Lowden shook his head. "The good news," he said, his voice drip-

ping with irony, "is we don't need much juice for the electronic equipment at the moment."

It could have been worse. The weather was clear, and they were at no risk of running aground. They also had backup handheld radios with limited range, though Lowden was not about to broadcast any pleas for help with the commando ship still nearby.

"Captain, I found one." Noriku entered the bridge with a hard plastic briefcase.

Lowden had to admire the woman. Minutes after nearly having her head blown off, she had regained her composure and was helping aid their situation.

She set the case on a desktop and opened it, revealing a satellite phone.

"I knew we had a portable one aboard somewhere," Lowden said. He activated the phone and waited for it to establish a link with a constellation of low-orbit satellites. When a connection appeared, he dialed a number from his logbook.

An early riser, Rudi Gunn had beaten the morning rush hour traffic to work and was just entering his office when his desk phone rang. He didn't have time to flick on the lights as he lunged for the receiver. Standing by his desk, he listened in dismay to the details of Pitt's discovery of the *Surcouf* and the assault on the *Havana* by the French-speaking commandos.

"They were French?" Gunn asked, linking the incident with the attack in New York.

"Yes," Lowden said. "And their leader seemed to know Pitt and Giordino."

Gunn took a seat at his desk and powered on his computer. "I'll check on the nearest vessels that can render assistance."

"Don't bother," Lowden said. "We'll be operational within twenty-four hours and can make our way to Panama for repairs. But they've got Pitt and Giordino and are likely headed to Martinique."

"Why Martinique?"

"Pitt spoke with St. Julien Perlmutter, and it's where they think Napoleon is buried."

"I'll do everything I can."

Gunn's office was still dark when he hung up the phone, which matched his thoughts. He remained in his chair a long while, wondering what, in fact, he could actually do.

91

As the *Moselle* sped east, Pitt and Giordino remained bound in the galley, under the eye of a guard seated near the door, a rifle cradled in his lap.

"You'd think they'd let us order something off the à la carte menu while we waited," Giordino said as a cook clattered some pans in the kitchen.

"I think some *poisson du jour* will be coming up shortly," Pitt said, pronouncing it *poison*.

Giordino casually rubbed the zip ties against the edge of his chair, checking for signs of abrasion. He found none. "Does Perlmutter actually think Nape is buried in the slave cemetery on Joséphine's estate?"

"It's the most likely spot. Julien first believed he would have been planted near Joséphine's parents, but he learned they are buried at a small church in town. He thinks it would have been too visible a location to bring in Napoleon quietly. Besides, Little Guinea specifically refers to the estate. So it's a good bet they buried the coffin in the cemetery on the grounds."

"I guess we're done once they find it."

"Or if they don't."

Giordino glanced at the guard. The commando stood attentively, his eyes fixed on Pitt and Giordino.

"Our pal at the door doesn't look like the sentimental type," Giordino said.

"I don't think he's going to fall asleep on us, if that's what you mean. We'll have to hope for a play in Martinique. Hopefully they'll take us ashore with them."

The galley door swung open and Brigitte stepped in alone. She sat down opposite the two men, a tentative look in her blue eyes.

"Seems just like old times," Giordino said. "Except for the rigging," he added, flexing his arms against the zip ties.

"I'm sorry," she said in a sober tone. "I had no idea events would unfold as they did. I never wanted you two, or anyone else, to get hurt."

"But you helped murder Captain Boswick," Pitt said.

"No." Brigitte vigorously shook her head. "I never called the reporter Vogel, but when he arrived on the boat, I agreed to help him take the diamonds. He was an associate of my . . ." Her words fell away. "That fool shot the captain for no reason."

"But you helped him escape," Pitt said.

"I didn't want him to shoot you, too."

"You played us for quite some time."

Brigitte sat grim-faced a moment, silently admitting the deceit. "The diamonds. They are simply too valuable to some."

"Nothing," Pitt said, "is so valuable as to commit murder. As your boyfriend has done repeatedly. In France, in Israel, and in America."

She knew it to be true, but the words stung her with anger. "And what do you know about it!" She stood, took a deep breath, and leaned over the table. "Just so you know, I made him promise to release you," she said quietly, then exited the room.

Giordino watched her depart, then looked at Pitt. "What would you say are the odds of him keeping that promise?"

Pitt gave a humorless smile. "About the same as the *Surcouf* rising from the seafloor and sailing herself back to France."

92

The native Carib Indians had called it Madinina or Island of Flowers when Columbus set foot on it in 1502. The Italian explorer had heard rumors that fierce Amazon warriors ruled the land and rowed ashore with trepidation. Finding instead a tranquil island, he named it Martinica. When no hint of gold was found in the landscape, he departed, never to return.

French colonists arrived a century later and claimed the island, introducing sugarcane and slavery. A French territory today, Martinique is better known for its dense tropical forests, its volcanic Mount Pelée, and some of the best beaches in the Lower Antilles.

The *Moselle* approached the island's west coast at twilight and entered Fort-de-France Bay. The huge inlet appeared like a five-mile-wide bite taken out of the island's pill-shaped outline. The bay's northern coast was twinkling with the lights of Fort-de-France, Martinique's capital and largest city, as the ship reduced speed.

Nassar strode across the bridge of the ship, his eyes focused on the darker, less-populated coast to the south.

A narrow peninsula, Pointe du Bout, jutted into the bay from the southern shore off the ship's beam. On the inland side of the point,

tucked along a wide cove, was Trois-Îslets, one of the island's quainter villages. On a hillside barely a mile inland from the small town stood the remains of Joséphine's family estate at La Pagerie.

Nassar watched with dismay as a raked pleasure boat sped close by the survey ship, its occupants gripping cans of beer and waving drunkenly as they raced to a small marina embedded at the tip of the peninsula.

The captain noted his displeasure. "There are some fancy resorts on Pointe du Bout, but it is almost dark. The waters ahead are clear."

A minute later, the helmsman refuted him. "Sir, radar shows a vessel off Fort-de-France running on an apparent intercept course from the northeast."

"Identification?" Nassar asked.

"The *Sokan*." He checked its registry. "It's a customs patrol boat."

"Stop engines," Nassar ordered. "See if he adjusts course."

The helmsman cut throttle, then shook his head a moment later as he eyed the radarscope. "She's adjusted her heading. Definitely coming our way."

Nassar cursed under his breath. This was no random customs check. The NUMA ship must have alerted the authorities. He looked at a digital map of the harbor. Pointe du Bout lay just ahead. If they reversed course and ducked around its headlands to the seaward side, they'd be out of the customs boat's radar and visual range for at least a few minutes.

He stabbed a finger at the concealed position. "Put us here immediately and prepare to launch the RIB," he ordered. "Stow all weapons in the hidden compartment. When they board to inspect, tell them you are stopping for provisions before crossing the Atlantic. Then head offshore, but return to pick us up in exactly twenty-four hours."

"You are not staying aboard?"

"No, I'm taking Brigitte and two crewmen with me."

CLIVE CUSSLER THE CORSICAN SHADOW

"What about the Americans?"

Nassar thought a moment. "They'll be joining me, too," he said. "But they won't be coming back."

The thirty-one-meter fast patrol boat *Sokan* was a recent addition to the French customs fleet in Martinique, used for surveillance, interdiction, and search and rescue missions around the island.

Standing on her expansive bridge, her captain tracked the *Moselle* on his radarscope. "AIS is not transmitting, so still no identification."

He spoke in English to two men in civilian clothes at the back of the bridge. Both men nodded.

"They're slipping behind Pointe du Bout," the captain added, "but they won't outrun us."

A few minutes later, the *Sokan* reached the peninsula and swung around its tip. The lights of the *Moselle* appeared a half mile ahead, near a small bay dotted with moored pleasure boats. The ship was motoring slowly, parallel to the tourist beach of Anse Mitan.

"They've turned on their AIS," the captain reported. "It's the *Moselle*, as suspected."

He hailed the survey ship and ordered it to halt for a boarding inspection. The *Moselle* readily complied, drifting to a stop as a detail of armed customs agents motored alongside in a Zodiac. A powerful searchlight mounted on the *Sokan* bathed the survey ship in a cobalt glow.

The customs agents were thorough, herding the crew onto the stern deck, then inspecting every nook and cranny. Several minutes later, the lead agent radioed the *Sokan*'s captain, who turned to the two civilians on the bridge.

"The entire crew is now on deck," he said. "Are your two men among them?"

Rudi Gunn raised a pair of binoculars and scrutinized the assembled men. Under the spotlights, their faces were easy to see. They

were a tough lot, he thought, doubting there was a geologist or engineer among the bunch. He searched every face, but Pitt and Giordino were not to be seen.

"No," he told the captain. "I don't see them."

Beside him, Charles Lufbery was performing a similar examination, searching for Henri Nassar. The commando had been linked to the Israel, Paris, and New York attacks after Hiram Yaeger had connected the dots to the Lavera-owned sea vessels involved. Video surveillance of Nassar and Villard with LeBoeuf had tied him to the shipping company. Investigative teams were now on the hunt in Normandy for Lavera Exploration's chief executive officer, who was in hiding.

The French police captain was bleary-eyed from a hurried transatlantic flight. He sagged with disappointment at not seeing his man. "Captain," Lufbery said, "can you have the crew's passports brought aboard for inspection?"

As the request was forwarded, Gunn peered through his binoculars. He no longer focused on the crew, but on the survey ship itself. He held his gaze on a stern crane that was angled over the side with a line trailing into the water.

"Cancel that request, Captain," Gunn said. "I'd ask that you release the crew and retrieve your inspection team as quickly as possible."

"What do you mean by this?" Lufbery asked.

"The satellite photos," Gunn said. He took Lufbery's arm and guided him to a laptop at the rear of the bridge. Gunn had used satellite photos to identify and track the *Moselle* after its assault on the *Havana* near Panama. The laptop displayed an overhead shot of the vessel on approach to Martinique.

"Look at the quarterdeck." He pointed to the aft end.

Lufbery studied the fuzzy photo, then glanced at the ship itself. "The inflatable boat. It's gone."

"I noticed it only because the crane is positioned over the water. They must have just deployed it."

Lufbery called to the captain. "Do as he says. We must put in to port at once." He turned to Gunn. "If it is Nassar, we must find him."

"There's only one place he would go," Gunn said, silently hoping that Pitt and Giordino were alive and with him.

93

The inflatable boat touched ground on a rocky ledge at the end of Anse Mitan beach. Farther east, where the sand was softer, the waterfront was dotted with motels, apartments, and restaurants.

Nassar had come aground at a quiet point between two darkened, foliage-covered houses. Pitt and Giordino were herded beneath the shadow of a concrete retaining wall and ordered to sit under guard of the two commandos. Brigitte followed Nassar past the houses to the front road.

"Stay here and wait for me." He tucked a pistol into his coat pocket. "I'll find some transportation. Figure out how to get to the estate from here."

She nodded and slipped from view beneath a palm tree and consulted her phone, while Nassar moved down the road. He had two options: either carjack a passing motorist or make his way to a tourist resort on Pointe du Bout and steal a car from a careless parking attendant.

A safer option appeared after he strode past a deserted package store. A wooden sign proclaiming *Réparation Automobile de Michel*

dangled above a two-bay garage, surrounded by used cars in various states of repair.

Nassar walked around the back and peeked through a garage door window. A white sedan was elevated on a rack with its wheels off and hood open.

He slid to the next door. The second bay held a green pickup truck with a mashed grille and a large dent in the front fender. Its wheels were on and the hood closed, indicating the repairs had yet to begin.

Nassar found a side door, checked its seam with a penlight, and found no evidence of an alarm system. With his suppressed pistol, he fired a round into the lock, then kicked the door open.

No alarm sounded. He made his way to a small, cramped office. He checked the desk drawers for the keys, but came up empty. He retreated to the garage and poked his head in the truck's side window. The keys were sitting in a console cupholder, and Nassar reminded himself he was on an island. There was no place to hide a stolen vehicle.

He opened the bay door, started the truck, and drove it out of the garage as if he owned it. Down the road, he pulled to a stop near the palm tree and waved to Brigitte.

She backtracked along the side of the house to the waiting commandos and motioned for them to follow. Then she hurried to the idling truck and climbed inside the cab.

Pitt and Giordino were marched to the back and ordered into the truck bed. Pitt stepped onto the bumper and over the gate and took a seat just inside. Giordino followed on the opposite corner.

The two commandos climbed in on either side, using the rear tire as a foothold and sat with their backs to the cab. They held their rifles at the ready, while their eyes were in constant motion.

Nassar stepped on the gas, and the truck lurched forward. "How do we get to the estate?" he asked Brigitte.

She held up her phone, displaying a satellite photo. "I believe we're

here, at the west end of Anse Mitan. We need to cross the town on this road and turn left on Route 38, which leads to Trois-Îslets. From there, a small road will lead inland to La Pagerie. It's about five kilometers."

Nassar followed the road through the sleepy beach town, which had turned even quieter in the evening hour. He reached a roundabout and followed the exit toward Trois-Îslets. The road grew pitch-black as they left the town and wound through a sparsely developed section of the island. Visibility was a challenge, as the truck's right headlight was inoperative from its collision damage.

The other reason the truck was in the shop was more evident to those who rode in back. Broken rear shock absorbers sent the occupants flying every time the truck hit a dip or pothole.

One rut sent Giordino sprawling sideways at Pitt's feet.

"Feels like we're riding in the pocket of a deranged kangaroo," he muttered.

Pitt noticed the two gunmen were being equally jostled. "I think we may want to spring out of here," he said under his breath.

"Say the word," Giordino said as he retook his seat in the corner.

The truck climbed a long rise, then descended into a clearing. Pitt noticed corridors of low grass on either side of the road and realized they were crossing through a golf course. He recalled seeing it in the data from Perlmutter. The course had been built on land that was once part of the La Pagerie estate.

The truck continued north, passing small drives on either side that led to hillside houses. Brigitte searched the dark roadside for a sign to La Pagerie, but was hindered by the truck's bouncing and lone headlight. The glare from an oncoming car distracted her view, and she missed the turnoff.

Nassar drove on, following the road as it gradually turned toward the coast and into a more developed landscape. A break in the trees showed the distant lights of Fort-de-France sparkling off the black

bay waters. More disconcerting was a congregation of lights behind and to their left.

Brigitte looked at her phone and enlarged the map. "Those closer lights have to be the town of Trois-Îslets. I think we've gone too far. We should have turned right after the golf course. I'm sorry, I didn't see the road."

The narrow road didn't offer enough room to turn around, so Nassar continued until reaching a turnoff that angled to the bay. He wheeled onto the lane, which led to a small industrial park. Corrugated tin-roof buildings and warehouses fronted the road, leading to a large complex on the waterfront. The truck bounded through a drainage ditch as Nassar pulled into a gravel parking lot to turn around.

As the truck circled, Pitt saw they were again approaching the ditch on the way out. He turned and whispered to Giordino. "Let's make like a marsupial on the next bump. Meet you at the bayfront."

Giordino gave a faint nod, keeping his eyes on the gunmen. The truck began to accelerate and this time struck the ditch faster. All four men in the bed were tossed from their seats, but Pitt and Giordino went much higher, pushing off with their hands. They vaulted over the tailgate and landed in the dirt on their feet.

Unaware of their escape, Nassar kept on driving until the commandos in back shouted to stop. One stood and fired at the fleeing men as Nassar stomped on the brakes. But his shots flew high as he was thrown back against the cab when the truck skidded to a hard stop.

As Nassar hopped out of the driver's seat, the second commando knelt and fired a burst at one of the fleeing figures. Nassar glimpsed Pitt round the corner of the nearest building as the shots trailed behind him. Across the street, Giordino sprinted toward the safety of a large steel shed. Nassar reached for his own pistol, but realized he was too late.

Just like that, both men had disappeared into the night.

94

"Hunt them down," Nassar yelled.

The closest commando jumped out of the truck and ran after Pitt, the target whom he had missed. The other commando, who had been flung against the cab, gingerly regained his footing in the truck bed. He clutched his shoulder and winced, one arm hanging limp as he climbed down. The man had fractured his clavicle.

"Take a seat in the truck." Nassar pointed to the passenger side. He stuck his head through the driver's window and looked at Brigitte. "Where is the road to the estate?"

She slid behind the wheel and showed him the photo on her phone. "It's this one, just by the golf course."

"Take the truck and locate the site. We will catch up with you there."

"Why don't you let them go? You said you would."

He considered the request, but knew it was impossible now. "I'll see you soon," he said, then sprinted in Giordino's direction.

Brigitte watched him through the rearview mirror until he van-

ished in the darkness. Her stomach churned, but she took a deep breath, put the truck in gear, and slowly drove away.

———————

Fifty yards away, Pitt felt like an ice pick was jabbing his knee with every step. He'd wrenched the joint when he leaped from the truck and landed awkwardly. The spasms soon lessened, but there was still a fireball of pain whenever he put weight on the leg.

He shook it off as best he could and continued around the front of the first building. The approaching crunch of boots on the gravel sent him scurrying ahead.

The complex around him was a series of industrial buildings that faced the dirt road. He skirted around to the side of the building and hobbled down its length, hoping to escape into the woods beyond. There he saw a high chain-link fence surrounding the exterior of the industrial park. With a bad knee, he doubted he could climb it quickly enough to escape.

An adjacent warehouse lay a short distance away and Pitt headed for its back end. He nearly reached it, when the commando appeared around the first building. Widely spaced light poles along the road gave just enough light for both men to spot each other at the same instant.

Pitt raced for the building. He was steps away when the gunman opened fire with his assault rifle. Pitt saw the ground burst around him. He dove forward, rolled behind some broken pallets, then scrambled to the cover of the building.

The tumble didn't help his knee, but he rose and kept running, crossing the back end of the building. Pitt threaded his way past several large trash bins and empty barrels to the next alleyway. Across the open gap stood one more structure—a long brick building painted yellow with the words *Pneus Usagés* painted in cursive along the side.

Pitt's real estate was running out. Beyond the yellow building was

just one more, the large complex on the waterfront. His eyes caught movement across the road. A blur rushed by the back of a steel warehouse. It was Giordino.

Pitt's partner had taken a similar tack, looping around the back side of the opposite buildings and speeding toward the bay. Somehow, somewhere, they'd both need to make a stand.

Pitt felt a stab in his knee, looked at the yellow building in front of him, and decided it would be his Alamo.

He ran to the corner and, using the exposed edge of the bricks, sawed through the zip tie until it snapped free. He glanced up at the wall inscription. *Pneus Usagés*. While his French was wanting, Pitt knew the term from owning an antique French sports car. The meaning was demonstrated by a massive wall of used tires that lined the side of the building like a garden terrace.

Pitt limped to the barricade, knowing it was time for the rubber to hit the road.

95

The commando paused and listened. He even held his breath, but heard no movement nearby. He had wasted precious time searching around the pallets and bins at the back of the second building, but he wanted to make sure Pitt didn't slip by him.

He'd seen Pitt limping and knew he couldn't have gone far. With the waterfront blocking his path to freedom, it was like an Old West cowboy herding a mustang into a box canyon. There would be no escape. But there was one more alleyway to clear, sided by the yellow brick building.

He approached the yellow building cautiously, gazing at the piles of worn tires stacked two and three meters high. Packed close together and tucked against the brick wall, they offered little refuge unless a man was foolish enough to climb inside. The gunman searched the near end, then slowly made his way along the wall. Every few feet, he'd stop and poke his gun barrel into the crevices between the columns of tires.

Midway along the building, he quickened his pace as he approached a dark stretch beyond the reach of the streetlights. Above him, he heard a sudden squeak of rubber. He looked up toward the

sound, only to observe an avalanche of rubber bearing down on him. Three huge truck tires toppled off a high stack and plunged through the darkness. They were followed by the outstretched body of Pitt, who had wedged himself behind the upper tires on a shadowed section of the wall.

The commando jumped to the side, but was clipped on the leg by the first tire and knocked forward to the ground. A second tire smacked the back of his shoulder as he tried to crawl forward. Pitt arrived an instant later, landing on the gunman's lower torso and driving a fist into his kidneys. With his legs pinned, the commando swung his upper body around with his weapon and squeezed the trigger.

As the muzzle erupted near his face, Pitt shoved his left elbow into the man's back, driving the commando and his weapon flat against the ground. The gunman's finger was caught in the trigger guard, and the weapon kept firing into the stacks of tires until the magazine emptied.

Pitt pulled back and launched a right hook that caught the gunman flush on the side of the neck. The blow pinched the carotid artery, and the commando lost consciousness.

"*Jean-Luc, il est mort?*" came a shout from across the road.

Pitt glimpsed in the distance the silhouette of a man with a pistol. Nassar. But his own position was obscured in the dark alley.

"*Oui,*" Pitt said in a guttural tone.

The man nodded, then resumed his pursuit of Giordino around the far building. Pitt rolled the gunman over and took his rifle, then checked his pockets for a spare magazine or extra weapon. He found neither.

He tossed the empty gun atop one of the stacks of tires and limped toward the end of the building, hoping he could find a way to save Giordino.

96

Nassar turned from the yellow building and sprinted toward a steel storage shed on his side of the street. Jean-Luc had done his job, killing Pitt. Nassar would finish the job with the other American.

With a head start, Giordino had not needed to play cat and mouse. But Nassar was a strong runner and closed the gap as he pursued Giordino around the back side of the buildings. A tall perimeter fence also hemmed in this side of the grounds. The industrial park was not so easy to flee.

Nassar reached the last structure facing the dirt road, a white stucco building. As he scurried along the rear, he heard the squeak of a rusty hinge nearby. Turning the corner, he faced a large compound along the waterfront, secured by a separate chain-link fence. A small office building stood to the side of a massive, open-ended warehouse that stretched the length of a football field. To the left of the building was an exposed yard full of pallets topped with blocks wrapped in plastic. A wooden dock stretched into the bay beyond, where the pallets could be loaded for sea transport.

A sign over the gate proclaimed *Briques de Martinique*, confirm-

ing that red clay bricks were manufactured here and stacked on the pallets. A pedestrian gate clanged shut and Nassar caught a glimpse of a dark shadow moving toward the warehouse. He raised his pistol and fired two snap shots. He then rushed through the gate and approached the warehouse entrance, hoping to find Giordino's body on the ground inside.

Instead, he found a maze of silent shadows under the corrugated roof. Massive conveyors and mixing equipment, interspersed with pallets, forklifts, and stacks upon stacks of drying bricks, stretched the length of the dimly lit building. Somewhere in the crowded confines, Giordino was hiding.

Nassar found pleasure in stalking Giordino as if he were wild game. It reminded him of hunting Islamic rebels in northern Mali in 2013, when he and his Foreign Legion regiment searched street by street through the dusty city of Gao. Only now, no one was shooting back.

He moved methodically down the wide center aisle, avoiding the opportunity for ambush. He stopped under one of the widely spaced overhead lights and spotted something on the concrete floor near his feet. He knelt and rubbed his finger through a dark spot. Wet blood.

He saw a similar spot a few feet ahead. It, too, was freshly spilled. Nassar smiled as he rose and followed the droplets on the floor, a red trail leading to the kill.

97

Pitt heard the twin pops of Nassar's gunshots. He crept around the corner of the yellow building as Nassar entered the compound under the fuzzy glow of a light above the entry gate.

Pitt waited a few seconds, then moved forward, keeping the gunman in distant view. When the commando stepped into the warehouse, Pitt slipped through the front gate and took cover behind a pallet of finished bricks. From that position, he noticed a mini utility truck parked facing the dock.

He peeked around the bricks and saw Nassar briefly kneel. The commando was near the middle of the brickworks factory.

Pitt looked through the warehouse to the far end, where a pyramid of raw clay towered into the night sky. Long conveyors carried the clay inside the building, first to a crushing device, then into a huge mixing vat. Water was added to the dry clay, and the mix fed through an extruder, which spit out the individually formed bricks.

Midway through the building, the newly formed bricks were placed in high, crisscrossed stacks to air-dry for a day or two. It was near these drying stacks that Nassar was studying the floor. Closer to

Pitt, and abutting the side wall, was a huge walk-in kiln, where the bricks were fired at over a thousand degrees.

While the huge oven was impressive, something next to it caught Pitt's eye—a large white upright tank that rose to the rafters. Positioned near the oven, it had to be a storage tank for compressed gas that fueled the kiln's burners.

Pitt considered the tank, then moved to the small utility vehicle parked nearby. He searched the interior and the cargo bed until he found a small toolbox. He grabbed the box and proceeded toward the warehouse, moving quietly from pallet to pallet.

Nassar had his back to him as Pitt reached the warehouse entrance. He slipped inside and found refuge behind the protruding wall of the kiln. At the back wall, he approached the large tank, which was marked with a red diamond-shaped warning label with the number 1075. It signified propane gas.

Pitt ran his hand across a thick rubberized line that ran from a base valve to the kiln. In the toolbox he found an assortment of wrenches and screwdrivers, brown with rust from the humid climate. None of the wrenches were large enough to turn the hose fitting on the valve, but Pitt's luck improved when he found a rubber mallet.

He retrieved a small Phillips screwdriver with a sharp point and aligned the tip against the hose. He took the mallet and gave it a whack, driving it into the line. The muffled blow was barely audible, so he quickly punched several more holes.

He expected a rush of compressed gas to blow out of the holes, but he felt nothing. Pitt traced the rubber line back to the tank and saw the main valve was closed. He opened the lever, and immediately the punctures whistled with a flow of gas. Even from a few feet away, Pitt could feel the cold of the compressed gas and smell its foul odor.

He crept to the corner of the kiln, where he saw Nassar had

advanced toward a large section of drying bricks on the opposite side of the aisle. Pitt moved to the warehouse exit, noticing a light switch panel inside the doorway. As he rushed by, he flicked the switches off, plunging the interior into darkness.

He had no way of knowing that act would save Giordino's life.

98

After jumping from the pickup truck, Giordino had expected Pitt would beat him to the waterfront. But the rattle of gunfire by the yellow building told him that wasn't the case.

Giordino's instinct was to run toward the sound of gunfire to render help, but absent a weapon, he knew it would be too reckless. The better option was to keep moving. There had to be something in the brick factory, even if just a shovel or some bricks, he could use to fight.

He reached the pedestrian gate to the factory, but found it locked by a drop-down metal fork secured by a padlock.

An overhead light revealed the mechanism was heavily rusted. He slipped his hand beneath the outer prong of the fork and pulled. The metal bent a fraction of an inch. He applied more pressure, moving it enough to slip both hands behind it.

Pushing one leg against the post, he leaned his mass into it and flattened the prong. He shoved the squeaky gate inward and ducked inside. A glance over his shoulder revealed Nassar taking a bead on him with his pistol outside the fence.

Giordino dove to the ground as two shots whistled by. He gauged

the defensive merits of an open brickyard versus the factory building and opted for inside. With his head down, he sprinted through the entrance and lost himself inside before Nassar could enter the compound.

The large kiln offered little cover, so Giordino ran down the center aisle to a broad maze of drying bricks stacked in eight-foot-tall squares. He ducked behind the first block, slipping out of sight an instant before Nassar approached the building and peered inside.

Giordino moved farther into the stacked bricks, spying through gaps in the pallets to track Nassar's approach. Sweat ran down his neck from his extended run in the tropic air. The shirt sleeve on his forearm also felt damp, and he found it soaked with blood. A light gash near his elbow marked where a bullet had just grazed him.

He kept moving, angling back until he reached a wall that supported the extractor machine. It was too high to climb. He realized he was partially cornered. Moving deeper into the warehouse would mean stepping into the center aisle, which risked exposure.

He pulled two bricks off the top of a drying stack, then crept to the aisle corner and searched for his pursuer. Nassar was nowhere to be seen.

Giordino froze, straining to hear over the sound of the breeze blowing through the rafters. He detected a faint pad of leather on concrete close by. He turned just as Nassar, having followed his trail of blood, rounded the stack of bricks behind him. The commando raised his pistol to fire.

Then the lights went out.

99

N assar aimed where Giordino had stood and pulled the trigger twice. The muzzle flashes revealed he fired a hair too late.

Giordino lunged around the corner at the first sight of Nassar, just as the building went black. He hesitated a second and lobbed both bricks over the stack, then took off running down the center aisle.

An artilleryman could not have computed a better mortar trajectory, as the bricks flew over the stack and rained down on Nassar in tandem. The first brick struck his outstretched right arm, nearly causing him to drop the pistol. The second landed on his left shoulder, bruising his collarbone.

Nassar dropped to his knees, wincing in pain before slowly shaking it off. He rose and groped along the wall of bricks to the end of the stack. He stepped into the aisle and looked toward the bayside opening. While the interior was pitch-black, the ambient light outside gave a faint illumination to the entrance area—just enough to see the dark figure of Giordino running for the exit.

The building's open end seemed miles away from Giordino as he sprinted across the concrete floor. He ran in a slight zigzag pattern, expecting to feel a bullet thud into his back. Instead, he detected a

sputtering ahead. It was the rattle of a small motor starting, then quickly revving. The outline of a dark object appeared outside, moving across the brickyard toward the warehouse entrance.

As Giordino ran toward the kiln, he put the shape and sound together, identifying it as the mini utility truck that had been parked in the yard. A second later, its headlamps popped on, blinding him as he ran.

Farther behind, the lights revealed Nassar raising his pistol in a two-handed stance. As the vehicle burst into the warehouse, it swerved to one side, then lurched back to the other as the driver turned the wheel hard over. The vehicle spun in a perfect arc, its rear tires screeching across the smooth concrete floor as the truck reversed direction, its nose pointing to the exit.

Giordino didn't need to see the driver to know Pitt was behind the wheel. He sprinted for the tailgate as Pitt accelerated the truck forward. But Giordino was moving faster and Pitt had executed the turn perfectly in front of him. Giordino took a long step and lunged for the open truck bed as a gunshot rang out.

The metal bed clanged from a bullet hitting the frame, followed by two more shots that whistled high. Nassar's numb right arm gave him a weak grip on the pistol, degrading his accuracy. He lowered his arm, tried to shake awake the nerves, and took off running after the vehicle.

Lying on the short truck bed, Giordino had a tenuous grasp as Pitt exited the warehouse. The small truck weaved around several brick pallets before Pitt pulled to a stop. Giordino slid off the bed and leaned against the vehicle while catching his breath. "I thought I called for an Uber Black."

"Afraid the limo's in the shop today." Pitt noticed Giordino's bloody sleeve. "You okay?"

"'Tis but a scratch," he said in a British accent. "But perhaps we shouldn't keep the meter running."

He plopped into the passenger seat, but Pitt looked back at the warehouse with other designs.

"I'll be right back," he said.

Pitt left Giordino in the truck and sprinted back toward the warehouse, using the brick pallets for cover. He stopped and knelt behind a stack near the entrance and peered inside. With the lights off, the interior was like a black cave, too dark to see Nassar. But Pitt heard the tap of the commando's shoes on the concrete floor as he jogged closer.

Pitt kept his eyes glued to the entrance as he felt the side pocket of his cargo pants and retrieved the flare he'd taken from the inflatable boat. When a silhouette appeared in the doorway, Pitt jumped to his feet, yanked the igniter cap off the end of the flare, and sparked it alight.

Just steps from the entrance, Nassar instantly saw the burning light, which cast Pitt in a red glow. He was surprised yet again to see Pitt alive, but now he was the gift of an easy target. Pitt might as well have painted a bull's-eye on his chest.

Nassar raised his pistol, but Pitt was faster, taking a step and flinging the flare directly at him.

The harmless glow of the airborne flare still allowed for an easy shot, and Nassar took a second to collect his breath as he aimed the pistol at Pitt. Then he noticed an unusual rush of cold air at his side and smelled the bitter odor of propane gas. As his finger tightened on the trigger, he heard a loud whooshing, then his world exploded in a sea of yellow flame.

Even standing outside the building, Pitt felt like a hydrogen bomb had detonated. A deafening boom sent a mushroom cloud of smoke and fire into the night sky. The propane tank, half the kiln, and a large section of the building's roof rocketed into the air, then came raining down in fragments.

Pitt tucked his body against the base of a pallet of bricks as a blast

of hot air and shrapnel surged around him. When the debris stopped falling, he made his way back to the truck, where he found Giordino crawling from beneath the truck bed with a wide grin.

"Caught our pal inside?" Giordino asked.

Pitt nodded. "I wanted to light up his life."

"You did that and more." Giordino pointed at a dark clump near the truck.

Pitt gazed at the smoldering object. It was a leather shoe, with the owner's foot still inside.

100

Sirens wailed in the distance as Pitt and Giordino climbed into the mini truck. The explosion had knocked down a portion of the fence surrounding the brickyard, and Pitt drove over it to escape the compound. A section of fencing rebounded against the underside and caught the muffler, ripping it off the tailpipe.

The exhaust bellowed, but Pitt didn't bother slowing. He drove down the dirt road, glancing to the side as they passed the yellow brick building and the wall of tires. The commando he had leveled was still sprawled on the ground unconscious.

Giordino caught Pitt's gaze and noticed the gunman. "What happened to him?"

"I believe he got tired."

They reached the paved road and Pitt turned right, retracing their original route.

"Can you locate Joséphine's estate?" Giordino asked over the truck's loud exhaust.

Pitt had nothing to navigate from other than his recall of a satellite photo sent by Perlmutter. "I know it's inland from the golf course, off

a road that runs along its northern boundary. I think I can put us in the ballpark."

Had it been daylight, he could have navigated his way there in minutes. But the darkness of the hills above Trois-Îslets made it like searching blindfolded for a penny in a cave. Pitt turned down several roads leading inland, only to find they weren't roads but winding driveways to houses hidden in the trees. He gave up guessing and drove to the golf course, pausing as a speeding police car passed by with its lights flashing. Pitt turned onto the course and drove across the grass of the driving range.

He sped past the marker flags to a fairway that sloped uphill to the east. The lightweight mini truck wasn't much bigger than a golf cart and bounced across the grass as Pitt whipped around a green and onto the next fairway. A sand trap appeared out of nowhere and Pitt had to swerve sharply to avoid it, digging the rear tires into the soft turf.

"Poor form," Giordino said, "not to replace your divots."

"I suspect my membership privileges were revoked about a half mile ago."

When the fairway took a dogleg to the right, Pitt cut left through the rough, having spotted a road beyond the course. He had to barrel through a small irrigation ditch, flooring the accelerator so the truck splashed through a foot of water before bounding up and onto the road. It wound through a dark, narrow valley dotted with small wood frame houses.

A short distance up the road, they approached a pair of stone pillars with an open gate. Pitt wheeled the truck through the entrance. The pillars were overgrown with vines, and the rusty steel gate was permanently wedged open by the roots of a tree.

The truck's exhaust rattled off the walls as he approached a large stone house at the end of the drive. Even in the dark, it appeared

crumbling and neglected. Beside it were two long buildings that re-sembled Army barracks, equally weathered with peeling paint and frayed tar-paper roofs. None of the structures resembled the photos of La Pagerie, and Pitt realized he had the wrong property.

As he swung past the house to turn around, a dog in the yard be-gan yelping and a porch light flicked on. Pitt stopped the truck as a tall Creole woman opened the door and stepped outside. She wore a long colorful skirt and a bright blue blouse with the name *Doris* em-broidered on the chest.

After glaring at the loud idling truck, she quieted the dog, then admonished Pitt and Giordino. "The children just get back to sleep after the big boom and sirens, and now you go and wake them up again."

Pitt smiled at the woman's feistiness, then felt bad when he noticed six or seven small children crowding around the doorway. An even smaller boy pushed to the front, clutching a worn soccer ball.

"La Pagerie?" Pitt asked.

"It is up the road another half mile." She waved her arm. "But it is not open in the middle of the night, you fools." She noticed Giordi-no's bloody arm and took a quick step back.

"Thank you," Pitt said.

He drove slowly out of the yard as Giordino waved at the children. Pitt had to weave around two buckets and some palm fronds, which he realized were set up as a soccer net.

When they reached the gate, Giordino pointed to an overgrown sign they had missed that read *Caribbean Children's Rescue.*

"I feel even worse now," Pitt said.

"Look on the bright side," Giordino said. "At least Doris doesn't know you were the one responsible for the big boom."

101

Exactly one half mile up the road, Pitt and Giordino reached a sign proclaiming *La Pagerie Musée*. Pitt drove past the entrance a few hundred yards and parked the truck on the edge of the road.

"Stealth was not our best friend tonight." Giordino patted the fender of the noisy truck as they abandoned it.

They returned to the entrance and entered the grounds on foot, spotting the stolen green pickup truck in front of the museum building. The stout stone structure had originally served as the plantation's kitchen. To the left stood the skeletal remains of the estate's main house, along with remnants of other structures destroyed in a 1766 hurricane.

Behind the museum, Pitt eyed the overgrown walls of a sugar mill, built to process the plantation's sugarcane.

Giordino tapped him on the arm and pointed in the opposite direction. "The cemetery would appear to be this way," he whispered.

Pitt looked past him to see the glow of a cell phone flashlight bobbing in a clearing through the trees. He and Giordino crept into the woods and quietly approached until they could get a full view of the clearing.

It was a small cemetery surrounded by a crumbling rock wall. The bouncing cell light was held by Brigitte, who was examining tombstones near the center of the graveyard.

Pitt and Giordino remained frozen in the brush, searching for signs of another presence.

"Were all three gunmen left at the brickyard?" Giordino whispered.

"I saw only the two."

They waited in silence another few minutes until convinced she was alone, then strode out of the woods and entered the cemetery. They approached within a dozen feet of Brigitte before she detected their presence and turned the phone light on them.

"Where . . . Where is Henri?"

"In the brickyard," Giordino said. "And in the bay. And in the trees. And in about a thousand other places."

"No!"

Brigitte had heard the explosion. She had seen smoke and flames above the treetops and knew it had come from the area of the industrial park. She sunk to her knees and let out a sob.

As she dropped down, a figure arose from behind the rock wall to her side. The third commando leveled his rifle at Pitt and Giordino. He kept the rifle on point as he awkwardly climbed over the wall and moved alongside Brigitte. "I told you," he said to her, "Henri would have driven into the estate."

He held the rifle loosely, his left hand resting on the barrel. Pitt could see from his grimace that he was in pain.

Brigitte took a minute to compose herself, then rose to her feet, her eyes damp. "This is the slave cemetery. The grave must be here. What more do you know?"

Her politeness did not extend to the commando, who raised his weapon toward Pitt's face.

Pitt looked down at the tombstone next to Brigitte, its weathered

engraving nearly unreadable. He crossed his arms and stared at the commando. "For starters, you're looking in the wrong place."

"What are you saying?" Brigitte asked.

"This graveyard was used in the eighteenth and nineteenth centuries. There likely weren't any unused plots in the center of the cemetery. If Napoleon was buried here, he would be along the perimeter."

Brigitte accepted the logic and led them around the outskirts with her light. There was little difference in the age of the tombstones as they completed a full circuit, and doubt began to creep into her mind. Then she stopped in front of a grave marker at the lower end of the cemetery that caught her eye. Like the others it was weathered and moss-covered, but the engraving was different. The letters were uneven and carved in a cruder fashion, yet looked crisper than the surrounding engravings.

Only the date was legible through the weeds, but it made Brigitte hesitate. It read *1821.*

As she stepped closer, her light flashed on the back side of the stone.

"It's been reused," the commando noted.

Brigitte looked at the back of the stone. "Noah, twelfth September, 1787," she read, then moved to the front of the marker.

She pushed the weeds aside and brushed her hand across the surface. Her fingers wiped away decades of dust and moss that had accumulated over the light engraving, exposing additional words. "Jean d'Éppé, 1821." Her hand shook. "That was the year Napoleon died."

She looked up at Pitt. "It's him. It has to be. The crew of the *Surcouf* must have carved the gravestone reusing an old marker."

Her anguish over Nassar's death was swept aside in a rush of excitement. She spoke to the commando, who stepped to the stone wall and returned with a pair of rusty shovels he had taken from a museum exhibit.

"Dig," he said. He tossed the shovels at Pitt's and Giordino's feet, then resumed his grip on the gun.

The men picked up the borrowed tools and began probing the ground. The soil was soft from recent rains and turned over easily. They dug near the headstone and had excavated a hole four feet deep when Pitt's shovel contacted solid wood.

Brigitte held up the light while Pitt scraped away the loose soil. A wood slab and crossbeam had been exposed, looking nothing like the smooth surface of a coffin.

The two men continued removing dirt, working around the edges until they had exposed the entire top surface. It was a crate, about double the size of an ordinary coffin, built from white oak in remarkably stout condition.

Brigitte walked back and forth beside it, studying the surface as Pitt and Giordino took a breather. Sweat dripped down both men's shirts from the muggy night.

"It must be the shipping crate," Brigitte said with excitement. "They would have used it for transport."

Pitt noted the French words *Ne Pas Ovrir* and *Hasardeux* printed on the surface and had to agree. It wasn't the grave of a slave.

Examining the top side, Brigitte noticed the lower end showed damage. "Please dig down to the bottom and expose the end panel," she said. "So that we can remove it and look inside."

Pitt and Giordino moved to the end of the crate and began to excavate. After digging down a foot or two, there wasn't enough room for both men to work, so Giordino climbed into the trench and dug solo.

His curiosity was as great as Brigitte's, and he dug without letup until he reached the base of the crate. He cleared away a large space behind it, then climbed out of the hole, breathing hard. "Why don't you finish it off," he said to Pitt and leaned on his shovel.

Pitt climbed down and wedged his shovel into the seam at the base of the crate. Putting his weight against the handle, he pried open the end piece an inch or two as several nails squeaked in protest. He slid the blade to the next side and repeated the effort, gradually working loose the entire panel. He dropped the shovel, gripped the wood with his fingers, and pulled it free of the crate.

Brigitte leaned over the side with her light and peered inside. The contents were covered in a rotted tarp. "Pull the covering off," she said.

Pitt grabbed the ends of the tarp . . . and a dozen lights suddenly snapped on around them. They were small flashlights, judging by their wavering beams, and formed a loose ring around the cemetery. The people holding the lights began moving forward, closing in on the group at the open grave.

The commando took a knee behind a tombstone and raised his rifle to his shoulder. As he took a bead on one of the lights, Brigitte cried out behind him, "No!"

It wasn't a plea to the commando, but a warning. The commando turned to Brigitte . . . and only then saw Giordino swinging his shovel like a baseball bat in the hands of Aaron Judge. The blade clanged against the gunman's head, and he slumped to the ground.

Giordino scooped up the man's weapon, then tossed it aside a second later when a cry of "*Lâche ton arme*" rang from the darkness.

A squad of Martinique police officers descended on the group, surrounding them at gunpoint. The circle widened to let two men through. Pitt and Giordino were shocked to see it was Gunn and Lufbery.

"I never pegged you two as grave robbers," Gunn said with a smirk, delighted to see his friends alive.

"Maybe if you weren't so tight with the payroll," Giordino replied.

"We were actually digging our own graves," Pitt said. He motioned toward the prone commando, who sat up, regaining his senses.

Two policemen cuffed him and dragged him to his feet. Another grabbed Brigitte and locked her hands behind her back.

"We saw the whole thing." Gunn held up a pair of night vision goggles. "We've been monitoring the scene for the past thirty minutes."

"Why didn't you move in sooner?" Giordino rubbed his calloused hands. "You could have saved us from getting our shoes muddy."

"Because we wanted to see what you found," Lufbery said as he eyed the crate.

The police began to drag Brigitte away, but she struggled in protest. "Wait. I have a right to know what's there." Tears flooded her cheeks.

Pitt looked at Lufbery and nodded. "We wouldn't be here without her."

The policeman released her arm, and everyone looked to Pitt, who still stood in the grave. He renewed his grip on the tarp and tugged it away.

Illuminated by a ring of flashlights, an oversized oak coffin appeared. Pitt rapped his knuckle against the top surface, next to a painted fleur-de-lis.

"Looks a little large for someone Napoleon's size," Gunn said.

"No, it is just right," Brigitte said, her eyes aglow. "He is buried in six coffins that fit into one another. And the outer coffin was made of oak, as this one appears."

"It can only be," Lufbery said, reverence in his voice. "It can only be."

They stared in silence at the emperor's tomb. Their thoughts were broken by a moan from the injured commando.

"Take them away," Lufbery ordered.

Brigitte resisted a second time. "Is there . . . Is there anything else in the crate?"

Pitt poked his head into the container and groped along the sides

of the coffin. His hand bumped into two dust-covered objects wedged against the side. He gripped their handles and pulled them from the crate, exposing them to the multiple flashlights. They were a pair of aluminum cases with Eduard Martin's initials on the side.

"What are they?" Gunn asked.

Pitt held them up, then looked at Brigitte. "For some, the luggage from a journey to Waterloo."

102

In his secret refuge in Le Havre, Yves Villard waited patiently for the courier to leave. From a small upstairs window, Villard had watched the young man approach, alerted to his presence by a motion detector. The courier was patient, ringing the doorbell for several minutes before finally giving up. He left the package by the door, then climbed aboard a scooter and rode away.

The note inside the package on the doormat was brief. *Midnight. 134 Rue du Hoc. L.*

Villard crumpled the paper in his fist until his arm shook. While the authorities may not have known the location of his safe house, LeBoeuf obviously did, and that was just as dangerous. Villard stepped to a narrow study in the small penthouse, poured a cognac, and fell into a stuffed chair.

He had watched the reports from America and knew that Nassar had failed spectacularly. The entire team had supposedly been killed, which was a saving grace, although it was unclear if Nassar was among the dead. There were no published links to Villard or his company, but they would come. Eventually.

And now there was LeBoeuf. The fat man wanted his money and

would know now that it wasn't forthcoming. Villard sat in the chair, staring at a photo of his wife until the cognac was gone. At eleven p.m., he dressed in a three-piece suit, removed a gold watch he normally carried in the vest pocket, and replaced it with a compact Baby Browning .25 automatic. The eighty-year-old pistol had been carried by his father on the docks of Le Havre, once used by the old man to shoot a drunken stevedore who threatened him with a pike.

It was a two-mile walk to the waterfront address listed on the note. Villard elected to travel on foot, hoping to walk off the effects of the cognac. He slipped on a light overcoat to ward against the chill of a misty evening and left his apartment.

Twelve miles east of Le Havre, a police surveillance team monitoring LeBoeuf was stiff with boredom. The suspected mafia kingpin had been holed up in his hillside compound for nearly two weeks. The old stone residence, surrounded by a high thick wall, stood atop a ridge that afforded no close concealment for their surveillance vehicle. The police had been forced to remain in a park at the base of the hill, where their listening devices proved useless.

But at 11:15 p.m. the gates had slid open and LeBoeuf's black BMW sedan rolled out of the drive and down the road. The surveillance team watched the car, but didn't dare follow immediately, given the minimal late-night traffic. Fortunately, they didn't have to.

A GPS tracker had been affixed to the car weeks before, while LeBoeuf was stopped at a traffic light. The police team let the BMW disappear before starting their van and giving chase, using a laptop to guide the way.

The BMW drove to a scruffy part of the Le Havre commercial waterfront and parked at a large warehouse used to store export goods waiting for shipment. LeBoeuf and two burly security men paid no heed to the tailing van as they casually entered the building. The surveillance team found a utility road that ran on a low bluff above the warehouse. The van driver parked next to a surplus

concrete mooring block that offered a perfect vantage for visual and acoustic monitoring. They barely had time to set up their equipment when a spotter called out.

"I've got a man in a gray suit approaching the building on foot." A minute later, he provided an update. "He just entered the building through an open side door."

Villard was met inside the door by the two toughs. One, a bald man with a thick neck, frisked him roughly, but not thoroughly. Villard's vest pocket pistol was left untouched. The bald man escorted him past a barren foyer and through a swinging door that led into the rear warehouse.

The cavernous space was empty, save for two office chairs and a small table positioned starkly in the room's center. LeBoeuf was wedged into one of the chairs, which strained under his obesity. He wore a baggy purple shirt and black pants. To Villard, he looked like a giant grape.

"Right on time." LeBoeuf motioned for Villard to take the other seat. "You came alone?"

"Quite. I walked a circuitous route here."

"Perhaps the authorities don't yet know of your little hideaway," he said in a knowing manner. "You are hiding from the authorities, are you not?" LeBoeuf smiled, which drew up the flabby skin hanging from his cheeks. When Villard failed to reply, he continued.

"I saw an account of the attack in New York. It seemed to share some hallmarks with the recent attacks in Paris, wouldn't you say?"

Villard relented and gave a grim shrug. LeBoeuf knew more than he thought, but it didn't really matter now. "We were hoping to accelerate demand for the offshore aquifers that we control."

"Perhaps the police will trace it to you and perhaps they won't. Nevertheless, that brings us to the matter of your loan," LeBoeuf said, "on which you are now delinquent."

Villard gave a heavy nod, dropping his chin to his chest.

"I have drawn up the sale of your company's remaining assets," LeBoeuf said. "The price is thirty million euros, which puts us even."

"The revenue stream from our offshore leases and infrastructure," Villard said, "would potentially cover that amount in a matter of weeks."

"Not likely under your management, unless your boy Henri has kept his hands extra clean. Be that as it may, it's a buyer's market at the moment, and that is the price. I've drawn up the papers right here." He motioned toward the table. "I've also made arrangements for your travel to a discreet location in Greece, should you so desire. I'm told one can live under the radar there quite affordably."

Villard knew it was the best he could hope for. Perhaps it was even generous. But it still left a vile taste in his mouth.

He picked up the contract. Flipping to the signature page, he signed his name and tossed the document back onto the table.

"We had a profitable run for a time," he said with a sigh. "But smuggling was never really the business for me."

"No, I don't believe it was." LeBoeuf nodded at the bald enforcer.

The thug stepped to the back of Villard's chair and, with a flick, dropped a rope garrote around the old man's throat. He pulled it sharply, yanking Villard from his seat.

Villard grabbed helplessly at the rope. He felt his windpipe collapse and saw spots before his eyes as the oxygen flow to his brain constricted. He let go of the rope, groped at his vest pocket, and felt the Browning. Wrapping his fingers around its grip, he raised the pistol alongside his ear, pointed the muzzle behind him, and squeezed the trigger.

The shot struck the bald man square in the forehead. The garrote slipped from the strangler's fingers as he keeled over backward and struck the floor.

Villard gasped and coughed, sucking in precious oxygen. His vision crystallized on the gelatinous form of LeBoeuf, who remained in

his seat with an alarmed look. Villard heard the swinging door open behind him with the approach of the second guard, but the man was too far away to protect his boss.

Villard turned the pistol on LeBoeuf and fired four shots. The fat man wallowed in his chair and raised a flabby arm toward Villard, uttering a stream of profanities in his last moments.

Villard didn't wait to watch him die. He pressed the barrel of the Browning against his own heart and squeezed the trigger a final time.

At the sound of the first gunshot, the French surveillance team called for backup, and a patrol car responded instantly. The uniformed policemen caught LeBoeuf's second bodyguard fleeing the building, then investigated the bloody scene inside.

"*Trois hommes morts,*" the lead officer reported, finding all three men dead on the floor.

EPILOGUE

1939 Bugatti Type 57C

103

Four weeks later

Saint Louis peered down at the empty sarcophagus a hundred meters below him. The painted image of the thirteenth-century French king had adorned the interior cupola of the Invalides since 1692. For the second time in history, Louis IX was about to oversee the internment of Napoleon Bonaparte.

A select group of French dignitaries and visiting heads of state, all in dark suits, took their seats in the lower crypt. Pitt and Giordino had a prime view in the front row, while Dirk Jr. and Summer were seated behind them. The two men displayed red-ribboned medals pinned to their lapels, the Legion of Honour. The five-armed white cross, created by Napoleon in 1802, represented the highest civilian and military award bestowed by France. Pitt and Giordino had received the honors from the French president in a private ceremony minutes earlier.

Elite members of the Republican Guard wearing starched blue uniforms stepped quietly into the room, guiding Napoleon's multilayered coffin on a flag-draped gurney. With flawless precision, they transported the coffin up a temporary ramp and into the open sarcophagus.

The archbishop of Paris recited the Rite of Committal, followed by a speech from the French president. It proved so long-winded, Pitt

had to nudge Giordino awake before it was over. Finally, the lid to the sarcophagus was resealed and the great emperor was allowed to resume his eternal sleep.

Charles Lufbery, overseeing a security detail at the building, approached the Americans after the ceremony. "May I offer my congratulations," he said, eyeing the medals. "It is a momentous day in the history of France."

He was interrupted by the French president, who stepped in for a final word with Pitt and Giordino. "I hope that NUMA," he said, "will continue to assist our country in the identification of new water sources."

"A silver lining to the whole affair," Pitt said. "With Captain Lufbery's permission, we have examined Lavera Exploration's survey records. We've identified numerous offshore aquifers around the world that they located in their oil surveys. One of those, as you know, is off the coast of Normandy. NUMA will be investigating the sites in detail and providing assessments as how to responsibly access the fresh water in those locations."

The president thanked Pitt and Giordino and shook their hands. An army of aides then whisked the president out of the building.

Giordino turned to Lufbery. "It seems we've come a long way from your jailhouse."

"We were operating without all the facts, as is often the case," Lufbery said. "But with your help, we unraveled a case that has even brought down a mafia operation in our country." He turned to Dirk. "I am especially glad that things didn't deter you from returning to France after your release."

Dirk waved an arm around and nodded. "The sights have been much more enjoyable than on my first visit."

Pitt stepped over and rubbed the base of the sarcophagus. "A lucky thing he was not left on the *Surcouf*."

"I'm told," Lufbery said, "a memorial will be added to the Invalides to honor the sailors lost aboard her."

Pitt turned to the police captain. "And what of Brigitte?"

"I have word she will receive the minimum sentence for conspiracy and two lesser charges. She proved very cooperative to the investigation, readily admitting her involvement and apologizing for her misjudgments. The court is inclined to show some leniency as a result."

"I believe she was primarily a victim of love, rather than a criminal at heart." Pitt glanced at his watch. "I'm afraid I must get to the airport to meet my wife. She's due at Orly in an hour."

"Do you need a ride?" Lufbery asked.

"No, I have a car waiting." He shook hands with the captain, but Lufbery held him up a moment longer.

The French policeman leaned close and lowered his voice. "I know it was against procedure to leave the Belgian diamonds out of my report, but after all you have done for France, I thought it justified. I am curious to know, what did you do with them?"

"The diamonds? We left them where we found them. In Martinique."

Lufbery gave him a baffled look.

"*Vive la France*," Pitt said by way of farewell.

Pitt exited the Invalides and strode down the front steps. Waiting for him on the sidewalk was Allain Broussard, his bright blue Bugatti parked at the curb. Broussard passed the keys to Pitt, and they both climbed into the car.

Pitt started the Bugatti and listened to the rumbling exhaust as he revved the motor.

"Are you ready for your test-drive?" Broussard asked.

"*Mais oui*." Pitt gave a devious smile and dumped the clutch, leaving a pair of long black tire marks trailing from the emperor's abode.

104

Sweat poured off the crane operator's brow as he lifted the large, ornate gable into the air. It was less the Martinique humidity that made him perspire than the headstrong woman overseeing his every move. She had dogged the construction team from the first day, supervising the renovation's every detail.

"You gonna let it hang there all day?" she called out as the pediment dangled in the wind.

"No, ma'am. Just waiting for it to settle."

He eased the lift lever higher and raised the triangular facing to the top of the building. Two workers on a scaffold guided the monolith into place like a piece in a jigsaw puzzle. It was the capstone on the two-story school building. The roofers would now be called in to complete the job.

When the lift lines were released, the operator lowered the boom to the ground.

"Well done," Doris said. "Now, please, get this vehicle out of here, and don't drive over our new soccer field on the way out."

"Yes, ma'am," he said.

The Creole woman in the flowered skirt stepped out of the crane's path and looked up at the nearly completed building. It was built in the French Plantation style that matched the two new boardinghouses nearby. They had replaced the old tar-paper dorms that once stood on the grounds of the Caribbean Children's Rescue.

The new houses were painted a bright dandelion yellow, the happiest color she could find. The school building, she decided, would be a dignified cloud white.

She reviewed the clipboard she always carried that contained the plans for the site's refurbishment. The new boardinghouses and athletic facilities were completed, and the school building would be finished in a month. The last job was the restoration of the old stone estate house, which would be remodeled into a nursery and faculty housing. It had all come together quicker than she expected.

At the bottom of her clipboard was the simple, handwritten instruction that had guided everything. It had been tucked into the two cases of diamonds she found on the doorstep, left by an anonymous donor.

One of the charity's board members, an attorney in the Virgin Islands, had set up the orphanage's endowment after the diamonds were sold through a reputable broker. Ten million dollars was earmarked for capital improvements at the Martinique site, while the balance of $47 million remained as an operating endowment. The donation was as transformative as it was unexpected.

With the capital improvements nearly complete, Doris reviewed the short list of remaining directives that had come with the donation. A bus was to be acquired to take the kids on field trips around the island to study its nature. French history would be taught to all of the children, along with a course in oceanography.

She mentally checked off those items, as a new bus was on order and she had hired qualified teachers for both subjects. Just one item

remained on the list. It was a curious request, but one she had no intention of neglecting, especially since the specified date was on the horizon.

An invitation was to be extended every year to an American gentleman by the name of Pitt, who was to be welcomed as a guest lecturer at the school. For some reason, the visit was to occur on the ninth day of March: the anniversary of Marie-Josèphe-Rose de Tascher de La Pagerie's marriage to one Napoleon Bonaparte.

When African jihadis attack a Nigerian regiment using American weapons, Cabrillo and the *Oregon* crew are on the case, investigating from Afghanistan to Kuala Lumpur to track a mysterious arms dealer—a genius, or perhaps a devil—known only as the Vendor.

Cabrillo goes undercover to find the Vendor's base, but his adversary isn't just an arms smuggler. He's an arms maker, and Cabrillo just walked into a lethal military game alongside the most dangerous mercenaries in the world, designed to test the Vendor's cutting-edge AI arsenal.

And yet, surviving an arena full of flame-throwing robots isn't even his biggest problem. The Vendor has an army of high-speed drones headed for a pivotal military site, and if the *Oregon* crew can't stop them from releasing a deadly neurotoxin, the entire globe will erupt in conflict.

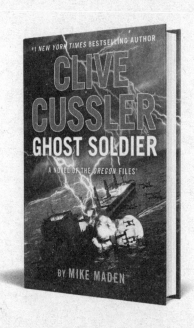

1

NIGER, AFRICA
Present Day

The long convoy of armed Toyota pickups loaded with Nigerian troops raced north in a line through the desert on a hard-packed road bracketed by thick stands of gnarled acacia trees. A howling wind clouded the air with fine powdery sand, red as rust in the late-afternoon sun.

The column was still three hours away from the village where the regional commander of the Islamic State faction was reportedly hiding. The Nigerian soldiers were far beyond the safety of their fortified base, but they were coming in force. The local fighters were armed with little more than AKs and rode air-cooled motorcycles. Their preferred targets were unarmed villagers and helpless farmers, not soldiers.

"*C'est comme la surface de Mars,*" said the driver, a first sergeant. He wore the scorpion patch of the 1st Expeditionary Force of Niger (EFoN). His American military surplus camouflaged uniform was covered in dust.

Lieutenant Wonkoye, the mission leader, grinned at the sergeant's comment.

"So you have been to the Martian surface, Sergeant?"

The sergeant flashed a blindingly white smile beneath his oversized helmet and shook his head.

"It's what the Americans used to say."

"Americans used to say a lot of things."

Wonkoye instantly regretted his comment. He actually liked the Americans, especially the operators he trained with. But American soldiers were mostly gone, thanks to the military junta that now ruled his nation. The only Yanks left occupied the massive American-built drone base in Agadez, but its personnel were forbidden to leave it.

The American Special Forces trainers were fearsome warriors with great knowledge and combat experience, yet they were humble, unlike the French *paras* who had fought alongside them over the years. Wonkoye remembered the big Americans training them hard, but still coming down to the Nigerian camp and playing *le football* with them—unlike the swaggering French who, despite their easy smiles and common *langue*, held the Nigerians in quiet contempt.

No matter, Wonkoye thought to himself. Those days are long past. The Americans and the French had been expelled on the orders of Niger's new president, himself an Army general. Wonkoye, a fervent patriot, quite agreed with that decision, perilous as it was.

The Islamist plague was exploding across the region. Over the years, both the Americans and French had spent a great deal of money to fight the jihadis in Africa. Their efforts were nationalistic, not humanitarian. They fought the terrorists in Africa so that the war would not be brought to their own homelands.

Both Western countries had partnered with Niger, one of the poorest nations in the world, in the long, bloody struggle. It might have been better if the West had sent aid instead of guns, Wonkoye had often thought, but those were matters for his superiors. He was a warrior and his only duty was taking the fight to the Islamist enemy, whose numbers grew daily.

Rumors of a grand alliance between competing Al Qaeda and

Islamic State factions swirled in the capital, Niamey. Guinea, Burkina Faso, and Gabon had all fallen to military juntas in recent years, all driven to act by the corrupt and incompetent governments supported by Western powers in the name of security. Other African governments were on the brink of toppling as well, including mighty Nigeria. The jihadists were poised to exploit the pending chaos.

So were the Russians.

Now the precarious future of all of Africa lay increasingly in the hands of Africans. Even Mali—now also led by military men—had expelled the fifteen thousand UN peacekeepers based there. Niger's fate would be determined by Nigerians, and the EfoN was the tip of his nation's spear in the war on jihadi terror. The proud young lieutenant well understood the risks. He was a professional soldier.

Wonkoye turned around and peered at the young faces on the other side of the pickup's small rear window getting jostled around in the truck bed. Their eyes were shut tight against the choking dust, their bare faces raw from the sting of the whirling sand. The back of every other pickup was crowded the same way save for the one hauling spare tires and ammo. Each man clutched an AK-47 or RPG launcher. With their free hands they held on to whatever they could, including the bed-mounted Russian machine guns, as they bounced along.

"Do you hear that, Lieutenant?" the sergeant asked.

Wonkoye paused. Over the roar of the Toyota's diesel four-cylinder engine he could barely make out the familiar sound of helicopter blades beating the air. He had put in a request for air cover, but it had been denied due to the shortage of aircraft.

Wonkoye stuck his head out the window. The stinging sand scoured his face and watered his eyes, but he could still make out the form of a helicopter in the distance to the east, high above the tree line. It was heading north, but circling back around.

"That's a Black Hawk."

"Americans!" The sergeant laughed. "I thought they were all gone."

"They must have seen my request." Wonkoye brimmed with pride. He had been a star pupil of the American operators. Perhaps his reputation was even greater than he knew and his old friends had decided to join the fight after all, even against their orders.

The lieutenant's radio crackled with a message from the lead vehicle.

"Sir, a Humvee is up ahead."

Wonkoye and his sergeant shared a confident look. With the Americans at their side the jihadis stood no chance whatsoever.

Capturing the bloodthirsty enemy commander might even earn Wonkoye a promotion.

The lieutenant raised the handset to his mouth.

"Attention convoy. This is Wonkoye. Everybody come to a halt. The Americans are here. We will break for ten minutes. Food, water—whatever you need. I will confer with the American commander. Wonkoye out."

The lieutenant pointed up ahead. The brake lights of the lead vehicle flared as soon as Wonkoye had given his order and skidded to a stop in the road. The vehicles behind Wonkoye had done the same.

"Go around him," the lieutenant ordered. "I want to parlay with that Humvee."

"Yes, sir."

Just as the sergeant eased the wheel left to leave the road, the lead scout truck erupted in a ball of flame and shredded steel. A burning body leaped from the bed and dashed blindly toward the tree line to the west.

Before Wonkoye could process the fiery image, the same stand of trees erupted in a stream of streaking rocket and machine-gun fire.

Instantly, half the vehicles in his convoy were shattered. Heavy 7.62mm rounds thudded into Wonkoye's truck. Blood splattered the rear window, his soldiers' screams muffled by the adrenaline flooding his system.

The sergeant jerked the steering wheel hard right and headed for the opposite tree line for cover as Wonkoye shouted orders into his radio.

"Head east for the trees. Get to the trees!"

But it was too late. More anti-tank missiles mounted on Humvees hidden in the western tree line had already turned nine of the eleven trucks into burning hulks. The other two were riddled with gunfire and stood dead in the sand, their tires shredded as badly as the thin steel of their doors. The few men who survived the initial attack were cut down in their tracks as they ran for cover.

The sergeant's boot mashed the throttle to the floorboard. His skillful driving avoided hitting the flaming wreck in front of them, and the shattered truck behind them blocked the rocket targeting their vehicle. Wonkoye turned around to see the bloody face of a young private now pressed against the window glass, his lifeless eyes accusing him of utter failure.

Wonkoye watched a corporal in a blood-soaked uniform rack the Toyota's Kord 12.7mm heavy machine gun with its T-shaped handle and open fire just as their pickup dove into the tree line.

Wonkoye shoved the door open and dashed for the trees just as the bleeding corporal was tossed from the truck by a burst of well-aimed machine-gun fire. The lieutenant caught a quick glance of the six lifeless bodies heaped in the truck bed like canvas sacks of butchered meat. He bolted away, his face streaked with tears of shame and rage, his sergeant hot on his heels.

Fifty feet above the treetops the hovering Black Hawk's deafening rotor blades threw blinding clouds of choking sand. Wonkoye screamed as machine-gun bullets stitched into his spine, but it was a skull-shattering round that killed him, plowing his corpse into the sand at a dead run.

2

Juan Cabrillo stood on the *Oregon*'s deck, his clear blue eyes fixed on the distant speck in the achingly bright cobalt sky, one hand upraised to shade his face from the searing sunlight. The *Oregon*'s thundering tilt-rotor aircraft, an AgustaWestland AW609, had begun its descent.

A gusting wind suddenly nudged his strapping six-foot-one-inch swimmer's frame. The blast of wind ran its fingers through his closely cropped sun-bleached hair and his vintage 1950s Hawaiian shirt snapped like a flag in a hurricane.

"Where's that wind coming from? No storm in the forecast," Linda Ross said in her high-pitched voice. Her green, almond-shaped eyes were hidden behind a pair of oversized aviator glasses and a black ball cap. Though strong and lean, she was battered so hard by the breeze she had to grab on to Juan's thick bicep for stability.

"Came out of nowhere," Juan said. "I don't like it."

───

Callie Cosima's tall, athletic frame sat comfortably in the tilt-rotor's copilot seat. Her shoulder-length honey-blond hair was pulled into a

ponytail to accommodate the tilt-rotor's headphones and Oakley wraparound sunglasses protected her eyes from the sun's harsh glare. She wore her natural beauty with an unadorned and easy grace and her toned body bore the healthy glow of a woman who had spent a life outdoors, especially on the water.

George "Gomez" Adams piloted the AW609 tilt-rotor, currently configured in helicopter mode. The three touchscreen cockpit displays were straight out of a video game and provided anyone in the dual-control pilot seats complete situational awareness. They'd been in the air nearly two hours.

Gomez had picked Callie up at the private jet terminal at Dubai World Central airport—one of several with which the Corporation had long-standing, discrete arrangements. With piercing brown eyes and a stylized gunfighter's mustache, Gomez was roguishly handsome, but it was his charming cocksureness that cut most women to the quick.

Callie frowned as she pointed through her side windscreen. The Gulf of Oman was dotted with cargo vessels and oil tankers.

"Hey, Gomez. Is that the *Oregon*?"

A pale blue freighter with a white stern superstructure was anchored several hundred feet below. She saw a 590-foot break-bulk carrier with four pairs of yellow cranes towering over five large green cargo hold doors. She'd seen dozens of such vessels over the years. It wasn't at all what she was expecting.

"Yup. That's the *Oregon*." Despite the electronic microphone, Gomez's voice was deep and smoky as a plate of West Texas barbecue brisket.

"Doesn't look like much."

"That's kinda the point." He flashed a leather-soft grin as he eased the aircraft into a gentle descent.

"Hate to ask but . . . Where are you gonna land this thing?" Callie asked.

Gomez opened his mouth to answer, but alarms suddenly screamed in their headphones.

Callie's eyes widened like dinner plates. Her blood pressure spiked into her skull as her stomach puddled in her boots.

They were plummeting out of the sky.

"Wind shear," Gomez whispered calmly in his mic as he simultaneously advanced throttles, mashed rotor pedals, and worked the cyclic and collective to generate massive lift without stalling—and yet, still maintaining control. The twin Pratt & Whitney turbines screamed as the tachometers crashed into the red zone.

The sudden burst of power pinned Callie into her seat as the AW's nose launched skyward. Skeins of high clouds sped across the windscreen.

The aircraft yawed and bucked in the turbulence, but Gomez never broke a sweat. His deft handling of the controls was deceptively fast.

The wind shear alarms suddenly cut off as the tilt-rotor stabilized. Gomez eased the big bird back into a landing approach. Callie sat upright in her seat, a little green around the gills.

"You good, miss?"

"Been in worse situations. Just not up in the air."

Gomez smiled. From what he'd heard about her, that was true enough.

The tilt-rotor's three small wheels touched down on the disguised cargo hold door that served as the *Oregon*'s helipad as gently as a feather on a velvet blanket. The whining turboprops cycled down as two aircraft technicians—"hangar apes" in *Oregon* parlance—scurried to secure the vehicle before it descended belowdecks on the elevator.

Juan pulled the cabin door open and Callie descended with a large waterproof duffel in hand. The two had never met, but there was an instant affinity between them, like twins separated at birth.

And maybe something more.

Cabrillo noted the copper tan of her skin, like the Hawaiian surfer girl she was—at least in her spare time. Cabrillo had the same kind of tan when he surfed the beaches up and down Orange County, California, years ago. He still got a lot of outdoor sun, but surfing wasn't the reason.

He extended his hand. "Welcome aboard. Juan Cabrillo."

Callie took it. "Callie Cosima."

Juan felt heat pass between them—and it wasn't from the warm weather.

"I see you bought the e-ticket up there," Juan said. "Heck of a ride."

"We hit a downdraft—or it hit us. By the way, your pilot was truly amazing."

"Gomez is a decorated combat flier. He flew AH-6M *Little Birds* with the U.S. Army's Night Stalkers—the 160th Special Operations Aviation Regiment—before he came to us. He's the best of the best."

Callie frowned quizzically. "I know his name is Gomez, but the tag on his flight suit read 'Adams.'"

"Gomez is his nickname," Juan said. "He has a certain effect on the ladies. Well, one of the many ladies unable to resist his considerable charms was the courtesan of a Peruvian drug lord who looked a lot like Morticia from *The Addams Family* TV show—"

"And Gomez Addams was her husband." Callie grinned. "Got it. Better than getting called 'Lurch.'"

"True that." Juan gestured toward Linda. "This is Linda Ross, my Vice President of operations, and third in command on the *Oregon*."

"It's a real honor to finally meet you," Linda said. She and Callie shook hands.

Callie noted Linda's shockingly bright mane spilling out beneath her ball cap. "Love the neon hair."

Linda pulled off her sunglasses, revealing a spray of freckles across her petite nose.

"Kinda crazy, I know. I change my hair color as often as I change my socks. Can't break the habit."

"Linda was a Pentagon staffer and blue-water naval intelligence officer before she came to work for me," Juan said. "I think she's trying to color away all of those Navy regulations she used to keep."

"Thanks, Dr. Freud," Linda said, pulling on her aviators.

"I might have to borrow a bottle," Callie said. "I understand you're a sub driver as well?"

"Best on the boat—except for the Chairman." Linda nodded at Juan. She caught the eye of one of the hangar apes, a barrel-chested fireplug in blue utilities. He jogged over.

"Ma'am?"

Linda pointed at Callie's enormous duffel.

"Please take Ms. Cosima's luggage to her guest suite. It's number 311, two doors down from mine."

"That's not necessary," Callie protested. "It's rather heavy. Gear, mostly."

"Happy to, ma'am." The deckhand snatched up the heavy bag as if it were filled with cotton candy and turned on his heels.

By the time she said, "Thank you" he was already speeding off toward the superstructure.

Callie turned back to Juan and flashed a curious look.

"So why do they call you 'Chairman'?"

The big hydraulic motors of the aircraft elevator whined as the tilt-rotor disappeared belowdecks.

"We run the *Oregon* and its operations like a Wall Street company, not a military organization. In fact, our business operation is called 'The Corporation.'"

"You need a better marketing department."

"I don't disagree," Juan said, chuckling, "because I am the marketing department. I'm the Chairman of the Corporation, Linda is

Vice President, and Max Hanley is the President. You'll meet him later."

"I've Skyped with him several times. Supersmart guy."

"He helped build the *Oregon*," Juan said. "He's one of the best engineers I've ever known."

"But the *Oregon* was Juan's idea," Linda said, "and he was the original designer."

Callie nodded. "Impressive."

"That's quite a compliment coming from someone like you," Cabrillo said. "I'll take it and run. I bet you want to see your baby."

"Sure do."

"Then follow me to the janitor's closet."

CLIVE CUSSLER was the author of more than seventy books in five bestselling series, including Dirk Pitt®, NUMA Files®, *Oregon Files*®, Isaac Bell®, and Sam and Remi Fargo®. His life nearly paralleled that of his hero Dirk Pitt. Whether searching for lost aircraft or leading expeditions to find famous shipwrecks, he and his NUMA crew of volunteers discovered and surveyed more than seventy-five lost ships of historic significance, including the long-lost Civil War submarine *Hunley*, which was raised in 2000 with much publicity. Like Pitt, Cussler collected classic automobiles. His collection featured more than one hundred examples of custom coachwork. Cussler passed away in February 2020.

DIRK CUSSLER is the author of *Clive Cussler's The Devil's Sea*, and coauthor with Clive Cussler of eight previous Dirk Pitt adventures: *Black Wind*, *Treasure of Khan*, *Arctic Drift*, *Crescent Dawn*, *Poseidon's Arrow*, *Havana Storm*, *Odessa Sea*, and *Celtic Empire*. He serves as president of NUMA, where he continues his father's legacy of searching for important historical shipwrecks. He lives in Connecticut.

VISIT CLIVE CUSSLER ONLINE
CusslerBooks.com
CusslerMuseum.com
CliveCusslerAdventures
CliveCussler_
TheCliveCussler

CLIVE CUSSLER

"Clive Cussler is just about the best
storyteller in the business."
—*New York Post*

TITLES BY CLIVE CUSSLER

DIRK PITT ADVENTURES®

Clive Cussler The Corsican Shadow
    (by Dirk Cussler)
Clive Cussler's The Devil's Sea
    (by Dirk Cussler)
Celtic Empire (with Dirk Cussler)
Odessa Sea (with Dirk Cussler)
Havana Storm (with Dirk Cussler)
Poseidon's Arrow (with Dirk Cussler)
Crescent Dawn (with Dirk Cussler)
Arctic Drift (with Dirk Cussler)
Treasure of Khan (with Dirk Cussler)
Black Wind (with Dirk Cussler)
Trojan Odyssey
Valhalla Rising
Atlantis Found
Flood Tide
Shock Wave
Inca Gold
Sahara
Dragon
Treasure
Cyclops
Deep Six
Pacific Vortex!
Night Probe!
Vixen 03
Raise the Titanic!
Iceberg
The Mediterranean Caper

SAM AND REMI FARGO ADVENTURES®

Wrath of Poseidon (with Robin Burcell)
The Oracle (with Robin Burcell)
The Gray Ghost (with Robin Burcell)
The Romanov Ransom
    (with Robin Burcell)
Pirate (with Robin Burcell)
The Solomon Curse (with Russell Blake)
The Eye of Heaven (with Russell Blake)
The Mayan Secrets (with Thomas Perry)
The Tombs (with Thomas Perry)
The Kingdom (with Grant Blackwood)
Lost Empire (with Grant Blackwood)
Spartan Gold (with Grant Blackwood)

ISAAC BELL ADVENTURES®

Clive Cussler The Heist (by Jack Du Brul)
Clive Cussler The Sea Wolves
    (by Jack Du Brul)
The Saboteurs (with Jack Du Brul)
The Titanic Secret (with Jack Du Brul)
The Cutthroat (with Justin Scott)
The Gangster (with Justin Scott)
The Assassin (with Justin Scott)
The Bootlegger (with Justin Scott)
The Striker (with Justin Scott)
The Thief (with Justin Scott)
The Race (with Justin Scott)
The Spy (with Justin Scott)
The Wrecker (with Justin Scott)
The Chase